BENEDICT KIELY

Benedict Kiely has come to be regarded as one of Ireland's most admired literary writers. Born near Dromore, in County Tyrone in 1919, his long and successful career spans the writing of novels, short stories and memoirs. He is well known as a raconteur and broadcaster on TV and radio.

His novels include *The Captain with the Whiskers*, *Honey Seems Bitter* and *The Cards of the Gambler* (also available from Wolfhound Press), among many other works.

REVIEWS

'Benedict Kiely is the Irish Balzac.' Heinrich Böll

Dogs Enjoy the Morning

'*Dogs* is picaresque…it recounts the adventures not of a single, central rogue, but of a whole community of rogues, picara and picaroon alike, all residents or wayfarers in the imaginary town of Cosmona.' Kevin O'Sullivan, *The Recorder*

The Cards of the Gambler

'An astonishing book…What is uniquely Kiely's, his thumbprint, is his easy mastery of the lyrical, and the feeling of felt life, felt experience, just beneath the surface of his prose.' Thomas Flanagan, author of *The Year of the French*

Drink to the Bird

'Anecdotal, hilariously funny, and replet̲ ̲ ̲ ̲ ̲ ̲ ̲ this memoir has the cadence ̲ ̲ ̲ ̲ ̲ ̲ ̲ ̲ ̲ cean resonance…It is immedi ̲ ̲ ̲ ̲ ̲ ̲ ̲ ̲ ̲ r of outstanding achievement. ̲ ̲ ̲ ̲ ̲ ̲ ̲ ̲

'Mr Kiely is one of the las ̲ ̲ ̲ ̲ ̲ ̲ ̲ ̲ ̲ ̲ ̲ ning is extensive and he is excit ̲ ̲ ̲ popular as by high culture. If in one chapter he is recalling the effect of Irish rebel incursions on the writing of Spenser's *Faerie Queene*, in another he salutes the Everton centre forward Dixie Dean as the only footballer ever to establish a hairstyle: the sleeked-back, middle-of-the-skull parting...A charming and civilised book.' *Sunday Times*

A Letter to Peachtree

'There are so many Irish people who write short stories, and so few who are real storytellers. Ben Kiely is one, and he should be preserved in aspic or crowned high king or just bought in huge numbers.' *Sunday Independent*

'Stylish, gabby, using language like a fallen angel, he mixes his feeling with a true storyteller's verse that looks like superb skill but is in fact something better. Call it instinct.' *Guardian*

Nothing Happens in Carmincross

'Written with zest and grace, humour and irony, in a style that is totally individual...It must be read by everyone interested in Irish writing and the peculiar tragedy of the Irish situation.' Kevin Casey, *Irish Times*

'I have been waiting for a novel as full of rage about contemporary Ireland as this one. And this is the book I have been waiting for.' Frank Delaney, *BBC World Service*

Proxopera

'Nearly flawless as a piece of literature.' Anthony Burgess

'Compare him with whom you will, the gentle Gogol, the percipient Gorky, Benedict Kiely defies comparison.' Dominic Behan

Also by Benedict Kiely

NOVELS

Nothing Happens in Carmincross (1985)
Proxopera (1977)
The Captain with the Whiskers (1960)
There Was an Ancient House (1955)
The Cards of the Gambler (1953)
Honey Seems Bitter (1952)
Call for a Miracle (1950)
In a Harbour Green (1949)
Land Without Stars (1946)

NON-FICTION

God's Own Country (1993)
Yeats' Ireland (1989)
Ireland from the Air (1985)
Drink to the Bird (1981)
Poor Scholar: A Life of William Carleton (1947)
All the Way to Bantry Bay — and Other Irish Journeys (1978)

SHORT STORIES

A Letter to Peachtree
A Cow in the House (1978)
A Ball of Malt and Madame Butterfly (1973)
A Journey to the Seven Streams (1963)

For Nuala MacDonagh
and to the memory of the poet,
Donagh MacDonagh

Dogs Enjoy the Morning

a novel by

BENEDICT KIELY

I wolde go to the middel weie
And write a boke between the tweie,
Somewhat of lust, somewhat of lore.

John Gower in the
'Confessio Amantis'

WOLFHOUND PRESS

This edition published 1996 by
WOLFHOUND PRESS
68 Mountjoy Square
Dublin 1

First edition Victor Gollancz Ltd., London 1968

Wolfhound Press receives financial assistance from The Arts Council/An
Chomhairle Ealaíon, Dublin, Ireland.

This book is fiction. All characters, incidents and names have no connection
with any person living or dead. Any apparent resemblance is purely
coincidental.

A catalogue record for this book is available from the British Library.

ISBN 0 86327 528 1

Typesetting: Red Barn Publishing, Skeagh, Skibbereen, Co. Cork

Cover design and photography: Slick Fish, Dublin

Printed in Ireland by Colour Books Ltd., Dublin

— ONE —

The rooks at noon left their hunting in the fields, their talking around the Tower, the ruined abbey, the churchyard trees, and crossed over for lunch to the coloured balconies. You could time the sun by them. The lighter troops, the jackdaws, grey heads twisted sideways with cunning, came with them. Hungry birds benefited, and bedridden boys and girls who mightn't relish that day's menu had the services of nimble scavengers.

One of the jokes of the place was that the boys were in the pink and the girls in the blues. The hospital was all on the ground floor and shaped, facing south, like a crescent cracked across the middle. To heal diseased bones the boys lay under pink coverlets in one half of that crescent, the girls under blue coverlets in the other half. Student nurses now and again sortied from the cool shady wards behind the sun balconies to hunt the rooks and see that the patients ate their food whether they liked it or not. White veils and black wings all flapped together as the birds, hopping and fluttering, backed away a bit to dig in resentfully on the balcony railings until the nurses, who had nothing against the rooks anyway, went back into the wards. One ironic girl, a farmer's daughter, said that she had turned her back on chasing rooks from her father's Tipperary fields to carry on the good work in the nursing profession. She suspected that she was haunted and that they were the same rooks all the time.

The old miller came walking cautiously along the tiled antiseptic corridor from the Reverend Mother's office, more cautiously still across the polished floor of oaken blocks in Saint Joseph's ward where the bigger boys were. He felt terrifyingly insecure when he hadn't the grip of grass and gravel under his feet. No active man of eighty and the best part of seventeen stone could afford a tumble on a convent hospital floor. These toy nurses, fresh from all the parishes of Ireland and so clean and plump-faced and blue-and-white as to be almost edible, could never manage his broken-boned body on spine frame, hip frame, not to mention bed-pan. The idea gave him coarse amusement. He could see the Reverend Mother who bought her oaten meal from him assisting at the monstrous task.

On the pink sun-balcony he bellowed gamely at the nurses, telling them they were sunworshippers all and that the sun made grain ripe, and the pagan gods alone knew what it would do to them: set them running the roads in the dusk or eating the ears off their boy-friends. The nurses and the shouting, eating, bird-feeding boys knew him well. Cups and plates and tin trays sounded a salvo to honour his approach. He walked, with special words for everybody, from bed to bed. Bodies, all stripped to the waist and red and brown and even quite black from the sun, arched on spine frames or sprawled, legs wide, on hip frames or, less hindered by surgical appliances, bounced about in beds. A cheeky pet jackdaw had perched on the right arm, held up as stiffly in an aeroplane splint as the arm of an oratorical statue, of a redheaded boy whose face had long ago vanished behind a screen of uniting freckles. The neighbouring boy, naked except for a triangle of loin cloth, was deep mahogany in colour and hampered only by an ankle splint, and had moved his wheeled bed closer and was poking the bird under the tail with a long sally rod. The bird squawked, not unpleased, pecked at the probing rod, rose fluttering, returned again to its perch.

Savages, he thought with deep satisfaction. The sun will heal them.

There were bodies no sun could heal.

A vita-glass awning in a quiet corner behind a pink screen diffused grey liquid sunlight over the only adult patient in the boy's wing: a clerical student about twenty years of age who was tailor-squatting in bed reading a biography of the saintly Brother Nicholas of Flue in whose cell there was nothing to see but sack-cloth and ashes, a stone for a pillow, and no sound of laughter to be heard. The clerical student stretched his legs and leaned back on his pillows. Compared with that ancient Swiss eremite he rated pretty low in austerity. But he was glad beyond words, after seventeen months of orthopaedic treatment, nine months tied flat on his back on a frame, eight months in a swallow-diving position on a reverse bed, to be able at last to stretch his legs and bend them, to stand up, put on a dressing-gown and hobble to the bathroom at the back of the ward.

The first biographer of Saint Nicholas of Flue had praised the saint for eating little or nothing so that, his stomach not filled and made heavy with foodstuffs, he slept without snores, sighs or stertorous breathing, rose lightly without yawning or stretching, did not have to go searching for a retired spot to evacuate his body. There was damn all to be evacuated. Five hundred years later the retired spots were built-in and comfortably fitted with the best equipment. Every time he squatted in solitude between green tiled walls, cisterns singing around him like woodland brooks, the student sought and found something of the singular peace the saint had found in his fifteenth-century hermitage. No nurse, no nun, no fellow patient could disturb him there, no sound of laughter reach him.

He closed the book as the miller came into his corner of the balcony. He said: Rembrandt was the painter I was trying to think of, Mr. Mortell. He was born in a mill on the Rhine where the sun shone through a mist of flour dust. How is your son today?

The miller helped him into his dressing gown.

— He's no better. He's no worse. He's limp like a weed in the stream. Going the way time's taking him.

— He's had more than his share. He has suffered.

Because his suit even if he wasn't wearing it was clerical black the student felt guiltily that he should say something about rewards in heaven, purgatory on earth.

— Sister Thermometer, said the miller, is a great lady for the holy leaflets. She gave me one bundle of these for you to give to the boys and one for everybody I'd meet in the village.

It was another joke of the place that the little boys, baffled by the grandeur of the words, called Sister Grignon de Montfort out of her name.

— She is a tree of life, the student read, to them that lay hold on her: and he that shall retain her is blessed.

On the back of a blue and gold picture of a sweet youthful Virgin ringed around with woolly cloudlets and the upper halves of angels some anthologist had been lavish with fragments of Proverbs, Wisdom, Ecclesiasticus and the Song of Songs.

— No time like the present, the miller said. I'll pass them out on my way home. Any day now you'll be able to come and see my mill.

— Any day now.

— Water and stone as the Lord meant mills to be. The last of its kind hereabouts. And once there were forty wheels turning between here and the sea.

— I'm getting my clothes tomorrow. I've been trouserless now for seventeen months. And trying on my shoes. In a week I'll walk to the mill.

Pausing now and again to lean and rest on the bottom of a bed, to talk to its occupant and to give him a leaflet, the student walked to his stall in his hermit's cell. Squatting, he luxuriated in the smooth comfort of planed wood instead of bedpan enamel, generally chipped, against his buttocks. Alleluia he had arisen and Tony Lumpkin was his own man again and didn't have to be helped on and off. He pulled the chain and thought of Wordsworth and of waters rolling from their mountain springs with a sweet inland murmur. He sat on, eyes half closed, dreaming about nothing. He liked the nuns, the patients and, to an extent that disturbed him because he had after all been on the way to sworn perpetual celibacy if he hadn't been hampered by a lumbar spine, he liked the linen nurses. But by Nicholas of Flue solitude was sweet after seventeen months of enforced community life. Musical water fell from some reservoir in the hills, gurgled through pines, and sweetly the cistern refilled. The ward noises were far away but two voices had followed him. The young doctor was telling the charge nurse that when he and his wife were going to bed the night before he heard a noise in the wardrobe and when he opened it there was a man, peeping.

— As for me, he said, I would have left the poor curious divil there, but the wife's fussy.

The nurse was convulsed.

— Quite a surprise for both of us, the doctor said. Not burgling. Just peeping. Smoke.

The charge nurse said thanks and smoked. She couldn't smoke out in the ward. Everybody had their own use for a hermitage. She said: You're smoking again yourself.

— Only gave them up for a month and put on two and a half stone. The wife objected. She couldn't carry any more weight. Anyway it all depends on what you want out of life. Lung cancer or fatty degeneration. Lung cancer's painless. So I settled for lung cancer.

— Could it, do you think, have been our mystery man? He has the night nurses terrified peeping in at them over the balcony railings.

The young doctor was talkative but he was also kind and professionally discreet.

— No. A poor fellow from the village. He did a bit of gardening for me once, very badly, dug in the weeds. There's no mystery about him. He's just interested in how things work.

— Dear doctor, who isn't?

Smelling their smoke, hearing their laughter, the postponed celibate in the water closet reddened at a remark that might have been meant for him.

— When I came here from Dublin and Birmingham via my honeymoon, the doctor said, I was feeling idyllic. I said peace, everybody here is at peace, no nuts and no neurotics, a salmon river flowing under our gable wall lulling us to sleep when the night's good work was over.

The doctor's wife was small, plump, dusky-skinned and dark-haired as a South Seas maiden. She had worn on a visit to the hospital a tight orange skirt. Nightly by the river she carried weight, then moistly drifted asleep by the lulling salmon water.

— Then you open this damned wardrobe and here's a fellow peeping at you. What goes on? Everywhere?

— And peeping at night over the railing, at my young nurses.

— I'd do that myself. A fine clutch they are. But in God's name why should anybody want to peep at me?

— Not at you, doctor. At what you would be at.

Laughter, footsteps on tiles, died away. The smell of smoke faded. Brother Nicholas stepped out of his hermitage to meet a procession of four red-cheeked nurses marching in to discharge the cargo from the midday bedpans: motion at last carried, as the stale, very stale, joke about the hospitalised county councillor said. The rooks had flown back to the fields. The boys were quiet not because of any post-prandial somnolence but because, before the shellshocked, sporting chaplain came to the broad balcony to hear their weekly confessions, a white-robed nun was giving them an edifying lecture, and asking them to chant after her, rhymed lines about faith, hope, love of God and sorrow for sins. The sing-song of their voices suited the slumbering afternoon. The student drowsed on his pillows. He had cast aside Brother Nicholas of Flue and opened Wilfred Ward's life of Cardinal Newman which he hoped might be a livelier companion to digestion. But the print diminished and enlarged, diminished and enlarged before his heavy eyes. So he began to count magpies. One for sorrow, two for joy and three for a wedding they played, if magpies are not too business bent ever to play, around the square top of the old abbey tower. When he had first come from the seminary to the hospital the student had uncovered to the chaplain his scruples about his new way of life, his difficulties in making his morning meditation and following the monastic routine of prayer and self-denial in uncontemplative surroundings, of controlling his thoughts when ringed by shouting boys and chattering women.

— Eat your food and get better, the chaplain said. Pray when you can. Play games with the boys, and the nurses – within reason. You may never have another chance. A bit of mothering or sistering will do you good and put the marrow back in your bones. You can't live like a monk here. Not with all those blue skirts and white aprons around you.

Seventeen months later those scruples seemed bloody funny. Bed baths carried out by two young women had continued to embarrass him, but then anything that caused so much embarrassment could scarcely be a yielding to the concupiscence of the flesh.

The chaplain was an honest choleric man but not much given to spiritual reading. He had been shellshocked as a Flanders chaplain and had a nervous sideways twitch of the head. Three devoted gundogs always followed at his heels and his housekeeper who knew the nuns complained that she couldn't keep dogs or the smell of them out of any room in his house. They followed him now on to the balcony. For privacy and the preserving of the seal of the confessional the beds were placed as far away from each other as they could be. Like playing dominoes, the crow-chasing nurse from Tipperary thought it was. But what sins these boys had to hide from each other was more, she said, than she could comprehend: they ate, slept, woke again, sinned, if at all, and did everything else in community.

From bed to bed then, sealing each sin in his shellshocked mind, the chaplain, now an old man, moved, who as a young man had crawled in mud from one dying soldier to another. But once to call to the student and to stir his following dogs to barking, he leaped to his feet, pointing, waving his purple stole.

— Peter Lane, he called, there's a shot in a million.

— Ego te absolvo, he shouted at a penitent boy before he remembered to lower his voice.

Brightening the leaden afternoon a white gull came gliding from the soft land of meadows between river and canal. Against the dull sky it seemed as large as a swan. It circled above the hospital, then perched, not resting so much as surveying, on the Tower, as if the grey friars who seven hundred years ago had placed stone on holy stone had been thinking only of the comfort of a bird and of that single moment.

§

The miller stood surrounded by lawns and flowerbeds and looked at the seagull and the old abbey tower. Walking to his car the doctor caught up with him and stood beside him. The doctor said that the first thing that had drawn him to the practice in the village of Cosmona had been the Latin name the monks had given to the ancient holy place and the legend that went with it.

— The Island of the Living, he said. Insula Viventium. The dead need no doctor. I read in the guidebook that the village was also distinguished by possessing one of the few still-working specimens of an old water and stone mill.

— They had me in the newspapers, the miller said. They had me on radio and television. They recorded every noise the mill made. They even wanted me to sing a song.

Miller and doctor, two heavy bewhiskered men, one grey, one brown, walked along a winding gravelled path that cut across the fifty yards or so of grass between the pink and blue balconies and the grey wall that surrounded ruin and graveyard.

— It's a wonder all out, the miller said, how a legend grows. This very ground we walk on was a lake until two hundred years ago the lord of the land drained it. They say that when the saint came to found the abbey on the island he went over dryshod, without boat, without ship. He could dance on the water.

— One better, said the doctor, than the Lord Jesus who like the tenth hussars didn't dance.

The miller's laughter was a brazen bugle call, suddenly beginning, suddenly ending, bizarre against the birdlike chirping of the children from the balconies, more surprising still in that it left no echoes. Then, laughter ended, he returned to legend.

— Bodies buried here didn't corrupt and in the end they said that the man who lived to pray here would never die.

— Where are they now, asked the doctor. Did they stop praying?

They negotiated a wicker gate. Tombstones flat with the ground were dominoes, like the balcony beds, on well-clipped grass. The miller's bell-voice chanted: No woman, no not even a female animal, was allowed onto the island.

— A sore country always for bestiality, the doctor said. There are parts of Tipperary, appropriately around a place called Rearcross, where the goats and donkeys never get a night's sleep.

— No female bird ever alighted.

— Fair enough. I'd say that gull was a cock.

— Doctor you're a heathen, the miller said. But if you stay long enough in Cosmona we'll make a Christian of you yet.

Without doubt the ground they walked on was holy. Even the jesting doctor felt that so keenly that he hadn't been a week in Cosmona when he had joined the local committee formed by the miller for the restoration and preservation of the abbey ruins. Now as they walked their examining eyes studied the clipped grass, the cracks recently sealed in the old walls, the fragments of carven stones that had once been scattered in disorder and were now lined in exact rows. Patches of weeds had been uprooted and the ground covered with fresh gravel. A stonecutter from Crooked Bridge had, with imitative skill and deep reverence for the work of men dead for centuries, restored as much as he could of the cloister. Rubble and twigs scattered by jackdaws nesting in the Tower had been cleared away and one could comfortably climb the spiral stairway.

The doctor said: They did a good workmanlike job.

— But what's this, said the miller.

Just inside the narrow doorway and at the foot of the stone stairs somebody had sacreligiously abandoned an empty incongruous bottle. The doctor picked it up, sniffed, grimaced. He read out the label: Finest Old Red Wine.

— Red Biddy, said the miller. The devil's milk. If I had my toe at the ass of the vandal who left it there.

— I'm thinking, said the doctor.

He slipped the offending bottle into a wide tweed pocket. With the miller in the lead they spiralled upwards.

— I'm thinking, Mr. Mortell, that by night a mystery man could have a fine view from the top of the Tower at the lighted balconies. Peering across the summer darkness at all that light and the flapping white aprons of the nurses. To a man who had once been buried in mud all that starched linen antiseptic cleanliness must have a big attraction.

— Buried in mud. By the heavenly father I know who you mean.

The miller's laughter spiralled up and down as he leaned against old stone and saw the fun of the mystery man and said, half-choking, that little amused the innocent.

— Harmless enough, said the doctor, if he does nothing more than peep. But it alarms people and we'll have to caution him about the bottle. On Red Biddy a Peeping Tom might do anything.

They stepped out into brightness on the top of the Tower. The great gull was gone. The battlemented parapet had long fallen away and for safety the restorers had replaced it with an iron railing.

— There's my mill, said Mortell, all ready for the beginning of harvest. More than sixty years of my life have gone into it. When I was a boy myself and the other boys of Cosmona thought the millwheel was a monster would gobble us all up. Turning and splashing and dripping with water and the mill-building making its own peculiar growling noise. A mother would threaten to put a disobedient child in a sack and bring him to the miller to have him ground. When we saw the sacks of corn going on drays down the corkscrew road we were sure they were full of bad boys.

— You may have been right, the doctor said.

The semicircular hospital and the abbey ruins stood on the gentle northern slope of a river valley. The hunched grey bulk of the old mill was a mile away and in between was the village of Cosmona, the main road that came from Dublin and went on ten miles to the village of Crooked Bridge, the canal that was carried over the river by an aqueduct. To the west there was an abandoned railway line and, rising like another village, older, ghostly, out of the green fields, the buildings that had once been railway station, canal warehouses, one of them even a hotel in the slow plodding days when people travelled by canal. The railway, rusted and grassgrown, was dead. The weedgrown canal was dead to everything except an occasional barge or a pleasure boat struggling westwards to some elysium of wide waters where propellers would not be fouled in green slimy tentacles: a misfortunate Englishman had once had his propellers ruined by a discarded wire mattress.

Late sunlight glittered on motor traffic rising and falling like surfboats over the humpy canal bridge at the eastern end of the village. A double row of beeches lined the sleepy lost Square where the fishing hotel no longer functioned much as an hotel. The fishermen came and went in their cars and didn't stay overnight.

The doctor said: How is Stephen today?

— He's like a doll in the bed. He's like a trailing weed in the millrace.

— I'll drop over tomorrow, even if there's little I can do.

— The jungle did for him. And the Japs. As they did for many a good man. And it breaks my heart to think that my anger ever sent him out to work among strangers and get mixed up in wars. But he was restless and he couldn't thole the work at the mill.

The rising and falling of the distant glittering traffic had a mesmeric effect on the young doctor. He said after a long silence: His life went to save others.

— I try to think that. But his poor wife looks at me when she thinks I'm not noticing as if it was me, not the jungle and the Japs. As if it was I sent him.

— There he goes, shouted the doctor. By God, the flying cyclist, the man of mystery.

Hunched low over the handlebars, his legs frantically working, a figure on a racing bicycle came from the east, rose with the traffic over the bridge, vanished behind the village and its beeches, reappeared as a tiny speck on the rising road that went on westwards, then stopped, dismounted, bent over the bicycle, came walking slowly back towards the village. Their melancholy forgotten or pushed aside, the doctor and the miller hugged each other and laughed.

— He won't break it this time.

— The world's record from Cosmona to Crooked Bridge, said the miller. I asked him one day wouldn't the bus do it quicker than any bicycle. He said: Mr Mortell, with all due respect, it's man and muscle I'm testing, not the machine.

— We'll go down, the doctor said. I'll meet him in the village and talk to him.

But on the way down they saw, half hidden in an embrasure, the book that in that place was even more incongruous than the bottle. The lurid paper cover said that it was all about Solomon and Sheba and that one thousand women burned to share his bed. They left the book where they had found it.

— If those nurses only knew the eyes that watch them, the doctor said.

— 'Twould take the starch out of more than their aprons.

They were still amused when they came to the doctor's Jaguar. He drove the miller to what had once been the fishing hotel.

§

The young doctor drove an expensive Jaguar because his wife's people were able to afford it and he had no quarrel whatever with that circumstance. Looking back on his life and loves he was well pleased that when love had at last led to matrimony the girl happened to have money as well as physical and other attractions. He could have loved a poor girl perhaps as intensely, but not in such comfort.

When he left the miller he drove twice round the Square looking for Gabriel Rock.

The doctor wore a brown wide-brimmed hat, a large brown moustache and whiskers; and his happy cheeks plumped out like tennis balls. His wife had been a nurse and, as an intern, he had proposed to her, sitting during a stolen moment on one of the hospital fire escapes over a bucket containing amongst other oddments a recently amputated diabetic leg. There was no point in waiting for the surroundings to be more propitious since she was pretty and willing and he was in the humour, and the leg had belonged to some sad stranger who wasn't going to have any share in their lives; and so far things had worked out very well.

He listened to the pleased purr of the Jaguar and thought of the car he had driven when he was an undergraduate. It had had no brakes and little floor, and while it had seemed a daring idea at the time, and while it was still fine in convivial places to tell about it for laughs, it had in truth been most uncomfortable and draughty.

Gabriel was not to be seen in the Square so the doctor drove up a narrow laneway of low whitewashed houses, dishwater slime in cobbled vennels, and turned right towards the canal to pass a patch of wasteground where the village smith still shod cartwheels; and there, the butt of the almost certainly doubtful jokes of five or six graceless young loafers, was Gabriel. The doctor saw him or at least he saw the little that was to be seen since, dressed for record-breaking, Gabriel was as mysterious as any masked man. He came to the doctor's signal, wheeling his bicycle, bowing down to look into the car.

— You didn't make it today, Gabriel.

— Broke a chain at top speed.

A pimpled chin, dark with cathairs, a mouthful of irregular teeth, were visible below helmet and goggles.

— Don't think I'm scolding you, Gabriel. But you left some of your belongings up at the Tower.

Low down in the car so that the loafers couldn't see it the doctor exhibited the bottle.

— It's not mine.

— There's a book there, too.

— I don't read much.

— Gabriel, you know what I know. Leave the booze alone and don't annoy them at the hospital. You'll be in trouble and I won't be able to help you. You know my wife wanted to send for the police.

Under the double carapace of helmet and skull the mind of Gabriel was confused for, when he looked at people, he saw and remembered the names not of the people he was looking at but of other people associated with or related to them. He couldn't call the doctor by his title because when he looked at the doctor he could see only the doctor's wife and when the doctor, looking like his wife, also spoke about his wife, confusion was piled on top of confusion. He sweated under leather jacket and corduroys double-seated by his mother to stand the wear and tear of the saddle. He gripped more tightly the tubular steel reality of his beloved red racer that some day would take him from Cosmona to Crooked Bridge at a speed never achieved by Bertie Donnelly or Alo Donnegan or any man who had ever ridden a racer in Ireland or anywhere else.

The doctor said: No hard feelings, Gabriel. Come up Tuesday and I'll give you a day in the garden. But Red Biddy's bad news. So are those Cawley boys you're with now. Watch them, Gabriel.

Gabriel knew as well or better than the doctor did that the Cawley boys were bad news. Their persistent black-eyed malevolence, their gibing tongues, cut sharply at times through Gabriel's dreams of winged speed and fair women. Only one of the three Cawleys was dark, sleek and sharpeyed. The other two were fair and had blank blue eyes. But to Gabriel, peering through goggles from his everlasting confusion about people, they all looked alike and spoke with the one voice. They called, jeering, to him now as he stood in the roadway, one knee bent in a fragment of a curtsey to the back of the car that carried the doctor's wife away from him.

— Gaby, was he asking you up to see his wife's operation?

— A fine cut she has too.

— Her little bum's like a pudding in a rag.

— Tighter than Nora Duckarse there.

The bicycle chain was mended and with one leg across the machine he was ready for flight but, impaled by the sharp tongues, he paused to look after the slatternly simpleton of a girl who passed, bucket in hand, to the iron pump at the corner of the patch of wasteground. At every fourth step or so she stamped her left foot as if she were angry, or squashing beetles. Her lowslung hips waggled like shutters hanging from half-broken hinges.

— Gaby, carry the lady's bucket.

— Take an eyeful, Gaby. The wiggle-waggle.

— Gaby, when a girl walks like that it's a sure sign she's wide open.

With a mutter that was almost a moan Gabriel was in the saddle and riding away furiously, laughter behind him, before him a vision of tiled walls reflecting bright lights, of white aprons rustling around firm bodies.

On the spokes of the wheels he had fixed leaden wights at differing and carefully calculated distances from the hub. The idea was that when the wheels started moving the weights would add momentum and set him travelling faster and faster, faster even than any man ever rode in the great race round France that the miller had once told him about. The miller was the one man in Cosmona that Gabriel Rock didn't confuse with anybody else.

§

From one of the leaflets the miller read in the rising and falling singsong of a school of elocution long gone out of fashion: My sister, my spouse, is a garden enclosed, a fountain sealed up.

The meaning dawning on him as he read he could have bitten out his tongue with embarrassment. Dear Sister Thermometer and fat little Sister Bruno who had compiled the devout voluptuous anthology didn't know a lot about life. But the woman behind the bar in what had once been the fishing hotel wasn't following him with any particular attention. She accepted a bundle of leaflets without looking at them and left them on the bar beside a collection box for the foreign missions. Guarding the slot of the box a miniature Saint Martin de Porres knelt, and nodded his head like a Dixie coon to acknowledge every contribution.

— Last week, she said, he nodded for two miraculous medals and some francs that one of our pious citizens brought back from Lourdes. For a saint of God he hasn't much discrimination. If leaflets could keep people happy Sister Thermometer would be the world's greatest benefactor. Those imps of schoolgirls have me annoyed.

Entering the hotel the miller had heard behind him the giggle, the quick sharp footfalls of little girls. They came, trying to tiptoe, through the cobbled arched entryway that cut into the heart of the big sixteen-windowed house and then sloped down to a grassgrown courtyard. Long ago stagecoaches had passed that way.

I see in the chamber above me, he thought, the patter of little feet: for Longfellow's poem about the children's hour and the Bishop of Bingen in his watchtower on the Rhine had been in the Sixth Reader which, prose and poetry, he in his schooldays had learned by heart and still remembered. Voices soft and sweet, the voices of grave Alice and laughing Allegra and Edith with golden hair plotting and planning together to take him by surprise, followed him as he turned right down three steps from the entryway and left down three more steps into the cellar bar-room. Increased in numbers to six or seven the giggling girls paused at the top of the second three steps and looked down at himself and the woman.

— Please, Mrs Hanafin, can we go to the toilet here?

— Go home, Mary. Go home, Minnie. Go home the crowd of you.

Grave Alice and laughing Allegra and Edith with golden hair scattered giggling. In apology for her asperity she said: I used to allow them, Mr Mortell. But they'd be in there for ages in deep silence apart from the odd fits of giggling. Then when they'd go

I'd find the whole carpet splattered with water. Standing on dirty feet too on the low seat before the dressing-table. It's a game.

The saccharine lines from the Sixth Reader pleased the heart of the old miller. He said: Aren't they young girls on the way home from school, living in a magic world and playing at being women?

— A poor game to play, she said sourly and read from a leaflet: She glorifieth her nobility by being conversant with God. Yea, and the Lord of all things hath loved her.

— Are you for Dublin for the wedding?

She picked up a second leaflet. She said: I suppose Sister Bruno by diabetes doth glorify her nobility, the poor old duck. She never married. I was at one wedding too many.

— Shadow and Substance are going?

— They're in the yard, tinkering at the car. My father and mother went yesterday.

She picked up yet a third leaflet. She was a small demure woman, tiny by contrast with the bulk of the miller. She led the way out of the bar. Business, she told him, was so slack that the place could look after itself for a while; and indeed the ancient room had about it a close, brooding, self-protecting personality. It had been the cellar of an older house that had been on the site even before the coaching inn that had preceded the fishing hotel. Now, with barrels for seats and dim alcoves lit by weak bulbs in old coach lanterns, it preserved an antique secretive appearance. Across the entry it was matched by a cellar dining room, just a little less sepulchral.

— Trade in Cosmona, she said. Snakes in Iceland. No wonder Gabriel Rock is always trying to get to Crooked Bridge in less time than it takes to tell.

Substance, or James Tarrant, the dominant brother of twins, dominant because it was said he had come second out of the womb pushing Shadow, or John, before him, sat stout and solid, a farmer and man of business in good dark broadcloth, behind the wheel of the car. He listened, pious head to one side, while the miller told him that his oats were ground and in sacks and ready for removal. Struggling under the weight of two suitcases Shadow, thin, stooped, prematurely grey, came from a back door.

First in and well planted, the folklore of Cosmona said, is last out and lucky for life. First out is last in, the dribblings of the ammunition bag, the sort of man who'd be wearing boxing gloves if it rained threepenny bits. Panting and peevish, always aware that he was fired from the second barrel and could expect nothing, Shadow took his subordinate place behind his brother and primly folded his shabby grey overcoat about his knees.

— Cathy won't come, Substance said. She says she was at one wedding too many.

Her brown eyes, under long lashes and behind thick-lensed spectacles, surveyed her prosperous complacent brother who had once, he said, been inspired to settle a trade dispute by making a novena to that charming little lady of the bourgeoisie, Saint Thérèse, the Little Flower. To Cosmona he was sometimes known as the Little Flower.

She said: The young couple will have the benefit of your bachelor's experience and advice. Give her this too with your prayers.

She reached him a leaflet.

— And one each for John and yourself. Compliments of Sister Thermometer.

— My beloved is gone down into his garden, Substance read, to the bed of aromatical spices, to feed in the gardens and to gather lilies.

— It does sound a bit odd, he said, but the nuns bless them must know.

— As much as yourself, she said.

The miller, happily, had an honest infectious laugh. He laughed now at the discomfiture on the face of Substance, and even Shadow smiled – but weakly.

— Cathy's tongue, Substance said humbly.

Standing side-by-side the miller and the woman waved the car away to the Dublin wedding. The grassgrown yard was quiet all around them except for the tick-tock of light hammering from the hut where Peejay, the hotel's handyman, lived.

— Peejay's at the carpentry now, the miller said.

— Or the painting. Or playing the fiddle with the bow in his teeth.

— Peejay's a born genius.

— And a poet and a little saint. Much more so than that pious bullock of a brother of mine.

— Don't be too hard on him.

— He means well you mean. Oh, he gave me a home, or rather my father did, when my own home went up in smoke. I'm duly grateful.

They walked back through the entryway. He rested his hard heavy hand on her shoulder. He said: No word of Christy?

— No, thank God. We've heard nothing of him since his last appearance in the newspapers. That was enough, wasn't it?

— But oh look, she said, here comes Tumble the Town.

Slowly along the Square, pulled by a weary saddle-backed piebald, went a light, brightly-coloured springcart. The driver was a ragged black-bearded man wide in the chest and shoulders almost to the point of deformity. The shawled woman who sat beside him smoked a pipe and replied in kind to the greetings of the three Cawley boys who pranced at the tailboard of the cart.

— I dread the sight of him, she said.

— Patrick Hoban, strong man, of no fixed abode and prone to bate the police.

— We'll have poor Annie dancing on the seat of a chair in every pub in the village.

— 'Tisn't many husbands, the miller said, could hold the backrung of a chair in their teeth while the wife hoofed it on the seat.

— A model husband, she said, like my Christy.

Responding to a remark from the shawled woman the following boys raised a shout.

— He's sober, she said, or he wouldn't suffer those terrible boys.

Walking to his mill, on down the sloping road past the last low cottages and gardens of the village, Martin Mortell meditated on those terrible boys. His own son, now limp as a weed in the millrace, had once been a terrible boy, not vicious like the Cawleys, but wild and alive.

In the old ramshackle building he climbed the first wooden ladder to the stone-loft and touched gently the heavy millstones that meant as much to him, he often feared, as children. The stones were warm almost and living to his touch; and all his aged melancholy, his helplessness before the inevitable maladorous approach of death, begotten by suffering and disease in a faraway green jungle, vanished before his pride in his ability to dress and swing these stones. Great industry had passed him by and left his mill and himself museum pieces on the side of a salmon river. But how many men living today could cut those curving marks in stone and balance the stones so delicately that, revolving, they could take the print off a visiting card without much damaging the pasteboard. Towny visitors with cameras always marvelled at that one. These stones were his undying children and through them, and the grain drying on the perforated earthenware floor of the kiln, he was a god on his own ground or at least a better man than a whole chartered company of men owning a million new-fangled machines.

Consoled by the touch of the stones he went down from the loft again, laughing to himself. There had been that day when he played the trick on the Cawley boys and their followers. He hadn't intended to be mean but they had pestered him for handfuls of dry oats from the kiln floor to munch and chew. The crisp grain was rated a delicacy among the boys of Cosmona and the best boys in the world they were, even the Cawleys, but for their own good you had to chasten them now and again. So he gave them a large bowl of oats treated with glauber salts, and from the top loft of the mill saw them afterwards, seven of them on their hunkers beside the roadside hedge, pants down, bare bottoms and shirt tails exposed, pained expressions on their faces. He was fond of the young but even the Lord himself chastised those he loved, and they had had him pestered, and on the previous day one of the Cawley boys had broken a valuable hammer, the property of the mill.

He walked round the building to the head of the millrace. That loodheramaun of a television photographer had asked him one day how you started the mill. So the miller had said, suiting the action to the word: You turn on the river.

He did now as he had done then. One twist of an iron bar and the water from the opulent panting millrace was beating rhythmically on the paddles of the wheel and the belly of the mill was half-grumbling, half-laughing, devouring grain, grinding out oatmeal, sweet with the smell of water and the taste of stone, for man and beast. He was content for a while as the master of at least two elements. But the released and redirected water stirred and altered the position of the submerged weeds in the race and set them helplessly trailing. Limp like a doll in the bed, he thought, like a weed waving in the salmon water.

§

On the morning of the day on which Shadow and Substance set out from Cosmona to the Dublin wedding, Teresa Fallon and Dympna Cawley, two fair maidens of Cosmona, covered the same road – but not to any wedding. Teresa had had the idea on the previous night, a sultry harvest night that threatened rain, when the pair of them had decided they were browned-off for all eternity working as wardsmaids in the hospital. The nuns scolded them and lectured them and expected them to be spotless little angels in white shifts. The nurses looked down on them and pranced past them as if nurses, in blue-and-white, were fashion models and wardsmaids, in white and grey, were dung, although it was the nurses had to carry the bedpans and that was the only reason they had for having a stink in their noses. The nurses had rooms and the wardsmaids only dormitories and this night, instead of lying down behind white cubicle curtains, Teresa and Dympna stayed out after the evening walk that came between slavery and supper and went to spend the night in Cawleys' which was open house. But that was only the beginning of the plan. Teresa was mad about Enda Cawley, and Dympna knew that Teresa and Enda might as well be married as the way they were, but Enda was the last person in the world they could tell about the plan because when a fellow had That he thought he was entitled to everything else too and Enda was a very bossy fellow and only looked easy and laughing and happy when he was playing the guitar which he did for the Blue Nuggets, the show-band of Cosmona. He played the tin whistle and the melodeon as well and while that wasn't romantic like films about Monterey and down Mexico way it was lively and funny. All the Cawley boys were musical.

Cosmona called the Cawley house the Ranch not because it was a ranch or because the Cawleys were in the cattle trade, they were really in the scrap metal trade, but because it was a long ell-shaped one-storeyed wooden structure bought out of surplus army stock and ornamented at each extremity by bus bodies that had exchanged their wheels for stilts and been transformed into greenhouses. At the rear of the house seven more bus bodies had exchanged most of their glass panels for plywood or corrugated iron and been transformed into sheds for scrap, and one of them into a henhouse, so that when you stood high in Cosmona and looked over the mill and the river valley in the direction of Crooked Bridge the Cawley place looked like a shanty town.

Two hundred yards further upstream along the valley slope was the white thatched cottage where Teresa's grandparents lived, and that was a most important part of the plan. Teresa said the plan would be an adventure or, at least, a change. Teresa, since her parents were dead, lived with her grandparents who were feeble and half deaf and had no more control over her and her adventures than they had over the wind that blew. When Teresa was up before the court for the larceny of cigarettes from a shop in Crooked Bridge she would have been sent to a home, she wasn't quite sixteen, if Sister Thermometer hadn't offered to find her a job and keep an eye on her. As if Sister Thermometer could keep an eye on Teresa. The thought of what that eye might see often gave Teresa and Dympna a laugh.

Half asleep in bed that night dreamy Dympna half-laughed at Sister Thermometer's eye, as big in the darkness as a plate and seeing with holy horror what was going on in the bed beside Dympna between Teresa and Enda who had slipped in as soon as the house was quiet. Dympna's own eyes were blank blue like the eyes of the two younger Cawley boys, but larger and liquid like saucers of a delicate duckegg blue china whose shallow bottoms were swimming in water. Pushover, dreamy, come-to-bed eyes Teresa called them; and a few bright boys at the street corners of Cosmona said, and some of them from experience, that if you simply stared long enough into those eyes Dympna would unhitch her drawers and go down backwards like a zombie. Teresa on the other hand was tall, with long red hair veiling one eye, and freckles, and teeth that protruded a little and shone and bruised Enda's lips, and a slight tendency to bow-leggedness which the wise men of the street corners said could be a good sign, except that Teresa was only for Enda. Nobody cared to challenge his title.

Pretending to be sound asleep Dympna lay unmoving while Enda on his own territory exercised his rights and once, when the moans were sharpest and the breathing heaviest and the buck-jumping wild enough to unsettle the bedclothes, Enda made a glawm sideways and through a rent in her tattered nightdress found Dympna. It was part of the plan that Teresa and herself would soon have better nightdresses. The contact, as long as he left That alone, gave her a warming pleasing feeling of community. Teresa was, after all, her best friend even if she was never so certain about Enda being her real true brother. For in a house where father and mother, two sons and a daughter were all easy people, flaxenhaired and content with what came their way, Enda, the eldest son living, was dark, sharp, glittering, always grabbing the best of what was and then restless for what wasn't there. He ruled the Ranch. You couldn't tell him about a plan or he would want the entire proceeds for himself.

When he had slipped away like a thief or something in the night Dympna asked if now wasn't the hour but Teresa, panting, said to give her time to get her breath and gather her wits, that night-duty was harder on her than on the nurse they called the Mouse who was in love with the clerical student. Then they laughed and hugged, they were sisters in a way, and dozed until the first harvest light dripped green from the fields into the wooden room. They dressed without washing, they combed, applied cosmetics, made and drank strong tea, ate leftover cold sausages, and set out along a narrowing boreen to the cottage where Teresa's grandparents lived. High hedges hid them from the world and the birds were as cheerful and busy as if they were paid for it.

The back door of the cottage, which stood at right angles to the boreen with a garden before and a netting-wired hen-run behind, was fastened on the outside by a chain linked on to a nail. Teresa quietly unfastened it and they slipped out of their shoes and tiptoed into a kitchen from which they could see through an open doorway old granny in her bed and a nightcap on her head and a smile on her face that would have vanished like smoke if she'd known what was going on around her in the land of the waking. The old woman was a renowned miser.

Breathless, Dympna stood in the kitchen and admired the deftness with which Teresa took from under a corner of the mattress a brown cardigan rolled in a bundle, from the cardigan an old-fashioned black handbag, from the handbag a roll of notes from which she peeled one fiver and five singles. The click of the bag's metal clasp seemed loud enough to waken Cosmona but greedy granny went on smiling – Teresa said afterwards that in her dreams she must have been winning the Sweep – and granda grunted and turned but didn't matter because he could neither see nor be seen, being only a lump under the bedclothes. Teresa said to Dympna that here was a pound for herself just so that she would have something in her pocket and not feel like a pauper, and that her granny would never miss the money because she had plenty of cheques and wasn't too good at the counting. Dympna said nothing but took liberty to doubt the bit about the cheques.

From the flat flagstone by the back door they lifted a can with a pint of new milk in it. A few early worm-hunting hens looked at them curiously. They drank the milk as they walked along and threw the can into a disused quarryhole in a field at a twist of the boreen on a high place from which they could look across the river towards the hospital. A few lights showed palely on the morning balconies and the Tower was black and solid. Lazy rooks rose slowly from the trees behind the nurses' home and one brute of a white seagull circled the top of the Tower. Teresa supposed that Gabriel Rock would be gone home now from his night's work of peeping over the railings at those stuck-up good-for-nothing nurses. He had little to look at and somebody should show him something to ease his mind, and she might herself some day out of pity give him a peep if she had time and Enda's permission. Gabriel anyway could only see one half of a nurse or one half of anything because he had the use only of his left eye since Ignatius Cawley, the youngest of her brothers, pasted him on the right eye with a rock, and that was why he was called

Rock. His mother's name was Orr and as far as anyone knew he
never had a father. But if he saw only one half of a nurse it would
certainly be the half that the apron covered, and if he peeped long
and hard enough he might see one half of what happened when
that so-called clerical student with the grand airs, and the revolving bookcase that had the wardsmaids killed pushing it from
place to place, tried to hoist the blue skirt of the Mouse who was
on night duty. Through chokes of laughter Dympna said that the
Mouse was crazy about the clerical student, the watery creature,
and serve her right, and that yesterday morning he hadn't hobbled
up the chapel aisle to communion and Dympna wondered were
they up to anything fancy. Teresa said as sure as shooting he had
set a trap at her mousehole and Dympna laughed until the blue
saucers overflowed and she had to wipe the water from her plump
pink cheeks.

   In high mirth with the propitious morning and the money in
their bags they walked back boldly past the Ranch and through
the awakening village, knowing that anyone who saw them
would think that they were two good girls heading off for a day's
slavery in the hospital. Half a mile east of the canal bridge they
waited at a sheltered corner under tall trees for the early morning
bus. Men coaxing a reaper and binder into the corner of a wheat-
field waved at them and they waved back. Ninety minutes later
they were walking the quays in the city of Dublin.

§

   From the deck of the *Hispaniola* he saw the island: two low
hills away to the southwest and rising behind them a third and
higher hill, all three sharp and conical. The persuasive voice of
Long John Silver assured him that the island was a sweet spot for
a lad to get ashore on, to bathe, climb trees, hunt goats, to be
young and happy and possess ten toes. On the glass walls of the
playroom between the ward for little boys and the ward for big
boys Sister Francis Regis had painted in the most radiant colours
the tale of the famous treasure hunt all the way from the old
seadog at the Admiral Benbow to Silver at his slaughter in the
grey woods, and back again triumphantly to the docks of Bristol.
For seventeen months Peter Lane had received his visitors in a

quiet corner of the playroom, little used by the up-patients in fine weather, and made so many times the same joke about how welcome they were to Treasure Island. Several times he had audibly wished that his timbers might be shivered, and tapped the fracture board under the mattress and impressed visitors with his good humour and resignation.

That particular evening he talked to the two young clerics, contemporaries of his in grace and wisdom if the third lump of his lumbar spine hadn't handicapped him, of what it felt like to learn to walk all over again. They still called each other Brother. Repeating a favourite quotation of the priest who had been their Master of Novices, Brother Keegan, who was literary, reminded Brother Lane that when the famous Dean Stanley came to his deathbed he said to somebody: Things seem so different when one assumes the horizontal.

— Different too when you reassume the vertical. I thought my head would never stop soaring. I felt like Tom the Steeple who thought he was a church. The nurses suddenly seemed so small.

The first time, the Mouse had helped him to his feet. Her lively grey eyes had mocked him when he said he would stand and take his first steps unaided. That was partly bravado and partly the last remnants of a monastic reluctance to touch a woman, to lean on her, his arm around her shoulders. But to his mortification he had been more than glad to depend on her while he painfully struggled erect, took two faltering steps forwards, went into reverse, sat down again, gasping, on the bed. She was so small and neat, but surprisingly strong. Looking down on her from his tottering eminence he realised that he had never seen her in ordinary clothes nor seen her hair unveiled.

— I had to be supported and led at first.

Brother Keegan said that another did gird him and lead him where he would'st not.

Brother Kennedy who was artistic said Brother Lane was a resurrection, like a painting by Stanley Spencer.

— My choice of hikes was limited. From the end of one bed to another. Hobbling. Clutching. Surgeon Behan said no sticks allowed. But one day I made the grand tour to the chapel and then on to the room where Sister Francesca gives advice to the poor people who come to see her. She has a green parrot called Andy. One day it hid under the table, then darted out and bit a wards-maid's ankle.

Brother Kennedy who was inclined to be facetious wondered if that meant that the parrot liked or disliked wardsmaids.

— She was very plump and innocent. Her name was Dympna Cawley. One day I got daring and walked all the way to the Tower. But not to the top of it. I'll do that soon.

He had warmly leaned on the Mouse all the way. She had been on day duty then. She had said: You can climb the Tower when you get your trousers. You'll be a man again, out of pyjamas and dressing gown.

To Brothers Keegan and Kennedy he said: It's fine for the first few days. Then the muscles start to grow again. Agony.

Obedient to rule, and edifying and being edified by the sick, they discreetly turned the talk to matters that had to do with the spiritual life. They talked of Christ, the life of the soul, and the writings of Dom Columba Marmion, O.S.B., Abbot of Maredsous. Brother Keegan said that he had read that, like Socrates, Dom Marmion did not actually write his own books. They were compiled from notes taken down by his disciples at his conferences. Indeed, his book about Christ as the ideal of the priest did not appear until almost thirty years after his death, having been edited by Dom Thibault and Dom Ryeland from notes on the priest and the priesthood which they found among Marmion's papers. Marmion disposed of, they were moving on to the French Jesuit, Père Raoul Plus, when far away along the tiled corridor that led to the nurses' home he heard her sharp quick breathless steps.

She was nineteen and always as if in a hurry, a child clutching a coin and running to spend it on some delectable toy. She brought back to him the excitement of the Saturday nights of childhood, the lighted crowded shops, his mother burdened with mysterious parcels, the feeling that the world was jelly and cream to be nibbled at and savoured and squelched in the mouth after Sunday's dinner. She didn't have to pass through the playroom on her way, before going on duty, to take the air with the other night nurses on the green, close to the Tower. But with a guilty delight he was aware that she came that way deliberately to talk to him, to be introduced to his visitors, to find out more and more about him. He said: This is Nurse Walters. I almost said the Mouse.

— Cheek, she said. Some people.

She stooped, laughing, to tuck in a trailing corner of the bed-clothes. Her pretty heartshaped face came so close to his that he could count the tiny dark freckles around her nose and feel one gentle warm spurt of her breathing. Her small firm breasts of white linen touched his right forearm and under the bedclothes he was aware of an uncelibate flutter of muscle, quite out of keeping with the company of the thoughts of the Abbot of Maredsous. Then, telling him that she would see him later to guard him against the ghost, she was gone through an opening in the glass partition – between the dark mouth of Ben Gunn's cave and the homeward-bound *Hispaniola*.

— The Mouse, said Brother Keegan, the ghost.

— Here, said Brother Kennedy, be mysteries.

— She's from Kenmare, he said, a lovely Munster accent and very good to the patients.

He felt with embarrassment that he sounded as if he were describing a property or a person in which he had an inordinate interest. He felt a hypocrite as he added unctuously: Only when you've been a hospital patient for a long time do you realise the bravery and self-sacrifice of nurses.

Brother Keegan said it was a hard but a high vocation.

Brother Kennedy said: The Mouse?

— Oh the boys call her that. One day one of the up-patients, a big wild Mayo lad called Durcan, tried to frighten her with a live mouse he had found in his locker. But quite calmly she took the timorous beastie from the boy, set it free on the grass and gave Durcan a scolding about cruelty to animals.

Three reverend minds in silence admired the intrepidity of the nurse from Kenmare.

Brother Kennedy said: The ghost?

— That's a curious story. It also concerns Nurse Walters and she's such a sensible level-headed young girl that I feel one may believe it. Look out there, just close to where she's walking now.

She was, in fact, running. She ran with an easy swinging of well-hung limbs. She was a good hockey player. She called and waved to two nurses who strolled in the distance.

— There's a bushy corner between the two wings of the hospital. By night it's not too well lighted. One night a week ago Nurse Walters was walking past there with another nurse. They're a little on edge these nights because of some mystery man who skulks about peeping in at the lighted balconies. Suddenly Nurse Walters stops the other nurse and holds her by the arm and says there's somebody standing in there under the bushes. But the other nurse could see nothing.

— The mystery man?

— No, a mystery woman. A third nurse. But this is the odd part of the story. The nurse in the shadows was a stranger to Nurse Walters. She was an old woman and not dressed as the nurses now dress. Her skirt was down to her heels. Her veil was knotted, not flowing free. So over supper that night the nurses told the night matron who crossed herself and said they must have a mass said for the repose of the soul of old Nurse Callaghan who died in the nurses' home ten or more years ago. She was a retiring eccentric old lady who never left the hospital even on her holidays. She'd sit at the window of her room looking towards the boys' balconies. Her dying words were: Keep them well tucked in on cold nights. Nurse Walters says that if I wake at midnight and find a dear old lady tucking me in I'm to know it's Nurse Callaghan.

His face felt warm as he said that, and the unseen flutter of muscle was at him again, for he remembered that the night she had joked about the ghost was the first night they had kissed. Bending, tucking in the bedclothes, she had pretended to tickle his ribs. He had responded by touching her soft armpits, and her face and fresh lips were so unavoidably close to him. Simeon the celibate fell on his ass from his pillar and although he knew the matter was not grievous enough to be mortal he could not hobble to the communion rail the next morning to welcome the Lord into the mouth that had kissed a woman.

Brother Keegan said: The mass?

— Was said, of course. And Nurse Walters had another mass said. And the chaplain quietly blessed the spot where the poor spirit had been seen. There has been no reappearance. Although for a few nights every nurse in the hospital was seeing visions and dreaming dreams.

Out of wide celibate experience Brother Kennedy said that we were all gregarious, only women more so.

As they talked and the dusk came he watched her walking with the other nurses. The light breeze fluttered blue skirts, white veils and aprons. This was a happy restful hour of the evening with night nurses meeting day nurses in a comradely ebb-and-flow. Because of her he was so conscious now that they were all soft-bosomed, sweet-breathing young women. The voices of the children, weary after the days talking and shouting, were muted on the balconies. Homing rooks flapped lazily over the roof of the girls' wing. He dozed when the holy brothers left him, and cycled off to a life that he had lived until seventeen months ago, and that now seemed more remote than Treasure Island or that summer of the black cat and the wonderful holiday that some night he meant to tell her about. He floated and splashed gently in shallow dreams of steep-walled mountains deeply cut by watercourses, the buzzing of summer heat on goat paths among deep furze, a black cat going wild in woods by a river, a freckled girl in a coat with a green cape, horse races on sands by a far western sea. He dozed until Dympna Cawley, a bandage around her ankle where the parrot had bitten her, came with another wardsmaid, gawky, redheaded, with protruding teeth, to wheel him and his loaded lopsided revolving bookcase back to his corner of the balcony. He always felt sympathy for the wardsmaids. They seemed under-privileged and overworked. To make talk he asked them when were they going on their holidays. They giggled. They wheeled around him the pink screen that Sister Camillus insisted should be around his bed to provide privacy for prayer, meditation and reading. Then the gawky redhead said they were going on holiday tomorrow to Dublin to see the big smoke and the bright lights, and giggling they left him.

§

With a thrilling sense of freedom and superiority Teresa and Dympna stood on the big bridge over the river in the centre of the city and watched busloads of girls going north and south and droves of girls, breathless, clutching bags of all shapes and sizes, trotting north and south on unsteady heels. Teresa chewed caramels with a squelching noise and a manlike or horselike jaw-movement and Dympna said the noise reminded her of the day her brothers had thrown a frog to a ferret on the bridge at Mortell's mill. Teresa had a wonderful knack of coating her teeth with a soft paste of caramel, then removing it with a deft flick of the tongue and displaying the imprint of her teeth. When she had done this three times she rolled the three impressions into one mushy ball and tossed it on the pavement in the hope that it might stick to the shoe of one of the trotting typists. It did. When the harassed girl had removed her shoe, scraped the sole with a comb and, flushed and anxious, thrown the comb into the river, they left the bridge contentedly and walked along the river wall. Teresa hoped that the fancy little bitch would be late for work.

They sat, taking the sun, on steps close to a bus-stop and speculated on the occupations, riches, sexual prowess and dispositions of the men going into and coming out of a nearby jakes. They talked to a baldheaded taximan who directed them to a basement restaurant, telling them to tell the man that Dick the Taximan had sent them. The most important thing, Teresa maintained, was a full belly. The basement restaurant was cosy, with a jukebox, red paper on the walls and magazine covers of girls in bathing suits or in their naked pelt, and oilcloth on the tables, and sausage, egg and chips and tea, and bread and butter by the hundredweight. At that early hour they were the only customers and had the undivided ministrations of the proprietor, a redheaded man with crosseyes, sleeves rolled-up off flabby freckled arms, and a long dirty white apron down to his toes. Teresa whispered to Dympna that if he ever ran out of food he could always cook and serve his apron and Dympna laughed until light blue tears rained down on the yellow eyes of her fried eggs. Then the proprietor said he was always glad to see young girls laughing, that, in fact, a hearty laugh was as healthy as a dose of salts. He was glad moreover to hear that Dick the Taximan had sent them because Dick the Taximan was a solid man, no better, always on the ball. They should come back at night when the place would be full of young girls like themselves and fellows all dancing. He played two tunes on the jukebox for them and refused to take any money for their meal and walked with them, when they were going, to the top of the stairs, his right hand on Teresa's shoulder, his left hand on Dympna's. He said that Dublin was a big place and a friend was a friend and toodlepip until tonight.

The mid-morning rush all around them impressed them with the realisation that he had only been telling the bare truth when he told them that Dublin was a big place. But the bustle of the shop they bought the clothes in excited them and made them proud with the power of money. They bought two of everything: nylons, pants, slips and bras, and Teresa was so delighted with her black, lace-fringed pants that she dragged Dympna back to the ladies' on the quays where, locked in one cubicle, they struggled into that much of their finery. Teresa flushed her discarded and battered pair down the bowl in the expressed hope that they would block the pipe and said that she wouldn't miss them, that they'd never been the same since one night Enda was in a hurry and reefed them on the night of the Blue Nuggets' annual spot-prize dance.

Across the road from the ladies' they entered the snug of a select saloon bar and sat for a while among dirty unshaven dockers washing coaldust out of their pipes with pints. But when they asked for two orange juices the ignorant lump of a barman said that ladies unaccompanied were not served in that pub and that they would have to go elsewhere. A well-dressed elderly gentleman with a lovely furry sort of a coat and a briefcase, but very drunk, said Timothy let the lassies have a tincture, for truth gleaneth in the field of booze, but the big thick said sorry Mister Mack no can do, rules of the house and you've had enough yourself anyway. Then Teresa rose to her full height and said that, as the man said about smoking cowdung, they were missing nothing by not drinking in that hole, and damn his impudence, and thank you sir a gentleman is always a gentleman, and she would go now and wash the dirt of the snug off her hands. The gentleman raised his hat and applauded. The dockers said nothing.

The mention of washing set Dympna thinking and she said she'd adore a lovely warm bath. Dympna was fond of the water and every chance she got at the hospital she was reclining and soaking and gently boiling herself. They found Dick the Taximan and he told them where the public baths were. It wasn't Hollywood or foam baths but it was lively running water. Dympna drifting off into one of her dreams said that someday she'd have a bath in milk like the film actress in Cork who kicked up hell because the hotel she was in wouldn't give her enough milk to bathe in, and right they were Teresa said, for nobody would ever drink milk in the place again and if fat Dympna had a bath in milk she'd wind up with curds and whey between her legs and a pound of butter up her bum. As they were sharing a wooden cubicle they splashed cold water on each other and laughed. Teresa, red hair in a white rubber cap, pranced like a wild goat under the shower. Dympna, a plump white porpoise, lolled in the tub until Teresa turned on the cold tap and froze her out of it.

The old woman who took the money at the door had sharp brown eyes and a throat swollen with goitre, and solemnly she warned them not to give or accept a loan of soap. Soap carried germs. Under questioning, after they had dried and dressed themselves, she went into further details. There were young girls today, dolled-up as fancy as queens, on the streets of Dublin but with bandages around their ankles and sores all over their bodies. She'd like to see the day she'd lend soap to one of those. They were beyond the benefits of soap. When her own husband, God be good to him, had died of agony of the heart, the doctors called it, she had knocked around for money for seven years and thank God she never got a spot although her own brother who had been in the British navy had caught gonorrhoea in Gibraltar and his penis, saving your presence, swelled up as big as your arm. She knew where her own good luck came from and that was the night she had refused the priest who offered her thirty shillings with his coat turned up to hide the white collar but you'd know him a mile off, and God help him she had advised him for the best and asked him most respectfully did he not think of the consecrated fingers. But luck she knew from that moment and the goodness of God, for the finest man you'd meet could be a walking monument of decay and girls couldn't be too careful, anything but clap.

Dympna said you'd never get a dose if you didn't sit on the timber of the toilet and that the old witch was raving. Yet the two of them leaving the baths were silent and chastened and a little homesick for the familiar men and ways of Cosmona. By night on these streets a black giant went about scattering disease. Babies wouldn't get too bad because Cosmona was, from all angles, well used to babies being born and sometimes, on the quiet, buried, and if a girl was careful and did it standing as much as possible, and chewed and ate blotting paper, and drank boiled water that had rusty nails in it, and wore her miraculous medal around her neck she would be safe always.

After that they paid a shilling each to see the girl on ice in the basement of the Fun Palace and Teresa put sixpence into a fortune-telling slot machine that told her on a printed card that she made friends easily, might expect changes in the month of September, and that a dark stranger was coming into her life.

The girl on ice wore nothing but a bra, blonde hair and the skimpiest of pants. She lay flat on her back inside a sort of ice coffin open at her head and feet and smiled, and as they looked at her the boozy voice behind them said could the public feel her to see if she was centrally heated; and there was the gentleman with the furry coat and the briefcase. Since he asked them most politely they went with him to another publichouse where they drank orange and he drank whiskey after whiskey and told them how much he loved his daughters, his wife was dead, and what were two lovely young girls like them doing wandering around Dublin. Teresa said this was the way of it: that they came from Donegal and had been badly treated at home, that they were looking for jobs in the city and for a room where they could live and entertain their friends. The gentleman approved. What they wanted now Teresa said was a few pounds, the price of shoes and stockings, because nothing went against you so much if you were job-hunting as to be down-at-heel and have laddered stockings. The gentleman said that was true, and, moreover, unfair to the poor since the only reason for job-hunting was to acquire the means for getting up at heel. He gave them a fiver and said he would be here when they came back. Speechless, but laughing, with the sense of good luck they went like hares along the quays to a cinema leaving their benefactor luxuriating in Turkish dreams of a room, secret even from God himself, where he would be entertained by two capering scampering girls, one fore, one aft, or one above and one below. His money, he was delighted to think, would case four thighs in nylon right up to the furry fringes of bliss.

When the barman who was sympathetic told him he was half-asleep and should go home to shut-eye he explained with great precision, for he was quite sober, that a dreamer in bed is behaviourally asleep but mentally awake in contrast to the alcoholic who is behaviourally awake at the bar but mentally in delirium tremens, and that while a dreamer may remember his dreams a drunk may not even remember where he has been, what he has done nor what has happened to him. Then he fell asleep and forgot all about Teresa and Dympna who were smoking, eating chocolates and holding hands at the pictures.

It seemed to be their fate that day to meet rare drunk men, and the second man was a wonder to see. He was a saucy sailor bold, he wasn't black, he wasn't white, he was a deep, deep brown. The pants he wore were tight and made of leather shiny black, his shirt was red as blood. He said room ant coke, but the barman who was a kind old fellow shook his head and smiled. His face was brown, his hair was curly black, and both his cheeks were marked with scars in distant battles won. Dympna thought he was a dote, a black and red and brown doll, his teeth so shining white when he turned round and smiled.

When he realised that he wasn't getting any more rum and coke he didn't run amok and wreck the house. He smiled more than ever and said not droonk and to prove it sprang off the floor, turned the wildcat in mid-air and landed safely without ever losing his breath. When he had done this three times the old barman relented and gave him rum and for Dympna and Teresa the sailor bought orange. In his five or six words of English he tried to work out the geographical position of the pub in relation to the dock where his ship had tied up. He waved his hands. He said thees way and thataway. He said nord sood, and when Teresa told him he had come in through a hole in the wall he laughed like a happy boy although he didn't understand a word of what she said. He said loov, and lay back in his chair and made his stomach muscles undulate as if he had a bag of struggling serpents under his shirt. Dympna was thrilled. She said to Teresa that she liked nothing better than being french-kissed by a man with the smell of rum off his breath, and Teresa said that she never knew Dympna was fond of rum, and they laughed and the brown sailor laughed with them. With the stub of a pencil he wrote on a dripmat the name of Liberia and Dympna wrote beside it the name of Cosmona. Then he said eets, food, loov, and made chewing movements and smacking and sucking noises, and Teresa had another idea. With one of them hanging on each of his arms they walked to the basement restaurant.

Teresa sang do you want to dance, baby, come hold my hand, baby, because you're my man. Baybee, said the brown sailor to Dympna, baybee, dansay, dansay. This was the life and Dick the Taximan, who was there, was a true friend to tell them about it. The place was crowded. The cross-eyed redheaded man was in a black suit, white shirt and bow tie. The jukebox was heavenly, and girls of all shapes, sizes, hairdos and colours swinging and rocking and rolling and twisting, and Dublinmen and sailing men, sober and drunk and drunker, dancing, eating, drinking red wine out of cups, buying for the girls at prices that got bigger as the buyers got drunker, and hoping that in the end they'd get value of their money in fun. They sat with Dick the Taximan and the boss sat with them for a while and then sent over to sit with them a tall brunette called Amantha who said she was a fashion model which Dympna believed but Teresa didn't. The brown man bought wine and steak and chips for all and danced again and again with Dympna, and every time he danced with her he rolled a pound note up thinner than a pencil and pushed it down the front of her red low-cut blouse. Dympna was well-upholstered and Teresa said there was room between those tits for the full of a safe. Dick the Taximan and Amantha were most observant.

Then like the King of the Turks the brown sailor sat with Dympna on his knee, Amantha to his right, Teresa to his left, while they drove far out of the city on a road that Teresa recognised as the road to Cosmona. Ten miles out or so they came to a roadside pub with a backroom and another jukebox and girls and men but not as many as in the restaurant. Dympna in the taxi kept screaming with laughter and beating back the hand of the brown man, and Teresa was worried that dreamy Dympna had drunk too much of the sour red wine but, in the roadside pub, Amantha who was a fast worker moved in on the sailor who by that time was too far gone to tell which was which and who couldn't now say one blessed word in a language that anybody could understand. After a while Amantha led him out of the backroom and then all of a sudden Dick the Taximan raced Teresa and Dympna back to the taxi, and Amantha darted out of the gateway that led into the yard beside the pub and sat in beside Dick and off they were again on the rocky road to Dublin. The sailor would have a walk to himself.

Dick told Amantha that was smart work. Amantha said it was as easy as eating cake, that Browny was too drunk to be any danger to anybody, that he was still waiting for her outside the door of the ladies', that he had parted with a packet for a pull and a promise. But she asked Dick to halt at another publichouse while she washed her hands for there was a boatload of bad news in the port at the moment and even to handle it might give a girl chilblains.

At night, Dympna thought, the black giant went the street scattering germs.

Dick and Amantha split the takings in the taxi and Dick told Amantha she was a hard girl, but Amantha told Dick they said you were hard if you didn't let them and if you did they said you were soft, and she'd rather be hard than soft – except, Dick said, she liked the fellow and he was hard too.

Amantha told Dick he was a scream but she didn't actually laugh to prove it. She didn't, indeed, laugh much at anything and Teresa was beginning to wonder about her and to envy her a little. She was no fashion model although she was tall enough. She had black steady eyes and a scar on her left cheek.

That night the three girls shared one room in a bed and breakfast place where Amantha was known. They planned that in the morning they would all go down to Cosmona. Amantha said she had a little money to spare now and a trip to the country would do her no harm and, just in case, it might be as well to be out of the way until the brown man's ship sailed.

With the wine and the travelling and the long day Dympna had fallen asleep in her clothes and Amantha and Teresa had laughs counting the notes, seven in all, that fell out of her when they stripped her.

§

He lay in the evening, drowsy, and knew, lulling his sense of guilt by narrowing his eyes and drifting with the yellow light fading beyond the dark tower that he was merely waiting for the Mouse to come on duty.

Her coming would be marked by her quick eager steps and by the rattle of bottles and bedpans as the nightnurses directed the last general release before sleep. For the first three months of his hospitalisation he could never bring himself to say bottle, but always urinal, and thus as he discovered afterwards, causing much amusement among the nurses as if, the Tipperary nurse said, he wanted an entire public convenience, penny in the slot and all.

Tickling was no sin and kissing could be harmless enough and on the Continent people kissed in the most formal and sinless fashion but, in this case, even to touch was surely an evidence of inordinate attachment to the creature. It was a violation of the ne tangas rule that in the seminary had even forbidden brother to touch brother. What was the point in talking in confession about such delicate matters to a shellshocked secular priest who slept with gundogs and meditated less on grace than on grouse.In the garden the risen Jesus had said to the holy woman: Noli me tangere. How would the little heartshaped face of the Mouse have looked if when she had started to tickle him he had tripped her up with those three words?

From the other side of the screen the gravelly voice of a fifteen-year-old, an incurable tubercular spine whose body was bent like a bow on a high frame, said: Listen to the melodeon, Mr Lane.

He listened. The sound came from the still fields far on the other side of the Tower. It came in the company of laughter and voices calling. It moved from east to west as if the man with the melodeon were leading a march. The boy said: They're walking to the music. You're happy, Mr Lane, to be up and walking again.

— You'll be up soon yourself, Paddy Loftus.

— Do you think so? I hope so. But six years now and no sign. I can read the X-rays now as well as the surgeon when he holds them up to the light.

The music, the laughter, the voices faded into the darkening pool of the fields.

For fun he must tell Sister Thermometer about a passage in the Canticle of Canticles that would have to be included in the second edition of her leaflet: There are three score queens and four score concubines and young maidens without number. One is my dove, my perfect one is but one. She is the only one of her mother, the chosen of her that bore her.

From shadowy fields and memories of his cloistered reading Saint Francis of Sezze, an obscure fellow, a mystery man, told him that the three score queens were the souls most pleasing to God His Majesty: patriarchs, prophets, apostles, martyrs, doctors, founders of orders. The four score concubines were saints who had reached a lesser perfection. The young maidens without number were all the other chosen saintly souls. The One was the Virgin who came terrible as an army in battle array, bottles and bedpans clattering, bugles for eternal beauty quickstepping breathlessly on her way.

She said: Time for the rosary, your reverence. The bedpans are gone and the dear little boys are ready to pray.

She lifted and looked at one of the books on the top of the bookcase. She said: Saint Nicholas of Flue. A sooty character. Lived up a chimney.

She suddenly poked his ribs, advised him to pray loud and plain so that she would hear him from the far end of the ward, said she would see him later, and laughing left him blushing, his heart beating painfully, embarrassed too because ever since they had fallen to tickling and kissing this had come for him to be the most humiliating moment of the day. Eighteen months ago when Sister Camillus had suggested that he should lead the boys in the evening rosary, giving them good example by the tones of his fervour, it had seemed a good idea. But the bigger bawdy-minded boys had quick jealous eyes and their own imaginative aspirations. Big Durcan from Mayo had once muttered to his next door neighbour: Thou, Oh Lane, wilt open her legs.

The neighbour responded: And my tongue shall anoint her braes.

A smaller boy squeaked, attempting to imitate the quick pert voice of the Mouse: Rub my back with methylated spirits so I can sleep on the fracture board.

Big Durcan responded: The Mouse'll need a rub now that his reverence is on his feet.

They had meant him to hear, so he hadn't heard. What, guilty or not guilty, could he do about it? Using his will fiercely to close his understanding against Durcan's lascivious parody he clutched his rosary beads and began: Thou, Oh Lord, wilt open my lips.

From the cracking hoarse voices of miserable curious manhood knocking at the door to the thin pipes of little boys who were no more than birds they announced the Lord His praise. From his pink-screened monastic cell he bellowed, with a fine carrying voice that a famous preacher had once predicted would make Brother Lane a famous preacher, about the five sorrowful mysteries of Christ's passion. He tried as he roared to meditate on those mysteries, to shut his ears against the repetitive cacophony that responded to him, and once against the Mouse admonishing a patient to stop playing with that jigsaw and to say his prayers because God was watching. Then exhausted he dozed and dreamt that God was watching, the mystery man was watching, so that he wasn't in the least surprised when she shook him awake and said: There's somebody out there. Over by the Tower.

There was no visible moon yet it was up there somewhere above a helmet of thin but unbroken cloud and the night was half bright with its concealed lighting.

— It's so warm, she said. I'm choked with the smell of wall-flowers from the beds out there.

— Better than Dettol or bottles from the beds in here.

She helped him into shoes and dressing gown. Leaning on her shoulder he hirpled to the balcony railings, ashamed of his dishonesty in limping more awkwardly than he had need to so he could lean on her more heavily. They peered into the night.

— We'll chase him, Peter Lane said. We'll give him a fright.

That way he could lean on her longer, his right hand drooping down the white linen slope and gently rising and falling with her breathing. As if to entice and guide their steps the melodeon music began again.

— Faery music, he said, leading old men away to grow young and dance with the immortals under a hill.

She laughed at him as they left the path and softly crossed the grass, winding around glimmering flowerbeds: You're young enough yet, your reverence, even if you're as stiff as ninety. That melodeon's the Cawley boys, the greatest scruff in the county, a sister here as a wardsmaid, a juvenile delinquent.

He laughed at himself and at the happiness of walking with her, feeling her, smelling her, listening to the little ripple of her voice; and walking too on a fool's errand that was only an excuse for travelling to the Tower. For unless the mystery man was a monster who would roar out of the shadows to attack them they hadn't a hope in the world even of seeing him. Behind her, she hoped, the wards were asleep, her assistant nurse vigilant, the night matron at her supper telling the nurses who sat with her about ghosts or her days in Guy's Hospital.

— A star, the Mouse said, and two and three.

High light wind unfelt on earth breached the clouds, revealing stars trailing grey gauzy wisps. Stepping carefully around the flat gravestones they counted seventeen stars.

— Stars are dotes, she said. What are you?

— What am I? A man, I hope, when I get my trousers. Not a star nor a dote.

She slapped his face lightly: Smarty, I mean stars. Your horoscope. I'm Gemini. That's twins, isn't it? You know Latin.

— I'm Capricorn the Goat.

He made appropriate noises and horns on his head with his hands. The moon came placidly out, discarding grey veils, to catch them kissing on the Island of the Living where no female should walk or kiss or graze or fly. Laughing she ran, he hobbled, from the light, under an arch into shadows that moon and stone had made for centuries. Sleepy squeaks of startled jackdaws were above them as they slowly ascended the spiral stair. Twice they rested whispering, leaning against each other, the firm round backs of her thighs against his left shoulder.

— Did you hear something? A step?

— No nothing, he said.

— Suppose he went mad and attacked us?

But there could be no fear in the joy of their being together in moonlight and shadows of stone, and crouched by an embrasure they laughed at the idea of that other person hiding somewhere, peeping out of his own life at the lives of the nurses.

— There's a book here, she said.

— This is his study.

That was matter for more merriment. On the dim stairway he tried, and failed, to read the title of the paperback then, following her lead, he went by a side passage and a few low steps to an open grassy battlemented space on the roof of what had once been the sanctuary. Here, halfways up the Tower, they were hidden from the hospital, safe from the betraying reflection of moonlight on white linen, and on a stone block they sat together while he read: One Thousand Women Burned to Share His Bed.

She snatched the book. She said: It's for me. Sister Camillus would have kittens if she found Solomon and Sheba on your bookcase with Saint Nicholas of Flue and Cardinal Newman.

Still seated they wrestled for the book. Deftly she tucked it between her blue skirt and the white linen band of her apron and his hands pursued it and they sat mouth to mouth for a long time. He said: I feel your heart.

— Then it's not in the right place. It must have dropped a foot. I've a prolapsed heart. Like the wombs the nuns have. Sister Raparata who was two years on that reverse bed keeping it warm for you has a prolapsed womb now, poor thing.

— I'm spared that.

More laughter and another long mouth-to-mouth rest.

— I'll swear I heard a step.

— Me too, he said. Down at the graves.

But when they peered over the low battlemented wall they could see nothing. A field away there seemed to be a rustle or a movement but it could have been man or beast or nightwind or a trick of the moon. The music of the melodeon was very far away now and melancholy and slow. She said: It's wonderful how such scruff as that Cawley boy can be so good at music. Playing. Singing. Wicked people you'd think shouldn't be musical.

He said: The first time I heard your voice you were singing.

— Tra-la-la-la, she said. A gypsy coming through a meadow spied a bird upon a tree.

She had a good soprano voice but she tossed it up and down the scale in mock hysteria and said she was Amelita Galli-Curci and held out her skirt and stepped trippingly like a shepherdess. Seriously he said: No, it was last Christmas Eve, you were singing with the other nurses, the carol singers, it was the Adeste.

With only his head and arms – hands in woollen gloves and holding a book – outside the bedclothes, he had listened, deeply moved, to the Latin words sung by young women who stood outside the balcony railings. They carried lanterns and wore dark-blue half-length cloaks over their uniforms. Verbum caro factum, they sang. Monastic fervour still strong in him he felt he had never before fully understood the meaning of the words. Then the young women who sang had passed by his bed and she had stopped to ask him what he was reading and he had noticed her and spoken to her for the first time.

She was flesh by his side now on the sanctuary roof. He said: I never knew any girl like you except one.

— Flattered, I'm sure, honoured and privileged with only one rival.

— No joking. I was on this holiday when I was fourteen, over Sligo way, she was a sort of cousin of mine. She wore a green coat with a cape and she had brown hair and a fringe and dark darting eyes and ankle socks.

— Love's young dream.

— She was thirteen.

— Just the right difference in ages.

— Don't laugh.

— I'm not laughing. I'm so serious I could cry. I'm jealous.

— Why did you cry that day when you were taking me off the reverse bed and I got mad and barked at you.

— My own business, your reverence. But if you must know it grieves me to hear men barking like dogs.

— There were dogs of all sorts in this place we holidayed in, a big farmhouse in a wooded glen between the mountains and the sea. Up on a hill above the house goatpaths went through deep furze and it was the warmest summer ever. The farmer, an uncle of mine, bought a horse from tinkers and in the dusk we went twice round a field of grass trying the brute in harness. The corn-crakes went wild. They couldn't make out what we were at, mowing and the moon coming up. One broiling day my aunt sent me to the Black River at the foot of the mountains to drown a black cat that was a thief. It was two miles by paths across bogs and meadows. But I hadn't the heart to drown it and set it free and there may be wild cats there now for all I know.

— Back to bed, she said, for you and back to work for me. They'll have a search party out for us.

— That stretch of the Black River was good for trout but not for bathing, the banks were crumbling clay.

— Easy does it, she said.

She went down before him into the darkness.

— One sunny day I walked to the seaside resort five miles away. At a crossroads a country fellow left the crowd and came with me. He had a navy blue suit and yellow shoes and a red face and buck teeth and a squint and he wore bicycle clips although he had no bicycle. Another day I cycled up behind two old men walking and by accident knocked one of them down.

In and out among the gravestones, in and out among the beds of flowers.

— But I always think of it as the summer of the black cat.

— Men, she said, men. Why not the summer of the green girl?

Laughing and wrestling she bent over him to tuck the clothes around him. That was the signal for the start of the tickling game. It was a ritual as exact as a Spanish dance: her hands, fingers wriggling on his ribs; his fingers gripping hard in her armpits, the heels of his hands against her breasts. At each succeeding performance the ritual became more perfect, the dance advanced by one new step. All along the balcony the boys, she hoped, slept. The pinkwalled house intended by a nun for his privacy and prayer, roofed by vita-glass that all day long attracted and concentrated and at night breathed out the heat of the sun, had so easily become a nest for private fondlings. Blood in his head hammered like drums, then one more step and they were racing away together. The thin fabric of her pants shifted like slippery muslin curtains between her flesh and the tips of his fingers. Together they had travelled to a magic moonland and halfways up the Tower. When he felt the moist cleft and the crisp warm hair he knew what the mystery man, hunched slavering in the night, was after. Verbum caro factum, indeed. She lay heavily on him, sobbing softly, moaning. Her veil had come unpinned and her hair, seen for the first time, was in his mouth and over his pillow. His longest finger probed and pushed and his twisted wrist was aching but when he tried to change position and draw her down beside him in the bed she stood up suddenly, smoothed skirt and apron, repinned the veil. She was no longer sobbing and moaning. She said: Smarty. Some people. The cheek.

Then she was gone swiftly and silently on the soft slippers nurses wore on night duty and only the salt odour on his fingers lingered to tell him what had happened to make them sinners. He regretted nothing except the concealing of some dark truths when he had told her of the summer of the black cat and the green girl. She was fair and young and a woman and he was a monster of a man, a sable sepulchre. Going asleep, he remembered how Fra Bernadino of Siena had once, in a crowded sunny Italian marketplace, told his most devout and frantic hearers of a woman who had slept with the devil for a whole year before she realised from the scales on his belly who he was. He investigated, but there was no crustation on his own belly, only sticky warm moisture and muscles relaxing after strain. The creatures of the coven had testified that the devil's penis and semen were cold as ice: an American refrigerated thrill on rocks. Fleeing from such images he prayed for sleep and wearily told his God he was heartily sorry.

§

The beat of the millwheel bouncing like a flat skimming stone downstream along the salmon water was a metronome for the plungings of the doctor, the sighs, in the big bed, of the doctor's dusky wife. Every night now before the light was dowsed she made him examine the interior of the wardrobe. This late August night was sultry and, no matter how fit a man was, the fourth time over the jumps took the sweat out of him. He rested. She wriggled, purring, her muscles contracting around him. Some lord, he reminded her, Lord Curzon possibly, or was it Lord Cromer, prince of imperialists, had given it as his considered opinion that a gentleman supports himself on his elbows and no lady moves. Pouting, mock tremor of tears in her voice, she said she'd be ladylike and stiff as a broomstick from that moment out, and kissed the coarse hair on his chest, and he was aware almost as if never before of the mingled odours of Paris perfume and removing cream and excited bodies in the heat of friction. Then the bedside phone rang. He stayed where he was but rising a little, leaning on his left hand, lifted the phone with his right. She said sullenly: It's as if somebody was listening. If they're not looking, they're listening.

A woman's voice, very shrill, spoke into his ear. It said: He's banishing me to the island of Crete. He's roaring round the house, doctor. Come down, doctor, before he has himself and myself roasted.

— I'll come, he said.

— When I complain of the heat, the voice said, he tells me that in 1531 a servant maid was by law boiled alive like a lobster in King's Lynn in England. Think of that, he says. And that when the household of the Bishop of Rochester was poisoned by his cook at his palace in Lambeth Marsh, the cook was boiled to death without benefit of clergy. I ought to be grateful, he says.

In fury, flattening her legs with a flap on the bed, his wife spat up at him: Again. That madman, Charles Roe. Again.

He kissed her back into the mood and the voice went on until her knees rose again and he and she laughed together at what the voice had to say: A hot August night and all the electric heaters in the house blazing. Six of them in the dining room, dining room, I mean drinking room. Nor will he deem or dare to sit on the toilet until I first pour a kettle of boiling water down it. Draughts, he says. I'll admit he had a terrible winter with the bronchial pneumonia but that he should come home to me wheezing with the cold, his clothes sodden from crawling through wet grass with the driver of a hackney cab.

— With a what?

— You know when he's drunk enough nothing will satisfy him but confession in the friary at Crooked Bridge and to nobody less than the prior, officer class to officer class he says. Poor saintly Peejay from the hotel had to drive him over at midnight. Then second thoughts or semi-sobriety took hold of him and he contents himself with crawling on his belly through a hundred yards of sopping meadow grass so that he could see the light of the red lamp in the sanctuary window. To make certain, he told Peejay that the Lord Jesus was safely abed. Crawling on his belly as if he were back in the jungle wars and forcing pious Peejay to crawl with him. Cathie Hanafin says the least he must do is buy Peejay a new suit. Practising the draw now round the house with that holster of his and the officer's pistol he never surrendered.

— I'm coming, the doctor said.

He put down the phone.

— I won't lie down again, he said. Rest after that and I sleep for hours.

Curling into a bundle like a woodlouse touched and tampered with, his wife said drowsily: Doctors and doctors' wives get no peace.

But there was contentment in her voice.

— Three times lucky, he said. It was too much to hope for a fourth clear round.

— You're not at the Horse Show.

Dressing, he raised the blinds and looked down on galleons of curdled foam drifting downstream from the weir. The beat of the millwheel was louder, steadier, now that he was distracted by no other rhythm. Cosmona slept and old Mortell too, but the river flowed on and the wheel set going turned with the river in the darkness to grind the first fruits of harvest.

— Granted he can be a nuisance, he said, but he's a gentle-man and a scholar.

— And beastly rich

— We're all rich, thank God. But he's an interesting man. Inherited the learning from his father who in his time was the greatest living authority on the old abbey of Cosmona.

— So what? From what you tell me he's mad. Locking him-self into his room and won't let that dreary housekeeper in unless she can give the right answer when he shouts who goes there.

— He was in the war. We're all entitled to our little oddities.

— Oddities? He went to bed for six months and nothing wrong with him. Just refused to get up.

— It's a common ailment. There's a Russian name for it. He said he felt safer in bed.

— Who wants to feel safe in bed?

She was cosily kittenish now so he kissed her, tucked the clothes around her and sat beside her for a while, his fingers groping in the thick dark hair on the back of her head. She was asleep before he left the room.

Virilitee, fertilitee he found himself rhyming and repeating as he drove to the house of raving Charles Roe. Virilitee, fertilitee, a fine pair in harness when they set off in such galloping fun and when the wife's people had money to burn. Virilitee was fond of fat, fertilitee was seldom lean. His windows open, he sang to sleeping Cosmona. He and she were healthy, non-stop, horse-show animals, happy, hilarious, repetitive, sometimes a fault or two, a stone sent spinning from the high wall, a wooden bar struck with a ringing thud, a slip and a plash in the mud and water, but more often than not a perfect jumping round. That was, indeed, most satisfactory. Some whisper in the air on a warm night must have inspired Gabriel Rock to hide in that wardrobe in the hope of a really good show. She was away now, and being a doctor he knew that she'd be regularly fertile and easy in delivery, popping them out like peas from a peashooter, glorying in fertilitee; and since her father was a born grandfather if ever there was one, every arrow into the quiver would be of solid gold. Virilitee, fertilitee, he sang and pulled up at the high house of Charles Roe.

§

— Domhnall the Horse Robber, a giant of a dark man, was hanged in the Square of Cosmona in the sultry August of the thirty-fifth year of the eighteenth century. That's history, doctor. But there are other stories about how Dark Dan, the Black Man of the Moat of Cosmona, went to his end. He robbed the rich and served the poor and lived above the Moat in a cave where he stabled his stolen horses. The people loved him as they love all Robin Hoods until he grew weary of his sensible bachelor's life and abducted a woman of the people to keep him warm in the smell of his horses in a corner of his cavern. Riding home one autumn day at the head of a stolen herd, he stooped when a farmer's daughter reached him a noggin of milk, swept her to the saddle before him and away. The pursuit was up and after him: her father and lovers and affianced lover. But he baffled them by holding a pistol to her head and threatening to blow out her brains, assuming a woman has any, if the pursuit came closer. So, helpless, they watched him ride, holding her face down, ass up, heels kicking, across the back of his beast, into his cave and the herd following him. They could hear her screams above the noise of the hooves. The pair never came out again.

The doctor made ready the needle.

— Reminds me, he said, of the tough old widow on a mountain farm. She had one watery son. He led the life of a slave. Up at five to see to the cattle. He lived in a loft above the hearth, climbed up a ladder to it every night, crawled down every morning. Then, a world's wonder. He marries without permission, climbs up with his lady, pulls up the ladder and, when summoned next morning to see to the cattle, sticks out his turnip head and says he's never coming down again,

— That, dear doctor, would suit you better than me. Fornication forever in the loft, in the cave. Years after the girl and Dark Dan vanished the people, for the protection of bullocks and sheep, blocked the hole, one of the caves above the Moat. Yet the books say Dan died dancing at the rope's end and was mourned on the great day by a sorrowing throng that included his lawfully wedded wife, matrimony being his one frail link with the law. The voices of centuries before books were heard of say the dark god seized his woman and went forever back to his own kingdom in the bowels of the earth. Behind the pathetic figure of Dark Dan I see the shape of someone greater, more terrible, the unconquered god of the shadows, Pluto, our Crom Dubh, our giant Balor of the Evil Eye, champion of our ancient faith in stock and stone, taking refuge in the earth and leaving Lugh, the young god of Christian light, to be king of the castle. But Pluto has taken Love with him to uproarious rape in the belly of the mountain. Will the god of light now descend singing like Orpheus in pursuit of his Eurydice? It would seem so, doctor, because for centuries before my drink and your damned crucifying needle the young men went up to the Moat in early harvest to pluck blayberries and maidenheads, if they could, and to crown their loves with garlands.

— Miller Mortell tells me, said the doctor, the old custom still survives.

— Faintly and only among a few unknowing people. Miller Mortell, the benevolent bore, would if he were blackskinned be a most excellent Pluto, Jehovah sentencing his son to the cross.

— A libel surely, said the doctor.

— Yes and no. I knew the son. He was doomed from birth. Even as a boy he was nicknamed the Dead Man. He was a sallow morose boy younger than me by fifteen or so years and most of the time he was alone. In church at his devotions he knelt stiff as a ramrod with his lips unmoving. His dark brown eyes, I feel, were also unmoving, never restless or lighted or dancing. He never laughed, that I remember. One night a month or so after he was married he went berserk. Threw most of the crockery in the house at his wife, cursed his father, took to the fields where I found him and brought him here to taste his first drink and to drink until he fell asleep. A few weeks later he ran off to the army to escape from marriage and millstones and grinding oats, and in the fullness of time the Japs got him and ground him as they did to many a more likely lad, to be in the heel of the hunt ground themselves. Oats and millstones, doctor, nothing but oats and millstones. Bullets and bombs I've faced and yet I dread the prick of the paraldehyde needle. Did Dark Dan in his cave give his captive bride the needle? So we may safely assume, doctor. Yet there are other – pardon my wincing – versions of the story, legends of a maiden who to escape from a marriage being forced on her by her father grew wings and flew across the valley from Crooked Bridge to Cosmona, faster than Gabriel Rock could cycle, and the cave behind the Moat opened wide to take her in. Others say that at her bridal feast a dark stranger danced with her, then flew with her up the chimney and into the heart of the mound. A giant hound once chased an enchanted doe all around this valley. When the doe, to escape, sank into the earth the hound in a slavering fury tore a hole there and burst seven springs of water and Lough Cosmona as we know it today, with marsh and reeds and wild duck, came into being as a barrier between the doe and the hound or between the maiden and the black man. Images, doctor, images filling the minds of your people and mine, helping to shape us the way we are. My mother believed that Jesus was the Son of God and also believed that sudden death, a vengeance of the spirits of the earth, would lay low anyone rash enough to cut down a lone whitethorn. Could the hempen cravat choke Dark Domhnall, the predestined child of shadows, or as the image of an everlasting shadow was he immune to the sting of death? We'll debate it, doctor, for days when this drinking bout is beaten. Take my stick and knock on the floor for that gloomy ghoul, my guardian cousin and housekeeper, so that I may offer you a drink as a recompense for taking you at this hour from your fleece-lined nest. Knock, doctor. A female ghoul, a mistress of gloom, may the gods send Dark Daniel to gallop with her to Tipperary and rape her in the belly of Galtymore Mountain.

§

In the days when passengers travelled by canal barge the house of Charles Roe had been an hotel built tall and thin, Scottish baronial, with rooms either as spacious and draughty as hangars or stuffy and cramped as coffins, and with a cylindrical and quite useless turret. A madhouse, Grace the housekeeper kept saying, to fit a madman. A useless house, she wailed, for an idle bachelor who, his life long, has done never a stroke of useful work, lived all his student career at a high income rate, wearing suede shoes and leading marches on embassies when he should have been taking his degrees. Wars and armies, she complained, were invented for the like of him, but you can't have wars all the time. Floating all his life, and his father before him, on drink and the money his grandfather made easy, the grandfather that was honoured as a papal count for tailoring drawers for nuns during world war one and he used such flimsy material the poor things were perished. He also owned sawmills.

— Nothing in the world, she said to the doctor, gives that man pleasure. When he thinks that other people like food his teeth ache.

Her dark hair was going grey but she still wore it long and looped by a red ribbon as she had worn it when twenty years ago at the age of twenty she had won a beauty competition: for a melancholy but undeniable beauty. She waited for the doctor at the foot of the stairway. She was a depressed unmarried maiden, a faded beauty, a distant cousin, a poor relation, a voice of lamentation, a martyr to hot flushes.

— Did the heat overpower you, doctor?

— I persuaded him to switch off two of the three heaters. When he sleeps now he'll be all right.

— Is he trying to bring the heat of the jungle here to Cosmona? There he lies like a lord dreaming dreams, seeing drunken visions, raving about fairy stories and reading books. It isn't that I object to books.

The doctor said yes he knew. He had heard so often about the literary tastes of this gaunt greying woman: Manon Lescaut, I read, doctor, and Madame Bovary and Brave New World all in one week when I was at home before Mummy died. Every book then was a new adventure. If Mummy had caught me reading Brave New World she'd have put me out of the house. My friends used to say to me: Grace, we know you're broadminded, but. Little did I know.

— Little, Miss Grace, do any of us know.

The floor, the panelled walls, echoed and re-echoed into baronial gloom the sound of their footfalls.

— Cousin Charles means no harm, I know, and it's a roof over my head. But he's such a waste. He should marry. He should have children. But he's afraid of women. He's half afraid of me, his cousin. Who goes there, indeed. The naked stone statue in the back garden's enough for him. She can't move any closer to him.

— He tells me, said the doctor, he got another of those postcards today.

— Perhaps he really should have stayed when he was in the seminary and become a Jesuit priest.

— Another of those postcards, the doctor said.

— Oh that's some local joker who knows his weakness, post-ing him bathing beauties from Crooked Bridge. They shouldn't worry a man who's been to the wars. Soldiers must have seen a lot of dirty pictures.

— And in Cairo, said the doctor, things not to be spoken of.

He laughed into the warmth of his tweeds and whiskers but, to his embarrassment because he was an infectiously genial man and accustomed to being accepted as such, he found himself laughing alone. She held out her hands, displaying them to him palms upwards.

— Dyed all colours, she said. Dyeing my underwear, of all things.

— All colours?

— Well that is an exaggeration. Not exactly all. A sort of crimson. I know I won't make a married man blush, and a doctor.

— Doctors blush continually, he said. That's why I wear whiskers. I never knew ladies dyed their underwear.

She giggled, she really did. She said that it was a fad or a fancy and that she did it for variety. But he still wondered with a schoolboy's wonder why any woman should and why, above all, she.

She opened the door. Across twenty yards of green the smooth canal water caught the awakening timorous blink of morning, then fell with a weary soothing sough through the old sodden wood of the lockgates. Up the dark slope the lights of the hospital, although dimmed to ease the sleeping patients' eyes, still made a faint halo around the black bulk of the Tower. Birds were awake and already travelling.

— Tomorrow I must go up to the hospital to return some books to that charming young Mr Lane. So intellectual.

— Seems a bit of a prig to me, he said. The boys don't like him.

Nor did the boys, he thought as he spoke, much like the dis-tant female cousin of Charles Roe. Sometimes they referred to her, with reason, as Miss Tippity Toes and sometimes, with no reason, as the afflicted mother. He was a little ashamed of him-self to find, as he drove back through the Square of the sleeping village that he was still absorbed by the image of Miss Grace dyeing, for variety, the fabrics she wore close to her lonely body. Did she pray prayers and cast spells above suds and crimson water? Somewhere he had read about Victorian young ladies folding drawers and shifts and suchlike around lavender, but that was something else, something different. Gabriel Rock possibly had read matter much more exotic in his book about Solomon and Sheba and had been sniffing in the wardrobe for odours of musky Arabia.

His wife was snug and drowsy but ready instinct reawakened her as much as was necessary and no phone rang to mar the fifth and faultless round.

§

Nine hundred cars or so, Christopher Hanafin thought, had ignored his cocked-up thumb. Behind him was the torment of the tramp along suburban roads, doors closing against the night and such strollers as himself, lights dying in windows, bushes in gardens crouching into the shadows. Behind him also was that straight mile of concrete with girders, scaffoldings, trenches, on either hand, where the city's new fringe of factories was rising. For a hundred rugged yards on a road as yet unsurfaced he had walked between parallel lines of red lamps, feeling for a while how much he belonged to all that untidiness and unfinished mess. At a watchman's brazier he stopped to light one of his last three cigarettes, then another fifty yards and he was on the main road west where cars swept by, blinding him, ignoring his pathetic cocked-up thumb as if they knew who and what he was. He reminded himself that a poet had said the summer dark was but the dawn of day and laughed sourly at poets and cursed without exception all owners of cars. There were lights still in the windows of some roadhouses even if the doors were closed and from one roadhouse came the sound of singing. He slaked his dry mouth at a wayside pump.

Ten miles out and his blistered feet were on fire. Bed in a bush would be his lot with the stars to see and, more poetry, bread to dip in the river. What must certainly be the last car blinded him and snorted contemptuously back towards the city. Then, as if his thinking of a river had created one, he heard the sound of falling water, felt roadside grasses and hedges rustle with the breeze that comes only over water. But it wasn't a river. It was the half-dead canal that went westwards, most of the way in the company of the road, to Cosmona and Crooked Bridge and beyond. The sound of water came from a roadside lock where the lock-keeper's cabin was no longer inhabited. Leaving his shoes and socks, such as they were, on the bank he sat on the lockgate's catwalk, dipped his sore feet into the blessed coolness, heard in the darkness the cluck-cluck of a waterfowl, then a startled cry and a splash to show him that even in that place of rest and peace the vicious rat lurked. At that moment the black man came along the towing path. He held a bottle in his hand. He waved it at Christopher Hanafin. He stepped with sure feet along the catwalk. He proffered the bottle. He said: Room. Trink.

— No better words, Hanafin said, were ever spoken in a stranger place. We haven't been formally introduced but here goes. Excuse my gravelly voice. I've a sort of laryngitis.

The warm rum went down like the blessing of God except that it couldn't be God's blessing for this surely was the beginning of the way a man sold his soul to the devil: night and despair, a black man, a bribe. Encouraged by the apparition he swallowed a second gulp and accepted his doom. Sooner or later life had to come to this. Then, limbs bending as easily as if they were rubber, the black man was squatting beside him on the catwalk, showing to him a white circle of cardboard. Peering in the shadows Hanafin saw that it was a dripmat from a bar table.

On a low hill on the far side of the canal there was a graveyard and the dark bulk of a ruined church. Dry reeds in the light breeze rattled like bones. Somewhere in the darkness the rat was feasting hellishly, bloodsucking on the hapless waterfowl. This was a most suitable place for a meeting and the making of a deal with the prince of darkness and if Christopher Hanafin had been a young and hopeful man he might have felt fear, or at least uneasiness. As it was, the most he could muster was curiosity. What in hell was a black stranger who spoke no English doing here at this hour, offering him rum, displaying a dripmat, pointing to it with a finger as thick as Hanafin's wrist, looking at him earnestly and saying slowly, syllable by syllable: Lie-beer-ee-ah?

But the rum, Wedderburn's rum with a sailor on the label and a sight to be seen in any bar nor to be associated with hell-fire, was real. He drank again. Under the light of a match the black man struck—of course he was a sailor like the man on the label—he studied the dripmat. It carried a printed verse in praise of porter. Hanafin read it out loud. The black man helplessly shook head and hands and made negative noises. Hanafin said: Very good. There's a noble lord who writes verse in that brewing family.

The black man, whose teeth did not shine in minstrel fashion when he laughed, clapped Hanafin on the shoulder and laughed and said again: Trink. Liberia.

He tapped the dripmat with the great finger and struck another match until at last Hanafin saw written on the cardboard the two words: Liberia. Cosmona.

— You're not asking me, I know, to admire the poetry. There are two words written here, two proper names. They can only mean that you're coming from Liberia and going to Cosmona or coming from Cosmona and going to Liberia.

Several times and slowly the black man said: Cosmona.

— Just as well, if you want my assistance, for I don't know the way to Liberia. And as it so happens I am going to Cosmona myself.

Rapidly and in a language that seemed to be largely French the black man talked and talked.

— No good, I'm afraid. The little bit of French I know doesn't make contact with yours. And the other stuff you're talking's a mystery.

The black man borrowed back his bottle, drank deeply, then rolled rum around his mouth, swallowed, and thus inspired, said: Cosmona. Girls. One. Two. Three.

He held up three fingers.

— Now I read you, said Hanafin. The old old story. You're off to Cosmona to see three pretty girls.

He drank more rum and sang that there were three pretty girls in Cosmona and made, for the black man's benefit, that international symbol of concord: the Spanish fig. Then they stood on the catwalk and laughed together like brothers akin.

— West we'll walk together to Cosmona on the path the patient barge horses used to plod. The old towing-path will be softer under our feet than the road. That should suit you, my nigger of the Narcissus, because I see you're wearing what seem to be carpet slippers, fragile footwear for a walk from Liberia to Cosmona.

— Cosmona, the black man said. One. Two. Three.

To the echoing night he roared one brazen roar. On the towing path he jumped and turned the flying wildcat and, back on his feet, roared again.

— A fine salmon leap you can give. A fine bellow, God bless you. It could be lust and if so you'd make three or thirty girls happy. I'm going to Cosmona myself but there's only one girl involved, a married girl, my wife, semi or totally estranged remains to be seen. I'm a poor companion for such a leaping roaring lover of three girls. But your humble guide I can be as long as you've the rum to pay me, man of Liberia.

— Liberia, said the black man. Cosmona.

They fell into step along the towing-path.

— Cosmona, said Hanafin.

He pointed west along the still water.

— We could follow this soft path all the way home. Home. There's a funny word for you. But then the path might here and there be overgrown. And there'll be no chance of a lift. No barge will ever come this way any more. I could talk now for a week to you about the sad fate of the old canals and you wouldn't contradict me once. You're the only really attentive audience the degenerate Christy Hanafin has had now in a long time. God bless you, my friend, with your shadowed livery of the burnished sun, for so hanging upon my every word.

The rum was the fire his eloquence came from. He stoked it with another swig. The smooth water shone all across the land to the village where morose Cathy waited. The shining path led the prince and his black servant to the fortress where the princess pined.

— Cosmona, Cosmona we come, he shouted.

— One, two, three, said the black man.

— A lift on a barge now would be a blessing and you could

end your journey, sailor boy, as you began it – by water. But the last of the barges has been towed off into eternity. Look here now at the deep grooves in the stone of this bridge. Straining ropes cut them as the horses pulled through. This old stone tank overturned in the grass was once a watering trough for horses. Those ruins over there were the old stables and the room where passengers waited. All rubble and ruin now, and back there where they're building a new edge to the city there's nothing but rubble and confusion. That's life for you, my black beauty. From one bloody mess to the next. Do you see that harbour there, that wide spread of water, you could hardly miss it?

— Harbour, said the black man.

— Harbour, haven, the end of the journey. It was famous once for the number of suicides it attracted. If a man had sense enough he could still drown himself there. But not while the rum lasts.

— Room, said the sailor.

From his jacket he produced another bottle and Hanafin embraced him and they laughed and together shouted: Cosmona. One. Two. Three.

— Some supernatural agency has surely sent you. Some higher or lower power. Your flowing breasts spurt rum. How you leaped like that and kept the bottle still in your pocket is a wonder. Just simply how you leaped like that is a wonder. The girls must love it.

— One, two, three, said the black man.

— And Bob's your uncle.

They walked on, away from ruined walls and abandoned harbour.

— Sixty miles they did in about eighteen hours. Halts for locks and changing horses. Manacled prisoners used to be brought that way because they weren't in a hurry going anywhere. At least they had fresh air and the sight of the green fields. When the lock-keeper at the harbour saw the barge coming he rang the passenger bell. Not to hustle the people. Sweet Jesus, no. That was a leisurely world. The bell was to tell the people in fields and cabins to drop their work and come along and chat to the passers-by. A time for talk and changing horses and hearing hot news from Dublin town. No bloody shouting at people through loudspeakers as they do now in stations and airports. Oh, man from Liberia, have you ever travelled or been led in hand-cuffs through a busy railway junction and all the decent people taking a good long sympathetic look at you? If we rang the old rusted bell back there at the ruins I wonder would the ghosts come dandering out of the fields. Ghosts would frighten you. All comic niggers are afraid of ghosts. But not me. I'm a ghost myself. The spectre of Cosmona.

— Cosmona, said the black man. One. Two. Three.

At the harbour the road had left them. A mile further on it returned to them and faraway they saw a light and heard a rumble and ran to a humpy bridge and waited. When it came it was slow and enormous, sailing so high above the road that it was with dif-ficulty that Hanafin, concealing his half-empty bottle, clambered aloft to the cab. The black sailor, his full bottle gone again as mys-teriously as it had appeared, followed him effortlessly.

— Going west, said Hanafin. Cosmona.

— Crooked Bridge, said the driver's mate.

— No better place, said Hanafin. For my friend and myself, thanks. He doesn't have the English.

The cab of the great galleon of a truck was as big as a fair-sized room. The black man and Hanafin sat at the back of it on two boxes. They drove through one, two, three sleepy little towns, then a big town with bright empty streets branching off into the night and a market-house like a toy in a wide square and one civic guard shining a torch at a shopdoor or at nothing in par-ticular. The desire to talk was gone from Hanafin. There were the vibrations of the cab, the engine noises, the taciturnity of long-distance truck drivers. Then it was so much more satisfying to talk only to an audience who didn't understand a word he was saying. After a long silence he said that it was a big truck.

— Mares, said the driver's mate, for a stud farm at Crooked Bridge.

After a further silence the driver said: Why would the like of your friend with no English be going to Cosmona? They speak English there?

— Girls, said Hanafin. Mares.

The driver's mate asked: Can he make them understand?

— The one language, said Hanafin, they speak in the stud farm.

He made again the symbol of the Spanish fig. The driver's mate laughed and the black man laughed with him but the driver who may have been very proper or very slow, or who may just have had his eyes on the road, did not laugh. That was life for you, no unanimity.

At the far side of a wide ocean of silence they came to Cosmona, passed through the village and, at Hanafin's guidance, pulled up beyond the bridge at Mortell's mill.

§

— Here is the mill, oh my Liberian, with the humming of thunder, here is the weir with the wonder of foam, here is the sluice with the race running under, friend of my darkness I quote you a poem.

— Cosmona, said the black man.

He pointed to the village on the road above them. He was asking a question. The rumble of the truckload of mares died away towards Crooked Bridge.

— That is indeed Cosmona. But asleep now, asleep, dead. Cosmona awake in the morning. Sleep now, we, in the mill. Morning, Cosmona awake. Sleep here in the mill. Rum. Drink rum.

His eloquence had deserted him. He gulped rum, burning the back of his throat, for inspiration.

There was the mill with the humming of thunder.

Somehow or other his pidgin message had crossed seas to Liberia and found the black man. When he pushed the old sagging door that he knew was never locked and walked into the humming mill his companion followed him.

— A mill's an orchestra if you listen long enough. The wheel and the river harmonise. Every loft of the mill is a different instrument. On the first loft the rat-tat-tat of the hopper. Follow me. One more ladder. To the upper loft. We can drink and sleep here on these sacks in the warm room above the kiln. A fine view of the village. My wife's in that big house jutting out back there. But seeing that she's waited so long she can wait until morning.

I wish I knew who your one, two, three girls were and when this rum was drunk I could send you on your way rejoicing. But it could be that their mothers wouldn't appreciate your turning up at this hour of the night, or morning, or at any hour. The mothers of Cosmona may not approve of black men for their daughters and so far I'm the blackest man any girl of Cosmona ever found in her bed. No, that light up there isn't a premature sunrise. It's a hospital, hospital, hospital.

He kept repeating the word. He made mimes of men in beds, legs slung aloft in splints, men hopping on crutches, spitting, choking, hugging painful distended bellies, mimes of surgeons slicing, anaesthetists drugging, nurses bandaging. Then they sat on the warm sacks and unwrapped and uncorked the second bottle of rum. The floor vibrated pleasantly. The mill hummed and was busy around them. Far below the wheel and the water kissed and splashed.

— Come to think of it, sailor boy, the children up there in the hospital would love you, the way you can leap the flying wildcat, your battered black friendly face. They'd think you'd stepped straight out of the pictures of Treasure Island one of the nuns painted on glass. But you should have a parrot or a monkey, my man Friday.

— Parrot, said the black man. Monkey.

He drank rum. He made monkey faces and parrot noises. He passed the bottle to Hanafin who drank and settled back, easing his tired limbs into the sacks. The rum, the warmth, the oaten odour, all combined and came over him like a cloud.

— Sounds of the village, he chanted, grow stiller and stiller, stiller the notes of the birds on the hill. Black sailor of Cosmona, I had the memory when I was young. Dusty and dim are the eyes of the miller, deaf are his ears with the moil of the mill. How do you start the mill, Mr Mortell? Just turn on the river. But who made the river run? Who made you? Who made the world? She's grinding now. Listen to the beat of the damsel that strikes in the feed, one damsel you couldn't fuck, my fine leaping friend.

— Much fuck, said the sailor with the sadness of a man in want yet still savouring a word as well known to the nations as the symbol of the fig.

They laughed and drank more rum and passed the bottle round. They were sworn brothers sweet.

— Dressed millstones are the image of a happy union between woman and man, revolving and grinding together, upper and nether, a happy marriage if you want to be polite about it, and I'm sure you don't. The faces of the turning stones must run true to each other, no hollows or mountains on either stone. Old Mortell would test the faces with a trueing staff of mahogany. He'd coat one smooth side of the staff with red paint or lampblack. Do you follow me? He'd rub the coated side on the stone. But you're not interested. More rum? Not even interested in rum?

Curled in a corner and happily drunk on the grain sacks the black man was sleepily masturbating off to the heaven where the girls, one, two, three, lay before him and bound to his will.

— Trueing staff indeed, Hanafin said.

He finished the rum in silence. He tossed the two bottles out into the night. They went spinning far over the wheel to splash in the deeps of the river under the sallies on the far bank. An object moving through the fields over by the hospital could be a spot before his drunken eyes. He rubbed his eyes and peered. It could also be a man in a zipper jacket and crash helmet. Who cared? The black man, appeased, was asleep. He slept beside him.

— TWO —

Martin Mortell walking in the dawn past currant bushes,
black and red, and beanrows to the wooden closet that he
called the House of Parliament considered that once he had been
a great lover and that he had nothing now to show for it but a
dying son. He strode trouserless, unlaced boots on his bare feet,
but covered beyond even the requirements of decency in a long,
striped, flannel nightshirt. A faint star delayed in the sky above
the village. He knew he cut a comic figure and was sorry there
was no one to be amused and made happy by the spectacle of a
huge, white-bewhiskered man dressed up like Lady Macbeth and
heading in a hurry for the jakes. But his drugged son slept away
the last of his life, and his son's wife, even if she looked out and
saw him, resented him so much that no matter how comic he
seemed he would not amuse her. She made more out of her wifely
grief than he could ever make out of the agony of a remorseful
father watching his only son die.

With the door of the jakes open to the breezes of the garden
he watched that last star vanish. It was there one moment, then
gone, as if a great hand, plucking the morning star, had snatched
it from the sky.

In the days long ago of the Kaiser's war he had left his mill
for a while and gone to work in Wales in a munitions factory near
Carmarthen. He and thirty other Irishmen had lodged in one
Welsh street of one-storeyed houses sloping dourly up the side of
a hill. The darkfaced singing religious people had been hospitable.
The loveliest girl he had ever seen had lived in that street. He had
worshipped her but although he was never slow with women —
millers had a name for women — he never could establish with her

one moment of understanding. Then one evening the Irishmen came home from work to find the door of every house fast shut, their belongings in a row in neat piles in the middle of the street. No door opened to their knocking. While they stood bewildered and fortunately sober, or they'd have wrecked the street and Carmarthen too, the minister came and told them that Margiad Jones had a big belly and, in the fullness of the devil's time, would have an Irish bastard; and they were to go. Looking hate at each other they picked up their bundles and left, and never knew which mystery man of their crew had violated hospitality and plucked that morning star.

Walking back by beanrows and currant bushes, pausing under apple trees and by orderly beehives, Martin Mortell still felt sick and weak with loss because he hadn't been the one to play the devil.

His son still slept: a stick in the bed. His son's plump, red-cheeked wife slept on a converted couch at the foot of the bed of death. Through the window he watched the mockery of bars of sunlight forcing their way into the garden, almost stirring plants and leaves with their living power. Relieved from the lethargy of deep summer the birds sang bravely for sheaf and fruit and grain. He dressed and ate and walked the mile through sunlight to the mill, leaving the sleepers behind him.

An unknown soldier or, better still, a maker of thunderbolts had plucked the morning star. With that Welsh woman he knew he could have made sons strong enough to defy the jungle. He could have rescued her from that mean street where such beauty did not belong, shown her this bountiful valley, two streams meeting to make a river.

The field path he followed, rubber knee boots cascading dew, led down the slope to the meeting of the waters. Slow as a canal, deep and dark, the main stream came from miles of level chalk-land. Clear, sparkling with life, a giggling girl meeting a severe matron, the tributary came from the mountains where in the morning brightness the new forests shone on the slopes, light green of larch, dark odorous spruce. He followed the right bank downstream, the ramshackle shanty town of the Cawley place above him, no smoke yet from any chimney in the village, sprawled still sleeping, along the northern slope of the valley.

To make a mill you must also make a weir and a waterfall and a millrace defining an island all your own.

By a wooden footbridge he crossed the main stream below the weir, followed the path along his bushy island and by the edge of the race. He said to himself that he was monarch of all he surveyed and for a moment felt proud as a king as he always did on this patch of wild ground. It belonged to him. It was his republic, free and independent of all the farms in the valley. It existed only to ensure that canalised water flowed with force and the wheel turned. But the sight in a corner of still water of the flat floating pads of lilies diminished him with the nearness of death. His son had gone round the world to eat such pads in frenzied hunger.

— Pads as big as pot lids, father, and not knowing whether they'd poison us or not, you'd be amazed at the number of growing things that aren't poisonous, the brute beasts have the secret.

Round the world, following the road that passed east and west at his father's door, to eat grass like the beasts of the field, to watch limbs swell with beri-beri, to be poisoned so that no doctor on this side of the globe could name one quarter of the diseases that destroyed his stomach. From a green hell of yellow devils he had returned to poison the common things of life with his story, to prove that in hell everything, sunshine, birdsong, laughter, had another meaning. Even the beloved river would never flow the same again. Mirrored in the millrace water Mortell saw his son's gaunt jaundiced face, sweating forehead, crown hairless from some disease of the scalp, his dark staring eyes loose as if they might rattle in their sockets. His head was a reptile's head darting from side to side from a carapace of wrinkled bedclothes already stinking of death, no death for a soldier, no death for his son.

— I used to dream about the river, father. We had no soap and little water, hot or cold. Only a trickle of a stream through the camp and sometimes it dried up. If you lived faraway from where the water came in under the wire you hadn't a hope in hell.

— But you built a bridge, son.

— We built a bridge. Hundreds of us. It was a relief to get into the water even if you were kicked in. The first time I was kicked in I was shocked unconscious, I fell thirty feet, far worse than the way you'd be here if you fell in with your clothes on. Then I came to and thought this is water, lovely water the same as at home, and dreamt that I was floating in the pool above the millwheel.

Pure strong western water shot as if muscled into the cut-stone conduit to touch and set turning that wonderful delicate instrument, his greatest joy, his millwheel, the child that would never leave him. No man could keep his son at home forever. Even God Almighty couldn't do it. Round and round went the wheel and round the world went his son and the very snails on the morning grass were polluted with the son's remembering: We cooked grass and the snails on it. Soon you couldn't get a snail. Either they were all eaten or they sensed danger and cleared off. Eating thorny leaves too that tore the insides of stomachs and some poor hoors died in convulsions. Often the big strong fellows went first and slight wiry fellows like myself tholed. You thought of nothing but food and water and water.

His son's road having run round the world he had been returned home, the refuse of some grinding process, to lie dying, a skeleton in bed, to give every living thing in Cosmona a dark significance of evil. Even the old tabby mouser, so lazy and confident that she merely stretched herself and flexed her claws as he stepped over her to enter the mill, reminded him of his son's story of the prisoner who had stolen and eaten another prisoner's cat: He was all scratches the next day, father. The other prisoners flogged him. He must have eaten the cat raw, skin, guts, claws, the perishing lot. Nothing was ever found. Nobody smelled cooking.

Diseased beyond any doctor's definition Martin Mortell's son was, by his tainted memory, a canker in the body of Cosmona. In distant jungles the broken bodies of strong men, sons made by love, collapsed into clay. Everything that had life must be ready for a wretched end. He left his rubber boots to dry where sunlight fell through the doorway. His breath came short as he climbed the steep wooden stairs. Resting on the first loft he looked through the window at the mountains, at the rockface above the larch and spruce where, the previous winter, an eighteen-year-old girl, climbing, had fallen to death. The ancient mountains had devoured her. Dropping like a stone she had joined the bodies in the jungle. It was all the same earth, the globe God made, turning like the millwheel, opening green mouths of jungle, brown mouths of mountain, a mere crust covering the uncountable dead, the earth digesting them as it turned. The mortal agents who had destroyed his son were distant and unimaginable. One could no more strike at them than at furies of the air, evil spirits that for a while had taken the shapes of stunted yellow men. God in heaven had no control over them. They'd never heard of God who had sent his son to die for them.

Walking, deep in his thoughts, on the loft above the kiln he saw two men curled asleep on warm sacks and on the instant it seemed that the white man, if white he could be called, with his unkempt beard and filthy clothes, could have come from the worst hellhole in the camp his son had suffered in. The black man with the brutal scarred face, mouth open, snoring, showing red tongue and bad teeth, could be a torturing subhuman guard. They could also be John the Baptist, back from the desert and with no time yet to consult the barber, and a Nubian eunuch from the court of the Herod who had the saint beheaded. Then a closer look showed him that, merciful Christ, the sore pilgrim, Christy Hanafin, had come back to Cosmona, and he saw the serious little browneyed person, too wise to be a woman, and heard her read from the nun's leaflet: She glorifieth her nobility by being conversant with God: Yea, and the Lord of all things hath loved her.

The good smell of the kiln, the smell of harvest and oven bread was polluted by smells of body dirt and sour alcohol. On a less cursory inspection the Nubian was no eunuch, and in the climates he came from they must sleep with hatches open and mainmast high, and in his particular case there was some proof of the popular report about the physical proportions of black men. That acrobat must have made himself welcome in many places. It was a matter surely for mild surprise that, unlike his face, his credentials showed no scars of battle.

The miller touched Hanafin with his foot. It was no way to waken one of God's creatures but that way the nose was farther from the odour, the clean fingers from the dirt. In Martin

Mortell's mill there had never been any dirt graver than the mist of dust shining around the ground meal.

§

Cathy Hanafin knew that Peejay would prefer not to be visited in his hut. He had once told her of that most exclusive hermit of the desert who held that he who was too often visited by men would not be visited by the angels. But the empty desolation of the huge house drove her out for company. If it had been windy wintry weather the loneliness would not have been so unbearable. Creaking moaning noises would have kept her company from room to empty room. The voices of the ghosts of the old house had no terror for her. But with the warmth of late summer or early autumn moving in the morning fields she could not suffer the emptiness of the place, the absence of her parents and brothers – not indeed that she much appreciated them when they were. She could not that morning face into the room in which she kept the toys.

Her sleep had been drugged with tablets and red wine, the only drink she could drink, and in her solitude she drank it to liverish excess. She woke with heavy eyelids and a sour mouth. Beau Jolais, her cavalier, lay at the foot of her bed, drained and empty after their night of love. In their shabby courting days Christy had given her a taste of red wine and the splitting of the French word into what might be the name of some dashing fellow from a story of the French foreign legion had been a feeble courtship joke. She had never gone on, for she was no explorer, to gin or whiskey or the vodka girls drank nowadays when drinking girls came to the bar of the Cosmona Hotel and that, God saw, wasn't too often. Young ones, mostly, travelling by car with elderly men who didn't want to be seen with them in more frequented places. She took a weary vindictive pleasure in witnessing their lack of wisdom for in time they'd find out that the beautiful big world would reckon them only as women of the second class, not prostitutes completely, nor sluts like Teresa Fallon and Dympna Cawley, but certainly neither real nor prospective brides-in-white with porcelain backsides and fruitful futures.

Sometimes she drank Mâcon because of the eagle on the label and remembered as she drank the day in her girlhood when the rumour went around that a tinker man had killed an eagle at the caves above the Moat of Cosmona. Young and old had run up the steep road to see the wonder and met to their amazement a winged man in the dusk descending. It was only the blackavised tinker with his winged captive on his shoulders, the giant wings relaxing and opening to the right and left. But the image stayed with her of a man who was an eagle coming down to her, and later in life taking the bodily shape of Christy Hanafin. Her secret laughter was more sour than the aftertaste of the wine.

She washed, and rinsed her mouth again and again, pulled back her fading brown hair until her forehead ached, put on the little finger of her left hand the horseshoe ring that she wore no longer for luck but to mock the possibility of luck. Substance, the pious fraud, was scandalised because she would no longer wear a wedding ring. She made and drank strong tea in a kitchen that was old fashioned but big enough to cater for more guests than ever came nowadays since the cars had struck such a blow at the trade of the smaller towns. Substance, the clod, was more than content with the trade the place still did. He had no trouble with staff and he had at any rate, and as he said over and over again, always got the land behind him. Once he even had in his capacity as a client of the Little Flower barred women from drinking in the pub because he said he couldn't bear to look at the young ones being stupefied with vodka and then driven away to unmentionable pollutions. But he had readmitted them when his sister taunted him with jealousy of the men who were paying for the vodka and causing, perhaps, the pollution.

The hotel's trade now in drink or food was a passing trade. The cooking was rough and ready and done by infra-red heater behind the snackery that was across the entryway from the bar: chickens roasted and eaten whole; steaks that jumped on the plate or lay as if twisted with arthritis. They were too fresh. They were never properly hung. Inelegant truckers didn't give them time to die with dignity. It was a rambling house of irregular corridors and many stairways. She took the stairway that descended into the snackery's kitchen, saluted the shining expectant grin of the silent but ready and willing jukebox, opened the door to admit the help, two girls and a boy, who wouldn't be here for an hour yet. She had tied her apron on back to front. Turn your apron, she thought, and change your luck; and, turning it, looked out at Cosmona mostly asleep, two dogs moving, a man and a milch cow, an old woman in widow's weeds hobbling towards the church for a mass that wouldn't begin until his reverence had pulled himself out from his doss with his dogs. She walked back the entryway and down the silent innyard to the cell of the hermit who might expect angels but would see only a drab rejected woman. She could hardly be, even to Peejay, a temptation, a desert phantom to entice him back to the fleshpots. In a previous existence in Crooked Bridge he had had his fleshpots and his woman.

On the chickweeded patch of ground before his wooden hut Peejay was feeding and talking to his flock of hens and no doubt understanding what the hens said to him, and to each other. When he heard her footsteps he stopped talking. It seemed that the hens, too, had less to say. He squatted, a small man with baggy clothes, a cloth cap, a grey moustache, not unlike a great kindly cock supervising the ladies at table, sweeping now and again over their backs a fanshape of yellow oats. He didn't look round or stand up but, still studying his hens, spoke to her: They're hungry allout this morning, Mrs. Hanafin. 'Tis the crisp appetising air. I like to see them eating well to do God's work laying eggs until they're pensioned off. Only savages would kill hens to eat them.

— The world's full of savages so, Peejay.

— Who says it isn't? In the paper I read a mad fellow writing about the mating habits of birds. He made them out no better than Hollywood film stars. From my own observation, Mrs. Hanafin, the birds and the bees with them behave better than most human beings. That much I learned in Crooked Bridge. Crooked Bridge was my academy.

To Cosmona from Crooked Bridge Peejay had come as to a new planet. In Crooked Bridge he had lived at the town's end in a tiny box of a white house in a row of such white houses, played his fiddle in the evenings, painted his crude pictures (a trick he had picked up from a journeyman sign painter) and by oddjobbing for the farmers on the fringe of the town lived as happily as most until he had the misfortune to inherit five hundred pounds from the estate of an uncle who died in New Zealand. The money brought the woman like a seagull after fish. How was Peejay who lived in music and the fields to know that she was free with all and sundry and the soldiers in the nearest garrison town? He believed her when she said she loved the fiddle. To prove her words she sat listening for hours, her hands beating time, her eyes dreaming echoing pools. She sat like an angel, too, when he painted her picture on the fire-brace. Nobody warned him. He was far too funny. Mocking his five feet four inches a Crooked Bridge wit said: Peejay put off the marrying until he was man-high.

In a rare moment of reminiscence he had said: Mrs. Hanafin, before I married I couldn't keep her out of the house. Afterwards I couldn't keep her in the house.

He grew melancholy. He grew a beard. He played no fiddle and plied no brush. He listened dully when they came in kindly dozens to tell him how she was playing whack with his pounds, and with those other matters to which by matrimony he was supposed to have some claim. To enforce a demand for money the lady and a fancy man once gave him a beating. Once in a wake-house the uncouth Crooked Bridge boys asked him why he grew a beard and he said Jesus had a beard and felt in his heart that since the time of Jesus he was the man most crucified. In his silent tiny house his soul endured its dark night until Martin Mortell, who knew Peejay through farmers for whom he ground grain, came in his wrath, routed the lady under threat of heavy law and brought Peejay to haven in the half-grass-grown innyard at Cosmona.

Surveying the back of his shaggy head, big in relation to the body and the stunted legs, she considered that Peejay having had his woman and she having had her man were equals in experience. She said that the hens seemed happy and, rising slowly to his feet as if somebody somewhere were turning a handle to straighten his little legs, he said, as she knew he would, that hens and ducks would always be happy if people would only leave them alone, that happiness was in the mind and not in what you ate or drank or did put on.

— Regardless, she said, come up and have breakfast.

She needed his company. How sad and far had a woman come when she needed the company of a midget like Peejay?

In a basin of water at the door of his hut he meticulously washed his hands, entered the hut to dry them on a patch of sacking boiled and washed almost to whiteness. She stood in the doorway and watched him – she had never quite had the courage to cross the threshold – and thought that in novels about women in her situation there was always a lout of a brute of a stableboy to oblige, and not a sanctified mannikin like Peejay. Except that he moved and talked and painted and played the fiddle he would not have been out of place as a grandfather in her room of dolls.

The hut was bare as the inside of a box: an iron bedstead, a chair with the fiddle on it, no shelves, no cupboard, never any sign of food, not an odour, not a crumb. He was a starving recluse and once, countering one of her recurrent attempts to feed him amply, he had told her of the saint in the desert who for the whole of Lent stood in the corner of his cell, without kneeling, sitting or leaning, without eating a crumb or drinking a drop, or indeed eating anything except a few raw cabbage leaves on Sunday.

— Mr. Lane in the hospital told me so, he said. A deep young man that. As learned as a Jesuit.

But if that was learning, she told the pitiful little man, Mr. Lane, whom she must talk to some day, was welcome to it. Martin Mortell talked a lot about this Mr. Lane.

Peejay studied his hands as he dried them, reverently, like a priest on the altar. Those hands could paint and play. She looked beyond him to a gaudy painting that was the cell's one coloured ornament. Christ in white nightshirt and red toga gave a portentous pontifical blessing, tossing grain to the hens, to three kneeling nuns whose anatomy had gone all to hell. Was it a fancy or did she recognise in one of them the plump pleasant features of that leaflet raider, Sister Thermometer?

— Your eighth station of the cross, Peejay?

He said proudly: Sister Francis Regis has the first seven already on the wall in the wardsmaids' recreation room.

— Sweet recreation. Teresa Fallon and Dympna Cawley must be thrilled.

— Weep not for me Jesus said but for yourselves and for your children.

— How very true, she said.

But who did they weep for that had no children? For dolls, for dreams gone dead?

His full craw, crop, throat or first stomach arched like the proud prow of a ship, his red comb a pennant aflame, a gigantic white cock approached them as they walked, the woman leading, back up the innyard. He was the sultan of Peejay's seraglio. He was called by Peejay the King of Cosmona. He came readily to Peejay's invitation and sat, magnified by contrast with the mannikin, in Peejay's arms and, when asked, extended one claw to be shaken by the lady. Nervously she touched the claw. There were times when Peejay's closeness to birds and dogs and horses affected her with a sort of terror. Once, peeping into the ragged orchard behind his hut, she had seen him lead through deep grass a file of young and quite unperturbed pheasants. She forced herself to close her hand over the claw and laughed to hide her disquiet and heard behind her the deep voice of Martin Mortell: Christy's here. I convoyed him from the mill into the house. I doubt if a soul saw him.

§

In goldbraided winecoloured uniforms the nine ushers lined up facing the twelve usherettes who wore green skirts, white blouses and black boleros. Each usher, each usherette held an electric torch in the right hand and stood as stiffly to attention as redcoated guardsmen. It was unnecessary, it was ludicrous, but it was a rule made in London by the management of a chain of cinemas and every day at ninety minutes after noon in cinemas in Halifax, Hull, Liverpool, Belfast, Bristol, Glasgow, Birmingham, Dublin, and almost certainly in Manchester and Leeds, the managers and their uniformed staffs conformed. Christy Hanafin conformed in his own way. Sometimes he was Charles Laughton on the deck of the *Bounty*. Sometimes he was Charles Boyer playing Bonaparte to Garbo's Walevska. Ushers and usherettes played the game with him and did not laugh but felt pleasure because, in their names and in the names of all sufferers who worked for others for a living, he was blowing a hard fart at a council of clerks who gabbled of management in London.

She sat in the cash desk halfways between the cinema and the restaurant and enjoyed the pantomime, looking at it through glass as, for the averting of ill-luck, one was not supposed to look at the new moon. She liked his twisted sense of humour but was startled one day to see how startled he was when a little bunny of a blonde, new to the job, burst into helpless giggles. That day he was Philip Mountbatten stepping the regulation number of steps behind the Queen. When the blonde giggled it was as if a solemn treaty had been broken and the secret comedy betrayed to the clerks. His tanned face darkened. He walked angrily back into his office. The blonde was sharply talked to by the chief usherette. Cathy pitied his momentary weakness yet worshipped him, through glass, as the master of the house of dreams and visions to which thousands came, to the woodland paths of escape, the surf, the sea, the lovely women, the handsome men, the glossy apartments, the champagne on ice, the wide savannahs of the flesh. At previews in cool mornings she sat beside him: she was in a sort of a way his secretary. He came finally to hold her hand and once slipped his hand up her skirt to grip briefly the inside of her bare thigh. She felt the burn of his fingertips for a long time afterwards, but sitting in her glass box and, in spare moments, reading about love and Mr. Lewisham, she wondered had he touched her for lust or to have one over on the council of London clerks who thought they knew it all and who were yet but a few of the wiggling legs of the monstrous centipede of management. She didn't consider that the touch meant anything higher than lust which from her reading seemed more real to her than almost anything else.

§

The first words he said to her were: I could use a drink.

— You always could. Will it be Red Biddy or just whiskey?

— Unkind, he said. And I walked all the way from Dublin to see you.

He stood where Mortell had left him at the head of the steps that led down into the bar. Morning light and warmth had not yet seeped down so deep: the barrels looked too cold to sit on, the alcoves were dim dungeons. Sour self-wounding pride had held him standing in the one spot, refusing to move and help himself even when the bar was empty and his tongue thick and chalky from the black sailor's rum. But he drank the whiskey she poured him in four sharp sips, not caring to hide the shake in his hand, the panting effort to recover breath after the first warm bite of the malt. He said: I can talk now.

— I'm favoured. You were always one to talk.

— There was a black man with me, a sailor, but he walked off somewhere.

— Was he any blacker than yourself? He might have been a vision.

— We slept on bags above the kiln in the mill. Haven't slept so well or warm since I was in the womb.

— Fancy. You remember that far back.

— Could I have a second whiskey?

— Why not? It's cheap at cost price.

— Old Mortell woke us up, walking in his garden in the morning. He made food and then when we looked round the black man was gone.

— Did you walk all the way from Dublin to tell me a ghost story?

— No, honest, Cathy.

— Honest?

— If you see a black man today you'll know I was telling the truth.

— I've waited a long time for the proof.

— I saw about the Dublin wedding in the paper. I knew they'd be away. I knew you wouldn't want to go.

— You understand me so well.

— The miller told me it was safe to come home. Only for that...

— You'd have vanished like the black man. Forsake her not and she shall keep thee: love her and she shall preserve thee.

— What's the leaflet?

— Sister Thermometer gave a bundle of them to Martin Mortell to spread all over Cosmona. Did he give one to the black man before he vanished?

— The black man was real.

— As real as whispering Christy Hanafin.

— He was chasing three Cosmona girls.

— Then he should have had a leaflet: Search for her and she shall be made known to thee: and when thou hast gotten her let her not go. Why did you come here, Christy?

— To see you.

— You've seen me. Now have a third whiskey and go.

— No. I've had enough whiskey.

— Such self-control.

— I want to be able to see you, to talk.

— Whiskey always made you talk better, or faster. What have you to say that I'd want to listen to.

— Only that I'm tired.

— So is everybody ever had anything to do with you.

— There's a time when a man has to see somebody who cares, really cares.

— What makes you think I care?

— You told me once you could never stop caring.

— I told you that often. But that was a long time ago. You mean somebody you can hurt. But you can't hurt me any more.

§

Talking to her, fifteen years after he had first touched her bare flesh as if it were part of the cinema furniture and subject to his inspection, he was an altered diminished man: broken, shame-faced, no longer able to dominate or to be, with her, at his most eloquent best. It could be the after effects of rum. It could be crabbed dirt, weariness, an unshaven face. He knew, trying to be honest, that it was simply fifteen years and the emergence of a ruin still to him as inexplicable as if the carpeted floor of the foyer had cracked open and a monster stepped out. He had been a man of power of a sort. On the floor before it cracked the usherettes had lined up for his approval. But at the head of the steps where the miller had left him he had stood paralysed with a hopeless pride until she came and inspected him and poured the drink. He had once been the patron and now she was wearyingly, pityingly, his superior. He was ashamed; and angry and afraid for being ashamed. He had decayed. She had not changed. She was the same small woman with brown downcast eyes, spectacles, and slightly hirsute on the upper lip, who had refused to go out with him the first time he asked her even though she had suffered without protest the grip of his hand on her thigh. He was provoked to persistence. He was a handsome loquacious man. She was a dour, dire, little, silent nobody. With complacent irony he saw his pursuit of her as a parody of one of Love's stories: a prince (he wasn't a prince) in love with a toad (she wasn't a toad) if toads ever were female. Did toads make love? Her refusal sharpened the bitterness of his knowledge that never, in spite of his bronzed good looks, dark strong cleft chin, and the care he took of himself, had he had much success with the blonde busty ones or the slinky brunette ones, or the beauties of any shape or colour. Only later, in the sour leisure that prison gave him for self-examination, had he realised that something saturnine and sinister in him had frightened them away and that she – not beautiful, not easily frightened – had felt sorry for and motherly towards his uneasy bitterness. The toad had taken pity on the prince. With that knowledge, he reckoned, had come his complete dissolution.

§

In the living room that looked out on the Square of Cosmona she said: Sit well back from the window. Don't let Cosmona see you. They have X-ray eyes here.

— You're ashamed of me.

— Oh no, it's just that you're a celebrity. I don't want the autograph-hunters to rush the house.

— You don't ask me what happened to my voice.

— Should I? I read about it in the paper. It earned you a nickname.

— It went and never came back properly. Working in the winter fog in the bloody midland fields around the prison.

— Whispering Christy. It's like a name from a comic song. Whistlin' Phil McHugh has come over from Bunlahey.

— It's not comic. It's a permanent condition.

— I read it in the newspaper. I kept the clipping for the family album.

— I could do with a wash and a shave and clean clothes.

— Why couldn't you have stayed quietly in prison and kept your name out of the paper? But to escape and get caught again.

— Were you ever in prison?

— Should I have volunteered to do your time for you? Did you ever live in Cosmona knowing that the whole place was talking about your late husband, Whispering Christy the jailbreaker?

— I went mad for a while, I think, the doctor said.

— For a while? Whispering Christy was captured behind a hedge by two young Kerry guards. He was still wearing his grey prison clothes and without a necktie. In a half starved condition he gave up without a struggle.

— I know it wasn't dignified, or daring. But I was going out of my mind and this day I saw the chance to cut and run.

— The guards found him standing behind a hedge in the rain.

— I couldn't make up my mind which way to go, who to trust for food or shelter, to go on or to go back and give myself up. I could do with a wash and a shave.

— You certainly could, and you were so clean in the old days. Do you remember? Changing your shirt twice a day in your office. Freshening yourself up. The old lady in the cloakroom said you were very clean, you washed three times a day she said, and I thought you must be very dirty if you needed to wash three times a day.

— You would think that.

— Go ahead to the bathroom. I'll get you clean clothes. Shirts by Shadow and Substance. There are suits of yours here still.

— Waiting for the prodigal to return.

— The pathetic goes well in that voice.

— Ease off, Cathy. Can't you see I'm down?

— I can see that.

The uneven boards in the floor of the long corridor creaked under their feet. She pointed to the narrow stairs that, opposite the bathroom door, went up to an attic.

— If anybody comes into the living-room you'd better hide up there.

— Who'd come?

— My grandmother for one. She didn't go to the wedding.

— Good God, is she still alive? I shudder at the thought.

He tried to make his words sound like light mockery of the flinty old woman he hated as much as she hated him. But mocking levity was not easy to come by in his laryngitic croak. He had a voice now suitable only for complaints, the voice of a child afraid to talk out loud. When she left him he sat on the toilet seat and was taken, as if possessed, by a fit of real shuddering. In the chipped enamel of the large old-fashioned bath he studied the landscape of evil memories.

§

Descending to the bar she thought that she should have sent him for hiding to any other hole or corner in the rambling house but that attic. It wasn't good that the candid staring eyes of her dolls, the innocent expectant eyes of her toy animals, should have to look on that shabby wreck of a man whose filthy fault it was that they would never have children to play with them. She would run up again before he had shaved and lock that attic and find him another hiding-place where his presence could cause no hurt.

But the sight of wonder she saw in the bar put dolls and toys for the moment out of her mind: for sweet Christ, she said, he was telling the truth for once in his useless lying life, and the black man is here, and not only the black man but the bird.

He was a cheerful-looking savage in spite of the scars on his face, not black but rich mahogany. With red shirt, shiny black pants and carpet slippers he might set new fashions for the men of Cosmona. She wasn't afraid of him. He was a cleaner looking man than Christy, and Peejay was only across the passage in the snackery, and one was always safe with a saint in the house.

He said: Room ant coke.

He pointed to the bird and said: Lost.

From a shelf between two miniature dummy barrels the quite unstartled pigeon looked with bright eyes now at her, now at the mahogany man. It was a ringed bird, a homing bird wearied out in some stupid competition and dropping down to rest in Cosmona. On its breast in tired breathing the slate-blue feathers rose and fell.

His deep-brown eyes warm with laughter the black man sipped rum, held it in his mouth, raised his head and swallowed like a drinking hen. Contented, at rest, the bird snuggled its head sideways on a pillow of soft plumage. Hugely amused the mahogany man laughed from a liquid quaking belly, then, swift and agile as a monkey on a stick, leaped his flying wildcat, turning one complete turn in mid-air, to land neatly on light feet, finish his rum and coke and politely ask for more.

She thought it would not be extravagant to suppose that something quite out of the ordinary might happen in the course of that day.

§

In a peaceful corner of the long meadow by the canal lock and beyond Charles Roe's house the Cawley boys were amusing themselves by scything the head off a duck. They had a thing against ducks. Their deceased eldest brother, Albert, who had been a great cyclist and whose exploits had helped to plant an idea in the scrambled brain of Gabriel Rock, had swerved once at high speed in a road-race to avoid a duck and had fallen and cracked the radius in his left elbow. For days the brothers, having thus discovered the radii, had swivelled hands from elbows and wrists and marvelled at the mechanism that enabled the hands to turn. But after Albert's death a year later they had, since the fall had also injured his head, taken a grudge against ducks.

— There was a gangster in America, Enda said, rode about on a horse.

— Gangsters don't go on horses. That's cowboys.

— Bullet-proof limousines. Bang. Bang.

— He rode on a horse for style and appearance, said Enda who could read with a dark intensity that did not belong to his two blond vacuous brothers.

— One day, he told them, the horse threw him and he died. So his pals bumped off the horse.

The idea brought a faint flush to the fair cheeks of Ignatius and Owen. Ignatius once with a blow of his fist had knocked a sunning cat off the parapet of Mortell's bridge into the river and Owen by night had nailed frogs to doors in Cosmona.

Through a gap in the hedge they could look along the canal at the village tapering to the narrow humped bridge. A rare westbound barge was moored above the lock with a goat and a donkey chewing and dunging contentedly on the prow. The corner of the meadow was a trap for the grilling sunlight.

— Hoban the strong man, said Enda, is afraid of his life of ghosts.

He stood stripped to the waist, his skin dark brown, and swung the scythe gracefully, shaving the grass slowly and deliberately from a circle of ground around the spot where they had buried the duck up to its neck. Past terror, past wonder, the bird was mute and still.

— How so, said Owen.

Hips and thighs straining their blue jeans the two blond boys squatted and watched the duck and studied the sweep of the scythe.

— When I showed him in the shed last night the beam Albert hanged himself from he started blessing himself like a steam engine.

— Go on. He has no religion.

— He's a tinker.

— Sure as Christ. And the old one with him did the same before she flopped in the hay.

— It's not safe, said Ignatius, having them about the place.

The scythe blade came whispering closer and closer to the silent duck.

— He pays his way, Enda said. He says he'll coin today with the free mobile X-ray coming and all the country ones in to get something for nothing.

— I would let nobody, said Owen, X-ray me.

— Finish her, said Ignatius.

Only a curtain of grass thin as silk stood between the duck's neck and the blade. The skill of the game was to cut all the grass before beheading the duck. On all fours Ignatius and Owen closed in, mouths open, eyes staring. Crouching a little, Enda stabbed with the scythe at stalk after stalk of grass. Aware in the end that something untoward was in hand the duck quacked sadly, and the blade made a sputting noise and blood spurted and the head was down.

— Christ, said Enda.

He dropped the scythe. There was somebody else with them in the corner of the meadow. For half a second or so the Cawleys felt sick in the guts with a suspicion that other people might not approve of their secret delights. But it was only Gabriel Rock, the helmeted angel of outer space, stepping timidly as if unsure of his welcome through a gap in the hedge. So they laughed with relief and asked him would his mother and himself like a duck for dinner.

§

When the bedside phone rang the doctor surfaced from deep sleep that swayed with the lulling river. Sunlight reflected from the salmon water, part sunlight, part bright water, poured in at the windows and burned and bathed his opening eyes. He listened. He listened again. He answered. He said: Go jump in the river. I know of no such man. Even if I did I wouldn't tell you. What the hell do you think doctors are?

By the time he put down the phone he was as near to fury as it was in his nature to be. His escapades as a student, the suffering he had seen, had combined to teach him kindness, to make him prefer the curves to the corners of living, to bring him to appreciate, as the greatest good yet discovered, the warm plump girl who lay by his side. It was a sweet curve, too, and not a corner that her parents should have money. So that she was startled and surprised out of sleep to hear a hard note in his voice.

— What is it, darling?

— Some bloody Dublin newspaper newseditor had the nerve to ask me if there was a man dying in Cosmona who had been in the jungle at the building of the bridge on the River Kwai.

— What did you tell them?

— Now that's a silly woman's question. Jump in the bloody river, of course.

Leaning on a windowsill he looked down at the sparkling water and thought that he could have said something nastier, that the river was clean, enticingly cool, too good for bloody snoopers. Dozing again she murmured: Sorry darling. I wonder how they ever hear these things. Just think of Cosmona getting into the news.

— It won't if I can help it.

But she was asleep again and, watching the water, he saw the poor sweaty turnip-head of Stephen Mortell, eyes loose in swimming sockets and ready to rattle if the head were shaken. One day, with intense pitiful learning, Stephen had informed the doctor about tertian malaria: The medic in the camp drenched me with water, it was all he could do to cool the burning fever. Wood ash we used for soap and big green leaves for towels. Men had blackouts from hunger, doctor, and beri-beri and pellagra because of no vitamins. Here in Cosmona they never heard of such things.

When the phone rang for the second time the doctor was still leaning on the windowsill gazing into depths in which wraiths of men waved towels of green weeds, combed and set rippling by the water's flow. Half awake again she held out the telephone to him, sweetly surrendering the vibrating symbol of mastery and manhood. He listened. He listened again. He answered. He said: Are you out of your mind? Never heard such nonsense. Ask the Reverend Mother if you like. But if I was her I would, so help me, call a copper.

— What on earth, darling?

— Another newseditor. Or the same man. Or somebody pulling my leg. Or Dublin gone mad. They want to know about rumours that a nurse in the hospital has seen a ghost. And about a mystery man who has Cosmona terrified.

— How do they ever find out?

Rubbing breadcrumbs of sleep out of her eyes she was a child contentedly accepting the omniscience of God.

— Somebody tells them, I suppose, he said.

At the bedside of the miller's son two hours later he wondered how a journalist, if he could find his way into dying Stephen's room, would attack that story. It was most certain that Stephen was dying. A sickening eagerness to talk, to tell, possessed the whole wasted body, to pass on before it was too late the glad news of life as he and certain other fortunates from Belsen to Burma had found it.

Veteran Stephen Mortell blew nonchalant rings of cigar smoke at the ceiling, leaned back on his deathbed and said: This man I knew, a Scotsman, they tied him to a tree and burned his feet with candles.

With a quiet yet courageous smile he added: There were madmen behind barbed wire in one enclosure and lepers in another. The Korean guards were afraid to go near them. They threw food into them as if they were animals.

To peaceful Cosmona Stephen Mortell has brought back news of a bigger, wider, sterner world. He talked wisely to our reporter of malaria, dysentery and beri-beri. Laughingly he said: Don't I know more about them than any doctor?

In the prison camp, he said, he knew he had diphtheria when he saw in a mirror a patch of blood-soaked phlegm at the back of his throat. Then he found he couldn't talk or eat or drink. The polished rice and water came back through his nose.

Outside the miller's house the doctor's wife waited in the Jaguar made available by her parents' money. Every second day she visited the hospital as a member of the women's guild that taught housekeeping and handicrafts to the girl patients. He sat in beside her, aware of her as of a choice familiar warmth, diverted by her presence from thinking of the instructive Sunday morning reading the story of Stephen Mortell would make for happy families of the island breed. She wore a white sleeveless frock with crimson trimmings. Her small firm round knees shone and although he knew so well the pleasaunce the space between them led to, his mind idled fondly along the path, as a lord of the land might dream along a favourite walk in his Italian garden. The sun shone. The birds sang. The millwheel turning, tossing the water, made its own rainbow. She said: There's that idiot girl, the one who stamps her foot.

By a pump at the corner of a laneway of low whitewashed houses Nora had filled a tin basin and was making morning ablutions. Her hair was matted. Her dress was scanty.

— She has little on, said the doctor's wife, but a sort of overall.

— Overall is right, he said.

— It's a disgrace, she said. A picture postcard place like this and every time you go out of the house you must see either that idiot girl or those criminal Cawley boys.

He added cheerfully: Or the companion of our boudoir, Gabriel Rock.

But she was not amused: What are lunatic asylums for? Or jails? Good heavens, there's another, a new one.

On the street outside the hotel the ragged, blackbearded, malformed giant, Patrick Hoban stretched his long arms, yawned away the sleep of Cawley's shed, watched the mobile X-ray unit van, bigger than most of the smaller houses of Cosmona, drive slowly round and round the green to find the best parking place for the day's work.

Walking towards the hospital ahead of the doctor and his wife went Martin Mortell and when they had picked him up the doctor warned him to watch out for newspaper men. He said: Let them come. They can write my son's obituary.

— He talked a lot today, Martin.

— A change before death. His last testament.

There were no words of hope the doctor could say or the miller seemed to need so they talked of the purple aubretia – you could, if it wasn't there already, pump it into the crevices of the walls – that grew on the old stone of the ruin, softening its grey colour and harsh line, and when the woman had gone on to her guild activities they climbed the Tower again and noted that the book of Solomon and Sheba was gone, and the miller told the doctor about the black man and Christy Hanafin. With brotherly good humour they speculated on the sort of woman that a black sailor would follow all the way from Liberia to Cosmona.

— A dark secret out of Grace Roe's past, the doctor said.

Their laughter boomed down the stone stairway. Far below in the corner of a field they saw the Cawley boys and a helmeted figure that could only be Gabriel Rock.

— Because of a woman, Martin Mortell said, the first miller was brought to Ireland by King Cormae MacAirt. He fancied a female slave whose task it was to grind corn with a quern and the jealous queen had her killed, poor thing, night and day at the quern. So to circumvent the queen the King brought in a master miller.

— And here you are still, circumventing queens, keeping the young ones fit for fun and games.

Hairy, friendly men and very much at one against life and death they walked towards the hospital.

— I always prayed, Mortell said, to be able to help others, it was the only prayer I had. Then I look at my pitiful son and think was this the way it was answered.

The doctor had never needed anything enough to pray for it.

— Was that only the prayer of a proud man, doctor? Only God has help to give.

— Peter Lane might tell us, said the doctor. The answer must be in some of his holy books.

§

Through the gap in the hedge the Cawleys and Gabriel Rock had watched the doctor's car bump over the canal bridge. Enda had dug up the duck and Owen at his command had started to pluck it.

— White and plump she is, Gabriel, as a fat duck, Enda said. White with red trimmings. I hear tell she has a sweet pink little one on her like a mouse's ear.

Gabriel repeated hoarsely: A mouse's ear.

Then after deep thought he said: The mouse's a nurse.

— Leave the nurses alone, said Owen.

— They'll cut it off you, said Ignatius.

— They'll take the britches off you and paint it black with boot polish, said Enda who had more imagination than his brothers.

Testing the loudspeaker of the X-ray van some unknown person sent a blast of music over the fields.

§

— Jennie Orr is one of my charities, Miss Grace said to the priest as she tippity-toed beside him on the way to the hospital.

— A more deserving case, he said, could not be found.

Miss Grace was perturbed by the rough simplicity of this red-faced, badly-shaven big-booted cleric with the wide brimmed hat set so squarely on his head. She was superstitiously afraid of him because of the shellshock he didn't even know he suffered from, until one morning when the war was long over he collapsed on the altar saying mass. And why in God's holy name did he always walk like Fionn MacCool with three hounds at his heels? It wasn't easy for her to step with dignity or talk with sense and three brute beasts pestering her, sniffing in the rudest way at the most impossible places.

— Down Bishop, down Deacon, down Martha, said the priest absently.

But his muttered words didn't seem to have any effect.

Would they leap up and muddy her black costume? It fitted so absolutely to a figure that was still as slim as it was the day she was crowned a beauty queen. Anxiety brought the hot flush to her face and created further anxiety because she knew the flush would die away so slowly, lingering stubbornly in the tip of her nose and making her appear a fright before the polite and intellectual Mr. Lane to whom she was returning a book about the art of reading. It was by a Frenchman called Ernest Dimnet and she hadn't read a word of it. But God in his goodness sent a waterhen out from the canal reeds and the three brutes were gone, baying and splashing, in pursuit; and his reverence who, crude as he was, may have been more aware of her embarrassment than she could have hoped, let them go.

— Jennie tells me, she said, about her soft son, Gabriel, a lovely baby she says, but one day when he was four those villainous Cawleys who were evil from the start buried him under a heap of mud and he was never the same afterwards. The Cawleys threw stones at her door and fled and she ran out and saw mud moving and just rescued the child before he smothered.

— He lost an eye to those same Cawleys.

— They're an evil influence in Cosmona.

— You could say that, said the priest with a heavy irony that was quite lost on Miss Grace.

§

Following the music a voice as loud as the voice of God repeated three times: Calling Cosmona.

It called the Cawleys. Carrying the plucked duck in a straw basket and followed by the enigmatic helmeted figure they went up the fields towards the village, crouching for a while in the shelter of a hedge to allow the priest and Miss Grace to pass.

— That's a queer one, said Owen.

— Not as queer as her pansy brother, said Ignatius.

— They say he's afraid of women, said Owen.

— Small blame to him with that lamp-post in the house, said Ignatius.

— He should meet our Dympna, said Owen.

— Mind what you're saying, said Enda. Mind your mouth.

— Look, look, said Gabriel Rock.

They looked.

— Jesus, said Enda, you have great sight for a one-eyed man with cracked goggles.

On the top of the turret of his Scottish Baronial Charles Roe stood with binoculars to his eyes.

— What's he looking at, said Enda.

— Did he see us at the duck, said Ignatius.

— None of his pansy business, said Enda.

He poked Gabriel brutally just below the belt of the zipper jacket. He said: He's cutting you out, Gabriel. He's studying the nurses. You'll have to get spyglasses.

Awkwardly and all legs Gabriel ran ahead of them along the road to the village. They followed, laughing and hooting. A small crowd had gathered. The strong man stood in a publichouse door watching the coming of his customers. On the fringe of the crowd Nora stood, now and again stamping her foot. Three times again the great voice said: Calling Cosmona.

§

— He has nudes on his walls, Miss Grace said, all staring across the rooms at each other as if they were sharing some lewd secret. I don't see why a few postcards should worry him.

— Nudes are art, Miss Grace. Or so they say.

— Father you don't, thank you, have to tell me about art. I have read and studied and been to the galleries.

She held out more prominently Peter Lane's book on the art of reading.

— I wouldn't dare to presume, Miss Grace.

Those dreadful brutes were back and sopping wet from the canal. But praise God the balcony of pink beds was near and Mr. Lane's secluded cultured corner.

— Charles Roe, she said, like so many men of the Irish

should have been a priest. We make the most priests in the world.

He called the hounds gently to heel. He said with cheerfulness: And the best. Though it ill becomes me to boast.

— If he had been a priest he would have been a bachelor by nature, an offence to nobody.

— Not by nature, by grace.

But tall and flushed and self-absorbed she passed, on tippity toes, his little joke by: And it might have kept him from being a pagan. He wants everybody he knows, including Mr. Lane, to make a picnic party this afternoon to the Moat of Cosmona. For the sake, says he, of the ancient gods.

— Why not, Miss Grace. Martin Mortell told me he'd like to stand stretching naked on top of the Moat to worship the sun. Only the people of Cosmona would never understand.

She felt the hot flush increasing. She said sharply: He wouldn't be much to look at.

— The Cawley boys would be a more lively pagan sight, he said with what she could only describe to herself as a hoarse unpriestly laugh.

She was glad when she could leave him and, keeping a careful eye out for Andy the green parrot, slip into Sister Francesca's room to talk and sip tea until her breath returned and the flush faded.

§

Wonders would never cease, Teresa Fallon was always saying, and she said it not once but twenty times on the morning of the day that she and Dympna Cawley and Amantha who didn't seem to have a second name, but one name like that was enough for anybody, hitched the lift from Crooked Bridge back to Cosmona. Would you guess how they came to be in Crooked Bridge? It was Dympna, of course, who had a fellow there, and whinged and pleaded in the bus from Dublin that they would go on to Crooked Bridge for a visit, and Teresa and Amantha were so rich for Dympna never remembered how much money they had salvaged from her new bra, that they hadn't the heart to say no. So on to Crooked Bridge they sailed, holding their breath as they passed through Cosmona, although they mightn't have bothered for the place was asleep except for dirty Nora, with the matted hair, stamping about under the trees as if she were trying to kill a cockroach. Dopey Dympna had her journey for nothing for the fellow, he wasn't much anyway, had gone off to work in England and hadn't even bothered to tell her he was going. They weren't, though, much put out because often and often, for laughs, they'd take a bus to Crooked Bridge and hitchhike home, or to any other town within a fair distance, for you couldn't live in Cosmona all the time and a change was as good as a rest and you never knew who you'd meet or what adventure you'd have on the road.

Three wasn't as good as two for hitchhiking for one man in a car would be afraid of three women and two men in a car would think nothing doing with a sparewheel present. So they sat on a bridge over the same river that flowed through Cosmona – Dympna was so dumb she could never understand why it wasn't a different river – and Teresa wasn't too hopeful, but then Amantha stood up, and her mannequin's figure and legs and long black hair did the trick for, sure as Jesus, Mary and Joseph, the first car that came down the road stopped without even being thumbed.

— Press, said Amantha reading the one word from the sticker on the windscreen.

That made the three of them push and shove, laughing, into the back seat, for gentlemen of the press, as that old windbag Mortell called them, were said to be great sports and easy with money, and the driver of the car was a dote, young, small but not too small, with brown wavy hair that sure as God shone, and like Mickey Rooney only much better looking. For a mile or so they were all eyes for him, and ears for his wisecracks and his rhyming slang, and it was only when the other man spoke that Teresa and Dympna recognised him, and Dympna said afterwards that she came within an ace of wetting her new pants. For wonder of wonders, as Teresa said, and believe it who will, but who should it be only the gentleman with the furry coat and the briefcase, that they had taken the money from and left for drunk in a pub on the quays of Dublin, and thanks be to the Sacred Heart he was still drunk, or drunk again, and would hardly have known who they were even if they had reminded him which, dear Christ, they had no intention of doing. For a half an hour or so even Teresa felt ill at ease until she knew for certain that the kind gentleman, God bless him, was beyond sight or sound, rhyme or reason. He talked very grand and said things like this and Amantha, as she showed afterwards, was a fabulous impersonator and kept them laughing all that day—until hell broke loose. She could even remember his words and imitate the high-falutin' sound of his voice: I have the honour and privilege to come from the garrison town of the Royal Inniskilling Fusiliers. That town has produced soldiers, church-men and athletes of renown, two or more authors. And all those dear girls have ever heard of as coming from that town are two showbands called the Platters and the Polka Dots.

Mickey Rooney said Amantha reminded him of Gina Lollobrigida and Teresa said she'd rather have Sophia Loren, and Mickey said he'd take either one or the other on a butcher's board, that like God he was hard to satisfy but easy to please. They laughed at that until they were sore. Then Lord Muck, the gentle-man, set them laughing again by saying something about pale cold Ireland and, as Amantha remembered, Italy of the opulent tits. He also asked them if there wasn't a man in Cosmona called Mortell who had a son in the jungle with the Japs. Dympna said she didn't like Ava Gardner, she had a face like Sister Camillus, and Mickey said that must be some face but he'd bet Ava had a better ass. He was good at the rhyming slang but not as good, according to clever Amantha who thought she knew it all, as a Liverpool sailor she had met, and more than likely, Teresa thought, robbed, in Dublin. He said the struggle and strife when he meant the wife, and Scotch peg for leg, and elephant's trunk for drunk, and to Lord Muck he said he was looking for his bag of coal and the two of them laughed and thought the girls didn't know what they meant.

Teresa told them there had been eleven burglaries in Crooked Bridge in the last six months, that a very bad element lived in that town, and that she herself knew and was friendly with every civic guard in Crooked Bridge and Cosmona, and to prove her point she waved to Guard Kane when they pulled up outside the hotel in Cosmona and Guard Kane waved back, but Mickey Rooney said the guard was taking a hard look at the number of the car and it could be that he thought they were the burglars from Crooked Bridge.

— So we'll park the jam jar here, said Mickey Rooney.

— We'll all have a drink, said Lord Muck.

— Why not, said the girls, it's the end of a perfect day.

Up the entry with them to the cellar bar, Amantha and Dympna swinging out of Lord Muck and Teresa walking behind with Mickey Rooney. She liked Mickey Rooney.

That was one drink they were not destined to have. From the top of the three steps at the door of the bar Mickey Rooney raced down to greet with a shout two other men who were leaning on the counter and, wonder of wonders and this was the wonder of all time, there was a third man at the counter, a black man, and Teresa was so shook for a moment that the only thing she could think of was that he wore carpet slippers, something she hadn't noticed before. She pulled Dympna back into the entry. They ran like three blind mice. They crossed Cosmona without seeing it. It was the devil's curse that he was there and he was the devil. He was black enough. They ran. They didn't even pause to listen to the loudspeaker music coming from a big van under the trees in the Square. They ran. They headed for the Cawley place. Footsteps were following, overtaking them. Dympna screamed. But it was only Enda, Owen and Ignatius and far behind them, tripping over himself as he ran, Gabriel Rock.

§

The four pressmen were halfways through their first drink in unison when Ned Broe, the small dapper photographer with brown shoes polished so as, if you wanted to, you could see your face in them, said: Newsflash. Check. Three girls missing in Cosmona. What happened the three aces of hearts we had with us?

— Tarts is correct, said the woman behind the bar. Pressmen mustn't be particular any longer. Where did you pick them up?

Ned earnestly explained. He never looked more like Mickey Rooney except that he was, as the girls had noticed, better-looking. Quietly accepting his explanation the demure freckled little woman said: Can you look after yourselves for awhile? And the bar? And the black? And the bird?

She smiled at the black man who smiled back and said: Room ant coke.

Ned was already behind the counter, tying round his waist a white apron he found there. With the studied, painfully-articulate expression made necessary by excess of drink Larry Collins, Lord Muck of Ballymuck, was saying: All my life my greatest ambition has been to own a bar, to pull the pint, to place the elbows on the counter, to interject the occasional sapient, incontrovertible remark into the conversation.

From the doorway that led back into the belly of the house the snubnosed woman said: Then gratify yourself for an hour or so. I've a job to do.

— Three women with us and they vanish like snow off a ditch, Ned said.

He wrinkled his nose up into his forehead. He was a very perplexed Mr. Michael Rooney.

— You're losing your touch, Bob Gunning said.

He expanded his biceps. They were enormous. He said: Losing three women could lose you your job. They could have been three stories.

— One, two, three, said the black man.

Ned said: It wasn't stories exactly I was thinking of.

— Our dark friend, said Larry Collins, has some knowledge of the tongue of Chaucer and Shakespeare.

Art Finlan, the second photographer, said: He speaks six words fluently. More than you'd find on most editorial staffs.

With a beatific smile the black man said: Room ant coke. One, two, three, much fuck.

— Eight, said Art. I underestimated him. He's a born managing director.

— These three women, Ned said, were good things if I ever saw good things.

In a piercing falsetto Bob Gunning sang a blast of opera. After flexing his biceps, singing falsetto was his favourite party trick. He frequently did both together. He said: Edward, it is reported that you have seen good things in your time. There was that chambermaid in Cork.

— She followed me into the bath.

— Some slight guarantee that she was at least clean, Larry Collins said. I wouldn't say as much for our recent companions. Pantsfull of contagious itch.

— More likely of stolen spoons, Ned said. I never knew girls who talked more about burglaries or knew more police.

Larry Collins said: They keep a pigeon in this pub. That's an innovation.

— Nothing in the licensing laws against it, Bob Gunning said.

— The lady says, said Art, that he flew in this morning and she's been feeding him since.

While they drank and talked the pigeon cast upon them a cunning bird's eye.

— She added in explanation, said Art, that they all come home to roost. Now I know about birds, mostly to shoot and eat, but I know that's not true.

Glasses were raised. The black stranger was invited to drink. The four agreed that they were gentlemen of the press whose business it was to report and photograph the truth, that the dove from the ark and the man from Africa were inexplicable but interesting companions.

— If it would not, said Larry Collins, be an impertinence or an intrusion on your privacy to ask, but what in the name of Jesus are the two of you doing here?

Robert and Art were about to answer politely, simultaneously and evasively, when a voice of thunder from the Square outside caused everyone except the black man to lower his glass and listen reverently. The voice said: You won't have to undress and you won't be kept waiting. It will take only two or three minutes of your time.

— Could that possibly refer, said Collins, to Big Mary MacKenzie, the last of the old-fashioned whores?

— This sounds like the place to visit, Ned said.

He poured more drink. He said that something might happen here.

— For free we could have ourselves tuberculin tested, Robert explained.

Lord Laurence Collins said it was a most reprehensible

practice, this allowing comparative strangers an insight into your insides, it was worse by far than auricular confession.

— But in the presence of God with his unmistakable voice of thunder, he continued, let us tell the truth. We're here after a dying man we're told helped to build the bridge on the River Kwai.

— A hole in the heart story was what I suspected, Robert said. Your editor's fascinated with holes in hearts or hearts with holes in them or whatever the hell it is.

Laurence most reverently raised his glass. He said: Hic est enim calix. This is a hole in the heart story. The first good story of the sort was Jesus Christ and by all accounts this veteran of the Kwai is a much crucified man.

— This sort of talk, Ned said, gives me the John Knox.

— Pox, said the black man.

— Nine words of English, said Art. A natural editor-in-chief. I wonder can he read or write.

— Food would be good, Ned said.

The woman came back very quietly into the bar. Lord Laurence was reading from a leaflet he had picked up from the counter and the black saint was nodding his head to acknowledge a threepenny piece. As the saint's head slowly settled Laurence intoned: The joints of thy thighs are like jewels, thy navel is like a round goblet which wanteth not liquor: thy belly is like an heap of wheat set about with lilies. Thy two breasts are like two young roes that are twins.

Expanding his great biceps and crowing like a cock Robert said: That there's my sort of religion.

— Have as many leaflets as you like, she said. They're a present from a holy nun. The dining room, such as it is, is across the passage.

Laurence, Edward, Arthur and Robert crossed the entryway.

— That's a sad sour woman, Art said.

He was a kindly pipe-smoking man whose life was in cameras, guns, fishing-rods, and a devoted little wife and two children.

— She has a secret sorrow, he said.

He read from his leaflet: Put thy feet into her fetters and thy neck into her chains.

— The other bit was better, Ned said. The joints of her thighs were like jewels. I never saw a woman like that.

— It could also, said Laurence, have been a great running mare I recall, by the name of Serpoletta.

§

The managerial man from London who fired Christy for fiddling had had the thinnest scrawniest neck ever made, and around it a white collar that could have circled his waist. He said he had sat seven times through a film about a town like Alice and wept each time and, indeed that could be true, for Christy thought the film would have made Jesus weep. But then all films had come to make Christy weep tears of alcoholic fury when he'd step in for a moment from the bars and look at them through blurred eyes and wonder what he was doing there and why he was roped forever to a nonentity of a woman, like Cathy. The managerial man, and the little neck of him swelled and contracted again like the neck or whatever it was of a frog, said that, in spite of his sevenfold gift of tears in the town like Alice, there would be legal action about the fiddle which was of magnitude, and of vile example to all slaves everywhere, and that was that; and that was the beginning. Or was it the beginning or the middle or the bloody end?

He was for a while in the attic, one dirty dormer shutting out as best or worst as it could the light of the high sky over Cosmona, before he saw the thin-necked little bastard staring at him out of the shadows. Sweet God was he haunted, had the black man's rum been hooch, was he seeing little men that were mockeries on living nasty men? To make it worse still the managerial man wore a policeman's helmet. Beside him but six inches taller was Little Boy Blue, knee-breeches and yellow hair, and blowing his horn although no sheep could be seen in any meadow, no cows in any corn. But lifting their heads in pleasant meads on the attic floor in answer to the notes of the horn were cloth, stuffed animals: a cow and three bay horses, a tiger, an elephant, a black baby bear. An army of toy soldiers stood in the oval of a railway track on which the train was not, at that moment, running; a teddybear lay on his back with his feet in the air; a tacking yacht sailed across the knotted timber. There were blocks to build with, a ball to play with, a truck to carry freight, a gunbelt for a cowboy to wear and two pistols to shoot with. Here in the heart of this hollow echoing house a childless woman, lonely for the son she never bore, had made a playground, a toy world, for a toy man: and for a toy woman, too, because three blonde pink-cheeked dolls sat on one bench and gazed into a toy mirror. Beyond them there was a doll's house and at its door, that opened into nowhere, an array of tiny cups and plates and saucers.

She was standing behind him. She said: I hadn't meant you to see them.

She meant: Them to see you.

— Are you expecting a blessed event?

— It makes you feel better to say that.

— I always feel better when I've shaved and washed.

— You were always so fond of water and fresh air.

— Were you hoping for twins? Two of those dolls are the image of each other.

— You had that electric fan in your office. You went up to the flat roof so often to do deep-breathing exercises.

— Dream children, he said. I think of all the trouble we went to, playing careful before we were married. We mightn't have bothered. Even that way life cheated us.

— Who is life?

— It wasn't in you anyway, Cathy. He or she.

— Always the kind word, Christy.

— That pint of nourishing stout I spilt once over your summer frock in the bar in Liffey Street. It fell right between your legs. We had a joke that it might fertilise you.

— That was your joke, Christy. You were ashamed of me from the start. Hiding in that bar in Liffey Street. Why did you ever marry me? To make me miserable?

— Jesus, he said. How many women have said that?

There was no answer to her unanswerable question except to shout the name of an inoffensive man who had died for love. The son of God had had nothing to do with his reasons for marrying Cathy. He could not admit to her that the beauties wouldn't have him, that he sought his revenge by taking to himself this self-effacing Cindy Lou. He couldn't even praise her by granting that in bed she was better, possibly, than the beauties, her animal appeal emphasised by her very quietude, no groans of pleasure, no protestations. She spoke now, almost over his shoulder, and how gratified he was to hear the ache of tears in her voice. She said: There were clots of frozen snow on the ground in the park that night. But the grass behind the bushes was very dry. It was almost warm, like a bed, our first bed.

— Do you remember what you said, you remember so much?

— I said: I never thought this would be necessary. I didn't know then that that was necessary for love, if it was love.

— We agreed that it was.

— At least one of us believed it. When you touched me first I cried. I never knew why.

— You cried for love.

— You made jokes about the game called Twenty Toes that was played all over the town.

— The little girls play it with ten toes up and the boys with ten toes down.

— That wasn't the tender talk of love.

— It made you laugh at the time.

— I laughed to stop weeping. And to stop being afraid. It was the time of the month and I was afraid the blood would stop you.

— I never knew that. I thought you were just an easy bleeder. Women were deceivers ever.

— You should talk, she said. You should talk.

He had known that night that there was a quality in her body that he would be loath to deprive himself of, that catered, moreover, to his sense of power, and that the slim beauties were never, necessarily, the best rides. He could hear her weeping, her laughing, while they sheltered from the wind on dry grass behind laurels and a beech hedge, and the rustle of dry leaves on a pathway beyond the hedge, and the wind in the high swaying trees. For a few minutes away from offices and management, they had found their own enchanted woodland. Listening to the leaves and the swaying trees he was only half aware that she had gone away again from the attic. But he knew that she was weak and had gone weeping and that he was strong again because he had caught her at her dreams of unbegotten children.

A musical powder-box on the floor behind the doll's house tinkled, when he set it going, some sweet melody that he wasn't able to identify. To the music he saluted in mockery the dwarf image of the scrawny-necked man, the sevenfold weeper, who had had him sent to jail. He tickled the chins of the twin dolls. He laughed to think that surely no man ever had had more biddable daughters.

§

That morning the world and his mother, and that included even Sister Francesca and her green parrot, Andy, stopped to talk by the bedside of Peter Lane. Neither John Henry Newman nor Nicholas of Flue could get a word in edgeways. Andy's vocabulary was limited at the best of times but with a wickedness that could only have been deliberate he confined himself on that occasion to repeating again and again: Tippytoes. Tippytoes. The boys were openly hilarious. The nurses tried to conceal their mirth. Sister Francesca, on whose black serge shoulder the green demon perched, must have taught him to repeat that nickname. Yet the wrinkled saintly face of the old nun showed no sign of comprehension while poor Grace Roe flushed and fluttered and tried to talk about Cardinal Newman, and delivered her message from Charles Roe about the picnic on Cosmona Moat; and withdrew in confusion.

For Peter Lane a journey to the Moat meant manhood and the welcome return to trousers into which the Mouse would have to help him. The idea set his veins dancing.

After nun and green parrot and tall flushing spinster came the doctor on his rounds, and the miller who lingered to talk after the doctor had moved on, and to praise the doctor as a renowned healer: He has a high name in the village. They queue up to him as if he was a holy well.

Then the doctor returned to say he too would join the picnic on the Moat and that he'd ask permission for a nurse to accompany Peter Lane; and the priest came to talk about the prospects of the shooting that would open on the twelfth of August; and priest, doctor and miller talked sadly of the miller's son.

Over by the Tower the Mouse was walking with the other night nurses, taking compulsory air before they went to bed for compulsory rest. His thoughts went with them. Then two past-patients from Cosmona, one hunchbacked beyond description, one who had merely both legs stiff from the hips, came playing banjo and fiddle for the amusement of the boys. They were frequent welcome visitors. They reminded the bedridden that even the most afflicted could again walk. They reminded Peter Lane that, his ailment being so much less than theirs, he was unworthily lucky and made him feel even more sharply the guilt of a sin that must be dark ingratitude to the God who healed, but who wouldn't or couldn't go far enough, not even with the help of a holy well of a doctor, to straighten the fiddler's back or loosen the banjoist's hips or raise Stephen Mortell from the dying. Altogether, the fiddle, the banjo and remorse proved too much for him, so, wrapping himself in his dressing gown, he withdrew, hobbling, to his toilet hermitage. Going about his business he thought that he should find some peace there for peace came dropping slow. Closing his eyes and with the noise of the refilling cistern in his ears he sat on beyond his time and dreamed his way backwards to the summer of the black cat and the green girl.

Then, as now, he had found a hermitage or at any rate the most complete privacy in a jakes: a dry closet in a hollow steeply below the farmhouse. To get to it he went down a twisted rocky path through dark-leaved odorous bushes. He never knew the name of those bushes but he could smell their musky sullen odour, and smell the lime from the bucket in the jakes whose wooden walls blistered in the sun of that rare summer. He could hear still the continuous buzzing of flies and the slow drip of semen on crumpled newspapers and remember now, almost with amusement, how he marvelled with some pride at the size of this thing that in the last year of schoolboy conversation had assumed a sort of human character: comic when boys talked together; threatening and obsessive in moments of lonely brooding fantasy. He could have masturbated in as much privacy and with more pleasure up along the goatpaths that wound through the furze on a hill above the house. But the sizzling jakes, the iron bucket, the smell of corroding lime went better with the sense of sin. You offended God, and God was more likely, if He had any wit, to be up on the sunny hillside with the chewing meditative goats. The goats had their own idea of God: the strongest, gravest, most long-horned of the pucks who sat in the centre of the circle, no younger puck yet aspiring to the godhead, when the herd squatted to rest. Here in the hot wooden box was hell and it seemed unlikely that God who made heaven and hell would choose to live in the less desirable residential area. You could also, the boys said, go mad and even in extreme cases grow hair on the palms of your hands.

Looking back over six or seven years that included one of frantic piety and purity he accused the three women, the slavey, the woman of the house, the girl in the green coat, of his frenzy and fantasies, of all the shameful things he could not now tell to the Mouse with the heartshaped face. To the girl in the green coat he said: She isn't like you. She isn't a tease. You were a tease at thirteen. The three of you were teases: a child, a country slut, a middleaged married woman, banding together by some instinct, like witches, to tease a boy of fourteen. Greensleeves, do you remember the day of that long drive by pony and trap to the horseraces on the flat sands by the sea? Going to the races, as you may recall, yourself and myself walked the steep hills behind the trap, hand in hand or fingers locked in fingers when we thought the uncle and aunt weren't looking back. With glints of glee in your brown eyes you told me that you were sure your elder cousin, all of fifteen years, a fat girl who went to school with you, had done the deed. Did you really mean it, I wonder, or was that only your childish devilish way of sharpening a fourteen-year-old's curiosity?

It rained at the races. The black clouds gathered and burst and swept the sands and the flatland beside them. We crowded in the steaming tea-tent, the two of us as close as two peas in a pod. Then on the journey home your knees like a vice gripped my right knee. Who taught you that trick, the slavey or my malicious middleaged aunt? Or was she malicious or was she simply trying to be funny when she said that night that if the house got too

crowded with holiday-making relatives she could see no possible
harm in two youngsters sleeping in the one bed? Yet I did feel
that as she said it she cunningly watched my face for reactions. I
was sick with fear or hope, or hope and fear. The three of you,
very weird sisters, must have laughed your sides sore as soon as
my back was turned. In the high attic of the old house I lay sweating in bed, listening in agony to the giggles of yourself and the
slavey from the bed you shared. But when I stiffened my courage
and asked you what you laughed at on those warm stifling nights
– laughed so as the bed creaked – you showed me a silly paper-
backed book: the story of the film of some film about Don Juan
that had some rot in it about she giving he a proof of her love. On
the Tower the mystery man left a book about Solomon and Sheba.
I was afraid always to tiptoe across to the door of your room and
listen. I was afraid the woman of the house would hear me. I was
afraid of more laughter. So, three weird sisters, Greensleeves
with elfin eyes, a middleaged woman, a loose-lipped slavey that
I heard afterwards was free and easy to the point of outrage,
danced in a ring around a boy and made their mockery of all manhood: until nothing was left for a boy to do but go down to hell
through nameless dark bushes, hiding from the sun and God the
goat, to the sizzling box and the smell of lime and the slow drip
of life on crumpled newspaper.

Returning from his dream of that lost summer he listened.
The noises of the ward seemed far away from his humming ears.
The cistern had filled and was silent. Life dripped down again,
but this time there was no smell of lime, no dank bushes, no
newspaper, and the tiled walls were cool all around him. Sin piled
on sin. Walking back to his bed, talking to boys that he felt must
know, he blamed not himself nor the Mouse but three witches in
an old farmhouse across meadow and bogland from the place
where, by the black river at the foot of the mountain, he had set
the cat free. The convent bells chimed noon. Dark as his thoughts
the rooks and jackdaws came from their hunting in the fields,
their talking around the Tower, the ruined abbey, the churchyard
trees, and crossed over for lunch to the coloured balconies.

Charles Roe, tall, florid-faced, silver-haired, still as straight
as the army had made him, keeping in spite of drink the figure of

an officer and a gentleman, dressed in expensive but subdued tweeds, was by his bedside dipping into the life of Saint Nicholas of Flue.

— Curious fellow this, he said. Oddest dietary habits. Do you know that the Emperor Leo I and the Empress Eudoxia came to ask a blessing from a Byzantine Stylite called Daniel. I feel Cousin Grace and myself should ask a blessing from you now that you're descending from your pillar. It might bring wisdom to me and warmth to her. I'm so glad you can come on our little picnic to the Moat. The panorama. The bracing air. Do you more good than a month's convalescence. And I have so much to tell you about the legend of the black man of the caves of Cosmona.

Later on he said: Do you know, Mr. Lane, why I left the Jesuits? I could never make up my mind whether God was a square or an isoceles triangle.

— To goats he's a goat, Peter Lane said.

But Charles Roe was not listening. He seldom listened. He said: That was my great difficulty. It still is.

Bearing his difficulty with him he crossed the balcony, saluting the boys and being respectfully saluted in return. He carried a shiny blackthorn stick with a silver monogrammed band. The boys respected him for the lame leg that came from a war wound. He descended the few steps and went away over the smooth grass. Rooks and jackdaws scolded before him, then returned greedily to their free meal.

— THREE —

So between the jigs and the reels, Peejay said to Mr. Collins and Mr. Gunning, you got here at last.

— We thank you, Peejay, for the tip, said Larry Collins.

— If we only had an alert man like you in every village in Ireland, said Bob Gunning.

— We have drunk, said Larry Collins to Bob Gunning, from the same fountain of knowledge.

— It's always a pleasure to advise the Dublin papers, Peejay said. They sorely need advice.

— You should be a managing director, Peejay, said Bob Gunning.

— Did you get your cheques, asked Larry Collins.

— Small sums, said Peejay. I'm not so badly off that I need them. I have free bed and board here and fair payment for what work I do.

Eyes closed, he counted off his blessings with the stubby forefinger of his right hand on the fingers of his left hand.

— I have time to paint and play the fiddle and say my prayers. I have peace, the heavenly peace of Cosmona. I have my New Zealand allowance, what's left of it. Once a week I go to the bank in Crooked Bridge to collect it. That's all I want to see of Crooked Bridge.

— You're a happy man, Larry Collins said.

— Happiness resides in the mind, Mr. Collins. It isn't for the cheques I write you information. The things I tell you about should be known for the good of the world and the salvation of men's souls. It should be known what that Mortell buy has suffered. He bears the marks of the sufferings of Jesus in his broken body. It should be known that there is a life to come and that for His own reasons the Almighty allows the spirits to return from it and manifest themselves. The spirit of old Nurse Callaghan turned the minds of those young hussies up there to their prayers. So Mr. Lane tells me. A young man that's as clever as a Jesuit. Doesn't that make better reading for the people than what buck of a film star with a wig and a corset on him marries or divorces what other hoor of a film staresse? Let him read about suffering and the dead. Keep the straps of women out of the news.

— Peejay, tell us about the Peeping Tom.

— That's unimportant, Mr. Collins. That was merely incidental information. That was bait to make sure you'd come.

— Birds of a feather, Larry Collins said. You mean newspaper men are Peeping Toms.

— They could be evangelists, Mr. Collins. We're all Peeping Toms in the sight of God. God himself is a Peeping Tom.

— Jesus he's a rare one, Bob Gunning said and crowed like a cock when Peejay, he judged, had gone to a safe distance.

Ned Broe said: He's a nut. He's completely astray in the board and bed. No women, no news, is my motto.

— Here was a boy had hard luck, Larry Collins said.

He read out the details printed under a faded photograph, hanging on the dining room wall, of a young man in uniform.

— Twenty-one years of age, he said. An Irish boy in the Australian infantry. A relative of the house here, I presume. Killed in a German air-raid, tenth of September, 1918, when the bloody business had only a few weeks to go. Listen to these names, still recalled with sorrow in many sad shires: Ypres, Loos, Arras, Bethune, Saint Quentin, Neuve Eglise, Bapaume, Bourbon Wood, Péronne, Monchy. It says here, too, that on his eighteenth birthday he killed his first German, a Prussian officer, at the Battle of Loos. All who pass by pray for my soul and the souls of those who met death at my hands.

With a hand unsteady from drink Larry Collins was making notes on a roll of copy paper. He said: Good background for our story of the man from the Kwai.

— He's always alert, said Art Finlan.

— A newspaper man of the old school, Ned Broe said. Always on the baby doll.

With ageing dignity Lord Laurence said: Do you mind? I learned my trade from C. P. Scott of the *Manchester Guardian*. I've thrown away more good jobs than you young fellows will ever hear of.

— He also, said Bob Gunning, had five women shot from under him at the Battle of Balaclava.

Yet they were respectfully silent while Laurence finished his note-taking. He was, they knew, a survival from another, better age.

They finished their meal: arthritic steaks and roasted chickens. In memory of the dead soldier, Bob Gunning, as they walked back to the bar, stepped the slow step of the dead march and made with his mouth bagpipe noises more or less to the tune of the Flowers of the Forest.

§

The bird was still in the bar but it had flown from its eyrie on the shelf of bottles to pick at a saucer of grain that somebody had placed on a low table in one of the alcoves. The black man was gone. The woman was not to be seen, but two men, one drinking whiskey, the other pale ale, stood at the counter. The whiskey-drinker, florid-faced, white-haired, clothed in good tweeds, a blackthorn stick in his left hand, was making a speech. He said: The woman saint of Cosmona was a curious one. When the son of a prince offered her his love she asked him what he loved most in her. He said her eyes, and straightway she plucked them out and cast them from her, and thereafter walked in blindness.

Helping himself and his comrades to whiskey, dropping the cash into the old-fashioned till, Ned Broe said it was lucky for her that the son of the prince hadn't mentioned anything less detachable than eyes.

— A frivolous remark, said the orator and went on talking.

— Since, he said, I hear that ye are gentlemen of the press and, a brace of you, cameramen, you might be interested in a little expedition I'm planning for this afternoon to the Moat of Cosmona. It's of historical interest and most photogenic.

— If we wouldn't be too frivolous, said Ned who didn't take talk of that sort from anybody.

— Forgive me, said Charles Roe. There was no intention to offend.

Partly mollified, Ned drank and they all drank and the other man, old, bewhiskered, but a fine heavy figure of a fellow in a blue serge suit and wide-brimmed, clerical black hat, said: Good health and welcome to Cosmona. You've a voice made for the pulpit, Mr. Roe.

— Don't remind me, Martin, that I belong to the genus so widespread in Ireland – the spoiled priests. In Maynooth College they have a special society for them, for the men who put their hands to the plough and then turned back. They call it Vexilla Regis. Only organisation of failures in the world – that I know of. But I would like to draw the attention of our friends of the press to the legend of Dark Domhnall, the horse robber, the black man of the Moat of Cosmona.

Art Finlan asked: Where's our black man gone?

But Charles Roe didn't hear him and nobody answered, for the voice of Charles Roe droned on to describe the high heather-capped rock known as the Sentry Box or Dark Domhnall's Chair.

— It is, said he, a naturally-formed seat or chair of stone high up on the side of a rock. From it you enjoy an uninterrupted view of the country for miles around in every direction. Behind the chair is a ledge of rock which served as a shelf for Domhnall's gun, and below the chair is a long soft-shaped stone known as Domhnall's bed. Close to the chair, in a crack in the rock, there is a tiny well about two inches in diameter which has never been known to go dry even on the hottest day in summer…

From the Voice of God in the Square outside came the words: There is nothing to be afraid of. Ten to one you are in perfect health. But it's better to be sure than sorry. Step right in. It will only take you a few moments. You don't have to undress.

Startled by the conflicting currents of sound the pigeon rose from her grain, flew in violent circles around and around the low ceiling, setting the men ducking and cursing the whim of the woman for keeping a bird in a bar. In the confusion, and under the pretence of getting their cameras from the cars, Ned Broe and Art

Finlan were gone and when, twenty minutes later, they returned, the monologuist, knocked off his stride by the Voice of God and the circling of a dove, had departed, the bird was at rest again on the shelf, the woman was back behind the counter. Only Art Finlan, the kindly, noticed that she had been crying.

— What happened that windbag, Ned Broe said. Did he blow himself up?

— He's a gentleman, said the stout old soul with the whiskers. But he'd talk the ass out of a pot.

— He's big when he's out, said the woman.

— Like a jackass's prick, said Ned and was reproved by Laurence Collins for using such language in the presence of a lady.

— Good day gentlemen, said Old Whiskers and he finished his pale ale. I'll go, before you beat each other. Come up to the Moat if you're still able to walk.

They refilled, and gave back to the bird in stares four times as much as it gave.

— A fine sturdy old type, a bold peasant, his country's pride, said Laurence Collins. Who might he be?

— It's sad about him, she said.

Her voice was hoarse with tears that might have been for another person's sadness.

She said: His only son is on his deathbed, wasted away to a shadow with diseases he got in the jungle.

There was a long drinking silence.

Then Art Finlan opened his mouth wide, his tiny moustache in danger of vanishing up his nose, and laughed a shrill sustained laugh, and the bird followed a careful parabola back to the alcove table and the grain.

— We're prize newspaper men, Art said. We're bound for the Pulitzer. First we lose three women and a black man who, in an Irish village, can't speak more than a few words of English. What's he doing here, for God's sake? Then we let the key man in the Kwai story walk away from us, just like that.

The woman said: I can tell you where to find him.

— We know, Ned said. Peejay told us.

— Peejay, she said.

She was puzzled. Bob Gunning said hurriedly: We met him in the dining room and asked him.

— C. P. Scott wouldn't like it, Laurence said. In the meantime we'll have another drink.

— Peejay's a wonder, Art said. He has a white rooster the size of a turkey that shakes hands like a human being or a dog. For my growing gallery of photographs of beasts and birds I got a shot of Ned and himself holding hands.

— Peejay says, said Ned, that the birds and the bees and the beasts behave better than human beings.

— Edward, that shouldn't surprise you, said Lord Laurence.

He raised his glass with both hands. He said: Hic est enim calix.

But as he was the only one of the five people in the bar looking at that moment towards the door, he lowered his glass again. He said: Is it the drink. Or do I see Quasimodo? Or Caliban? Or a djinn out of a bottle?

— You can go the way you came, she said to the strong man. You will not be served in this bar.

— For the love of God, ma'am, he said, a single pint. I'm crucified with the thirst. And a bottle to carry to the wife. She's too backward you see, sirs, to cross the threshold of this elegant saloon. We've a day's work to do and I'll pay you, ma'am, when the money comes rolling in. There's a crowd out there to have their lungs tested that's bigger, God be praised, than the Fair of Puck.

— That's a plea no woman's heart could resist, Laurence Collins said. May I have the pleasure, sir?

He pushed forward to buy the pint the silver change that lay before him on the counter.

— No, thank you kindly, sir. Herself here never has the heart to refuse me ragged as I am.

— Drink your pint and go, she said. And don't come back if you're drunk.

One swift swallow and the black pint was gone. With a gentlemanly farewell and a blessing Quasimodo lifted the bottle and went to his dancing wife and his feats of strength. The woman crossed herself. She said: God bless the mark. I wouldn't want to see him if I was pregnant.

Bob Gunning said: I've seen him perform. He can let lorries roll over his chest.

— His arms, said Ned, are as long as the arms of Donnelly the bareknuckle boxer who fought Cooper on the Curragh of Kildare. Donnelly could scratch the backs of his calves without bending. One of his arms is mummified in a glass case in Kilcullen.

— I saw Caliban there, said Bob, holding the back rung of a kitchen chair in his teeth while his tinker wife danced a reel on the seat of the chair.

Again Laurence raised his glass with both hands: Hic est enim calix. When I was young if anybody asked me what I was going to be when I grew up, I'd never have thought of that.

She poured herself a half tumbler of red wine and sipped it slowly. Girls, old Mortell had once said, need the blood of the beef to make up for what they lose every month. But he wouldn't say the same for the blood of the grape. She explained, though why she should bother explaining she couldn't see or say, that she didn't drink when Mortell was in the bar because his wife, now deceased, had been an alcoholic and he hated to see women drinking. The bird again curved back to the shelf of bottles. She thought: They all come home to roost. She thought: I could gaze twenty times a day on monsters and never bring forth a child, harelipped or comely. She said: I should have given him a leaflet for his dancing wife. Charles Roe took several away.

She read: I purposed therefore to take her to live with me: knowing that she will communicate to me of her good things and will be a comfort in my cares and grief.

From the Square outside, interrupting the music the Voice said: You have nothing to fear. Twenty to one you are in excellent health.

— Twenty, said Laurence Collins. The odds are improving. Another drink, my dear.

§

Gabriel finished his hedge-clipping for the doctor, and crossed the bridge and went, sheltered by a hedge along the far bank of the river to a muddy corner of reeds and brambles from which he could see without being seen. He knew what was going to happen as soon as he left the doctor's garden. While he was there clipping she would make no appearance or not, at any rate, the sort of appearance that Gabriel wanted her to make. She might call from a window or appear at a doorway, but wearing her ordinary clothes, to call to the doctor where he stood by the edge of the water casting a careful fly. He was an accurate but not a fanatical fisherman. He wouldn't dare weather or distance, no, not to capture the Old One Himself, the King of all the Brown Trout. But it was more relaxing than golf to own a riverside garden where one could stand in good weather and touch the fly down on a fruitful stream.

Gabriel crouched and waited and watched, for a start, the bedroom window. The doctor watched the water under his drifting fly for the white flash of belly that would betoken the rising fish. Gabriel watched the window, straining his one weak and goggled eye to try to peer far back into the room, hoping for the faint flash that would betoken the woman changing into the two bits of rag, they covered little or nothing, that she called her swimsuit. He crouched low in a small trench that in winter was a running stream. The smell of mud sickened him. A weight of mud seemed to press down on him as if somebody for hellery had tipped a lorry load on him to smother him. Only hope kept him from sickening or smothering, and hope had its glorious reward when she stepped out of the door, ran naked, or almost, down the path to the river, kissed the doctor whose big hairy right hand covered her rump, lay for a while airing herself in the sun on a rug on the grass, then trotted like a plump little pony downstream from the fisherman and plunged and splashed. In his trench, his fingers like claws stuck in the mud, Gabriel gasped with delight. He liked it better when the little thin rags and the bathing caps were black or red and you could see what was what. It wasn't so good when they were, as sometimes they were, yellow or white.

When angler and swimmer had gone indoors he stayed crouching, watching the window. It was a pity they always drew the curtain, yet still that was as good as telling him what was afoot. He could then lie on his back, his eyes closed, no longer smelling or feeling mud, but thinking and thinking, and laughing to think that Enda Cawley, smart as he thought he was, didn't know the half of it.

His bicycle was down the road towards the village, securely hidden in a corner of an oats field that had already been harvested. He mounted it, he stood on one leg, held the fixed wheel in the air and spun the pedals until the wheel sang. Then for sheer bravado he rode over the bridge and passed the door of the doctor's house. They'd never know what he knew about them. He turned and rode back again. The weights on the spokes ticked like a slow heavy clock.

From the front window of the bedroom the doctor and his wife, amusements over, watched him return, crest the bridge, increase speed and, pedalling like fury, race off towards Crooked Bridge via Cosmona.

She said: We shouldn't have him next or near the place. Not even clipping hedges. He's mad as mad.

He soothed her. He told her clipping hedges was a high form of curative therapy.

She said: The best cure he could hope for would be to break his neck off that bicycle. Does he never take off that helmet?

But secure from all contusion the Angel of Outer Space swept onwards. Once he had told the doctor that he wanted to fly. Hunched in hot frenzy he worked over the pedals and said to himself: I want to fly. I want to fly.

He almost did as he went over the bumpy canal bridge and shot past the priest and set the gundogs barking. Daft Nora, on her way to the hospital to beg from Sister Francesca, stamped her foot and called after him: Gabriel Rock. Gabriel Rock.

He heard her voice as the admiring voice of the doctor's wife hailing his speed and prowess, so he stiffened his elbows and pushed harder and harder.

Peeping from a dormer window at the scene in the Square Christy Hanafin saw Gabriel circle the crowd, and the Cawley boys race out to intercept him, only to be left behind leaping and dancing and cheering and waving their arms. Gabriel knew their tricks ever since the day, the big brother that hanged himself being still alive, they had offered to pace him and, because he was blind in one eye, had ridden him into a ditch. The big dead brother who wasn't so bad had laughed but had pulled him out again.

Clean wind by now had blown the smell of mud out of his nostrils. Sheer speed, the road racing backward beneath him had dazzled his one eye with the gleam of white linen. Halfways to Crooked Bridge he stopped, distracted by thinking of the nurses that the white linen covered. Something always happened to prevent him from cycling to Crooked Bridge in less time than it had taken anyone to cycle there before. Slowly he turned towards Cosmona. He thought of nurses on lighted balconies. He thought of the doctor's wife splashing in the water or drying herself in the curtained room.

From the green place where he sat on the lower slopes of the Moat of Cosmona the black man watched him pass. From the bar he had taken a parcel of sandwiches the woman had given him. He bared his chest to the sun, and lay back, and chewed at his ease, and swallowed and laughed. Music and now and again the great unintelligible Voice came to him across the fields. Over there somewhere were the girls who had taken his money and given him no value. He chewed slowly. He swallowed with delight. His glistening skin breathed in the sunshine. He made himself ready for the search.

§

— Jesus, Mary and Joseph, the miller said as, standing on his own bridge, he felt the rush of wind go by him and heard the whines of the spokes and turned to see Gabriel, his arse higher than his head, pedalling past for Crooked Bridge. He thought: That poor boy isn't right, and sooner or later something will have to be done about him before he bursts a blood vessel cycling or takes a mad running race at one of the nurses.

But the glittering flow of the river, the criss-crossing patterns, some always changing, some always the same, of eddies and currents, and the spray, tossed multicoloured from the turning eternal wheel, swept the thought of Gabriel quickly from his mind. The wheel was the world, and the spray the clouds around it, and he was God that, with the help of the river, had set it moving.

What did the daftness of Gabriel, or the misery of Christy and Cathy, or even the inevitable death of his own son, matter to something that went on forever and ever? He had had time in plenty to accept Stephen's doom: the years of absence, of imprisonment that was as good or as bad as death, of wasting illness that was worse than death. Looking up at the far mountain from which the most turbulent part of his river came he thought how much worse it must have been for the father of the girl that the mountain had devoured: to see her in the morning walking away, alive and laughing with her friends, to hear before nightfall that the slippery clay on the cliff's edge had betrayed her and the rocks crushed her. It had not been like that with Stephen and himself. Once long ago they had sat on the grass margin of the roadside and watched the traffic pass and Stephen had asked him to talk of the places the road ran to. Once during his illness Stephen had said: Do you remember, father, how when I was a boy you told me where the roads went?

But in Martin Mortell's memory there was little if any difference between the dying man and the brooding boy who had inherited moments of strange melancholy from an ailing mother: Boy and man, they were both dead.

On that day long ago he had spoken to the boy not of the great cities of the world that other men might think were the logical termini of all roads but – because such things ran in his mind – of old mills, many of them no longer moving to either wind or water, in Ireland and England and France. His wanderings in search of mills had gone no further. Of old mills he talked and the places they were in: of the peace of old Hoxie's place where the wooden overshot millwheel was now only a motionless relic of the past, of the tidy fields, the wooden feeding troughs for the calves, of dogs too lazy to bark in the June heat; then of an old windmill on parkland between deep woods and a lake's edge, rhododendrons fringing the woods in May, the first cuckoo mocking from somewhere beyond an early-opened meadow. Could the roads not have led his only son to such places of peace, to an interest in the ancient ways that belonged to such places, to the talk of old crafts, the loy, the fack and the spade, and of the nailmakers who were always proverbially busy?

— They were the busiest fellows I ever knew, Stephen. I blew the bellows for them myself. Twelve foot lengths of nail rods waving like sheaves of corn, and boots then at nine shillings a pair, the best of leather. On Saint Martin's Day in those times every mill-wheel stopped, some people said because Saint Martin was the patron of millers, others said it was a pagan memory of ages before saints were mentioned, and that the wheels stopped for a day because the god who had given the harvest died when the grain was ground. Charles Roe is the man to tell about such things.

But only last night, unconsciously recalling that lost moment of boyhood, the dying man had said: In the jungle the wicked yellow bastards have their own pagan gods. They're so far gone from God that they think, God save us, the snake is a god: they think the brute python that could swallow a bull, balls and all, is a god. I heard tell, father, God between us and all harm, a python seized a yellow man, wrapped its coils around him, crushed him and swallowed him. He was five feet when it got him and seven when it swallowed him and he still alive.

Green jungle and yellow men, a strange god, a green-and-yellow diamond python had coiled around Stephen until, no heavier than three stone, he was a stick in the bed, a weed waving at the will of the stream. The sweaty forehead was too big for the shrunken body. Dry lips babbled of horrors that came steaming from the jungle of the brain. The water of the rivers was vicious with leeches and crocodiles. Diseases grew with the rank grass. Bodies, almost skeletons, squatted in rows excreting into boreholes the remnants of their entrails. A yellow devil knocked a prisoner down and jumped on him until he was unconscious because, the guard said, the man had a look on his face that was an insult to the emperor.

— There were pools of muddy water, father, in the rice paddies that you'd love to roll and drink in, but if you did 'twould be the same as rolling in shit and the end would be typhus or cholera, and the guards threw cholera corpses on the pyres and burnt them and you'd see the dead bodies kicking and bending and dancing in the flames. The green jungle was all around you and nobody that escaped into it was ever heard tell of again. We ate rice, not much of it, watered down to go round until it was like wallpaper paste, and the prisoners tried to grow anything they could and you'd see a man with eyes like a mad dog watching over a sliver of sprouting scallion. This Scotch fellow he was a great joker, he said that his only ambition was to die of old age. When he said that, he was helping to carry out the corpses. There was no weight in them. They didn't take much carrying.

Nor would it take much effort to carry Stephen from the house to the hearse, like John Peel the huntsman, from the hearse to the grave. Those babblings by something that had once been his son destroyed even the heavenly patterns made by the mingling into one of his two rivers, by the play of clear bright water over sand and gravel. A lot we heard about what Jesus endured on the cross, accusing his father of forsaking him, but up there above the clouds, looking down on the clouds as if they were water moving over the earth, the suffering father stayed silent on how he felt, watching his son reviled and spat upon and nailed to the cross: the son who wouldn't stay at home and who wanted to know where the roads ran to.

Well, the roads that blessed day hadn't led Gabriel the Flyer far from home. Martin Mortell was glad to see him, his fixed wheel relaxed, cycling slowly towards Cosmona. This too was somebody's son, nobody's son, not yet tortured, not dying, daft if you like yet comic and seemingly happy.

— You didn't get far today, Gabriel.

To his amazement and yet to his happiness the cathaired half of a face under the goggles laughed.

— Mr. Mortell, you mean I wasn't long away. I think I broke my record but I forgot to time myself.

— Someday, Gabriel, I'll time you with a stopwatch from here to Crooked Bridge and back.

— Would you, Mr. Mortell. I'd appreciate that.

Happily, and thinking of the legs of the nurses moving like pendulums under blue skirts and white linen aprons, Gabriel cycled more rapidly up the slope to the village. The miller looked after his hunched leather shoulders. He said aloud: God help you, you witless boy. May the roads never lead you farther from home than Crooked Bridge.

He went down into his mill.

§

Limping a little, tall, soldierlike, silver-haired, wearing a panama straw and a white linen suit and leaning on a long bamboo staff, Charles Roe led his picnic party up the green slope towards the Moat of Cosmona.

— If he only had a beard and the snakes running before him, the Mouse whispered, he would be a sort of Saint Patrick. We should sing a hymn.

— We follow an ancient pilgrimage path, Charles Roe intoned. For this hilltop was holy even in pagan times. Christianity adopted it. It is known for certain that the monks from the Island of the Living led the local people up here to pray. To do this climb fittingly we should go on our hands and knees.

Peter Lane said: One of us damn nearly does.

He hobbled, he puffed, he perspired, but to his delight he leaned on the Mouse. She wasn't in uniform. She wore a red-and-white striped skirt and a white angora-wool blouse, and they and she were wonderful to the touch. Her hair, revealed as brown, blew free to the hillside wind. He said: This is real curative therapy. When I was strapped to my spine frame Sister Joan wanted me to make mats or try fretwork. She thought it morbid of me just to want to read and write. But this is better than mats or fretwork. Or reading and writing.

He expanded his lungs with the green lively air. He tightened his embrace around her angora shoulders.

— You're a real big man with your pants on.

— Do pants make the man? Black clerical pants?

She was sly. She whispered: Some men are better with their pants off.

Then the doctor said: Take it easy, Peter. Take a rest any time you need it. You are in the capable hands of Nurse Walters.

He patted her affably on the tail and in a way that maddened Peter Lane – all doctors thought they owned nurses, that they were a sort of furniture – and passed ahead of them up the hill, his wife's spherical bottom swaying beside him in bermudas tight enough to show the track of her scanty panties. Let him pat his own property if he felt so inclined. But forty yards further on and up Peter Lane was glad to take the doctor's advice. She called to the procession that the two of them would follow at their ease. They sat on the steps of a stone stile, she on the topmost step, he on the lowest. Cosmona was well below them, the two rivers meeting, the one great river glittering on across a patchwork of varied green and golden oblongs of ripe oats and stubble. Already they could see, rising up as if alive and in motion, the circle of blue mountains that defined the saucer shape of the valley and a smoke in the middle distance marked the presence of Crooked Bridge. One white cabin cruiser idled westwards along the canal, facing into the warm west wind that carried up to them the voices of the children, the loudspeaker's shouting of jumbled words from the village square; and that suddenly whipped the light red-and-white skirt up like froth around her face. Laughing, and with his ready help, she resettled it, tightening it primly around her knees. It was the summer of the black cat again but a cloud that he could not tell her about had come over the sunshine.

That country fellow who had left the crossroads crowd and joined him on the sunny day he had walked to the seaside resort five miles away from the house of his aunt had, indeed, been the funniest fellow he had ever met: red face, buck teeth, squint, bicycle clips but no bicycle. His conversation and his capers as they walked the dusty road had been a delight, but there had been more to it than that. The last two miles of their walk had been on a grasspath along the tops of low cliffs, groups of people, not too plentiful, scattered here and there and, behind one fence of grassy sods, a woman spread-eagled and asleep. So the redfaced caperer bends down over her, hoists her skirt and studies her undercarriage, naked thighs and skimpy blue pants, with the dispassion of a scholar studying a rare manuscript. Anything could have happened if they hadn't heard the voices of people approaching. The scholar dropped the curtain. The woman stirred in her sleep but did not awaken. After that there were no more capers, no more conversation, and they parted forever on the edge of the town. Times on his knees, at morning meditation or mass or benediction in his brief year of holiness, the picture of the redfaced yokel, teeth sharp as goats' horns, bending over the sleeping woman, had come brightly and it was to be assumed from the devil, between God and himself. Brightly again it came before his eyes, obscuring the image of the sweet brown-haired girl sitting on the stone stile and primly tucking her skirt about her knees, then rising and saying: Up and over, reverend sir. This must be the first stile you've climbed in a long while.

— Along with the pilgrimage, said Charles Roe, went a festival for the first fruits and the beginning of the harvest. It was a festival of the young, the vigorous, the high-spirited, those for whom life seemed about to offer its most fruitful joys. Boys and girls would come in parties up this hill, bringing flat cakes of oatmeal to eat, and milk and ale to drink. Musicians went before them and a youth carrying a great hoop decked out with flowers and coloured ribbons. Only unmarried girls gathered those flowers and wreathed the garland. The touch of any but a virgin hand was unlucky. A maiden, too, was always chosen to cut the first sheaf of harvest. On the heathery places above the Moat the young folk gathered bilberries and ate until their mouths were purple, and threaded berries into bracelets to see which youth could make the best bracelet for his beloved, and the girl with the finest bracelet was crowned queen for that harvest.

— Just like a beauty competition nowadays, Miss Grace said.

A sentimental song ran in her head: Just the kind of a girl that men forget, just a toy to enjoy for a while.

She was dangerously on the verge of singing it aloud as she walked, not now on tippity-toes but sensibly flat-footed and in serviceable tweeds, a stick in her hand, an Irish terrier at her heels. The depth of her sadness was that she had not even been enjoyed as a toy. After that beauty competition she might have modelled but mummy had considered that modelling was low. She might have married, but in mummy's estimation all the men who offered were low. Once she had almost had an experience with a young man she met at a huntball, but after an hour or so of ignominious wrestling – she never did know whether she had wanted to go on wrestling or to find out – he had desisted, said some rude things that placed him with the lowest of the low, and that was that.

So, mummy dead and life passing, she was left with Cousin Charles who wasn't low – how could he be and he of the same family? – but was mean about money; and a sort of a half-priest driven mad by the war; and so afraid of women that the Cosmona people joked that he travelled around like a monkey along the back-garden walls in case he'd meet a woman on the Square or on a street; and so bad-tempered that he presumed on his war-wounded leg to lie in his bed and knock on the floor with a stick when he felt he needed attention; and such a slave to drink that he'd stay abed for a week, reading or pretending to read Latin tomes, and wearing a Turkish fez, and drinking neat gin out of an earthenware hot-water jug.

She was at last losing hope that the postcards she had bought in London and put, at intervals, in envelopes for Peejay the Saint to post from Crooked Bridge, would awaken in Charles anything like a desire for the life of a normal man. She had once been a beauty queen and because of the meanness of life she was still eligible, with virgin hands, to wreath a garland or cut the first sheaf of harvest.

By the standing stone that was only thirty yards or so from the green mound of the Moat of Cosmona they waited until Peter Lane, leaning on the Mouse, came up with them. Miss Grace was opening the hamper that the miller and the doctor carried in turns. The doctor's wife was spreading cloths on the grass.

— This stone, said Charles Roe, was reputed to have magic qualities. It was said that if a bachelor in search of a wife walked around it sunwise three times his suit would be successful, however haughty the maiden.

— Mr. Roe, said the miller, you don't feel tempted to try.

Miss Grace laughed sourly. She said: He has his own maiden in the garden at home. She's a statue. She's a stone pillar too.

But Charles Roe hadn't heard them. The standing phallic stone, the green mound, dotted with faery white thorns, where men had lived before history, the heathery slopes rising to the caves, now blocked, where legend said the black man, the horses and the maiden had vanished, had bewitched him. For the benefit of his audience he recalled that the mother of a saint who had had some connection with that hill had been known to tradition as the rare possessor of four paps.

— How embarrassing, said the Mouse.

— How vulgar, said the doctor's wife.

She had a feeling that nurses shouldn't speak even if they could. It seemed a long time since she herself had been a nurse.

They looked down the slope and, to the horror of Miss Grace, saw the curate following them, his sniffing hounds at his heels. Martin Mortell, remembering Wales, was looking with young eyes at the tight blue blouse straining across the conventional twin paps of the doctor's wife.

— It only meant, said Charles Roe, that she had four sons by four different husbands.

— Oh, said the doctor's wife.

— She could, of course, have been confused with the mythological hag, really hunger, that was conquered and driven out by the harvesting of the first fruits. There's a story that at a harvest festival once in Balla in the County Mayo three hundred sheep were eaten.

The Mouse whispered to Peter Lane that the sheep were safe today, and together they had a fit of the giggles for Miss Grace was not renowned for her lavish larder.

Leaving for a while the learned monotone of Charles Roe, the miller and the doctor climbed together to the flat top of the mound. Startled rabbits raced around whitethorns and scuttled into burrows. The west wind sighed and swayed all across the great saucer of the valley and the far mountains were the rim of a wheel turning around the hub of the Moat. From the picnic place by the standing pillar stone a fragment of the dissertation, capriciously distorted by a freak of the wind pursued them: So many people used to make this climb for the festival of the first fruits that once when a hare was started from its form the boys made a great ring about it and captured it.

— To the hare, said the doctor, they must have seemed like the mountains.

— You could still hear their voices on the wind, Mortell said, if you came up here on your own. This is a haunted place.

— By God, Martin, you stand there like Jehovah in a navy blue suit surveying the world he made.

The miller was hatless, his long white hair waved sideways by the wind.

— It's round like the world, he said. It's a golden valley. I recall ten wheels working on the stretch of water that you see. They're all gone now except my own, as dead and silent as my son will be, as he is.

— You did better to walk up the Moat, Martin, for the sun and fresh air. There's nothing more you can do for him.

— God himself couldn't save his own son.

— The story goes that he rose from the dead.

— Birth and death and rising again, said the miller, it's a good story. It's all a good story from the moment on that the angel came to Mary.

Miss Grace called them from below. The doctor's wife was pouring tea. The Mouse was uncapping bottles of lemonade.

— Down below there, said the doctor suddenly, there's something going on, no, not at the standing stone, at the Tower.

They looked.

— Lord of Almighty, said the miller.

— This couldn't have happened before, said the doctor.

— Ladies, roared the miller, for God's sake look this way.

But being of the mettle of Lot's wife they paid no heed to him. They looked over their shoulders and down directly at the top of the Tower. Fifty yards further down the green slope the curate, great black pot of a hat in his hand, wheeled and saw and set off half-running towards Cosmona, his bellowing hounds making round and about him excited figures of eight.

§

With the best intentions in the world Gabriel Rock was on his way to remove the book from the Tower when he met daft Nora in the graveyard on the Island of the Living. He would have taken the book away the previous night if he hadn't been disturbed by a nurse and somebody, and if he hadn't been disturbed by night he wouldn't have met Nora by day and nothing might ever have happened. He came cautiously up the sloping fields from the river. He was hidden from the village by high hedges and from the hospital by the graveyard wall and by the old jagged walls of the ruined abbey. The sound of the river came up the slope and made a sort of humming music under grey arches and around old table tombstones. He liked that sound. It was better still by night. He stood for a while listening to it, postponing the glad moment when he would climb the stairs to peep through the angle of an embrasure at blue-and-white nurses walking on blue balconies and pink balconies. He heard Nora before he saw her. She was humming. Since his two ears could often be as confused as his one eye he thought at first that the humming was part of the sound of the river. Then she came in sight around a high corner of old grey stone. She hopped from one foot to the other as if she were dancing. The idea of daft Nora dancing as if she were the belle of the ball seemed funny for a moment even to Gabriel. She wore a pair of men's boots laced with twine. It was one of her notions to cast a boot now and again and to walk Cosmona with one bare foot. Her thick legs below the knees were bare and mottled and measled from toasting herself too close to the fire. Her orange cotton frock was ragged and tight to the point of bursting. She hopped and hopped until she was quite close to him. She peered out at him, shaking her head, giggling, tossing corkscrew twists of matted brown hair. A mangy Irish terrier ran at her heels, darting away to sniff around tombstones, to puzzle over the odour of age in ancient corners, returning to circle silently around his odd mistress.

— Gabriel Rock, she said. Ride a bicycle up and down. Gabriel Rock's a big black beetle.

She stamped her foot and spat. But the long shrill laugh that followed the speech, the stamp and the spit, was friendly. Curiously he reached out to touch one of the bursting orange breasts. A low neckline showed white skin clean from scrubbings at the village pump. She washed a lot. He touched the other breast, poking with one finger. She didn't stop laughing. So he laughed with her.

— Hopping Nora, he said. Hopping Nora.

Then they were silent like any other pair that had spoken of love. In that ancient holy place where no woman should walk the sound of the river sang around them.

— Gabriel Rock, she repeated and elaborated, is a big dirty black beetle.

But it was all in fun and they laughed again. They sat down together on a table tombstone. The terrier sat before them, a suppliant, looking up inquisitively, panting for play. With a sudden twist of her body she was squatting like a tailor on the top of the tombstone, bending to unlace or untwine one boot. Her matted hair, clean even if it was matted, wasn't more than twenty-four inches from his one eye. He looked down through corkscrew twists of hair to see as a shock and a vision the insides of her wide white thighs and the tight elastic limits of white pants. Before his eyes those pants turned a splendid crimson. He was away out of the mud like a bird from the nest, flying faster than his bicycle to the memory of that greatest adventure of his life: the night of the doctor's house and the bedroom and the wardrobe. Then as now the sound of the river had been in his ears. Up a downspout he had gone like a monkey on a stick, in through an open window, tip-toeing in the dusk into the big enchanted room that must certainly be their bedroom. Nobody heard him. Nobody knew a thing. It was as dark in the wardrobe as it had been under the mud, but the lovely smells, of warm cloth, of perfume, and the feel of slippery dresses between his fingers had kept his heart up with expectation. In his pocket he had the tiny crimson pants he had picked up from the back of the chair, he had them still, for when the doctor, half-laughing, had herded him gently to the door he hadn't troubled to search him.

— Hopping Nora, he said, I'll give you a present for Christmas if you do something for me.

— What present, Gabriel Rock?

— Pink drawers, little tight ones.

With sudden giggling she bent down until her head was between her knees and his one eye bored down between the bursting white breasts. Her left boot was off. She wriggled her toes.

— What do I do to get a present? Ride your bicycle?

— No. That.

Feeling as big or bigger than Enda Cawley he pushed a hand up between her thighs. That was where it was.

— Gabriel Rock, she said, ride a bicycle.

She leaped off the table tombstone. On one foot she went hopping away from him as quickly as anybody else might run. But she was laughing wild. As she hopped she swung the boot by the twine, then sent it like a slingshot spinning high between the

abbey's grey roofless walls to fall somewhere on a green patch
where the grass was yet unclipped around flat gravestones.
Delighted at last in finding play the mangy terrier went barking
after the boot. Over her shoulder she called: Gabriel Rock, my
boot, my boot.

As a great game they went searching for it, cunningly creeping on hands and knees because if they stood straight on that
green patch they could be seen from the hospital. Then the terrier
found the boot and Nora found the terrier and Gabriel the Flyer
found Nora, grasping her, as they crawled, by the bootless foot,
struggling to hold on to her so that his hand could climb higher
up her bare leg. But she laughed and she kicked and rolled over
and over until his grip slackened. Her ankle was too thick to span
or to grip securely. The orange dress rumpled around her waist
like a hoop, her great thighs bare, the raggedy pants on full display, she rolled away from him. She was redfaced and choking
with laughter. Then the terrier raced back with the boot to the
shelter of the cloisters and, disregarding all caution and conceal-
ment, they stood up straight and raced after him.

— Hopping Nora, he called, hold your horses.

Echoes of the taunts of the Cawleys cried at him all along the
cloister: Nora Duckarse there. Gaby, carry the lady's bucket. Take
an eyeful, Gaby. The wiggle waggle. Gaby, when a girl walks like
that it's a sure sign she's wide open.

Like shutters hanging from half-broken hinges the lowslung
hips waggled away from him. Their elusiveness infuriated him.
The echoes of the Cawley voices taunted him until he sobbed and
no longer for him was there any laughter in the chase, even if
Nora was still laughing and the terrier, the boot abandoned, merrily barking. He cornered her in a dark room off the cloister that,
although he neither knew nor cared, had once been the abbot's
cell. On the dry soft clay floor they rolled and wrestled, the dog
hilariously yapping around them, until bit by bit the raggedy
pants came away in his hands. Stuttering breathless promises of
gifts of pink drawers he lay on top of her and tried to kiss her,
pushing aside a curtain of matted hair, but she bit his lip until it
bled, and then she was laughing shrilly and away again, round
and round the cloister, playing thread-the-needle in and out under

fragments of arches, around fallen stones now carefully arranged along the line where the perfect arches had once been. Hotly pursued, not as fast a hopper now as in the beginning of the race, she went upwards, yet hardly seeking refuge for she was still laughing. White thighs spiralling above him in the half-darkness gave him the speed and strength of ten men and when they came out on the grassy space on top of the Tower, in full view of the world, he was a better man than all the Cawleys put together. The dog was there before them, their herald and trumpeter, barking, making certain that nobody who was near enough and had eyes to see could miss the spectacle. He was no longer a flying angel. He was a beetle-headed demon. Hot from the chase and the friction of his fighting hands she lay gasping, still laughing, submissive, inviting him. The tight orange dress rolled up with an elastic snap. He curtained her face in it. Growling a little he worked away like a beaver, let the nurses look if they liked and the same to them, and proudly he took possession of the doctor's wife.

§

Teresa, Dympna and Amantha had meant to keep well out of sight until the black man in his carpet slippers had shuffled off to Buffalo. But wonder of wonders and this was a day of wonders and what could be more wonderful than Gabriel and Nora going at it hammer and tongs on the top of the Tower? Curiosity killed the cat, as Dympna often said, but that sight was enough to make more than cats curious, so Teresa dropped the dish she was drying and the cloth she was drying it with, when she saw through the scullery window what was happening, and out through the door with her, pulling on her blue coat as she ran and with the rolls in her hair, and calling on Dympna to follow, that this beat Duffy's circus. Well indeed, as the song says, Dympna did, and so did Amantha but, pretending to be a Dublin lady, Amantha wouldn't run. Teresa said afterwards she was too tight to run, afraid to tear herself. Amantha was all airs and graces. Amantha, I might as well tell you, was getting Teresa down. It was Dublin this and Dublin that and Dublin all the time until you'd think to listen to her there was nothing in the world outside Dublin.

Well they ran and they ran like three blind mice except that Amantha walked, although in the heel of the hunt and to keep them in sight she had to smarten up to a sort of a canter. They ran along the boreen past Teresa's granny's house, by a fieldpath and two wooden footbridges that crossed the two rivers before they became one, by another fieldpath that sloped up towards the Tower, and there behind the graveyard wall, well hidden from the hospital, they saw a sight that would have made a dummy split his sides laughing. For there was Gabriel Rock running round in circles trying to button the fork of his trousers and his shirt tail sticking out behind him like the minstrel boy in the song, and the reason why he was running in circles was that Enda, Owen and Ignatius had him cornered the way men at a coursing match, jumping and clapping their hands, would corner a hare and frighten it back to the dogs. Every time he'd try to break out Enda or Owen or Ignatius would leap at him with a roar and a grab and frighten him back the other way, and he was crying out something but with the helmet and the goggles you couldn't hear under God what it was, and the boys were roaring laughing, and the girls, even Amantha who had caught up with them, laughed as well. Oh Jesus, who could help laughing?

Teresa said where's Nora and we'll have some sport out of her but just as they were starting to look for her that bull of a priest with the red face and a stick in his fist came roaring like the bull he was round the corner of the graveyard wall, and his brute dogs roaring like lions at his heels, and seized Owen who was the nearest to him and began to batter hell out of him with the stick. Enda and Ignatius and Teresa and Dympna, and Amantha, they all ran. They had no choice because nobody could stand up to that madman with his head split nine ways in the war. They ran away, and Amantha ran as fast as any of them, saying suffering Jesus get me back to Dublin where the like of this doesn't happen, away in a circle around the back of the hospital to the corner of a quiet field where Enda had been playing his melodeon when the fun began on the top of the Tower and, as they ran, they could hear behind them the roars of Owen as the mad priest hammered him. They lay down hiding breathless in a dry ditch and Enda said Jasus that man was a savage and somebody should report him to the police, and Teresa said the police would be useless, that only the bishop would serve, the police would be afraid of him. They hid in the ditch, until Owen, black and blue and a sight for the cruelty man, limped half-crying and half-cursing to join them and told them the priest struck him until the stick broke and he shouted that he'd cut a bigger stick and deal likewise with the rest of the Cawleys male and female. But serve him right, while he was hammering Owen didn't Gabriel Rock, the real culprit, slip away as sly as a fox, his shirt-tail spinning like a brush, and the Cawleys in all their career had never equalled what Gabriel Rock had done on top of the Tower and in full view of the world.

§

— We were met at the door, said Lord Laurence Collins, by a stout woman with a cherry blossom face. She seemed amiable but she had, in truth, a tongue like a whiplash.

— The worst I ever heard, Ned Broe said. Christ help her father-in-law.

The woman behind the counter supposed that at the moment the miller's daughter-in-law had enough on her mind and could very well do without the gentlemen of the press.

— Quite true, Laurence said. But the truth is often bitter.

— We have a job to do, Ned said. She called me a little over-dressed fart.

— In your brief time, said Laurence, you have been called many things.

— But nobody up to this day ever called me a little over-dressed fart.

— Travel, said Laurence.

He sipped a fresh whiskey.

— Travel broadens the mind. Among other things she asked us had we no respect for the dying. For Edward and myself that posed a mighty pregnant problem. Our editor, you see, like all of us respects the dead and mostly forgets all about them. But the dying can still be news, the more so if the cause of their diminishing is interestingly revolting or terrifying.

— Holes in the heart, said Edward, are this editor's favourites.

Twice, as they watched in silence, the bird fluttered round the cellar and returned to perch on the shelf of bottles.

— Yet Edward, he prefers people laid low by polio or twisted by terrible cancers. He says the public loves them. He loves them. Holes in the heart, madam, are too cheerful. They preclude resurrection. There was that case of the boy who until a year ago suffered from a hole in the heart and who the other day was accepted as a student by a top seamen's college. The boy said laughingly: Who ever heard of a sailor with a hole in his heart? Too cheerful by far for my editor.

Into the ale he was drinking to cool the whiskey he had drunk Ned muttered, but nobody paid much attention to him, that sailors found their holes in other places. Out in the Square the loudspeaker, to rally the lungs for inspection, played stirring martial music.

— My editor, said Laurence, said to me with unction: a six-millimetre diameter hole in the heart's dividing wall. But his face fell when the boy was cured. And he lost sleep when that English chap who was dead as Jesus for two hours and twenty-two minutes woke up again.

— There's no fear, said the woman, that Stephen Mortell will rise again on the third day.

— But get there we must, madam, before they close the tomb. We are not angels. We can't roll the stone.

— We're just sent out, Ned said, to do a job.

They considered whether they should or should not follow the miller up the Moat to ask permission to see his son. While they considered they had yet another whiskey and the miller and the dying son and the job they had been sent to do drifted farther and farther away from them on an amber tide.

— If we went up the Moat, Ned said, we'd have to listen to that gasbag.

— True, Edward, true, and who wants to listen to a gasbag deflate especially when there's wine and whiskey in the cellar and the darkies may have fun.

— Here come your friends, said the woman. I'll leave you for a while.

And indeed, there came the two friends, the kindly Art Finlan and Bob Gunning of the biceps, holding each other up and red-faced with drink and laughter.

— He's a man in a million, they said.

— Two nine inch nails, by God, between his teeth.

He says: Develop your neck muscles and save your teeth. Then he crosses himself, exerts pressure, and out come the nails as right-angled bends.

— Then we met this little boy, said Bob, and Art says we'll take your picture and put it in the paper and he says what for.

— That was a wise kid, said Art who had two lovely children of his own.

— If everybody was like him, Tom said, if they asked themselves what for. That boy saw through it all. Why should his picture be in the paper? Why should anybody's picture be in the paper? Why should there be any papers?

— We have a job to do, Ned said.

Back again behind the bar he poured drinks for Art and Bob.

— Mrs. Durand-Deacon, Laurence at his loftiest said, used to tell her nieces that ability to keep her picture out of the papers was the mark of a gentlewoman.

— Mrs. Who, said Ned.

— Your aged aunt, said Bob.

— She made the headlines nevertheless, Laurence said. She had the distinction of being dissolved in acid by that charmer, John George Haigh.

— That reminds me, said Ned. Where does that woman keep going all the time? And why?

— She may have something cooking.

— She may have a child in the house.

— I'm curious, Ned said.

It was part curiosity about where she went so often and why, and part curiosity about how she would react if he tiptoed after her through the door at the back of the bar, downstairs to a basement or upstairs to a bedroom or wherever she went. If she bridled he could always pretend to be drunker than he was or make game of the fact that in her absence he was acting barman and entitled to the run of the premises. She wasn't as saucy as the three he had so foolishly lost but he was old enough not to be taken in by spectacles and brown quietness, and he had noticed through her stockings the hair on her legs, and hair on the legs as the world knew was a good sign.

So he tiptoed, glass in hand and teetering slightly in case anybody was watching him, through the doorway to find himself in a stone-flagged corridor, its walls shelved for wine bottles but the shelves were empty, and cluttered along the floor with cases of beer and stout. Of course, he thought, he was already in the basement, in the cellars, and a stone stairway at the far end of the corridor led up to the ground floor. On that ground floor the reception desk was empty and the front door bolted. No guests any longer entered that way. Two sad dusty antlered heads stared at each other with glass eyes across the width of the hallway. The crumpled ancient carpet shifted uneasily under his feet but it did not effectively muffle the sound of his steps and he was halfways up the stairs to the first floor when he saw the mirror on the landing and the man and woman reflected in it and heard the sound of their voices, and hoped they couldn't see him as he could see them. The man was tall, blackavised, hollowcheeked. Only the sound of their voices not the meaning of their words carried to where Ned stood for a while sipping his whiskey and looking as drunk as he could just in case they spotted his image in the mirror. Then he backed slowly and silently down the stairs. Out in the Square the music, changed from martial to waltz, kept mocking time to his retreat. She had spoken in a murmur, never raising her eyes to the man's gaunt face. His voice had been a hoarse croak that troubled Ned with a faint painful memory, troubled him so much that to his annoyance he found himself still idiotically backing to music down the stone stairs to the cellar. But once on the level flagged floor he tiptoed with speed back to the bar and nobody any the wiser. It would almost seem that his three colleagues hadn't noticed his absence. He leaned on the counter and stared at them. He was a puzzled aggravated Mr. Michael Rooney. Somewhere in the dark he stumbled about in his own memory. He suffered because he almost knew something and couldn't remember exactly what it was. He said: She has a man up there with her.

Bob Gunning said she was entitled to a man if she wanted one, that it was a free country and Cosmona no mean city.

— They were whispering together, Ned said.

Then, of course, he knew.

— By the swinging tit, yes. Whispering Christy. I photographed him when he was on the way back to prison.

— Explicate, Lord Laurence commanded. And another drink.

Ned poured four more. He told about the man and the woman. He spoke in a whisper in case the woman, suddenly returning, might surprise and overhear him.

— She is Mrs. Hanafin, Art said. She is the wife of that poor derelict.

— Not always a derelict, Laurence said. Edward and Art, you are too young to remember his previous condition. One of the finest men in Dublin City.

— He was always, Bob said, very hospitable to the press. I was a film critic for a few years. I was amazed when they got him for fiddling. A very big fiddle.

— A cello, said Laurence.

— A big bloody bass fiddle, said Bob. I never could understand it. He put five hundred pounds one day on the bar of the Welsh House and said tell me when me and my friends have drunk the lot.

— Diamond Jim Hanafin, said Ned. The last of the big spenders.

— Though I have heard, Bob said, that he was never the same man from the time he had the blow on the head in a car crash. That always makes me worry about myself. I came off a motorbike once and landed on my head. Out cold for a fortnight.

— Now we know, said Art.

Raising his glass, closing one eye, scrutinising the dancing of light on the amber liquid, Lord Laurence was ready with a lecture: Dr. Pavlov at the age of seven fell from a balustrade and landed on his head, sustaining a severe blow to his skull, on a tiled floor. The shock to his nervous system was such that he was unable to attend school until he was eleven. He spent the rest of his life torturing dogs.

— When I photographed the poor bastard, Ned recalled, he was just recovered from a fit of cramps. They gave him a meal in a cafe beside the guards' barracks and he ate it too quickly, like a savage, and doubled up. He hadn't eaten for days. He drank ditch water. They charged him with stealing a coat and a pair of trousers from a roadworker's trailer. He whispered: They were given to me by a gipsy. He sat barefoot before the fire and told us how the gipsy had shaved him. We all laughed at the idea of a gipsy barber. He'd walked a hundred miles in five days.

— Enough's enough, said Art.

For from the stone corridor came the sound of the slippered shuffling steps of the woman returning and as Ned relinquished his post and the bird once again lazily circled the cellar the Voice from the Square said: You don't have to undress. It will only take you a few minutes.

— That reminds me, said Laurence.

He ostentatiously changed the subject and addressed himself to the woman.

— That in the course of my foreign travels in Nashville, Tennessee, the Athens of the South, I read this inscription in my room in a motel.

He read from a small notebook: For your added comfort we have equipped this bed with the famous Magic Fingers Massaging Assembly which quickly carries you into the land of tingling relaxation and ease.

— So I inserted the required twenty-five cents and waited for belles of the blackamoor brand to come weaving and waltzing to join me on my couch. But divil the one. Nothing happened. The mattress merely shook and shivered.

— Not a sound was heard but the sofa shook, said Bob and flexed his biceps and emitted a staccato whinny of lust.

He could hold the note for minutes. He held it until his voice was lost in the sound of many voices shouting from the Square outside.

— Sacred Heart, said the woman, is the village on fire?

Running she led the way up the steps out of the cellar, along the cobbled entry to the Square. There they stopped and looked the way the laughing cheering people were looking towards the top of the Tower. Ned with both hands firmly gripped Bob's left bicep. He said in mock faintness: Strong Bob, hold me up, I faint,

I fall. Bob, we must find those girls again. We'll have to get something in a place where they're even doing it on top of the bleeding church steeple, rhymes with people.

§

In the corridor on the first floor Christy had said to her: Why can't you stay longer with me?

— What for? To hold your hand?

— Can't we talk?

— What about? Happy old times? Or the lovely present? I have customers in the bar.

— Who are they?

— Are you jealous?

— How many are they?

— Four handsome pressmen. All drunk as Bacchus. And a homing pigeon that got lost.

— Like myself.

— Like yourself. They all come home to roost.

— I could talk to you about prison.

— We could swap experiences. Here in this house I'm in prison.

— Do you know how long it takes for a man in prison to crack up? Scientists have investigated the matter.

— I know that you cracked up before you ever went to prison.

— No, but seriously, Cathy. Some scientists say nine years.

— You didn't last that long.

— Don't gibe, Cathy.

— I've lasted longer than you.

— There's this thing called Gate Fever.

— I'm most interested. How do you catch that?

— It's the tension. Just waiting for the gate to open and set you free.

— Is that why you jumped the gun?

— That was why. You make all sorts of mad plans for the future.

— You must have made some very mad ones.

— Every worry you ever had is a million times magnified in prison.

— You left a few worries outside the walls for other people to magnify.

— A prisoner becomes a child again.

— Of such is the kingdom of heaven. A sweet baby you became.

— Prison is a place where you don't have a watch.

— Would the other prisoners steal it?

— That's not what I mean, I mean that in prison time doesn't exist.

— Weren't you doing time?

— A doctor said this. I read it and learned it by heart. He said: Some prisoners regress to a childlike dependency. Some, when they come out, just hear the noise of the traffic, decide they can't take it and heave a brick through a police station window to get themselves back.

— Why don't you do that?

— Have you no pity, Cathy?

— None for you.

— Only for your dolls.

She left him then. He saw her brown eyes darken, her mouth tighten, and he knew again with joy that he still had the power to hurt her, and felt in him a sickening urge to rush to the attic and smash all those dumb staring images of unborn children: Little Boy Blue, the three blonde pink-cheeked dolls who must be Boy Blue's sisters. He watched her walk away down the stairs. She had changed into a brown woollen suit that emphasised her small firm hips and now that he was washed and cleaned – it was amazing the difference soap and water made – he began to remember such things. All over she had been, considering the sunless Irish climate, a very brown woman. She tanned easily and smoothly. She had been a clean warm girl and inclined, and not to his annoyance because it flattered his sense of power, to fall when he had hurt her into sullen silences and to stare doggedly for long periods at the floors of the backrooms of the obscure bars in which they mostly met. Alone in that large empty house he was back again in one of those rooms, breathing the odours of old leather and porter, sitting in the warmth and brightness that the sun sent though a skylight and a burglar-grating. She had been silent for a long time and he had known why and in the end she had said: Mary Bee, that fat bitch of an usherette, told me you stripped her to the waist.

— What else did she tell you?

— She said nothing else happened.

— They all say that. No woman will ever admit the real thing to another woman. They're all untouched and untouchable.

— Why do you do it, Christy?

— One must do something with so much stuff lying around.

— Then why do you bother about me?

— You're different. You are different, Cathy.

He couldn't tell her that he had heard of a poet who lived with and on rich women and who captured and held them by cruelty and the suggestion of evil, and that he, Christy Hanafin, envied the man his success, but that his own sharp critical tongue merely offended or frightened off the beauties he would love to lord it over, and that he had to fall back on half-tarts who were already in a way in his power. Could it be that the women he desired were not rich enough or old enough, or that with the temperament that might have made a mint for a man as a beachboy in Florida he was misplaced as a cinema manager in a rainy religious provincial city.

— I'm out of place, he told her. Or I'm out of time. The moon was off balance when I was born. Some moment when the moon was blood then surely was I born.

She smiled, pathetically – if he had been in the mood for pathos. She said: What's that all about? Perhaps the moon was whiskey.

Then she was clutching his hand. She said: Thank you for saying I was different. You're different too. There's nobody like you.

He was touched. He was genuinely touched. The memory of that moment could still affect him, so that walking into the attic of the unborn children he no longer felt any resentment against the three blonde pink-cheeked dolls who sat on one bench and gazed without sight at their images in a toy mirror; nor even against his son, Little Boy Blue. The poor lost brown woman was entitled to her hopeless dreams, he thought, and then heard the roar rising from the Square and rushed to the dormer window. From that height the angle of vision was awkward and he could only gather from the swelling hilarious sound that the people were wildly excited about something. He saw the fringes of the village, the still canal, the baronial home of Charles Roe, and far on the slopes that led up to the Moat a party of people, transfixed, black still dots. He saw Mortell's mill and the glitter on the salmon water. He saw the pink and blue hospital, and the sun glittering on the vita glass of the balconies as it glittered on the water. Then he saw the Tower. He was so high that it seemed quite close to him. He was the one man in Cosmona who had a grandstand view.

— The angel of the Lord, he said, declared unto Mary. Cosmona is the world's most wonderful place.

— Daughters three, he said to the dolls, if you only had eyes that could see I'd raise you to the window.

— FOUR —

In spite of which the picnic on the Moat went on for, as the doctor said, the priest on his own, or at any rate with the help of his stout stick, should be able to look after the matter. It was in the province of the clergy and the police whose concern was with morals, public and private, and the keeping of the peace, and morals would go down the drain and the peace be forever unkept if other couples began to follow the example of Gabriel Rock and daft Nora.

— Please, doctor, said Miss Grace.

The doctor's wife squatting like a tailor, ripely filling her bermudas, looked at the picnic cloth and nibbled the picnic fare and said nothing. The miller laughed coarsely. He was not, Miss Grace decided, as saintly a man as his white locks might make him seem. The young nurse had a fit of sneezing that she said she feared was hay fever but that could have commenced as a fit of the giggles.

Nor was it a suitable time, Miss Grace felt, for Cousin Charles, as madly eloquent as usual, to tell how Lucian of Samosata had described a rite celebrated in his day at Hierapolis in honour of the goddess, Atargatis, in which a naked celebrant had to climb a stone phallus one hundred and seventy feet high and stay for a whole week on top of it so that all men would be nearer to the gods and all the land below be more fertile; or of a pagan rite practised in memory of Deucalion and the time when men climbed mountains and trees to escape the deluge; or of Heliodorus, spiritual guide to the young Simeon, afterwards to be known as the Stylite, who during his sixty-five years of life spent sixty-two in his Syrian monastery to which of course he had been admitted at the age of three and who had had no knowledge of the world and didn't even know how a cockerel or a boar was made; or of Serapion, an elder in asceticism, who went one day to Rome where he met a holy virgin and the two of them, to prove that they were dead to the respects of the world and the desires of the flesh, walked naked together through the city.

— Please, Charles, Miss Grace said.

She meant that there was a clerical student present; and a young nurse, not that the pert hussy had as much as blushed or turned away her eyes from that degrading sight, but had even begun to giggle; and a young wife who was showing the first tender and holy signs of pregnancy; and a lady, even if the lady was advanced and intellectual and a cousin of Charles Roe and used to his ways and his talk.

— Charles, please, she said. Talk to us about the history of this hill. Isn't that your favourite topic?

He needed no more encouragement, no second invitation to bring back to life again, from the scaffold where he'd danced his last dance, Dark Domhnall the horse-robber or to talk of that darker shadow, ten times the size of Domhnall and behind him in space and before him in time, who had snatched the maiden to the horse's back and ridden forever with her into the bowels of the earth; or to tell of the double echo, as if of a male and female voice joined, that answered back to anyone who called into the piles of rocks and rubble that now blocked the mouths of the caves. Don't the stolen horses also neigh, asked Peter Lane, and wondered if he and his beloved could ride like that into the belly of the mountain and find there a new land where the name of Cardinal Newman had never been heard of and the idea that to touch was to sin had never occurred to anyone. Across the picnic spread he watched the Mouse and was unaware how closely Miss Grace was watching him. By the twitching of her lips he knew that the Mouse was bursting with suppressed laughter but he remembered her, with veil unpinned and hair loosened, panting over him in the bed. Her tender tickling hand plucked blades of grass and he quoted to himself a translation of a warm Gallegan love lyric: Do you remember, my lass, that night in summer? You counted the stars and I the blades of grass.

Could she calmly count the stars if he lay on top of her on this hillside on a warm night?

— Please, Charles, Miss Grace was saying.

For Charles had drifted away from Dark Domhnall to talk of an ancient custom of the girls of the countryside who would go on a Halloween to the meeting place of the two rivers and there drag their shifts thrice upstream and thrice downstream and bring the wet shifts home and set them to dry before the hearth fires, and keep vigil beside them all night to see if the ghosts or fetches of the lovers or husbands to come would reveal the future by walking into the room.

— Please, Charles, she said again.

Peter Lane wondered what, if she knew his thoughts, would that poor dry stick of a woman say to him, and the doctor was tickled pink to think that a spinster who dyed her underwear all colours, well not all colours but only a sort of crimson, should object to legends of country girls dragging their shifts in the river and drying them by the hearths and hoping, perhaps as she still was, for something terrifying but yet delightful to happen.

— It must have been cold for them, said the Mouse and laughed outright to ease the tension of all that bottled-up merriment.

But what she was really thinking as she looked at that rubicund face – as much of it as was to be seen – and the brown whiskers and bullet-proof tweeds of the doctor was that he was teetotally different from the doctors in the stories in the nauseating religious magazines that had been forced on herself and her sister sufferers in their days of incarceration in convent boarding school. Those doctors had always been distinguished surgeons, tall, grey at the temples, well gone into middle age, and their scientific obsessions and prosperity in Harley Street had caused them to drift from the faith. Then in the operating theatre one crucial morning they were, each and every one of them, impressed by the calm courage of young Nurse Mulligatawny, fresh from the Irish bogs; and wondering, as they leave their various hospitals, about the sources of that courage they see the Nurses Mulligatawny, each and every one of them, slipping undemonstratively into the hospitals' chapels. So the surgeons are driven in their Rolls Royces by their liveried chauffeurs back to their Harley Street consulting rooms and all the time they are thinking of their aged mothers, for each and every one of them has an aged mother who sits, rosary beads entwined in gnarled fingers and praying for her wandering boy, in a cottage by the sea in County Kerry. The end of the story was always in conversions and wedding bells and visits to aged mothers, so that it would seem to be part of the whole duty of the good nurse to bring greyheaded atheistic surgeons back to the Catholic Church, but she herself didn't feel up to the part and couldn't care less and was at that moment in the process of dragging a budding priest away from the altar and, once again, she couldn't care less. Although the next time, she thought, it might be better not to allow him to put his hand inside her pants. That poor priest galloping down the hill to call a halt to the antics of Gabriel Rock and daft Nora was a clumsy bigbooted snuffling shellshocked thing yet she had heard about him from the night matron the oddest, most wildly romantic story: how when he was a young priest a woman had fallen in love with him and pestered him night and day – she was an ex-nun who had seen him for the first time when she had been a nun and he a convent chaplain – and when he resisted according to law, as her own father would say about coursing greyhounds taking a turn after a hare, didn't the woman kneel at the altar rails when he was giving communion and gash her throat but not, cute enough, so as to kill herself but just so as to make a mess and cause a scene, and what a scene that must have been. They put her in a home and, God help him, it was no wonder that now and again he preached to nuns and nurses in the hospital chapel the weirdest sermons about the sixth and ninth commandments. It could be that, from his experience, he thought the nuns needed the sermons more than the nurses.

But there was the Eloquent Dempsey, Charles Roe, off again and what could it be this time?

What was it but an historical note, to this effect: that when the lord of the land had drained dry the shallow lake around the Island of the Living the peasants of the place had used fragments of the mud from the lakebed to mix with cattlefood so as to induce fertility in their stock.

— Under a glasscase in my hallway, Martin, you have seen a few pieces of that clay preserved by my family for a good two hundred years.

— Wonderful, said old Mortell. Wonderful.

But Miss Grace wondered would a few grains of that mud mixed into his morning coffee make him behave like a normal man and not like a mixture of a mad professor and a spoiled priest.

Watching the three women, three corners of a triangle, facing each other across the picnic cloth, the miller was thinking that in ancient times when women worked the quern they sat facing each other and passing the handle of the quern from hand to hand, that oats was always ground in the husk and afterwards sifted, that, prior to grinding, the grain was often dried in an iron pot and stirred to prevent it from scorching; that millers in the old times had had a great name for being fond of women because their mills were at the town's end, with soft bags like mattresses and quiet dark corners convenient, where women would pass homewards half-tipsy at the tail of a market day; that he had once loved a Welsh girl with hair as dark as the hair of the doctor's wife, and that the doctor's wife must have, as that Welsh girl, the morning star, must have had, a bush as crisp as furze but not, pray God, as prickly; and that his foolish and wandering son, begotten on a weakly woman who drank and had made his life a misery, was dying of diseases that grew like animals in poisonous jungles far far from the wind blowing over this green and pleasant hillside.

— I should be making for home, he said.

Dipping away away back into the monastic world of the ninth century, Charles Roe was reciting: Bell of pleasant sound ringing on a windy night. I should prefer to tryst with it than to tryst with a wanton woman.

— And what, he said, would the monks of the Island of the Living, where no female was allowed to walk, have said had they lived to see this day.

— Charles, please, she said.

— Did Simeon, named the Stylite, climb up and stay to be quite literally closer to heaven? Or was his pillar and place of residence just another huge stone phallus?

— I should be heading homewards, the miller said.

But Charles Roe, who seldom heard anyone, asked why had the saints really climbed the mountains, and suggested that the picnic party should ascend to the caves. The doctor, who had as much for one day as he could take of Charles Roe, said that Peter Lane who was his patient wouldn't be able, and Peter Lane, greatly daring and hoping, said he could wait where he was while the party ascended, that he had a mouse to look after him.

— A mouse, said Miss Grace.

— He means a nurse, said the Mouse.

— At any rate, said the doctor, someone has beaten us to it.

— This hill, said his wife, is exclusive no longer.

A hundred yards away, emerging from the cover of a hedgerow that was shelter for cattle on a stormy day, was a single file of young people, three male, three female. The leader, a male, carried a melodeon and as they ascended towards the caves he began to play, quite well, the tune that had the words to it that went: There once was a troop of Irish dragoons.

To the complete disapproval of Miss Grace, the doctor and the miller began to sing to the music: I never will marry a soldier, oh!

— Those frightful Cawleys, she said. They shouldn't be tolerated.

— Sister Thermometer, said the Mouse, is looking blind and wild for Teresa Fallon and Dympna Cawley. They're missing.

The figures diminished as they ascended, the music was more faint. Emerging from the cover of the hedgerow a single figure stood and looked up after the single file of six.

— Do my eyes deceive me, said Charles Roe, or is that a black man?

— Impossible, Charles, she said.

The doctor looked at Mortell and Mortell looked at the doctor.

— It's time I was moving, said the miller, it's time I passed on. Will you come with me, doctor, even if there's nothing medicine or mortal man can do?

§

Three of the biggest men available in the crowd in the Square squeezed with no small difficulty into one large wheelbarrow.

Four of the strongest, with the exception of the strongest of all, seized the handles of the wheelbarrow. The strongest of all lay flat on his back and bare to the waist on a carpet of potato sacks.

— He has a square torso, said Ned to Laurence. I never saw the like. As thick one way as the other and take an eyeful of those belly muscles.

— An eyeful, Edward, is just what I can't take. If he went into that trailer, the sharp eye of the X-ray would be blunted.

— Ladies and gentlemen, said Patrick Hoban, to show you that there is no deception.

The rumbling sound of his voice went straight upwards from where he lay.

— Three heavy men in the barrow. Wonderful the works of a wheelbarrow. Four strong men at the shafts. The four strong men will raise the shafts and wheel the loaded barrow up on my chest.

They did so. His shawled wife, her brown tinker's hair trailing over her face, stood above him and smoked her pipe as if nothing whatsoever was happening.

— The barrow, he said, will remain in position for five minutes while I do my exercises, deep breathing and others.

The barrow and its cargo perceptibly rose and fell. He wasn't even puffed. He flexed his corded arms. He raised his legs and cycled like mad on an imaginary bicycle. He entreated the three men in the barrow to jump and stamp, but when they tried to do so in the confined space they upset the barrow and the chaos sent laughter roaring round the Square. A whitecoated radiographer looked out in wonder from the door of the trailer. Of the eight men involved the bearded monster was the least perturbed. He stood up and bowed. The crowd cheered. He took from the ground a bullwhip and set it twisting like a snake and cracking like rapid rifle fire. It was his bell, his trumpet.

— Ladies and gentlemen, now for the greatest trick of all, how a small man like me can make a mob like ye disappear.

He passed round the hat. Some few, the fainthearted, the parsimonious, took him at his word and slunk away but, for the credit of Cosmona, the majority fumbled in pockets, dropped coins into the battered black bowler he passed around. For the honour of the press, Lord Laurence contributed a ten shilling note and, with Edward a subordinate pace to the rear, camera box hanging from left shoulder, he moved off again towards the house where the man lay dying. There was, the woman had told them, a pleasant walk even if it was a roundabout along the towing path by the dead or dying canal. The Voice of God no longer spoke behind them. The X-ray people, exhausted from laying bare the cavities and cancers of Cosmona, were eating a late lunch. But music played from the loudspeaker and punctuating the music was the sharp crack-crack-crack of the strong man's whip.

With academic detachment, Lord Laurence, who knew a lot about buildings, surveyed the baronial hall of Charles Roe and pronounced it fine, nineteenth-century, canal-company Gothic.

From the lock beyond Charles Roe's place the canal sailed high, a Dutch canal, banked up over dun-coloured meadowland that was living with birds, then crossed the river by an aqueduct a half-mile downstream from Mortell's mill. The wonder of the aqueduct, water over water, entranced the learned lordly mind of Laurence. To Edward who half-listened and now and again whistled back to the birds he dissertated on the symbolism involved: the canal, ordered and rational life; the river, life lived according to nature, smooth and deep here, rattling over pleasant shallows there, torn in this place by vicious rocks, in the white tumult of cataracts in another place, swept this way and that by the tempest of the heart.

High on the embankment he sang to the birds of the sultry brown meadowland a bit about the tempest of the heart. His boozy bass voice sank so low that Edward made a great play of helping him back to a standing position. Quite unperturbed Laurence pointed out to Edward that the life of nature was demonstrably superior to the ordered life of reason because the river flowed free and the canal was mostly choked with weeds. A shoal of rudd came slowly in formation from one curtain of weeds, spotted briefly with red fins a clear sunlit space, then vanished again into greenery. Laurence told Edward about a photographer he had once known who had always travelled with a fishing rod in his car and every time he came to a river commandeered some passing peasant and made him pose for a fishing picture. The photographer himself had never fished and yet his fishing pictures were famous.

— I've a better idea, said Edward.

He had unslung his box and was pointing the camera at something.

— Would it be the farmhouse now you're photographing?

Below them, its barns and byres snug against the canal embankment, was a long, thatched, whitewashed homestead.

— Look again, said Edward. A rock. A fountain pen. Who in Christ's name would want to photograph a farmhouse?

— A cock. A hen. I see a cock treading a hen. It's little that keeps a man happy as the widower said when he saw a similar sight and he coming from his wife's funeral. But, Edward, is a cock worth wasting a plate on?

— This one, said Ned, is.

At the back of one of the byres a gigantic white cock was flattening a brown hen. Her sisters had gathered together at a distance to talk over the matter. They were fluttered, but curious. The onset was short, sharp and vigorous. Satisfied, the large white gentleman stepped aside, raised his head and proud scarlet comb and flapped his wings.

— It's Peejay's cock, said Ned, the one that shakes hands.

— A versatile chevalier. Should I shake to congratulate him?

Peejay will wring his neck if he ever hears this. He says the birds don't behave as badly as Hollywood film stars.

— But, as Humphrey Bogart said, he was misinformed.

Picking herself up from the dust the brown hen moved a little away from her ravisher, yet not far enough away to rejoin the harem. Coyly she pecked sideways at a stray potato, pretending, said Laurence, like most women, that nothing out of the way had happened.

— Laurence, said Ned, I see her tail-end. It's still opening and closing. Peejay's boy must pack a punch.

— Not unusual, Edward, and not confined to our feathered friends.

— She's winking at me, said Ned.

— That the anal area, Edward, is erotically sensitive may not be familiar to everyone. But stimulation of the genitals normally causes contraction of the muscles around the anal orifice and vice versa, and after orgasm the anal sphincter can be seen to open and close convulsively. That is, if anyone would care to see it.

— She's still winking at me. I'll try a closeup. Another plate for Peejay.

The shoal of rudd appeared again, going in the other direction. The white cock flapped his wings, a triumphant pugilist waving gloved fists over his head.

— Make a poem about that if you can, said Edward.

For it was well known that Lord Laurence could turn a verse with the best of them.

— Challenge accepted, Edward. With my genius and your gift for rhyme we could do something considerable. Listen to this: When lovely woman stoops to folly.

They walked on by the still, weedy water. Behind them although it was by no means morning the white cock crowed.

— He's laughing at us, Ned said. He's saying that unlike ourselves and the nuts on the church steeple he has a licence to do it in public.

— But then, Edward, he can't vote or drink whiskey.

Solemnly they agreed that in this life a man couldn't have everything.

By the catwalk at the next lock they crossed the canal and left it to follow a boreen that led back to the road and the house of death. Cool in the shade of the high whitethorns that lined the boreen Laurence stopped every few steps to beat time on the air and to complete his poem.

— When lovely woman stoops to folly.

— Get on with it. Take the finger out, as Prince Philip said.

— In fair Cosmona where we take our scene. No, that's too classical, perhaps too derivative. In fair Cosmona by the aqueduct.

— I see the rhyme, said Edward.

— She pecks a spud with melancholy. And thinks with great content. No, that isn't forceful enough. And thinks. And winks. And winks her sphincter and says, and thinks…

— I'm fucked, said Edward who couldn't resist the subtle appeal of the rhyme.

Then they were out on the road and the miller and the doctor were fifty yards away and walking towards them.

At that moment the miller was saying: Speedo. Speedo. In his nightmares, tossing and twisting and the sweat out on him like a heavy June dew, he keeps crying: Speedo. Speedo. That was what the Japs shouted, beating them on to work or to march faster: Speedo. Speedo. They hammered them with staves of bamboo as thick as your wrist: Speedo. Speedo.

All the way through the lanes and sideways of Cosmona interrupted only by the passing of daft Nora, proud as a queen and walking in a dream – he had talked of the Japs and the jungle who had crucified his son: of a fearful hospital that was no hospital at all but only a charnel house to dump men to die in when they were so sick with amoebic dysentery they could no longer work, for sick men were dead men to the yellow devils and, as they walked down from the Moat, the doctor felt that yellow faces, bucket-mouthed, buck-toothed, slant-eyed, grinned evilly out from the green hedges; of the laying through jungle of the hell railway where every sleeper laid meant the death of a white man, and of the hell train that travelled on that railway with trucks made of thin metal and normally used for carrying rice, thirty-two men to each truck and all stinking and shitting on the floor, and their bodies and their filth cooking for five days in the blazing heat, and at the end of all that to make on jungle tracks a forced march of two hundred miles.

To avoid the crowd in the Square they walked by quiet lanes of low whitewashed houses, and it was there they saw daft Nora docilely following Sister Thermometer and a nurse, and on the way, they guessed, to some place where the nuns would look after her. She no longer as she walked stamped her right foot. She didn't weep because Sister Thermometer was too kindly to scold her. She smiled at something not visible. She had her own thoughts and something to remember. She had been visited. No mocker, the miller said, would run at her heels because of the company of the sharp little nun in white nursing robes, but the creature would be lonely for her dog, and her dog for her, and she might also miss her frantic ablutions at the public pump. Until her great moment high on the Tower nobody had known because nobody had bothered much about her. Her life had been a sort of a secret and now, by God, she was, even if only to Cosmona, as famous as a beauty queen. Remembering the leaflet, as fine a poem as any in the old Sixth Reader, the miller said, half-laughing, that her ways were beautiful ways and all her paths were peaceable. But three paces later he was thinking of and talking about something he could never forget: the story of the man who in the prison camp ate the cat raw, skin, claws and all, and Nora was soon forgotten, and the green land beside the river was peopled, as hell was with lost souls, with sixteen thousand famished men squeezed into a space that could hold only a thousand, menaced by machine guns, left without shelter or sanitation, told that the sick who were dying of dire infectious diseases would be carried in among them unless they signed a declaration saying that they would not try to escape from hell. The doctor said that no just and punishing God could have thought of a better one unless he had been also a civil servant.

— Speedo, speedo, said the miller.

Then they saw Laurence and Edward on the road before them and the camera clearly signifying their profession and purpose.

In the morning the doctor had resented the attempted intrusion of newspaper men but matters were much altered now because, as it so happened, from his days in Dublin he knew both Edward and Lord Laurence and liked them, and they him, and the newspaper man you knew was always better than the one you didn't know. So the four men walked on together and the miller said: In the monsoon they slept on low platforms of split bamboo with rivers of mud oozing up around them.

Faraway, in autumn afternoon light, the mountain that had devoured the maiden was so calm, so venerable, so nobly purple.

— There's not much left to photograph, the doctor said.

— We won't worry him much, said Edward.

To the doctor's sensitive imagination the grassy roadside margins were horrible with voiceless wraiths of men.

— Yourself, Mr Mortell, said Laurence, could give us everything there is to know.

— Come and see for yourself, said the miller. It's never the same thing unless you see for yourself.

§

After the fiddle, of course, all hell had broken loose. Mary Bee, the usherette, the fat bitch, who admitted to having been stripped to the waist but to nothing further, told her story, weeping, to the scrawny-necked management man who was himself an authority on tears. She made it sound like criminal assault perpetrated by an irresistible tyrant: the forfeit for resistance being her job. There might, to add to the fun, have been a court-case for criminal assault if the scrawny-necked man hadn't in his time encountered many Mary Bees and if his concern had not been teetotally with money and management and not at all with the virtue of usherettes which he regarded as expendable. So the weeping Mary Bee merely got herself fired. There were other implications too numerous to mention and too painful to recall although Christy did recall them as he sat at stool, feeling painfully the burning after-effects of last night's rum, studying the patterns of the past, those landscapes of evil dreams, in the chipped enamel of the large old-fashioned bath-tub.

— How and why did you get there in the first place, he said to the diminutive pinpoint of a spider that crawled and crawled up the vast, dirty-white, fissured ice-floe that the side of the bath must have seemed to it.

He said: King Bruce of Scotland flung himself down in a lonely mood to think. 'Tis true he was monarch and wore a crown but his heart was beginning to sink.

There was nothing to wonder at in lonely men in lonely places seeing spiders. Spiders and lonely men fitted each other and, like true lovers, found each other out. The tiny atom ascended and ascended, then faltered and failed and tumbled hopelessly down, almost to the treacherous verge of a small lake that tap-drippings had made.

— If at first you don't succeed, he told it, try, try, try again. Are you yourself to blame for being there? Did you deliberately choose that bath? Or were you like the rest of us pitched-in arse first without as much as by your leave?

Slowly, painfully, patiently the pygmy spider recommenced the climb, faltered again, slipped back a few inches, climbed again until the halfway mark was reached. There it paused to rest and, mayhap, to consider. Fore and aft the remnants of the rum corroded Christy and he gritted his teeth at the burning and most undignified pain and cursed the black sailor and the chance, yet one more in a long procession of sad chances, that had brought them together.

— Think it over, brother, he said to the spider. Is it worth while trying? Is it worth going on? Sooner or later everyone except the imbeciles who make a success out of life realise there's no use in struggling. Slip down. Lie down. Fall down. Give up. Give it over. The morning that dawned on me I remember as well as if it were yesterday. I was sitting, spider, in a barber's chair being shaved, trimmed and cleaned-up to face a job that everytime I thought of it I felt ill and smelly, as if I had puked over my suit. Several times a day I had to wash the smell of that job, the smell of my life, off me. So I sat in that barber's chair and studied myself in the mirror and thought that whatever botch handyman was responsible for the human body had imposed on each and every one of us an awful, endless, idiotic task of cleansing, trimming, purging, dredging, flushing, so as to keep from offending eye and nose. Spiders may have to spin webs but as far as I know they don't have to shave. Do they? Go on, tell me. Say something in spiderese.

From his seat on the throne, his rectum still burning, he leaned forwards, puffed out a malignant breath, and the pinhead of an insect descended once again into the abyss.

— There you are, my mighty atom. God from on high has no sympathy with your struggles, no more than he had with mine. So why struggle? That was the inspiration came to me on that morning in the barber's chair. All that washing I did in my office. One day the door of the bathroom was swinging open and Cathy walked into the office and found me dripping and stark naked and didn't even pretend to register shock as you'd think a young maiden, and she was still a maiden, might have done. She was always a strange one. Her quietness I could never fathom. All that washing, all that fresh air and deep breathing up on the flat roof of the cinema, all that was a cowardly running-away from the condition of a Robinson Crusoe. Do you know what a Robinson

Crusoe is? One of those bearded ragged stinking bums that you
see a few of them in the gutters of every city in the world: proud,
solitary men, each on his own island of dirt, no treasure island I
can tell you, not caring any more, not struggling. But after that
morning I thought why not join the R.C.s. And I don't mean
Roman Catholics. The old Robinson Crusoes have the best of it.
Why fight? Why worry? Past forty you realise more and more the
finality of every action. So why take any action? Once, I remembered, when I was a boy I walked with a schoolfriend on a country road by the high granite wall of a lunatic asylum. Beyond the
wall there was a lunatic roaring like a wild animal. For a long
time afterwards I used to hear the roaring in my dreams and I'd
sweat with fear that someday I might go mad. But oddly enough
it was my friend who went mad. The roaring had been for him
and not for me and why should I have worried?

— That morning was the very first morning I didn't go near
the lousy cinema and Cathy sitting in her glass box, reading a
book, turning her wedding ring round and round on her finger as
if she were repeating spells. Life, spider, owed me beauty and I
had married Cathy. So I drank: in the early morning bar with
dockers and fruit-market workers, and with the silent men who
drank slowly and shook a little and spoke to nobody and stared at
the wall and were, either in mind or body or both, in the horrors.
The more I drank the closer I got to them and the bigger and better I felt. Oh, you clumsy hopeless little bastard, you've fallen
down again. Give it up and drown yourself. For all eternity you're
damned in that bath. I drank with an old soldier who had fought at
the Battle of Loos and I thought of Cathy's uncle, killed on the last
day of that war, doomed like yourself never to get out of the bath.
Cathy used to say that his pale young ghost walked the corridors
of this old house, the sort of silly fancy you could trust Cathy to
have. Loos, or wherever Cathy's uncle rotted, before she was born,
back into the clay is a longer longer ways away from Cosmona
than it ever was from Tipperary. Mortell's son might with more
reason haunt the jungles. In one bar I picked up a blonde with
black slacks and a cheap English accent, and did a pub crawl with
her and brought her to the exclusive fish-bar in the Red Bank
where, only it was funny, she would have made me blush through

my drink by asking, in a whine that carried, for fish and chips. Later I found myself rolling with her, slackless, on my coat laid on the grass in the Furry Glen in the Phoenix Park and, half up and half down and half in and half out, being interrupted by a plain-clothes policeman who demanded ten pounds for his silence and the privilege of a cut of the cake for himself. We argued about that, not for the honour of the lady but for the sacred rights of property, and while we argued she re-slacked herself and slipped away through the trees. So we laughed and walked out of the Park to the Angler's Rest and had a drink like gentlemen together or brothers akin and he gave me back five of the ten and I took it. No apprentice Robinson Crusoe could have had a nobler Man Friday to leave such a spacious footprint on the sands of his Island of Dung.

— Man if not cared for constantly, spider, is dirt and all life is paper.

— It was bloody funny, though, about that girl, although it's highly unlikely that a spider would see the joke. You see, that night in a bar I opened my briefcase which had been with me all the time and what should pounce out of it, like a jack-in-the-box released, but the tart's white silk panties. In the bar I was in, that made me a celebrity and for a long time afterwards if a strange floosie would wander in there some of the bright boys would say that if Christy Hanafin was at the top of his form at least they'd know the colour of her pants. Go down, spider, you'll never make it. Spider, remember rum burns. I feel like a jet plane, my arse is on fire. I felt big when the boys talked like that. Dear spider, I wanted living out of life and big hotels and South American sands, and all I had was morose Cathy twisting the ring on her finger, and the only romantic encounter that could happen was with a cheap tart who knew no better than to ask for chips in a good restaurant and who'd whip her slacks off and give away her pants to the first drunk who bought her a drink. Man was dirt and all life was paper. Do as I did, spider, lie down and give up trying. Spiders climb and spiders fall, kites go up but must come down, and a man can get giddy flying kites and living faster from one day to the next and treating all life as the paper that it is, no better than this bumf, and hoping that the paper money of Cathy's parsimonious people might be there in the end to save the day. It wasn't. Spider, those mean people were glad of the chance to sink me, and scrawny-necked management men don't think life is paper, they think paper is life, and they take a damned poor view when they find somebody has been making free with the paper they think belongs to them or, worse still, to the Company or Firm, or whatever they call it, because the bloodless bastards would rather be robbed themselves than see the Company or the Firm or the Corporation lose a ha'penny. Spider, my ass is sore. Nothing is ever going to be right, nothing for me, absolutely fuck all for you. You've done nothing for me, spider, you haven't inspired me, and look at all the great things the spider taught King Bruce of Scotland. Got his throne and crown back for him, it did. But you've taught me nothing except that there's no way out, and I knew that already. So I sentence you. You deserve to drown. So I carry out the sentence.

He buttoned his fly. He buckled his belt. He flushed the bowl, then turned on both bath-taps and in a roaring belching torrent washed his hapless companion down the drain. They said it was ill-luck to kill a spider. They also said: Thou shalt not steal. The same gang said both things, although they claimed some sort of established authority, a directive from management, for the prohibition on stealing.

He paced slowly and as quietly as he could along the knotted creaking boards of the old wide corridors and down the creaking stairs. It wasn't that he was trying to hide from or sneak up on anybody. But here, as in other places, in his stone and concrete cell, on a prison exercise yard, or herded along a railway platform in full view of the commiserating but remote and superior beings who were free, or hiding hungry behind a cold hedgerow from the relentless search, he felt or hoped that sheer silence might persuade material things, stone, concrete, clay, dripping thorned boughs, to absorb him into their anonymous repose.

Just then, because of his quietness, he was privileged to hear when he paused to stare at himself in the mirror on the first floor landing what They at that moment were saying about him.

§

The voice of Cathy's grandmother was the first voice he heard. She said, and Jesus, her vile voice made her visible: Don't deny it, Catherine. There is no smoke without fire. We have heard a rumour that the blackguard has been seen in the vicinity.

— Have you a warrant, Cathy said. Do you intend to search the house?

— We only came to warn you, Catherine.

A whining, long-nosed, male voice said: Just to warn you and protect you, Cathy.

The front door that was seldom or never opened was half-opened now and sunlight came in and the sounds of the Square. The voices came from a room off the hallway, that had once when commercial men stopped overnight in Cosmona been the commercial room.

— If he came here, Cathy said, I could deal with him better than the two of you put together.

So now, Christy thought, we know where we stand: She can deal with me. Yet, for some reason, she hasn't told them I'm here.

The long-nosed man whined: Don't be angry with us.

She said: I have less cause than anyone to welcome him.

That man had one of the longest of long noses, inclined to redness, frequently with a drip to it. Christy's sometime rival for Cathy's hand had been a rich farmer with a whining voice and a long nose with a drip to it. But at least he had been rich, really rich.

The grandmother said: A woman can be soft in these things.

Hear her, thought Christy, oh suffering Christ, the flinty bitch.

— I know, Catherine, what I put up with myself. A woman can be soft.

— Too true, said Nosy Connell.

— For in the latter end, said Cathy, thou shalt find rest in her: and she shall be turned to thy joy.

— What are you talking about, Catherine, said the grandmother? What is that thing you are reading?

— It's a holy leaflet, dear, put out by one of the nuns. Here's a copy, one for you, one for you too, Johnny Connell. You can read it on the way home.

— It's to be seen that you don't want us here, said the grandmother.

— I've the bar to look after. I'm all alone.

— I wish I could be sure of that.

— Search the house, so.

He marvelled that she hadn't even raised her voice.

— I've a good mind to.

— Go ahead then. I must go back to the bar.

She stood out where he could see her in the hallway. She was small and quiet and very angry. He wanted to touch her and be warmed by her anger. He wanted, absurdly, to stand by her side and defy them as she was doing. That domineering old woman, that unctuous whining man only wanted to see him broken and repentant. But he was quick to see the absurdity of his impulse. Drop down, spider, give it up, get yourself decently drowned. This was all unreal, and Cathy wasn't by any means defending him, but her dolls, or her dreams, or defying the old woman merely because the old woman was, no matter what, detestable. So when Nosy Connell spoke again Christy backed away from the head of the stairs not so much from fear of discovery as from, although he still listened, an argument that had nothing to do with him.

— Don't be so hasty, Cathy. Your grandmother and myself only came over for the best. We know the way that man imposed on you.

— That man, whatever he is, is my husband. He's mine. If you're yoked, the Scotchies say, ye maun pull.

— Religion is all right in its own place, Catherine, the grandmother said. But we're here to talk commonsense now, and there's not much commonsense in this. Listen, Mr. John Connell, for God's sake: Then she will strengthen him, and make a straight way to him and give him joy.

— Oh the holy bible be the holy, said Nosy Connell. Those nuns could lead a body astray.

— Not much pulling, said the grandmother, did he ever help you to do.

— Pulling the other way he was, said Nosy Connell.

— So you would compare us, Cathy said, to two yoked and spancelled goats.

He was abject. He said: No offence, Cathy. I ask your pardon, Cathy.

But the old woman, her metallic voice crackling in fury, burst in on him: What offence in God's holy name? It was the sorrowful day for you, Cathy Tarrant, you didn't marry a decent man like John Connell.

— Ma'am, I implore you, please, Mrs. Tarrant, said Long Nose. No acrimony.

— Hold your tongue, John Connell. I'll say my say and go.

— Go without saying it if you find that easier, said Cathy. The door is wide open.

She has life in her, Christy thought. He moved two steps towards the head of the stairs. He thought better of it. He paused. He was the spider on the cracked enamel. He tiptoed away from the voices, stepping so slowly, scarcely breathing, lest the creaking house might betray his presence. He was the ghost of that uncle, the lost soldier boy, killed so futilely by a spent bullet when the war was as good as over.

— He thought he was clever, said the grandmother. But tell him from me when you see him he was nothing but a windy bag of words.

— We all talk too much at times, John Connell wailed.

— Words, words, words, screamed the old lady. And a thief to boot. He couldn't talk his way out of the jail or away from the civic guards when they caught him. Sweet mother of Christ, Whispering Christy, a credit to Cosmona.

— Get out, said Cathy.

— Mrs. Tarrant, hush, ma'am, moaned Connell. Nothing, Cathy, I assure you, was further from my mind when I came here.

— Hush yourself you fool's head, John Connell. If you'd been a man at all you'd have married her quick and saved her. Not to let that devil from hell marry her for my money.

— She knows me, Christy thought with lighthearted pride. The old bitch reads me like a book.

— But no money of mine did he get. Or no money of mine will you get if you receive him in this house.

— Stuff your money, said Cathy.

Great girl, thought Christy. I taught her something, and she still hasn't raised her voice.

— Every single pound note of it, said Cathy, one by one.

— Oh, Cathy, Cathy, wailed Nosy Connell.

— You told me yourself about his violent fits of temper.

Did she by God, thought Christy.

— I did nothing of the sort, said Cathy.

But did she know that he was listening?

The grandmother said: Praises be to God the two of you never had children.

— Get out and go, said Cathy. I have the bar to attend to.

She still hadn't raised her voice. She was quiet, but she was rock.

— Drunks at the bar, the old woman screamed. Rabble on the Square.

But the front door slammed to cut her short. The old house shook. In that slam Christy knew that, much provoked, Cathy had at last spoken out loud. It was the sound of victory. But he didn't peep out of any window to witness the departure of the vanquished, again not so much from fear of detection as because he wasn't at all sure that, although she was protecting him, she was fighting on his side. He tiptoed up to the attic. He wouldn't pretend to her that he had heard a thing. He sat on a lopsided basket-chair and looked at the toys. He said: Be of good heart. She's down there defending you. She'll let nobody disturb you.

He addressed himself particularly to Little Boy Blue and the three blonde pink-cheeked dolls who so complacently studied their perfections in the toy mirror. He told them: She looks after you the way any good mother would look after fatherless children. And you don't even know who I am. I'm a black stranger. Now that I think of him I wonder what ever became of the black stranger. Did he find the girls? One, two, three. Much fuck.

An unaccountable lust stirred in his own washed weary body. Washing was unsettling. It reminded him of things.

He hated the three blank beautiful faces. He hated that blue hornblowing boy.

§

Up to that moment nothing much had become of the black stranger except that he had fallen asleep in the sun behind a hedgerow between the river and the hospital, had been awakened by the hoots and jeers of the Cawleys as they pranced around Gabriel. From his hiding and with glee he had observed the trouncing of Owen, had observed with interest the girls and the boys making, melodeon and all, up the green slope. Charles Roe's eyes had not deceived him and it was indeed a black man he had seen following and gazing upwards after the musical Cawleys. But the black man had also seen Charles Roe and his company and, his intentions being what they were, he had moved back into hiding to think and to plan. Three young men didn't worry him. He had already seen one of them whipped like a cur. But since he was a black stranger in a green land he had no wish to have the whole foreign world hostile around him.

In the corner of a field from which he could look upwards and still see his prey he came to a high rock that had a purple blossom growing on and overhanging its top, and cut by nature into the side of the rock there was a place where a man might sit and see and not be seen. It was no trouble for a sailor to clamber like a cat the six or seven feet up to that secure place. The part of the rock he sat on was soft with moss. He sat and waited and, silent, sank backwards into the silences of the hill and the advancing evening. He was grass and bramble, he was twisted wood and grey rock. He was a part of a patient people. He watched his prey. They sat on the hillside and one of the boys played the melodeon. Above them, where jagged rocks stood out in silhouette on the slope, a jet plane suddenly appeared, so far away as to be scarcely audible although it seemed as if it had arisen from a hole in the hill, a black buzzard soaring up straight, marking the sky, where blue faded to a shimmering grey, with white vapour shat from its tail. He was a sailor. He knew where the sun set. He knew the plane was hurtling west over an ocean he had often crossed to great cities of whose nether parts and the people in them he had happy memories. He waited and watched his prey and made simple plans for violence.

He said: Cosmona, one, two, three.

He inspected his most private possession in its half-risen strength and felt again Amantha's white hand on it as before she had fled with his money. He pissed transmogrified porter in a high parabola that carried it far from the rock to sink in deep grass, and waited with the calm of a lion at a pool where deer would come to drink, and was content with his anger and the certainty of vengeance.

§

She leaned her forehead for a while against the timber of the door that she had slammed with silent fury. Outside in the Square the Voice of God, growing hoarse with the dint of the long day's talking, invited, almost certainly, her mahogany grandmother to come in and have her innards, if she had any, photographed: She wouldn't have to undress, it wouldn't take her ten minutes. The loudspeaker crackled. God coughed and, it seemed, even spat, then repeated the invitation. But this time it must be for Johnny Connell with all the money and the drip to his nose and the oft-repeated wish, unknown to that dire grandmother, to have fun and games with the lorn grass-widow, Cathy Hanafin. At the thought of Johnny, one crystal pearl distinct on the tip of his nose, standing up bravely for examination, her anger broke and she giggled for the first time in a long time, choking with schoolgirl's merriment, crushing in her hand one of Sister Thermometer's luscious leaflets. When the fit was over she turned from the door, uncrumpling and smoothing out the leaflet and reading as her fingers worked over the paper: She shall give to thy head increase of graces and protect thee with a noble crown.

The last rippling wave of giggles shook her body. Christy would never credit it that I was in business protecting him with a noble crown from the fury of my granny that walketh by day and the nosiness of Nosy Connell that would lie by night. A long wet nose they said was always the sign of a dirty inquisitive mind and if the rest of the wet and long-nosed world was like John Connell what they said was true. I'm protecting Christy's honour, she thought, and mad laughter would have followed the giggles except that she saw then the young man standing in the corridor at the top of the stairs and felt instead of laughter the sudden cold steel of fear.

He said in a low gravelly voice, he was close to whispering like Christy: I came in through the bar. They were laughing at me out there.

That fear was because for a second she thought that the fable she had woven around the dead young soldier had at last come true: that he, young exile in Australia, sad victim of a battle that was over when it killed him, had in his Flanders graveyard heard her words or felt her thoughts and truly returned to haunt the house in which he had been born. As a schoolgirl she had been proud to lay claim to an uncle who had been killed in the Big War. He was a hero, wasn't he? She boasted about him to the other girls. She allowed the few who were close to her to look at his picture, at the strong young man's dark chin made stronger by the military chinstrap, at the eyes half-lost in the shadow of the peak of the khaki cap. As she grew older and her close friends became fewer and fewer until there were none left, either because she preferred it that way or because she couldn't hold them – she was never sure which – she studied the picture and gloried in it all alone. She talked to him, spending often as long as an hour at a time looking at the photograph, touching the face with her fingers, reading out the list of the names of those French places, Loos, Arras, Bethune, Bourbon Wood, Péronne, where brave men like him, men with the wings of eagles, had died in battle; so that it was not surprising that in lonely evenings she felt she could see or sense him walking in old corridors or silently up creaking stairways. But we may dream in comfort of the dead and yet be afraid to come upon them standing in the corner of a room. So she was startled for a moment until she looked closer and saw who it was and laughed at her own folly and fear.

— I'm not laughing at you, she said. Who was laughing at you, Gabriel?

— The strangers in the bar.

— The two of them?

— Two more came in. I ran in to hide. The whole place is laughing at me. They're after me. The Cawleys chased me and the priest bate the Cawleys.

— More power to his oxter. What did the strangers say to you when they were laughing?

— Just what you said about the priest, Mr. Tarrant. They said more power to my oxter and asked me to have a drink.

She wondered which brother he saw when he looked at her.

Was it Shadow? Was it Substance? To which one of the two would he run for shelter? Or was it to Peejay or the lost exile, the ghost, the dead warrior? She said to him although she wasn't really talking to him: I've a houseful of men now. I've a dwarf saint painting Christ's passion in a wooden hut. And a husband that's come home to roost although Johnny Connell once said he never would.

What Johnny Connell, drunk one night and fumbling to pull up the back of her blouse, had in fact said was: That bastard will never come back.

To hear Christy so spoken of had wounded something small and pitiful and tender in herself. For the twentieth time she had fended off Johnny's clumsy advances. Sex was in its awkward infancy with him, as the man from the village of Bunniconlon in the backwoods of Mayo said about Bunniconlon when he came back to it from the war and the kips of Cairo. She had said to Nosy Johnny: Someday he will. He's my husband. They always come home to roost.

He had come home. She had a secure feeling of triumph. The visit from Nosy Connell and that stinking old woman had made her feel almost kindly towards Christy. She led Gabriel down the stairs to the basement.

— And four drunk heroes from Dublin, she said. Hark to the roars of them. And a nut in a helmet who picks the most public place in Cosmona for his most private performance. All I need now is the black man and the strong man and Nosy Johnny Connell. Still a man's a man and Gabriel boy you've shown yourself as much a man as anyone in Cosmona. Not that Nosy Connell hasn't made the offer to me often enough. Someday when I feel the pinch I might take him at his word.

Outside in the Square, the loudspeaker, a quavery tenor voice singing, said that it was the end of a perfect day.

— Most apt, she said. I shall protect you, Gabriel, with a noble crown until the doctor or somebody decides what to do with you. Come on, Casanova. I'll hide you in safety. For the good people of Cosmona'll skin you alive for desecrating the old abbey tower. Although what did you do but do in public what they're all at in private. All except me, Gabriel. All except me.

§

A golfing bank manager in Crooked Bridge had once bestowed on Peejay a suit of blue-green, tartan-patterned plus-fours that had brought the manager ill-luck on the links as, it was said, the wearing of a white tall hat had once brought ill-luck with the grouse to a grouse-shooting gentleman of the locality. The golfer had been a small man but by no means as small as Peejay who fitted twice over into the striking cloth. Being, as musician and painter and part-time journalist, a man necessarily conscious of style, Peejay had made his image more striking with green stockings, tan shoes and a tweed cap that seemed lost and lonely without a fringe of trout flies.

When he came down the three steps into the cellar bar Bob Gunning leaped up, in mock amazement, from an alcove where he had been feeding more grain to the glutted bird, and said: Gorgeous Gussie. By the living God.

— The name of God in vain, said Peejay.

— The name of Gorgeous Gussie, said Art Finlan.

— That white cock of yours, Edward told Peejay, isn't the Christian Brother he puts up to be.

Peejay listened while Ned told him of the dirty deed done by the aqueduct.

— He was enjoying himself, Laurence said, like any Hollywood star.

— He was just acting according to nature. To do so is to do the Lord's work, said Peejay.

— Was Superman on the steeple, said Ned, doing the Lord's work.

— I wasn't here when it happened, said Peejay. I was in Crooked Bridge.

That was an unanswerable argument.

In soprano, contralto, falsetto and tenor Bob Gunning sang: I come, I come, my heart's delight.

But he reserved his royal bass to sing: Seated one day at the orgasm.

Quietly again returning the woman said: Leave Peejay alone.

— I can speak for myself thank you, Mrs. Hanafin.

But he was sufficiently shaken to accept the whiskey that Lord Laurence with a curtsey offered him. He sipped it. He said: It's the bad example of the well-to-do and the smutty stories in the papers that set off a soft lad like Gabriel.

— He wasn't so soft, said Ned. This blessed day he managed better than any of us.

Lord Laurence said: We have seen and hearkened to the son. We can go back by another way into our own country.

— Eating raw cats, Ned said. In the film about the Kwai there were bathing beauties by jungle pools. Too good to be true.

Art, removing his pipe, gave it as his opinion that if that had been the way of it every soldier from Omsk to Omagh would have volunteered for the jungle.

— Eating raw cats, said Edward.

Peejay, offered by Laurence a second drink, had taken it as if he needed some support other than his high principles.

The woman said: Peejay you shouldn't drink.

— Raw live cats, said Edward.

The woman said: You were a long time in Crooked Bridge.

— I had some special business to do for Miss Grace Roe.

He was proud that now and again Miss Grace asked him to post religious leaflets from Crooked Bridge to her cousin, Charles, to turn him, she said, from his godless ways. He had to address the sealed envelopes himself and he was a slow and careful penman, master of a controlled orthography as stately and dated as the crinoline.

The woman said: For Miss Grace?

She was puzzled again by Peejay as she had been puzzled to find that he had been telling the newspapermen where to find the miller. She could think of him only as blessing his flock with a sweep of golden grain, or tidying-up about the place, or in his hut painting the passion of Jesus or playing the fiddle. She said: Watch out for Miss Grace. She's looking for a man.

— We had a job to do, Ned said mournfully.

— We have heard and photographed the son, Laurence said.

— But we, said Bob, have done fuck-all about the Holy Ghost.

Art said: We must wait for nightfall. You can't expect me to get a picture of a ghost in broad daylight.

He fed pennies to Saint Martin de Porres who nodded and nodded. The woman said: He'll give you only the same nods for halfcrowns. For a saint of God he has little sense. Nor have you, Peejay. Is that your third drink? What's come over you?

— Saint Paul says drink a little wine.

Ned watched the nodding saint. He said, more to the saint than to anybody else: Where has our black man gone? Where, oh where, the ace of hearts?

She said: Paul said nothing about Jameson's ten year old. And tell us, Peejay, what was it you were specially doing for Grace Roe?

§

On his throne on the rock with the purple blossom high above him the black sailor sat and waited and unlike the black saint didn't even nod his head. In the shadow that the rock cast between himself and the evening sun he was truly black, not brown nor mahogany. A thin white line on the sky marked where the westering jet had passed. He sat and waited. He made no sound. He listened to the music. He listened when it stopped and when it began again and stopped again, and when shrill angry voices came down to him through the evening quiet. He didn't raise his head to look up the hill towards the place the voices came from. He knew they were slowly coming closer to him. He was, with the prey within hearing, the most patient of men.

§

Transformed by green of jungle, and blue of ocean across which the *Hispaniola* breasted splendidly, the evening sun shone into Treasure Island. The Mouse, aided by a tall, freckled, red-headed day nurse, who was gladly ending the day's duty, tucked in the bedclothes.

— Matron's orders, the red girl said. She said you had enough fresh air for one day. No balcony for you tonight.

— Some people, the Mouse said, are mollycoddled.

But in his own excitement and elation he could sense hers. Thanks to the pink screen, the corner of the balcony was a fine and private place but the playroom by night was as secluded as

Silver's island itself, no company except a half dozen grave, size-able rocking-horses that some of the luckier little boys bestrode during the day, no light except the muted rays of a night-light, in the ward outside, struggling dimly through the painted story-telling glass.

— Poor Father Jarlath, said the red nurse, was fit to burst. The purple face of him and the mad eyes.

— But not at Gabriel and Nora, said the Mouse. Sure what harm were they doing? But he was mad at those damnable Cawleys.

— It's enough to set the poor priest flying in the air again.

— He can't any more. The bishop won't let him. They forced him to give up his little aeroplane.

As nurses do they smoothed and tucked in perfect unison and talked to each other across the bed as if the patient, prostrate between them, did not exist.

The red nurse said that it wasn't silenced by the bishop, but grounded, that Father Jarlath was.

The Mouse supposed that he had learned to fly when he was a chaplain in the war.

They bent over the bed as if the two of them moved by the same machinery. They were in no hurry. He was a special privi-leged case. It was more titillating to work for him than for one of the boys who were not yet old enough to remind them that they themselves were young women. Then he was a cleric, or at least the makings of a cleric if he held together. He was forbidden fruit. It was a double, a triple pleasure, to tempt and tease and taunt him.

— The sermons he preaches, the red nurse said.

She explained that Father Jarlath was a hero and a caution and that she never knew whether to laugh or cry or cheer when he'd turn round on the altar and preach to nuns and nurses about the sins of sex and the cinema and the degrading passion of love.

— Sure as God that's what he said, the Mouse agreed. The degrading passion of love.

She blushed. She sang: Fall in love, fall in love says my heart.

The red nurse said that Father Jarlath had said that men and women falling in love would have second thoughts if they could see a picture of a nudist colony. She wondered, fairly enough, where Father Jarlath had ever seen a picture of a nudist colony, or where or how he had ever seen anybody, himself excepted, in the bare pelt. She was willing to agree that that spectacle might be enough to put his reverence or anyone else off love or sex or whatever you cared to call it.

The Mouse sang: Fall in love, fall in love says my heart.

She said: Wasn't he on the foreign missions?

She had once overheard the priest telling the doctor that when he was a young missionary in Africa he had watched black women diving naked for fish.

— Wasn't it a pity, Jarlath, the doctor had said, that you hadn't a camera.

And the priest had roared: What did I want with a camera? Didn't God gift me with two sharp eyes and a retentive memory?

Once again and with liquid laughter they bent to the machinery, then straightened up again, white aprons pressed against the bed, the hard edge of the fracture board defining, so close to his left hand, so close to his right, two gentle white mounds. Responding to their provocation, the flutter of stiffening muscle was at him again, so he closed his eyes and fled from it, from them, into darkness, only to come out at the far end of the tunnel on a summery road with the sea in the distance, and walking by his side the redfaced yokel, teeth sharp as goats' horns, squint, bicycle clips but no bicycle. There was no escape from the linen nurses and their teasing talk or from the redfaced goat bending down and studying without passion the undercarriage of the sleeping woman.

That magic moonlit night, travelling to and from the Tower, he had told her: One sunny day I walked five miles to a seaside resort and met on the road a country fellow with a squint and buck-teeth and yellow shoes and a navy blue suit. He walked on with me and I've never met a funnier fellow. He had no bicycle but like most country fellows he wore bicycle clips, even in bed.

Yet to tell her truly what Buckteeth, the laughing goat, had been and done would be as much as to lift the veils, white apron and blue skirt, from that rounded place he could touch if he moved his left hand a few inches. The thought of telling her, of uncovering and touching her, set those muscles off like brimstone butterflies and made his belly cold and empty with holy joyful sinful fear and desire.

On that walk to the seaside the merry yokel and himself had come to a humpy old stone bridge over a small stream. Two girls sat on the parapet of the bridge.

— What are you at, girls, the yokel asked.

Their faces were sallow from wind and sun and working in the fields. Their clothes would smell of peatsmoke from the cabins. With arch rural humour they said that they were fishing, Timothy, and Timothy, rising to the joke, said: Girls, you're sitting on the bait.

That moment of country manners came back so brightly to him, surrounded as he was, on Treasure Island. Wrapped up in white linen, warm as birds' nests, the bait was there to either hand.

— He's hell on the short skirts, the Mouse was saying.

The red nurse supposed that Father Jarlath's sermons about the evils of short skirts were meant for the nurses and not for the nuns, and only for the nurses when they were off duty. He made, and she asked God to give him sense, an unholy fuss about a few inches of material, and the reverend mother, she did believe, had to say something to him the Sunday that he preached the sermon against both cosmetics and short skirts and gave it as his learned opinion that if the skirts got any shorter the ladies would have four cheeks each instead of two to paint.

They bent over him, helplessly laughing. Opening his eyes he could see the red girl's freckles as if they were floating on her blonde skin, could see the faintest moisture on the upper lip of the Mouse and one wisp of brown hair that had struggled loose from her veil. They laughed. Buckteeth the Goat laughed. The girls on the bridge laughed. They called after Peter Lane: Young towney fellow, does your mother keep chickens?

Buckteeth called back: He'll tell you if you show him your nests.

The summer meadows were turning purple with ripeness and warmth. In the evenings the country couples, tumbling like animals, would flatten their lairs in deep grass.

That magic moonlit night, going to and coming from the Tower, he had told her: On that same road one day I cycled up behind two old men walking and by accident knocked one of them down.

The red nurse said that ever since Jarlath had read some new book or other he was holy hell for what he called medical ethics.

— As if, she said, Sister Thermometer was changing over to abortion.

— They're mad out and out, said the Mouse, when they try to be modern.

The old man lay groaning on the grass margin of the roadside. The other old man stood in the dust over the fallen bicycle, backwheel still spinning, and called Peter Lane a roadhog and a murderer. The names made no impression. Half-dazed from his fall he looked at the groaning victim, at the rip in the fork of his coarse frieze trousers that exposed something yellow-and-grey, and withered like a weed clinging to a rock left bare by receding waters. It was frightening to think that the rubber-tight resilient thing he wrestled with, his angel, in the hot limepit, the wooden jakes, down among the dark bushes, the salmon that leaped up now stiff under the bedclothes, rising to the lure of two baits, would one day shrivel into such ugliness, such helpless uselessness.

He had afterwards heard that the two old men lived in one cabin a most primitive existence, that they seldom washed and never shaved but only clipped the jagged bristle, that on winter nights they had their total livestock, three goats, tethered to the foot of their bedstead. His uncle, by way of compensation for the bump of the bicycle, had sent them a pound note and a bottle of whiskey.

Stopping to urinate from the cliff path, making proud patterns along the cliff's edge, Buckteeth had screamed apparently to the seagulls, and said that it was awful hard to have no bones in it.

The red nurse said that Father Jarlath said that it was the nurse's duty, and not the duty of the priests, to instruct married people without, Father Jarlath insisted, what he called unbecoming publicity. She considered the probable nature of unbecoming publicity and reckoned that that might have something to do with Gabriel and Nora.

— Let the married couples work it out for themselves, the Mouse said. Haven't they long nights and all the time in the world.

— As to the exact calculation of days, the red nurse said, you nurses are rightly expected to be well informed of this well-known theory of agenesical periods.

The Mouse held that nurses for their own protection would need to be.

The bed was made, the teasing accomplished. They left him before he could think of anything to say that wouldn't set them mocking at his prudery or betray to them, if they weren't well aware of it already, that they knew so much more than he did.

The green of the jungle, the blue of the ocean was a painful blur before his half-closed eyes. His face was burning from a tropical sun. Away from where he floated naked in the black waters of the River of the Black Cat blobs of sperm floated, white maggots, to be taken perhaps by a leaping female fish with the direst results in progeny. When the horse was bought and sold in the meadow of the corncrakes the farmers and tinkers sealed the deal by standing in a long line, one team of male brothers complacent in the moonlight, and pissing into a brambly ditch. With the Mouse he went walking up the green slope to the Moat, then blossoming burning furze closed around them but they came out at last, his arm around her, their eyes dazzled with gold, to a clearing where God, the greatest goat in the world, sat in the centre of a circle buck-lording it over a hundred black nuns and a hundred blue-and-white nurses who knew more than married couples about medical ethics and who all, nuns and nurses, chanted in upstanding medieval Latin that they were sitting on the bait.

The lights were on in the ward outside when the Mouse, pulling his ear and gently stooping to kiss him, awoke him for biscuits and milk and to tell him that Enda Cawley had been carried in roaring with his right jawbone tripping him, that this was a wonderful day all out in quiet Cosmona because a black sailor who came from nowhere had, up by the Moat, committed multiple rape on some slut of a girl that the Cawleys had brought from Dublin City, and that the poor thing, although she wasn't much, was so sore she couldn't walk.

— It was, she added, a man's world.

§

Of all things, the trouble began over bubble gum which Teresa and Dympna had never liked anyway so that in one way they could side with Amantha when Ignatius who was chewing bubble gum leaned over her and kissed her full on the bubble. They were all lying on the grass at the time except for Enda who was on his hunkers playing the melodeon, and they were all, up to that, as happy as the day was long, except for Owen who was still aching and complaining from the beating he got from the mad priest.

But Amantha made more fuss about that kiss than all the bubble gum in the world was worth, and pushed Ignatius away from her and leaped up and began spitting and scrubbing her mouth with the back of her hand. Ignatius rolled over and over on the grass, laughing, until he heard what she was calling him. She said that bubble gum was a filthy habit, and to say that was harmless enough and no worse than Sister Thermometer said once when she caught Dympna combing her hair in the hospital kitchen. But she went on to say that Ignatius was a filthy country brute, and no Cawley liked hearing himself or another Cawley described as a filthy brute, let alone a filthy country brute. Ignatius stopped laughing. Enda stopped playing. Dympna who was easily nervous tried to laugh it off by saying sweet sixteen and never was kissed, and it might have ended with that if Amantha, and serve her right for everything that happened to her afterwards except that she caused such trouble to everybody else and especially to poor Enda, screamed at them that she would let no man living kiss her or touch her. She said all men were filthy brutes and all she ever wanted out of them was money and a good time.

She's a whatdoyoucallit, said Dympna who couldn't credit her ears and couldn't remember the word, and Teresa said a virgin, and Ignatius said he had once heard Old Windbag Mortell who put the glauber salts in the oatmeal as if he owned the world, say that it was a right thing to keep a virgin cow in every herd.

Enda put down his melodeon on the grass and looked at Amantha and said he could give her the good time whatever about the money. And did you never, he says, get a rub of the relic at all and did you never among the sights of Dublin see anything like this.

It was funny in a way with Enda standing there with the staff of life in his fist and it as thick as a jam jar and Dympna laughed though Teresa for her own reasons was a bit peevish, but Amantha just turned her long back on the company and headed off down the hill, trying to trot but not able to on her high heels, but walking as hard as she could, her hips hopping up and down and her long black hair flying.

Well and good, and if she had just kept moving and her mouth shut they might all have been warned in time that Apeman was hiding in the bushes. Dympna was about to say come on up to the caves and the heather and we'll pluck some blayberries before the fall of night when Amantha who wouldn't leave well enough alone looked black and spat, and pulled her skirt up and kicked her legs in the air, and said she was off to Dublin where men were men. Teresa shouted back that a lot she knew about men with all her big talk, and Owen said it would be well done to leave her with a souvenir to display to her friends in the big city in nine months time. The rights of her country is what she's asking for, says Enda, and with that he ran, his melodeon in his fist and all he had exposed and dancing before him, and Owen and Ignatius ran and, although Teresa couldn't exactly approve of Enda doing it, still somebody had to teach the fancy bitch a lesson, so Teresa and Dympna kicked off their shoes and ran too, and Amantha who wasn't used to the wide open spaces and grass under her feet hadn't a hope in hell. She screamed and kicked and spat like a cat when they caught her, but Owen held one leg and Ignatius held the other and Teresa and Dympna held an arm apiece, and Enda slowly peeled off her swish black pants and said fancy meeting you here so that they all had to laugh, and put in his finger to warm and tickle her, he said, for a start, and was on his knees with his pants down when the angel descended from the skies, only it wasn't an angel but the black devil out of hell himself.

The first thing was the crash and the groan as he landed smash on the unfortunate melodeon and the second thing was the crack of bone as he made mincemeat of Enda's jaw, for with his pants around his ankles Enda hadn't a chance to stand up, let alone run. After the priest and all, Owen's nerves were so bad that he was halfways to Cosmona and roaring like a calf without even waiting to see what it was had descended on them, and Ignatius at his heels, and Teresa and Dympna as close behind them as they could manage, and screaming murder for the world to hear.

When the rescue party led by King Kong Hoban went back up the hill they were guided through the shadows by the groans of Enda as he tried to crawl away across the grass, and Amantha was by that time unconscious with the black man working on her for the forty-first time and getting in thundering fashion the value, and more than the value, of the money he had lost the night before. As Teresa said, if Amantha was late in starting she made up for it in one session and got in one fine evening as much as most hard-working women get in all their lives. It was the will of God, too, that Hoban was performing in Cosmona that day for not ten civic guards could have quelled his black lordship, but King Kong mastered him with a kick to the privates and a thud of the elbow on the back of the head. After that he came tamely enough, staggering and handcuffed and trying to speak but his mouth was bleeding. There could have been bad work when the shouting crowd got around him in the Square but old Mortell, as if it was any of his business and Enda and Amantha both on the way to the hospital where the doctor discovered he had a multiple fracture and she was lacerated inside and out, drove the crowd away, and Guard Kane put the black beast into the black hole in the barracks where Teresa said they'd never find him again in the dark.

But when trouble gets going there's no stopping it, for Owen said to Ignatius that if he only had had the starting handle of a car in his fist he'd have marked the nigger for life, and Ignatius said you'd have done fuck all, and Owen said you ran away too, and before Teresa or Dympna could stop them they were dug into each other and rolling like animals in the street, and blood was spilt.

That was the first time in history that the hand of a Cawley was raised against a Cawley.

§

With the lady Eustochium of noble Rome Charles Roe knew that he could have lived in perfect accord. She had the receptiveness to ideas that could never belong to poor Cousin Grace. She wouldn't have flushed or have had a nose at times red-tipped. Her skin would have been smooth, Latin, olive and her face well-fleshed and content. She wouldn't have had that maddening, nervous, tripping, short step or that weakness for bemoaning lost opportunities and remembering one crowded hour as a beauty queen. Nor would she have wanted to marry him, for Eustochium was a reverend mother before reverend mothers really got into business.

While the shadow of Aphrodite rising from a foam of grey stone lengthened over the grass of his garden he sat and communed with Eustochium. What a woman, what a marvellous woman to so invite and stand up to the confidences of old Jerome.

Low in his deck-chair, whiskey bottle and glass beside him on a low table, he read with enthusiasm, now mumbling, now silently moving his lips, now orating. Aphrodite and the nonchalant evening birds were his only audience. But he was also Jerome. Aphrodite's shadow draped by the decent grass, was the listening Eustochium.

— Your bridegroom is not arrogant, he told her, he is not proud. He has married an Ethiopian woman.

He repeated, lingering over the syllables: An Ethiopian woman.

— Subject to sin, he said. Therefore dusky in hue.

Then to the shadow on the grass he read: The king will conduct you into his chamber and when your colour has been changed in marvellous fashion this question will be applicable to you: Who is this that cometh up, being made white?

He stood up, the book in his left hand, his right hand raised, and hardened his voice and sharpened his note. By the blood of God, old Jerome could be a stern man, he could warn, he could denounce, he could fulminate. Charles Roe had always approved of Lord Byron because Lord Byron could not stand the sight of a woman eating. His life in the army had convinced him that women, like Cousin Grace, were wasteful and slovenly house-keepers. They were, indeed, dirty. So, savouring the whiskey and feeling like Lord Byron and using the words of Saint Jerome, he denounced them, one and all.

Take care I pray, he read, lest sometime God may say of you: the Virgin of Israel hath fallen, there is none to raise her up. I speak audaciously: although God can do all things he cannot raise up a virgin after she has fallen. He has power, indeed, to free her from the penalty but he has no power to crown one who has been corrupted. But if those virgins are also virgins, yet because of other faults are not saved by bodily virginity, what will become of those who have prostituted the members of Christ and have turned the temple of the Holy Spirit into a brothel. Straightway they shall hear…

Cousin Grace he knew had come out from the house and stood behind him. She was waiting to say something. She wore a black dress and a heavy grey shawl. She was repellent. She was funereal. Raising his glance from Eustochium, shadowy on the holy grass, he addressed grey sinful Aphrodite, shielded by her conch.

— Come down, he read, sit on the ground, virgin daughter of Babylon, there is no throne for the daughter of the Chaldeans, for thou shalt no more be called delicate and tender. Take a millstone and grind meal, strip off thy covering, make bare thy legs, pass over the rivers. Thy nakedness shall be discovered and thy shame shall be seen.

— She'll hardly come down, Miss Grace said. She's too long up there. She's too stiff to move. And as for grinding meal she's not the right shape to be of any use to Martin Mortell.

Miss Grace knew all about Eustochium and about Jerome, whom she had told the doctor she regarded as a spoilsport and no good influence on Cousin Charles. She had heard it all before so many times. She said: There have been dreadful events this day in Cosmona and you, the richest and most influential man in the place, stand here raving.

But her cousin regarded her not. He raved, he read: She shall be stripped and her hinder parts shall be bared in her own sight.

Roaring drunk again, she thought. God pity me that has to listen to him.

With venom she said: She couldn't see her own hinder parts.

— She shall sit by the waters of solitude, said Charles Roe, and putting down her pitcher shall open her feet to everyone that passes by.

— A second ago she was in solitude.

— She shall be polluted from head to foot. I entreat you as a bride of Christ avoid wine like poison.

— You haven't the countenance of a bride of Christ, Cousin Charles. But you could profit by that advice. You that once drank yourself bandy on brandy.

The memory of one humiliating week when, because brandy had done something to the balls of his legs, two male nurses had propped him round the garden to study anew the art of walking, and in an unguarded moment had dropped him so that they might chase the Cawley boys who were peeping through the hedge, never failed to bring him back to Cosmona, to Cousin Grace, to the drab earth and the present. He said: You are a cantankerous virgin, Cousin Grace.

He sat back into his deck chair. He poured another whiskey. He said: You know I never drink brandy now.

— We'll give you a red rosette, like a bull at a show, for self-denial. And while you sit here and sozzle, a nigger from nowhere has raped some slut of a Dublin girl up by the Moat.

— A Dublin girl. Impossible, Cousin Grace.

— He's in the black hole, impossible or not, waiting for a ship's officer and a detective to come from Dublin.

— It should have been a rural maiden, not a slut from Babylon.

— It was some young girl, she said. Some mother's rearing. Mother of Mercy, have you human blood in your veins at all, or only whiskey? You're worse than Mortell.

— Mortell?

His son's dead. He wasn't even in the house when his son died. He was down settling the affairs of Cosmona and rescuing the nigger, as if that was any of his business. You'd think a father could be present when his son died.

— There's precedent for it, he said.

He drank again. Cousin Grace drove him to it. He said: So the Dead Man as his schoolmates called him is now truly dead. Did he ever live in the flesh? I will go to that house, bringing consolation.

That was Jerome.

— Cousin Grace, wrap me up two fresh bottles for Mr. Mortell.

That was more in the style of milord Byron: Keep the hussies on the run, don't listen to them talking, don't watch them chewing, don't think of them digesting.

— You'll be an angel of mercy, putting the old man himself drunk.

He ignored her. She would do his bidding. He looked up at grey stone. He said: Aphrodite, was the holy place desecrated? Or did something return that was there before the Island of the Living?

— Make it Bushmill's black label liqueur, he said. A decorous drink for a funeral.

— The black man picked his queen of the mountain, he said.

— She feels complimented, I'm sure.

— You were crowned a queen once yourself, he said. But not in the same rough way.

That would rattle her. That would send her about her, or his, business.

— How much better these silly beauty queen competitions would be if the elected queen were publicly deflowered.

— Charles, she said. Please, Charles. Decency demands.

She was gone.

— Aphrodite, he said.

She screamed back at him, startling him so that he splashed his whiskey. Screaming was new. She called: Walk three times round her before the sun sets. She might come down and lie on the grass. She might do something for you.

§

Shivering and sobbing she locked herself into the bathroom. She had never before spoken so to Charles and now anything might happen, and let him wrap his own whiskey. But when she had sat for a while, reason returned and she knew that nothing would happen, good or bad. All would be hopeless and as before. He would never marry her. He could never afford to lose her. They would go on as they were until death did them part. The dogs on the street, the imbeciles on the top of the Tower could have their fun.

She had always had a persistent concern about the forbidden degrees of relationship. Cousins had married cousins. That was common. Uncles had also married nieces and that was certainly keeping it in the family. In one family of the best people in Irish history three uncles had married three nieces, with the proper papal dispensations of course, and no monsters had been produced, not so as anybody noticed or mentioned. Was a dispensation also a blessing?

Cousin Charles and herself were both so useless, both so wasted.

She went from the bathroom to her bedroom and back again, carrying a small velvet-covered box that she kept carefully locked on her dressing table. It was a deep red in colour, or a sort of purple. She was never sure which. Yet when she thought of velvet she thought of it as black not as red or purple, and black would be her colour from this moment forever: she was in mourning, she had given up all hope, she had surrendered, praying and reading and long-suffering and works of charity would henceforth be all her life.

From the box she took the last dozen of lascivious postcards she had purchased once in London and tore them to fragments and flushed them down the toilet bowl. They were merely lewd. They were not art. Art might have conquered where mere lewdness had failed. The triumphant stone woman was, after all, art.

There went her dreams on the water. There went the naked figures that Charles had once told the doctor were his Anthonian temptations in the desert. One dancing fragment survived the deluge. She rescued it, studied it bitterly. It showed a portion of a strong young thigh and a vee of diminutive panties.

She tightened her mouth and tore it again and again and again until the fragments were too small and wet and slippery to hold, and tossed them, wiping them off her finger tips, back into the bowl, and brought down on them again the watery wrath of heaven and smiled with sour satisfaction, and went down to the kitchen to wrap up the two bottles of Bushmill's black-label liqueur whiskey.

§

All that happened in the garden was that Charles Roe, moved by an inexplicable good humour or just by the joy of triumph over the dreadful sex, did gird himself with a brimming glass of whiskey and walk three times sunwise around Aphrodite.

She had come to his garden when his friend, the prior from Crooked Bridge, had had the pillars and porticoes of a dismantled eighteenth-century house carted away to make Roman backgrounds in his monastery garden for a set of life-size statues of the stations of the cross. Aphrodite, grey, lichened, assaulted by creeping climbing weeds on the abandoned lawn of the old house, had no fit place in the story of Christ's passion.

— 'Twould be as odd, said Charles Roe, as if the weeping women of Jerusalem went naked to meet the Saviour on the road to doom.

So he had opened his arms to her. He had given her a home as he had also given a home to Cousin Grace. The contrast diverted him. On sunny days his chair of meditation was in her shadow. He moved the chair as sun and shadow moved.

He circled her now in the dusk. He said to her: The King did conduct you into his garden.

She was a mother, a graceful mother from a pagan past. Grace now and then tried to mother him, but that was different.

— All men want the mother, he said. They could do very well without the daft son who got himself into trouble.

— Jesus died, he told her, on the day of Venus, lay in his grave on the day of Saturn, and arose from the dead on the day of Helios.

He had had the best intentions of going to the house of death, bearing whiskey and words of consolation but his meditations so beguiled him that he sat on drinking and muttering until the moon came up. He thought of death and burial. When his father and mother had died within a week of each other he had been so out-raged at the high cost of dying and being buried, that he had for a while considered willing his body to the knackers. He reasoned: there was a shortage of bodies for research, and few people were enlightened enough to give themselves thus to the furthering of knowledge. Wasn't it livelier to be chopped up, examined and talked about by zealous medicals than merely in darkness to rot and rot? And Cousin Grace would get, when his corpse was delivered, an extra twenty-five pounds.

— First, he muttered to Aphrodite who was beginning to glisten in the moonlight, they cut off the head, then boil it to bare the skull. In the grave the baring process takes fifteen days, in a pot a few hours.

Once in his student days he had seen a happy medical lifting a skull out of the pot, a prong of the tongs in each eyehole. He had known then too a man who died of cancer of the liver. He had heard that medical lament that the cadaver, uselessly corrupting under clay and floral wreaths, could have been a goldmine to researchers.

Not deigning to speak, Miss Grace left on the low table the two bottles of Bushmill's. He called after her: Tilly who sacked Magdeburg boasted he never tasted wine, lost his chastity or suf-fered defeat. With Pappenheim he was responsible in one night for the death of thirty-five thousand people.

Cousin Grace didn't answer.

— He was defeated, he roared, but killed, by Gustavus Adolphus. He kept his chastity.

Cousin Grace was gone back into the house.

With all those unnamed and unmentionable diseases the cadaver of Stephen Mortell should have been a special sort of goldmine, all the riches of the gorgeous east, gold and frankin-cense and myrrh, buried and lost forever in Irish clay.

He, Charles Roe, was the most influential man in Cosmona. His family was old stock. He should be out now, he thought, look-ing after Gabriel Rock, the Dublin girl, the nigger from nowhere, and advising the bereaved father. The Roes were ancient people.

That was why he had not willed his body to the knackers. Blood was blood. Blood was greater than any one body. Time out of mind the Roes, kings in their own place and their own way, had had hereditary right of burial on the Island of the Living.

He slept in the deck chair. The king for the moment had abdicated.

§

The doctor's wife, lulled to sleep by the salmon water, dreamt that she was a nurse again. But it wasn't a pleasant dream. She had been so uneasy and upset when in the dusk in the empty house she had fallen asleep. In her dream she was making a bed in which a British war hero with the name of some famous film actor had died. At first the dead body seemed to be in the bed, then it wasn't. There was an excessive number of sheets, all bloodstained. Her husband was in the next bed. He was sitting up, clipping his whiskers with a huge scissors. Then on the floor at the far end of the room she saw a small sort of alligator. It came creeping towards her. She dodged it. She fended it off with the long bamboo staff Charles Roe had carried when he led the picnic party up the slope towards the Moat of Cosmona. But the alligator kept following her. Then it seemed to have lost its tail. As it followed her it made grunting whining noises that were at the same time musical. To escape from it she leaped with a scream on to the bed her husband sat in, and awoke, all sweat, to see him silhouetted, undressing, against the window that looked out on the river. She said: I had the most horrible nightmare.

He didn't answer. She said: Such a hideous horrible nightmare. Where on earth were you?

He said: I didn't leave Mortell's house until the women came to wash the corpse. There wasn't much corpse to wash. The dead body hardly made a bump on the bedclothes. The head was far and away the biggest part of it.

— Must you, she said. This is as bad as my nightmare.

— Then I went searching for Gabriel Rock. I had some plans for helping him if I could have found him.

— Helping him? To lock him in a cage like the baboons in the zoo is the only help. A bullet in the head would be better.

— But I searched everywhere and no luck.

— Luck? And I was here having nightmares.

She thought: He hasn't asked me about my nightmare, he doesn't care about my nightmare.

— It's funny, he said. The poor divil wanted to see us. Instead we saw him.

— How can you be so filthy, she said. How can you be so complacent.

— Be sensible, dear. They only did in public what goes on everywhere.

She said nothing.

— Everybody, my dear, goes through the day with more or less a solemn face, retires at night to his cave to have a bash, comes up in the morning, solemn or smiling, as if he hadn't done a thing. Gabriel's trumpet has caught us all in the act. He's made Peeping Toms out of the whole ruddy place.

She said nothing. He had stopped undressing. He was looking out of the window. He said: Old Mortell saved the black sailor from a bad beating. He has great authority in this place.

— It would be like him, she said, out saving a savage nigger while his son lay dying. What business of his was it what happened to the nigger.

— He said to me that yellow men had killed his son so the best he could do was save a black man.

— Big talk, she said, big talk. Why can't we move to the city where it's civilised?

— The savage nigger, as you call him, came from the city.

Then she yelled at him: You never asked me about my nightmare. You don't care about my nightmare.

He turned from watching the river and came towards her. She yelled at him again: Don't touch me, you brute. You alligator. All you men are the same. Shave off those dirty whiskers. Go off and look for Gabriel Rock and the mad girl too. They're as good as we are, aren't they? They can do anything we can do.

Ridiculous in shorty pyjamas she hopped to the door. She shouted, sobbing: If I have a son how do I know what he'll turn out like? Gabriel Rock or Stephen Mortell?

She was gone, bouncing and sobbing down the stairs, to hide

somewhere in the lower part of the house; and he felt for a moment like following her not to console her but to beat her. He switched on the light. Considerately he hadn't switched it on earlier so as not to awaken her. His eyes blurred, then moistened with a fury that made him feel weak. Then he laughed, deliberately and without mirth. He had never felt like that before. A good trouncing with a cane would beat the notions out of her satiny hide. He was ashamed of the picture he saw and went on laughing so as to wipe away the picture, and the shame. But he didn't follow her either to trounce or console her. He didn't, for the moment, trust himself. He dressed again slowly. He wondered had he himself, had she, the bouncing girl, really wanted to be spied upon. She liked it so much, and he gloried in the easy, smooth, oiled push-and-pull of the piston and in the effects it could produce. He surveyed, as if it were a sun in a foggy sky, the enormity of his own complacence, for he knew that tomorrow their world would roll on as merrily as ever. Tomorrow? Tonight? He bore no grudge against Gabriel Rock for the momentary discomfiture. All along he had known that Gabriel like himself was equipped and crusted with the general issue – a general issue that gave rise to the saying that small jockeys had long whips and made nonsense of the stories of the physical superiority of some white and of all black men – and was madly curious about the use to which it could be put. His wife had never realised that daft Nora could be cleft like herself for the service and purposes of joy. His wife, bless the bouncing beauty, thought she had a monopoly. That was odd for a girl who had been a nurse.

By one bright dance Gabriel had united Cosmona, at least had made them all for one moment look in the same direction. Small wonder that the same dance, danced over and over again and always more or less to the same tune, could unite the world.

He went out of his house to recommence his search for Gabriel Rock. He had intended but didn't remember to slam the door.

§

When it was all over Dympna told Teresa that for a married man, the stout fellow with the big muscles that could sing opera, didn't know much, for he kept shooting below the bull's eye and trying to thumb it in too low down, and with the gruntings, jump-ings and rollings of him there wasn't a blessed breath left in her body. But Teresa said money was money, and it wasn't often in hungry Cosmona a girl got the chance or the half-chance of mak-ing an easy coin, and about Mickey Rooney she had no com-plaints, Mickey Rooney knew his way home, Mickey Rooney was as slick as a fiddler, and she had liked Mickey Rooney from the first moment she saw him and would have gone with him for nothing, but a pound was a pound and a pound's worth better than nothing, and anyway he had offered, she hadn't asked. Dympna knew but didn't say that Teresa was out with Enda because Enda had been just too cute taking advantage of Amantha when they had her laid low, and might have left the job to Owen or Ignatius who had no regular attachments; and Enda, and rub it into him, wasn't the big boss any more if he could be felled by one blow from a wandering nigger.

There was no peace but hell upon earth at the Cawley place that night for Sister Thermometer had sent messengers looking for them, and the mother was in a panic that the police would be in after Teresa, with her record, and the father in a rage and say-ing that Teresa was no person to have in any civilised house.Teresa afterwards said to Dympna that God saw the Cawleys were the ones to talk about civilisation, and Dympna hadn't the heart to argue with her. Then Teresa's granny, who wasn't so dumb and doting after all, had been over to blame the Cawley boys for stealing money out of her house and Teresa, cute enough, mollified old Cawley by telling her granny the Cawleys never laid a finger on what didn't belong to them and that, if any stealing had been done, the black brute who had caused all the trouble had done it.

After that, life was quieter for a bit but, when they heard that Amantha was being brought over from the hospital to rest and recover, Teresa and Dympna took off. The Lord Jesus only could guess what she might say, and Sister Thermometer might come with her. There was nothing for it but Dublin and this time don't come back. So they put on tight blue jeans belonging to Enda and Owen. That was to save their own clothes as long as possible.

They packed all they had in one suitcase and sneaked out the back of the house and away. They hid the suitcase in an old hayshed on the Dublin road where they could sleep in hiding until morning when the bus would come or a passing car, and then went by back lanes to have a last look at Cosmona.

Teresa said that only for that black bastard, as mad or worse than the priest, and it was Amantha anyway had stolen the money from him so why should they suffer, they could have had a fine time in comfort that morning in the cellar bar of Tarrant's Hotel. Even if Lord Muck was still there or able to stand he'd be too far gone to recognise them, and wouldn't have a chance at all because they were all different and all style in tight blue jeans with zipper forks on them like men's trousers, but the zippers didn't show as badly as buttons and at least stayed closed unless you wanted to open them. Dympna knew but didn't say that Teresa was mad all out to see Mickey Rooney again with his smart slang and shiny shoes and wavy hair, but Dympna went where Teresa went and, as she had seen that morning, there would be other men in the bar. There were indeed. There was Lord Muck and Charles Roe talking each other down, and a nice quiet man with a moustache and a pipe, and a thick butt of a man screeching opera songs at the top of his voice, and a bird flying round and round and crazy to get out and small blame to it, and Mickey Rooney as large as life with an apron on him behind the bar and smoking a cigar and pulling the porter and pouring the whiskey, and King Kong Hoban, well-drunk, holding the back rung of a chair between his teeth and his yellowfaced tinker wife doing a stepdance on the seat of the chair. The noise could be heard in Dublin. They were as glad as anything that sourfaced Mrs. Hanafin wasn't behind the bar for she never had the good word or welcome for them, not that she could look down on anyone with a husband that deserted her and went to jail for robbery on a giant scale.

Lord Muck bought the drinks and bought them twice over and welcomed to the bar the fair young ladies of Cosmona and had no notion in the world that he had ever laid eyes on them before. But he was a perfect gentleman, as Teresa said to Dympna, and generous, and not like that Charles Roe who had never been known to buy a drink for man or beast and had that

misfortunate Miss Grace half-starved as a cut-price housekeeper
up there in his dreary barracks of a house. He could talk all right,
wind was cheap but wine cost money, and Lord Muck with his
open hand and hearty way shamed him out of the bar. Off he went
like shit off a shovel, saying he was bringing a bottle to the dead-
house, but Dympna said when he was gone that it was a big day
and a big deal and Christ would rise again when Charles Roe, the
meanest man in town, bought a bottle for anyone. He was so
mean, she said, that Jesus Christ wouldn't be in heaven unless
Charles Roe was in hell. Teresa said to the whole bar that he was
well known to be a pansy and would take to his heels if he saw a
skirt, even one that was never lifted except in fun, flapping on a
clothesline. The stout butt of a man whose name was Bob
Gunning, Mickey Rooney's name was Ned Broe and a lovely
name Teresa thought, crowed like a cock and pinched Dympna's
blue bottom so that she jumped, and said that hard as he stared he
couldn't see a skirt in the room. Dympna would have preferred
the quiet man with the pipe to pinch her, he had a lovely yellow
waistcoat, but you couldn't, as she well knew, have everything,
and all the quiet man did was to smoke and laugh and buy another
round of drinks.

Teresa and Mickey Rooney had their heads together across
the counter, and Mickey was whispering to her and blowing cigar
smoke down her front. Then he kissed her a long sticky kiss, and
boy had he style, and Fat Bob Gunning crowed again and flapped
his arms like wings, and Hoban's wife jumped back to the floor,
as light on her feet as if she was seventeen. Bob Gunning, buying
booze for the Hobans, said to the Hoban woman that that man
ought to be a powerful man in the bed, and cool as brass the tinker woman answered back that times she felt like it and times she
didn't, and to Dympna she said, dear, always tell them it's great
because it's bad for them if you don't. King Kong Hoban didn't
look too pleased.

So Teresa, to move quickly before the Hanafin woman came
back and routed her and Dympna and the Hobans, steered dreary
Dympna to the ladies and put the proposition to her, and said that
if Gabriel and Nora could do it for show surely to God they could
do it for kicks and money. These gentlemen of the press were

well-dressed and would be clean as a whistle and not like the farmer that came back from the Isle of Man with the dose, and the old doctor who was there before the young doctor said to him: Sir, you put your prick where I wouldn't put my walking stick. Dympna said that only niggers and sailors had doses. A bit of a roll anyway would be no novelty to Dympna because she time and oft gave it away not because she was that fond of it but because she was soft-hearted and knew the boys needed it.

The funniest thing that happened that night was when Teresa and Ned after the first round came laughing from behind a haystack in a meadow near Mortell's mill and there were Dympna and Fat Bob hard at it, and Dympna's jeans hanging around one ankle and her heels, to raise her, hooked on the back bumper of the car that was parked in a quiet laneway, and wait, says Mickey Rooney, till you see his face when I tap him on the shoulder and say excuse me sir have you got a match and how's the holy family, the old hairy Henry Halls. That was a howl, and even Dympna had to laugh although she told Teresa afterwards that the fat man was so rough he bled her.

Ned wanted to sneak them into the hotel and that would have been real living, but Teresa was afraid of that Hanafin one, as like as not she'd call the guards and Sister Thermometer too. So there was nothing for it but the hayshed, but fun is fun any old where and, as Dympna said, you're only young once. They swapped mounts once in the night, not that Teresa much wanted to, but fair is fair and Dympna was her friend, and Dympna, to judge by the threshing noises, was working hard for her money in her corner of the hay. But Teresa was just as well pleased when Fat Bob was too drunk and played out to manage, and fell asleep snoring like a hog. Ned lay between the two of them with a hand on each and in the dawn saluted the two of them in style. He was a wonder and what he lacked in size he made up in speed. Speedy Gonzales he said was his middle name. Not one pound but a fiver did he give them, and helped them to tidy up and pick the hay off their clothes and out of their hair, and for fun left Bob snoring in the shed, and drove them five miles away for safety to a place where they could thumb a lift in peace, and kissed them both a fond farewell, and said he would see them in Dublin's fair city where the girls are so pretty. There was no one for sport, said Teresa, like the gentlemen of the press.

§

Except for Lord Laurence the cellar bar was empty. He thought to himself that even the bird had flown and that Art Finlan, who was building up a collection of photos of birds and beasts, had followed the bird, though that wouldn't do Art any good since the bird was high and flying to end its homeward journey and since night was over the land; and Ned and Bob had flown with the two fair birds of Cosmona. He leaned on the bar counter and regretted his age and recalled the glory of having learned his trade under C. P. Scott of the *Manchester Guardian*.

He sang loudly although there was no one to admire his voice: I feel like one who treads alone some banquet hall deserted, whose lights are fled, whose garlands shed, and all but he departed.

He reflected that Thomas Moore, the smug little man who had written that song, had visited the much-bestrode Princess Borghese, otherwise Pauline Bonaparte who, dirty tongues had said, might even have taken a tumble with her own brother, and who had shown to the songwriter her beautiful hands which he had then the honour of kissing twice, and had allowed him to feel her tiny foot, one of two in her possession, which he considered to be matchless. That was the world for a gentleman to live in. Feeling a foot would not, he felt, do much for Ned or Bob but then neither of them would ever have found themselves in the presence of a princess who had posed in her pelt for Canova. The gentlemen and C. P. Scott had long ridden by and there were people now who could never enter a noble house except through the pantry window.

He sang again: Some banquet hall deserted.

Then he made a discovery. He was not absolutely alone. His companion like himself was drunk. His companion was in fact a bumblebee gone stocious sipping at tiny pools of beer and spirits left behind by the wastage of a good day. Now it steered a wavery crawling course between one pool and the next, moving on from oasis to oasis across a desert of stained brown wood. Lord

Laurence sang that where the bee sucked there sucked he, and flicked with his finger and watched the boozed bumble, too far gone to spread its wings and fly after the bird, fall on the floor close to the door through which the demure little woman made her exits and her entrances. Then he made another discovery. The door like the door in a haunted house was opening on its own, slowly and with the proper creaks. No, not exactly on its own for further study revealed a human figure, a man, entering, creeping on hands and knees, reaching up and around the corner to grasp a bottle of brandy, then shuffling backwards in retreat.

— Do you mind, Lord Laurence, while you are there, so to speak, pouring me a glass of whiskey. My hand is a trifle unsteady.

The man straightened up but stayed kneeling to the image, to the bottle. He said: Mine's no steadier. So pour you own. This is Liberty Hall.

He had a husky gravelly voice. Lord Laurence blinked, and refocused. He said: Haven't we met somewhere?

— In Monte Carlo, the man said, the year we broke the bank.

Then he was gone, leaving the door swinging open. It was the oddest way, Laurence decided, for a barman to behave. The bee, too, had vanished quite away. Try as he would he couldn't see anywhere on the floor its coloured drunken body. Had the bumblebee stung the barman? Had the barman crushed the bumblebee? It was a grave question. There was no easy obvious immediate answer. He could ask the woman when she returned, if she ever did return that is, or if he remembered to ask her when she did return. He could ask Peejay. But where was Peejay? Where indeed was everybody? He had, however, the story he had been sent out to get in his notes and Ned, not a bad young fellow when he was under expert direction, had the pictures of the bed of death and of Old Chief Whitewhiskers himself in all his glory.

The day's work thus nobly ended, Lord Laurence needed only a bed on which to rest his weary head. Seeing no bed in the bar he, for the time being, dozed gently in one of the alcoves.

§

Mr. Lane was in the playroom for the night. The blue dim light usually left burning in his corner of the balcony, so that he could read if he felt like it, had been switched off by Nurse Walters because Big Durcan from Mayo said that now that Holy Joe was gone to Treasure Island to dig for hidden gold he, Big Durcan, didn't have to read, and the light got in his eyes when he was trying to sleep and, moreover, he could in the dark make a better grab at Nurse Walters when she walked around every hour to see that everybody was sleeping and comfortable. Nurse Walters laughed at Big Durcan. She liked him. She liked everybody, Paddy Loftus noticed. She liked Paddy Loftus and left the blue light burning at his corner of the balcony so that, emulating Mr. Lane, he could read and read and listen for the melodeon playing and the voices talking and singing from somewhere out there in the darkness. He heard no melodeon, no voices. It was lonely without them. He read and read. Over by Mr. Lane's corner, bare and lonely too because Mr. Lane and his pink screen and revolving bookcase were gone, Big Durcan and his cronies tired of whispering dirty stories and fell asleep. Everybody seemed to sleep except Paddy Loftus, his fifteen-year-old incurable tubercular spine bent like a bow on a high curved frame, head thrown back, reading and reading and the print almost upside down, about the man who had the crimson circle round his neck and kept a guillotine in the basement of his house to chop off the heads of hosts of enemies. Then a shadow came between Paddy Loftus and the blue light and the lights dimly burning in the ward behind. It could be Nurse Walters. Or the night matron. Or the ghost of old Nurse Callaghan except that if ghosts could walk through walls they'd be too thin to possess shadows. When he twisted his head around and looked he saw a man. He wasn't in the least alarmed. On a night of no melodeons any company was welcome. He said: Are you the mystery man?

The man said no, he was only a newspaper photographer chasing a ghost.

— Can you photograph a ghost, mister?

— It has been done, friend. Everything has been done.

— But this is only old Nurse Callaghan. They say she wouldn't be much to look at.

— She might be better-looking as a ghost than she was as a woman.

They joined together in thinking that that was funny.

— Who saw the ghost?

— Nurse Walters, mister. She's on night duty. There'll be hell to pay if she finds you here.

At which the soft rippling Munster voice behind them said there would most certainly be hell to pay, and Paddy Loftus time for you to be asleep, and who are you sir and what, may I ask, are you doing here?

Riding to the rescue of his new-found friend, Paddy Loftus told Nurse Walters there was no melodeon music tonight. He said: You'd miss it. It's lonely without it.

— The musician, she said, had an accident today.

She was lost in wonder to think that music played by such scruff as Enda Cawley could help a doomed boy in his endless illness. Art Finlan said: Do you read much, friend?

— Not as much as Mr. Lane, the boy said. Mr. Lane reads all the time.

— To come back, she said, to where we were. Who are you and what are you doing here?

So Art, thumbing the fuel into his pipe and sitting against all regulations, on the edge of the boy's bed, but looking so kindly that no soft gentle girl who didn't anyway put much heed in regulations could resent him, said who he was and that he was merely wandering about in the vague hope that he would, like herself, be privileged to meet a ghost, a chance that didn't so often come the way even of a newspaper man. He had hoped that he might perhaps see also the mystery man.

— Today you saw him, she said. The poor lad came out into the open. With a bang, too. He's no mystery any more.

— No mystery, no ghost, no nothing, he said.

— Nothing, she said. I don't know now if I ever saw anything. I thought I did and I said it and then they persuaded me I did myself. I mentioned it and they persuaded me that I did. But there's a cup of tea in the kitchen behind the ward if you tell the night matron that you're an uncle of Paddy Loftus and turned up late from Dublin City to see him. By the smell of your breath a cup of tea would do you no harm. If we meet Nurse Callaghan's ghost, I'll ask her to pose for her picture.

Then Art Finlan and the night matron, Nurse Walters and three other nurses had tea in the kitchen behind the ward. When the night matron heard that the uncle of Paddy Loftus was a newspaper man she told him in greater detail than usual the story of her life in Guy's Hospital. When he listened with polite intelligent attention she went on to tell him everything about old Nurse Callaghan and old Nurse Callaghan's ghost. He took all their pictures and promised to send them glossy prints. Somebody had to work round here if Bob and Ned were in the ditches with the village whores. He left a pound note with Nurse Walters to buy books or anything else he might need for Paddy Loftus who would never, Nurse Walters told him, separate himself in this life from that bow-bended frame to walk by moonlight after melodeon music.

Art Finlan walked back hastily, repentantly to find Lord Laurence. He shouldn't have left him alone drunk as he was. All newsmen must have a certain responsibility to a man who had learned his trade under C. P. Scott. That poor bent boy would die, and lie flat and straight in comfort only in death. Art had a son of his own and felt ill at the thought that he might ever be bent and helpless and, still young, resigned to death. It was a pity that the black man had broken the musician's jaw and deprived the bent boy, even for one night of his brief life, of the company of the melodeon. But then you couldn't blame the black man. It was rumoured that he wouldn't have been there to break the musician's jaw if he hadn't earlier on been clipped by the Dublin girl. This life was a game of consequences sometimes, and sometimes a game of comic senseless contradictions, and sometimes the two mixed up together and a lot more besides.

It was comic, whatever, that before he, Art Finlan, had got as far as the boy's bedside he had peeped, playing the mystery man, through a glass wall with some painting on it and seen that sweet little nurse bending down over a bed to kiss a patient. The patient's right arm was most undeniably hoisting a blue uniform skirt from a delectable pair of thighs. Above black stockings they showed delightfully clean and white. What a delicate lovely picture that would have made to crown the day's affairs, but from where he had stood at the time it would have been technically impossible to take it, morally impossible, too, alas, for Art Finlan was the soul of decency.

But by C. P. Scott Little Ned Broe would have gloated over that picture. What a caption: Girl who saw ghost finds man's hand – up her skirt.

Some day in Dublin he would torment Ned by telling him what he had seen when he went searching for the Holy Ghost. Was it possible that a dainty young girl with such lovely thighs could have been chosen to see, or ever been persuaded that she had seen, the uneasy spirit of a dry aged dead woman? He would ask Lord Laurence when, if ever, Lord Laurence was sober.

§

The night matron went as she always did after supper to sleep in Sister Francesca's office, having first made sure that the green and biting parrot, Andy, was safely in his cage and shrouded under cloth. Then the Mouse went back to Peter Lane on Treasure Island. He was reading. He was in fact reading what the Swiss eremite, Saint Nicholas of Flue, had to say about the sacrament of penance: And when your conscience is stained by sin ask God for repentance and endeavour without delay to purify yourselves by confession and mortification.

But far away from Saint Nicholas of Flue and mortification was the black silken cloth that under the bedclothes Peter Lane with his free hand was fondling. Now and again he raised it to his face and knowing that nobody, barring Jim Hawkins or Long John Silver could see him, kissed and sniffed and knew the taste and odour of love. Love tasted like artificial silk. Love smelled, he was glad to find, like some pleasant perfume. She leaned down over him and they kissed and she said: Some people. The cheek. If it wouldn't inconvenience the reverend gentleman could I have my panties back?

How could he tell her that sniffing and tasting he had thought, from poetry and hymns, about virgin mantles and virgin snoods unbound.

— If that photographer had only known, she said.

She told him about the photographer.

How could she tell him that all through supper she had been half-amused, half-afraid to think what the night matron would say if she knew that one of her nurses sat there pantless as the prostitutes that, she had heard, plied in Nassau Street, Dublin, or in Soho, London?

— You mustn't, she had said to him when the tickling game began earlier that night, put a hand or a finger inside these panties.

But what was a girl supposed to do with his hand rubbing and his fingers feeling and the world asleep, and all the quiet of night and the colours of the painted glass around her? All through supper she had kept her legs tightly crossed although the night matron who was a lady of the old school didn't approve of any lady crossing her legs in the presence of a gentleman, and that kind photographer with the fancy waistcoat must for certain be a gentleman. She had risked reproof because she could still feel his fingers, and after supper dried and dusted herself and went back with no fear to what she knew was going to happen. If Gabriel and Nora could play games in full view of the world was it over-much to demand that a girl might make love to the man she loved in the privacy of Treasure Island or, safer and more private still, in the cool quietness of the bathrooms where nobody but herself had any business to be at that hour of the night?

Two things he had read a man knelt for: to pray and to make love. He had thought at the time that that was a quare combination, yet here he was on his knees on the hard floor, and what he was at wasn't saying his prayers. Her thighs were open and the world before him, her buttocks propped against the rim of the lavatory bowl. It wasn't a couch for a princess and the hard floor was crucifixion to the kneecaps of the prince, yet he knew with wild pride that he had come out of the shadows into the light of knowledge, he had leaped the balcony railings and discovered the heart of the mystery. He had arisen. By God he had arisen. Tony Lumpkin was never more his own man than at this timeless moment. He ran first in a race. He rode the first horse on the Curragh of Kildare. He wrote a book. He won a battle.

On that Sunday by the sea, Buckteeth the Goat had said to him simply, and reached sideways as he spoke to grab at his fly:

Tell me, young fellow, did you ever have it out of sight? Did you ever get the ticket in that town you came from?

Now he carried it before him like the brave American boy in blue who rescued the flag, when it was in peril from the boys in grey, and brought it back to his captain, and died, and asked the world forever to just break the news to mother.

A soft button resisted him, then yielded before him as if its centre had melted and the circumference admitted him grudgingly, then gripped him. He drove, shrieking before him, three witches of women down into the shadows of the dark odorous bushes around the wooden lime-stinking jakes. She leaned back moaning against the tiled wall. He butted like a battering ram, hopping for comfort and better purchase from one knee to the other. Then his knees were off the ground and so were her feet and they were holding each other like wrestlers until they rolled sideways to the floor and trying to protect her, always the gentleman, he caught his head a most unmerciful thump against the wall, and found to his dazed fury that she was giggling even if there were tears on her face, and that he, ankles fettered in pyjamas, was splattering himself, as if he would never stop, all over the floor. She was in giggling hysterics. She said: We couldn't stay in the saddle. Oh, Peter darling, you look a scream.

She was pulling on her pants. In dumbstruck rage he mopped the floor with toilet paper. The great moment was all over. It was one of those dreams in which he tried and tried at some faceless nameless woman and woke up hideously alone and with wet pyjamas.

But when he stood up and flushed the paper down the toilet with a soft inland murmur she pushed him against the wall and kissed him over and over again and said: Peter love, that was lovely. We must do it every night.

He asked her had he hurt her. For his own sake he wanted to know. He had hurt himself and not only on the side of his head.

— No, darling.

— Was I in at all?

— I think so, darling. I feel you were. Something happened. I felt something that never happened before. Something lovely. I tingled all over.

The kissing, he felt, would have to stop. In the confessional the priest was supposed to ask the penitent had he caused pollution. That was a rare bloody way to put it. He said: Will you have a baby?

She told him, still kissing him, that it wasn't the dangerous time of the month. But then you never could tell. She hadn't any experience. Father Jarlath's little book of medical ethics didn't actually tell nurses how to do it and not have babies. She had heard of an army sergeant who got married on the strength of a book about rhythm, with an introduction by two Jesuits, and boasted that it was safe and no sin now, the pope said, not to have a baby every time you did it, and how the whole army came to know him as Sergeant Rhythm because as regularly as nine months came round his wife had a baby, and once had triplets, so that some soldiers even called him, behind his back, Sergeant Syncopation.

— But, she said, I love you, Peter. Never before did I do that with anybody. I'd love to have your baby.

His blood ran cold. She said: Say you love me, Peter.

He said he loved her. On Treasure Island she tucked him in and kissed and kissed until he thought he was going to suffocate. Then, when they rested for a while, he warned her against the bad men she might in the future meet in the world. She danced away from him as she had danced the other night in moonlight on the Tower. She twirled, holding out her skirt with one hand. She was Amelita Galli-Curci trilling up in the clouds: Tra-la-la-la-la-la. A gipsy coming through a meadow spied a bird upon a tree.

She said from the doorway: I'll have you, Peter love. Big Peter with the strength of ten to beat away the bad men.

Then she was gone.

He made an effort to banish the idea of babies, particularly when they came three at a time. What fearful consequences could follow a few minutes spent wrestling in a tiled toilet. It was safer by far to go it alone. But surely to God nothing could happen in this case. The floor had got the benefit of the full cargo. Or had it? One pellet, he had heard, no bigger than the head of a pin could bore through stone walls and make its contacts and grow up to be a baby. He had also heard of girls who had had babies by the simple love-touch, by long-range gun so to speak, a weird thing when you consider it religiously.

Think of something else, he thought. But the only thought that would come into his aching head was a recollection of his master of novices telling himself and his brothers in Christ a story about a boy of a princely family who was preparing to enter the Jesuits. Boys of princely families were always turning their backs on the world and entering the Jesuits. This boy's people threw him a big party in the week before he was to abandon the world. At that party he sinned with a woman, went to bed, whether with or without the woman the master of novices didn't say, and woke up dead and in eternal torment. That was a bloody sight worse than triplets. And here he was alone in the night on Treasure Island. Yet the Lord, as his mother used to say, had everything mixed with mercy, for who at that moment should walk into Treasure Island but the night matron who did sometimes waken up and take a notion to do the rounds. She liked to talk with Mr. Lane more than with anybody else about her days in Guy's Hospital. While she talked he, shaking with relief, thought that if that night he had got all the way to where he had been trying to go, they might still have been at it to be caught redhanded or whatever you might call it. The horrifying thought put both triplets and condign hellfire out of his mind.

When she had gone he dozed gratefully. Later, reawakening, he was to find that imagination and undercover muscles were reawakening with him. Feeling himself gently but saving himself he resolved that on the next night things would be managed better. Because of the way that he had twisted himself in action, and because those trousers that he wasn't used to wearing had that day almost cut the crotch of him, he could first of all persuade her to rub him down with some soothing cream. Then he would have her flat on the floor, hard as it was. They could take a few pillows, though, from empty beds. Her heels would be fixed on the ground, her legs wide but only a little arched, and rigid in the preliminary stages, later slackening, her knees rising as he burst in and in until she rocked under him like a cradle and whimpered for painful joy. Then he would feel downwards with his left hand to make sure he was as far in as any man could possibly go.

§

Christy had stolen the bottle of brandy while Cathy was in the bathroom. He had no intention of getting drunk, he told himself. If he had wanted to get drunk he would have stolen a bottle of whiskey, or rum, or even gin. He merely wanted to keep up his spirits for the night ahead and for what he intended to do, and brandy was the only man for keeping up the spirits. Brandy was delicate. Brandy was reviving. Brandy was good for the imagination. Brandy, the man said, was for heroes.

With the bottle safely tucked under his left oxter he tiptoed along the stony basement corridor and out to the grassy yard at the back of the hotel. Not all the prying eyes of Cosmona could find him there in the deepening shadows. From a previous existence when he used to visit the place with Cathy, away long before the earthquake had opened the crack in the smooth carpeted floor of the foyer of the cinema, he recalled a deserted wooden hut, a refuge for abandoned furniture, where not Cathy herself could ever find him, if she cared to look, or if she wasn't on her knees already thanking her Redeemer that Christy the Whisperer had gone again just as he had come. But, by God, she wasn't rid of him as easily as all that for after a day's deep thought he now knew that he had come back for a purpose that might have been in his head for months. Before a man ever knew what he really meant to do he needed food and, more important than food, a shave, a bath, clean clothes. He knew now what he really meant to do.

Satisfied with his own reasoning, he had opened the door of the hut before he realised that he should have noticed that there was a light in one tiny window. That was a change and strange enough, and could have been embarrassing, for God only knew who might be there, and he could have closed the door and cut and run into the dark with his stolen brandy if the sight of wonder that met his eyes hadn't held him there paralysed. No doubt about it, this wooden box was no longer a lumber room for distressed chairs and three-legged tables. This was a Dutch interior done with infinite thought by Salvador Dali. For who but some crazy Spanish painter could group together in a room as bare as

an anchorite's cell, a gaudy picture of what might be Jesus talking to the weeping women; and a spaceman or a hell's angel, but
a pathetic pimply-chinned hell's angel, in a leather jacket, helmet
and goggles, and sitting as still as a stone with a hand on each
knee; and at his feet a giant white cock stretched stiff and dead, a
splash of blood on its snowy neck. That angel he had seen before,
once mounted on a bicycle and careering through the village,
once high on a tower and mounted, according to Cathy, on the
village's female imbecile. But she hadn't told him this noted per-
former was on the premises. Or did she know?

— Kind sir, he said, may I walk into your parlour?

The angel, not turning to look at him, not moving his hands
from his knees, sitting as still as a statue, said: This isn't my parlour, I'm only sitting here.

— I see you sitting. You seem to have the only chair.

— The woman said I had liberty to sit here. I'm doing no
harm. It's Mr. Tarrant's chair. It's not yours.

— Be at your ease, my man. I can drink standing.

— You're all after me, Gabriel said. The priest and the
Cawleys and the whole place and the fellows in the bar. I only
wanted to break the record to Crooked Bridge.

— Be of good heart. I'm not after you. Have no fear. Have a
drink.

— I only drink wine.

— But this is wine. Fortified. Watch how smoothly it flows
down.

He demonstrated, then coughed a little, wiped his lips and
the neck of the bottle, held the bottle to the lips of Gabriel who
sipped and sputtered and pushed it away and said it was whiskey.

— Stupidity, said Christy, could not do better than that.

He was sudden angry with the statue in the chair. He had, he
told himself, merely been trying to be kind. Why, at any rate,
should the statue sit and he, Christy Hanafin, stand, who once had
ushers and usherettes, torches in hand, standing at attention
before him? He said: You're going to have grilled white cock for
supper.

— I didn't kill it.

— It would go fine with brandy, the best Martell.

— It's not mine. It was dead when I came in. The woman said I could sit here. They can't blame me for that. All I wanted to do was to cycle to Crooked Bridge.

— Of course they'll blame you. They blamed me. They have to have somebody to blame and you're the likeliest victim. You, and the black man. They have him in the black hole. He found his woman, one, two, three. And so did you. And you killed a fine cock.

— I didn't kill it. All I wanted was to break the record.

— You've broken it, too. You got up higher than anyone ever did. You showed them all. They'll hate you for it. They'll get you in the black hole with the black man, one, two, three.

There was no reason, except the way he felt, why he should have to be cruel to this creature; and he felt that way most of the time, pitying himself, pitying himself, until self-pity was a sour hatred for everything living. He said: You always wanted to get to Crooked Bridge as fast as a bird. But in the black hole you won't be going anywhere.

Brandy made the mind bright. Brandy washed away the bitterness. Brandy made the words flow like the Rhine. These could be another man's memories. This could be another man speaking. The plump weeping women bobbed and curtsied comically before a flamboyant crimson and white Jesus. The slain cock wore the same crazy colours. The room rocked a little, then spun slowly, pleasantly, bringing with it, in its easy round, the helmeted, hooded, goggled, pimply cyclist, the gaudy painted group; and setting the cock circling so that at any moment the wings might move, the head and neck rise up to crow.

— In the black hole, my fine fellow, they'll take everything from you, helmet, goggles, jacket, bicycle, the works. If you have a watch they'll take it from you.

— I haven't got a watch. Mr. Mortell said he would time me with a stopwatch.

— Then they'll take Mortell's stopwatch from you. They'll wind it every day but they won't let you see it. Time will pass but you won't believe it. They'll take everything from you. They'll take the sky from you. You'll have to stand on a table to look out through the bars in the window and you'll never see the sky.

When you sleep at night, if you do sleep, the weight of those bars will lie like a ton on top of you. If you do sleep, it will be a nightmare, not a joy, to dream about your bicycle and the road to Crooked Bridge. They'll take everything from you. They'll take your handkerchief, if you ever had one. They'll force you to strip naked and to spread your legs and touch your toes and they'll shine a flashlamp up your arsehole.

Some other victim, not himself, because the brandy now protected him, was bending down for that inspection. Through the arch of his legs the victim could see the red face of the warder, one eye closed, the other squinting, peering into intestinal darkness. Looking for gold the victim thought, and prayed to God for the power to muster a fart that would blind the warder and, alas, had his prayer blessedly answered. Alas, because afterwards in his cell he paid for his brief pleasure in the shape of a kidney-beating skilfully and quietly administered, outside the call of duty, by the offended warder and a colleague. To teach him manners, they said; and he was in no position to argue etiquette with them, and could only think, as the soft sickening blows fell like clockwork, that if it was bad manners to fart in a man's face it was worse manners to shine a light up his back passage.

He sipped more brandy to make certain that another man and not Christy Hanafin was remembering that gay time. He said: Grilled cock, Sir Malcolm Campbell, you mean to eat tonight.

— I didn't kill the cock. The Cawleys cut the head of a duck.

— But take it from me you won't dine so lavishly in the deep black hole. They give you plenty time to eat, though. That can be said for them. They don't make you bolt your food and ruin your digestion. Quite the contrary, Sir Malcolm. They give you an hour and a half to eat what you could eat at your ease in five minutes. A pint of porridge in a tin. Do you want to look at the day's menu, Sir Malcolm? Four ounces of bread. Nine-sixteenths of an ounce of butter. How in Jesus' name do they ever manage to measure it? A half pint of pissy tea. Three-fourths of a pint of milk. Very thin meat broth in which they put one pound of potatoes. Four ounces of meat. The same of vegetables. I'd give you brandy to wash it down only it seems that brandy would be wasted on the likes of you.

To his added annoyance the figure in the chair didn't even look towards him when he held up the bottle and shook it until the drink bubbled.

— They'll take everything from you, he said. If you have a mirror, and a handsome fellow like you, Sir Malcolm, would need a mirror, then they'll take the mirror from you. At breakfast time once in a while they'll give you a shaving kit. A wire brush would suffice for your cathairs and pimples. They'll loan you, under supervision, a broken fragment of looking glass. Then they'll not allow you to possess or see a mirror until the next shaving day comes around. It is an offence to have in your cell even the tiniest fragment of glass. Afraid you'd cut your throat or the veins of your wrist. So they won't even let you enjoy the company of your own reflection. They can't stop you, though, from masturbating. They can't stop you from dreaming. But they won't allow you, apart from that, to pick your own job. Your job, such as it will be, will be chosen for you. So that when they open the gate and let you out of prison you'll be afraid to walk, let alone cycle. And when you do get out, if you ever do, they'll give you your fare home and sixteen shillings to face the world, and search you again, back door and all, in case you'd be carrying anything away with you. That time you won't fart in their faces. Because the most fearful thing about what they'll do to you is that by that time you'll be grateful to them for all their kindness. You'll think, for instance, that the governor is God. He is God to the prisoners. Until you've been in prison you don't really believe in God. But there he is. The governor. To be seen once in a blue moon. God's the governor. You'll sing hymns to him in the prison chapel. You should hear the way the poor bastards strain their tonsils singing: Jesus Lord I ask for mercy, let me not implore in vain, all my sins I now detest them, never will I sin again.

— Peejay, said Gabriel, knows that hymn.

— And all the time they're singing to the governor. He's the only lord they know that might give them mercy. Prisoners can be so overwhelmed with gratitude that a man in the condemned cell once told a warder that he felt exactly the way he felt, thirty years before, when he made his first communion. A nice holy feeling, he said, not exactly understanding what lay ahead. Swallow a

wafer one day. Hang by the neck another day. It all comes to the
same thing. That's life for you, Sir Malcolm. And all the time
you're in prison, Sir Malcolm, you'll be afraid you'll die there.
That a warder will simply notice you stiff and stark, and say that
there's one off and stroke your number out of his notebook. You
could die there and nobody would give a damn. You could be
killed by another prisoner. They're a bad crowd. There was a fellow in the States, in like yourself for carnal knowledge, in Skagit
County, Oregon, was knifed by another prisoner just a month
before he was due for release and he had been in for fifteen years.
Prisoners don't like the carnal knowledge boys. You'll get so
afraid of dying there that you'll try to escape, and the closer you'll
come to release the more the fear grows. There was a fifty-year-
old man with only a week to go who lost his nerve at the last, held
a knife to a warder's throat and made a run for it. They got him in
half an hour. It's too late to run, Sir Malcolm, when the walls have
closed around you. Run now. Better still, leap on your bike and
ride. Break all the bloody records. Be absent-without-leave forever. Ride and ride and ride until they forget all about you. The
wandering Jew. The flying Dutchman. The cyclist from Cosmona.

In hellish black fury he shook the creature's shoulder. He was
glad to feel that, all through his talking, the creature had truly
been listening, hadn't moved because it had been frozen with
fear. It was crying now. The pimply chin, at any rate, was wet,
and it said, sobbing: I didn't do anything. They can't put me in
prison.

— What makes you think you're privileged? They can put
anybody in prison, Sir Malcolm. I was a big man once and they
put me in prison.

There it was then: the evil secret was out. He had been talking all the time about himself and his own memories. Yet not
exactly about himself. It was not the Christy Hanafin he liked best
who would torment this imbecile into a state of terror. You looked
into a mirror and saw yourself, but not exactly yourself. You drew
on paper what you saw in the mirror, but not exactly what you saw.
There was a shadow behind you, and a shadow behind the shadow,
and a shadow behind that, and so back and back forever. That mad
philosopher had in a dream seen his hand on the table before him,

the skin made of glass, the bones, the tissues, the blood, the moving muscles all easy to be seen. That was life at a good moment. Then a slimy toad squatted on the hand and, overcome by desire, the madman gobbled it up, and all his life, after that dream, he was so afraid of defilement that he dressed with a crazy extravagant care and cleanliness, just as Christy Hanafin, haunted by spectres of ragged, hairy, unwashed, stinking Robinson Crusoes, washed and washed and washed until the day came when, just like that, his efforts ceased. It was no strain to give up the struggle. He didn't even taste the slime of the toad. In the long line of shadows one of them simply took the place of the other. All life was paper, dirty paper, blowing along unswept Dublin streets.

— Run, he said, run. Ride while you still have time. As for me, Sir Malcolm, I go to bed with my wife. She expects me to. She hates me. She loves me. She loves me not. She hates me not. Whether for hate or love all women expect somebody to. But who am I to talk to you who rose higher to do the deed than any man ever in the long history of Cosmona? Run. Ride. Fly.

The creature was out the door before him and away running across the dark yard. He called after him: Wait, wait, Sir Malcolm. You forgot your cock.

He put down the brandy carefully. He raised the heavy white body. It was beginning to stiffen. He swung it by the legs and tossed it as far as he could into the darkness.

§

She remembered the pain with which one day, in the company of old Mortell, she had watched a dozen or so laughing little girls playing ring o' ring o' rosy. Round and round they hopped, and sang ring o' ring o' rosy, a bottle a bottle o' posy, round we go and round we go and all fall down. They all fell down. They may not have been, but all seemed to be, ringleted and red-cheeked. They rose again, danced again and all fell down, and all, the game over, ran home to their mothers. In the last half-dying wasp, Christy cried, the summer turns to poison, and round and round the bedroom he chased the frantic, buzzing exhausted atom until with a swipe, a lucky one for he was drunk, he captured and crushed it between his two palms, and showed her the dead wasp and his palms without a sting on them. Not even a dying wasp could pierce his leather skin, and she thought that everywhere he went he brought death with him, but thought also, because she had begun kissing Beau Jolais, hero of the French Foreign Legion, no sad ghost but a living red-blooded fighter, that she knew a trick that would yet cheat Death & Christy, his messenger. The liar he was, the total pretender. In the room of the toys, in the presence of the three little girls just sitting and staring and not at all playing ring o' rosy, he had said let me, let me, Cathy, and tugged at her skirt and tried to kiss her to give the skirt-tugging, she knew, some semblance of decency. She didn't mind the tugging or the attempted kissing. She had her own needs. Even daft Nora on the Tower could have her fun, and was Cathy Hanafin who owned a husband to be left with nothing except Nosy Connell? She could hardly consider attempting Peejay and his white cock as women, she had heard the doctor say, might do with dogs in the kips of Cairo. But she had to draw Christy and his putrid endeavours away from those curious innocent eyes. So saying not here, not here, that this was not the place, she led him to a musty bedroom not her own, and heard him say truculently that she was a stubborn sullen woman who loved a ghost, and said in return, mocking him, that he had always had too many words for the job in hand, that he was words and words, as dear grandmother said, and in the end couldn't do anything. To justify himself he argued that there were men who were born misfits, that he had known even of a good Christian Brother, a valued teacher in a religious order, who led the good life, thin neck, wide dog-collar, wide-brimmed black hat, chastity, big boots and all, who all day long for years taught the alphabet and addition to snotty urchins, until one day it dawned on him that he shouldn't be doing that, and out he walked and never came back and became a barman in Liverpool.

— But he didn't, she said, as you did, fiddle the till.

— You always had the shopkeeper's mind. Your granny's granddaughter.

She said in the darkness, in the creaking musty bed: Someday the two of us will be dead. What will our hopeless mis-understanding matter then?

— Or even, he said, a hopeful understanding. All air.

— But couldn't we leave the air cleaner for those coming after?

— In this case there's nobody coming after. Dolls. Dreams.

— You're so sure, she said.

— Even if there was anybody coming after they'd manage on their own to foul the air. Or break their hearts trying to find somebody to do it for them. Every room turns stuffy if you live in it long enough.

— Words, she said, you're so sure.

Then after a long silence she said: The miller's son is dead. Christy, could you give me nothing better than misery to remember you by?

— If you hold I'll marry you. If you don't you're none the worse. That's what the lads say to the lasses in Scotland.

She slept and awoke again and satisfied for a while said: I feel the way the saints would feel after they'd been to confession. And when I was young, she said, old Mortell told me I'd be the ripe girl after I had my first baby. Poor Christy, you could never make me the ripe girl.

But, perilously on the edge of the bed, he was asleep, one hand trailing on the floor, snoring slightly, and Cosmona, the day's work well done, also slept, except that is, for the night nurses and some of the patients, and for the people, who stayed awake to keep death company in the wakehouse of the miller's son, except for Peejay and Larry, Art, Ned and Bob, who were not, properly speaking, part of the real heart of Cosmona. Although Bob, as far as we know, may have been asleep.

§

Lord Laurence was awake again but quiet and sipping, and quivering a little with a malady that, to the quiet amusement of all, he called bronchitis. Art Finlan in another alcove was quiet and smoking. Ned Broe, aproned again and behind the bar, poured himself a restorative drink then with elbows on counter, lectured Peejay, who sat crouched like a performing monkey on a high stool. Bob Gunning was nowhere to be seen.

— Repeat after me, Ned said, a Barney Dillon equals a shilling, a half dollar equals an Oxford scholar.

Peejay repeated nothing.

— A Rosy Lee, said Ned, means a cup of tea, a tealeaf equals a thief, a piece of toast means the Holy Ghost.

— That's blasphemy, Peejay said. He shall come like a thief in the night.

— Peejay, Ned said, with infinite patience, you'll never understand, you'll never make the grade as a newspaper man. This is the world-wide code, the Morse, the Esperanto, the over and out. Lord Beaverbrook knew it all by heart. Told me so himself. Check, Art.

— Check, said Art.

— If you don't get with this, man, you'll never be anything bigger than you are now: just the Cosmona & Crooked Bridge Sentinel.

— The Vindicator, Art said.

From some faraway place of dreams Laurence said: The Sentinel. Peejay stands at the gate of Cosmona like the angel with the flaming sword.

— A Scotch peg, said Ned, equals a wooden leg, a bottle of water is the same thing as a daughter, a Jimmy Riddle is a piddle, an early morn adds up to a horn and that is frequently the case, and elephant's trunk means that you're drunk as we all were this blessed day, the Johnny Ross is another name for the boss, and the wife is the struggle and strife.

Peejay agreed that that was God's gospel truth.

He spat suddenly but not towards Edward. He leaped off the stool. He said: That kissing is a filthy business. If it weren't for the ones in the films slobbering over each other, poor eejits like Gabriel wouldn't be going mad in holy places. Kissing is filthy.

— Oh, I never knew, said Ned, that you cared so much.

— Leave him be, said Art.

— There's no purity left in the world, Peejay said.

— Your townhalls, said Ned, if you have any. Who wants purity?

— Well I was aware all the time it wasn't holy leaflets she was sending to her cousin from Crooked Bridge. I opened two or three. But I went on posting them all the same because she paid me. Thirty pieces of silver.

— Gravel and grit, Ned said.

— There were more necks than one that should be wrung. Before the cock crows twice thou shalt deny me thrice.

— Not me, said Art.

— Peejay, said Ned, I will join you in prayer.

He reached for the pile of leaflets. He read: For her conversation hath no bitterness, nor her company any tediousness but joy and gladness.

He said: I was with her tonight. Several times.

— It's a dirty world, said Peejay.

— Uncle Ned, said Art, means bed.

He came out of his alcove. He said: Peejay, come back to your seven wits and show us where our rooms are.

Peejay, staggering somewhat, led them across the entryway. Behind him, arming Lord Laurence between them, stepped Ned and Art. Peejay showed them the stairway that went up from the dining-room.

— One of our planes is missing, Ned said. Poor Bob's in the hay with the beasts of the field.

— Pray to your guardian angels, Peejay said.

Then he staggered on alone to stumble and fall in the darkness of the grassy yard over the white body he had slain to redeem the sins of Cosmona.

— FIVE —

When the shadow of a man darkened the early morning sunshine in the doorway of the old mill, Mortell, without turning round to see who it was, said: Whoever you are, you should know better than to come to the mill on a fine sunny day.

He was dressed in a good black suit. The mill was silent. For want of anything better to occupy his hands and thus his mind, he was stitching with a packing needle at a torn sack. He said: A good day is a day for the land. A wet day's good enough for the mill. The wheel's stopped anyway. I've a death in the house.

But when Christy Hanafin from the doorway said that he was sorry for the miller's trouble, Mortell dropped sacking and packing needle and turned to face the sunlight. He said: In pain as he was, he was better to go.

— We'd all be better gone, Christy said.

Under his right arm he carried a cardboard box.

— That's a good brown suit, Christy. You're in finer fettle than you were twenty-four hours ago.

In the pure crisp morning air, his nose that, because of his dead wife's weakness, was abnormally sensitive to the odour of drink, could get the sharp tang of whiskey, and he knew that Christy, the sad pilgrim, was on his way again. He said: You won't stay with us, Christy?

— No, Martin. There's no place for me here. Less place still when they'd return from the wedding.

— You should stay with your woman, Christy. Or bring her with you. And make sons.

— What for, Martin? To die like your son or to grow up like Gabriel Rock, the high-flier?

— Poor Gabriel. Sure what harm did he do? The doctor has a job for him as a groundsman at a men's home in Dublin where they'll be able to keep an eye on him.

— It's a cheery future. Never to be born was better. Never to own anything. Better to give it all up.

— You're a cheery man to meet, Christy, on a sunny morning by a clean river. It should be easy to be brave and cheery on a bright morning by a clean river. Even about death. That's why I walked down here to look at the mill. To get away from the smell of death and the weeping women.

— Yet you'd have me make life, just to end like that, a smell and weeping women, something to run from.

— You might be more lucky than I was.

— Don't I look the picture of luck, Christy said.

He perched to rest uneasily on the corner of a wobbly packing case. The sailor's rum, the pilfered brandy, and then on the top of that mixture the exertion and excitement of unwonted love-making had added up, as anybody including himself could have told him they would, to palpitations and trembling knees.

He had hoped to walk a mile beyond the mill and away from the village, towards Crooked Bridge, so as to confuse any pursuit, before he stopped to hitch the lift or to catch the bus – he had the money for his fare now – that would take him forever absent-without-leave to Dublin and places beyond. But he had felt the need of a rest, even of a bath to wash away the sweat that came in spasms, sometimes hot, sometimes cold. There was, though, no going back to Cathy and that desolate prison of a house. Mortell's mill offered rest and shelter, and even a refugee and runaway could always talk to old Mortell.

Not meaning to speak aloud he said: The living image of a man that would be begetting sons to shake the world.

He wiped his forehead. One moment it had been cold and dry. The next moment it was beaded and glistening with perspiration. The miller watched him. He said: Sit and rest yourself there on the straw. If it was good enough for the infant Jesus it's good enough for you. I'll brew you a pot of tea for the rocky road to Dublin.

He went up three stone steps into a little cave that he called his office. The sputtering, pumping noise of the paraffin ring on which he boiled the water was a lively cheery noise in the silence of the morning, a warm noise in the round well of old cold stone walls, a noise that was a mocking crowing contrast to the sleepy sound of the river. Above them on wooden floor after floor the simple dusty machinery was mute for mourning.

It's good to own something, old Mortell said. There was a day long ago when every workman owned at least the tools he worked with. The man who wove the cloth owned the loom. I've owned this mill for a long time. It's not much, it's not modern, the ways of milling have changed forever. But it was mine.

— Who'll own it when you die, Martin?

— A man should have more sons than one and by a strong woman, Christy. Or many sons by many women, like the patriarchs of old. There was a blackheaded Welsh woman once I fancied. She had a bastard by somebody. Nobody knew who. Except that it was an Irish bastard.

— Surely at least half Welsh, Martin.

— And the one son I had by a weakly woman went to hell and never came back. There he lay, as light as a feather, like a changeling in the bed.

— I saw a corner of hell myself.

— It could only have been a sort of purgatory, Christy. And God knows didn't you ask for it?

— Didn't Stephen ask for anything that might happen when he put on the uniform?

— It's not the same thing, Christy. He was a martyr, the world's martyr, he died that others might live.

— He wasn't the only one. It's been done before.

— Well I know it, but he was my only son that used to sit as a boy outside my door and ask me where the roads went to.

— He found out.

— He found out the hard way. The hard road round the world and straight through hell and back to the death-bed and the grave. There was no use in him trying to tell me what happened because unless you were there you could never understand. The father above never knew what his son meant when he cried out on the cross.

— This strong tea, said Christy, is a consolation.

With the paraffin ring silent the sound of the river, the only sound, it seemed, in the world that morning, was louder but still sleepy and soothing.

— That Welsh-Irish bastard might have followed the same road, Martin. If Nora foals after being so well served by Gabriel, there could be another bastard for the hard road.

— If breeding counts for anything, Christy, that would be the rare and unfortunate child. Nobody here, not even myself, knows who begot Gabriel.

— An angel, for God's sake.

— But there was a quare strain in Jenny Orr's family. She had a brother was put away in the end for religious mania. When his father was on his bed of death and anointed by the priest he thought the anointing should and could work a cure. But the father died and the son in a mad fury went to the priest's house to shout and harangue, and when the priest's housekeeper lifted the phone to get the police he took to the stones and smashed every window and pane of glass in the house, even the stained glass window in the room where the priest keeps the blessed sacrament. After that his road was a short one, straight, nonstop to the madhouse.

— He was a true believer, Christy said. There have been great days in Cosmona. It's a pity to leave the place.

— You could stay. You could be useful here. You could bring back life to that old hotel.

— That would be the resurrection, indeed.

— The tourists would come. They'd come to see the Tower.

— They would, after today. The pilgrims would come too.

— And to learn the legends of the place, to hear about the Island of the Living and the monks of old.

— And the black wise man that came out of the east following three stars.

— They'd come to fish the river and to climb the mountain, even if the young girl was killed there. You should stay, Christy. Face up to it. What road do you follow now? I'm old and I come from the house of death to find you running away from life.

— Here in this box I have something that will lighten the road.

— Drink by the shape and size of it, and the smell of you.

— Whiskey. Two bottles of the best. The Tarrants will never miss them.

— They'll miss them. They'll blame Cathy.

— She's a Tarrant. She's one of them.

— She was born that way. But she married you.

— She stayed a Tarrant. That's what I'm running away from, not from life.

If he had not that morning made the final step that had taken him forever beyond shame, he might, he thought, have been ashamed to tell such a drab trite lie to this old beefy white-whiskered man. But could an old countryman who had begotten a pathetic son on an ailing alcoholic wife and whose one dream had been of some blackhaired slut in Wales, understand visions of surf and beauties on Copacabana beaches? Or could he understand how Christy Hanafin had taken his revenge on Cathy for being a morose brown mockery of the scarlet vivid beauties denied to him, and revenge too for the quietude and resignation with which she had accepted herself as she was, and taken pity on him. He said, hoping to hurt: Everybody runs from life, nuns and monks and hermits, and timid travellers who won't fly for fear of crashing, and your son who ran from you and his wife and the river and the mill and the same view, day after day, of the same mountain.

— Sure as God, he ran from life. But he thought he was running towards it. Who am I to chide you that could do nothing to chide or guide my own son. Go your way, Christy, and God go with you.

— He might if you say so, Martin.

He stood up from his seat on the pile of straw: Turn on the river, Martin. Start the wheel. Start the world. The oats must be ground. I like the sound of the mill.

— No, the wheel must be silent today, Christy. My son's dead in the bed. He weighs forty-nine pounds. He was a big baby. His wheel has turned.

— My last request denied, Christy said. Nobody up there likes me.

He stood in the doorway. He raised his right arm and recited: Where is your mill with the humming of thunder, where is the weir with the wonder of foam, where is the sluice with the race running under...?

— It will run again, Christy. It won't stop forever until I stop. Even then you never know. Somewhere I might come on another man who loves the old ways.

— Sounds of the village grow stiller and stiller, stiller the notes of the birds on the hill. Dusty and dim are the eyes of the miller, deaf are his ears with the moil of the mill.

— There were many songs and sayings about mills. There shouldn't be much wrong, Christy, with a man that likes poetry.

— I don't like poetry, Martin. It's just that I had a memory when I went to school. What's poetry but words? What are words but wind? Ask Cathy. Ask her grandmother. Ask Shadow and Substance and John Connell with the drop to his nose.

The hot strong tea had had an enlivening effect on the mouthfuls of whiskey he had gulped in the chill morning darkness of the cellar bar to give himself courage to rifle the till and make love to those two bottles of the best. The cellar bar had had the lost weekend stench of stale drink. The shutters on the half-windows, set high in the thick stone walls, had still been closed to repel the morning. It was a worse dungeon than he had ever seen in prison. He sweated with a sick fear and his hands shook as he folded the notes and packed the two bottles into a cardboard box that he had found outside in the dank corridor. Cathy would be cute and quiet enough to pass the whole thing off as an ordinary burglary, if she wasn't so maddened when she awakened and discovered his deed upstairs as to set the pursuit on his heels. That for sure would be jail again for Whispering Christy. Yet he reckoned that shame would prevent her as it had not prevented him. 'Twas time, to take no chances, 'twas time he was moving, 'twas time he passed on. He nursed the cardboard box as if it had been an infant or a doll. He said: I'd better go so. I'd be better gone.

— I'll walk with you as far as the end of Cosmona, Mortell said.

— I'm going the other way.

— I'll walk you to the bridge, so.

Over there under the sallies, in water still and withdrawn from the current, the black man's empty rum bottle had sunk to rest. Cosmona, one, two, three. The mountain, pale blue in the early light, faded back into the sky. But a precipice shone like silver and above it rested a pile of cottony cloud.

— She must have searched the mountain to find that precipice, Mortell said. Or the spirit of the mountain found it for her. Elsewhere there's nothing but heathery slopes a child could roll down unharmed. It was nightfall, though, and she had strayed from her company and lost the mountain path.

— Like a lot more besides, Martin. How long do you live when you're falling? What happens in a doomed aeroplane?

— When I met her funeral on the road I walked the three steps of mercy with it. It was an old custom that, no matter how urgent your business, if you met the dead you turned and walked three steps of the road with them.

— Slipping and grasping at everything, and falling into nothing, and screaming. Was she still alive when she struck the rocks? In my former life I knew a man who was laughing and pinching girls at a party in Dublin on the eve of a flight, and twenty-four hours later he was portion of a mountain in Austria.

— Them that would die like that by fall or fire I'd say, Christy, would go straight to the footstool of God. All in an instant their purgatory and last day and judgment would be over.

— Thanks for the tip, Martin. I'll find a high place and jump. Upwards to God's feet. Defying all the laws of gravity. There was a man in jail with me who did jump from a height, a month after he came out of jail. He'd done a long stretch for killing a baby. It died, the doctor said, of acute peritonitis arising from stomach injuries and ill treatment over a long period. Its face was bruised and its forehead punctured, there were nine wounds on the abdomen, consistent, the doctor said, with the child having been burned on the bars of a fire. There were bruises on the spine and on both sides of the jaw and the baby's collarbone had been broken. A month after he got out of jail he jumped out of a high window in London, straight to God's footstool, suffer the little children.

— You're a sour man, Christy, this blessed morning.

— I never knew until this morning…

He was about to say that he had never known until that morning, and only then in a fit of sick fury against everything tangible, how a man might find it in him to batter a baby to death, or to find demoniacal joy in the idea of a fair young maiden falling, falling to shatter flesh and bone and spatter blood and forever stifle screams on the rocky road to God's footstool. But just as he started to speak and possibly to horrify the old fool forever he heard the rumble that once before in the night he had heard in the company of the black man. When it came it was slow and enormous, sailing so high above the road that it was with difficulty and the miller's help that he clambered on wobbly legs to the cab of the great galleon of a truck. The miller reached up to him the cardboard box. With the noise of the engine Christy couldn't hear what the old man was shouting.

§

— We heard the wildest stories in Crooked Bridge, the driver's mate said. Your black friend found the girls he was looking for.

— He wasn't exactly a friend.

— Oh, no offence.

— None taken. He found his girls.

— They understood his lingo well enough.

— He spoke out bold and plain.

The driver said: The world's in a terrible state. A bloody nigger can come out of nowhere and behave like that in an Irish village. To an Irish girl.

Christy hadn't suspected that the driver could make such a long speech. After a silence he said: She stole his money.

The driver said: Nevertheless. The world's not near settled.

— Gives the people something to talk about, said the driver's mate.

— If she was your daughter, said the driver.

— She wouldn't be Jasus, be out stealing money offa black sailors.

— Be Jasus is right, said Christy.

— Or white sailors either, said the driver's mate. Or her arse would be sore.

The driver said: The world's not near settled.

— The arse of the lady, Christy said, who stole the money is said to be very sore.

— If her father had given her a sore arse long ago she wouldn't be that way today, said the driver's mate.

— Fathers aren't supposed to, Christy said and regretted his remark. With their own daughters, I mean.

The driver glowered. He was a moral man. So did the driver's mate. He felt he was being mocked. Christy remembered uneasily that he was their guest.

— It's a painful topic, he said weakly.

There was no response. It was too early in the morning, perhaps, for talk and he, at any rate, had exhausted himself with old Mortell. But while they were talking he had sailed high and triumphantly through Cosmona. Was Cathy still asleep in that musty house? Or was she awake and did she realise, or would she admit, how fragile all dreams were? He was revenged at last, he told himself, on that scrawny, thin-necked little bastard of a management man in a policeman's helmet.

The mountain seemed closer now, a deeper blue. The precipice, as if it were glass like the glass on the balconies of the hospital up there, flashed sun-signals over the awakening valley. From a gateway leading out of a field and beside a hayshed a stout block of a man stepped forth, brushed hay off his clothes, expanded his chest, yawned, then walked back towards the village.

— Well-dressed he is to be sleeping in the fields, said the driver's mate.

— Out looking at his cattle, said the driver.

— He's not dressed for the farm, Christy said.

The air in the cab cleared. Debating merrily the mystery of the well-dressed man emerging, yawning and stretching himself, from field or hayshed at that odd hour, they drove on for a mile or more. Then the truck groaned and shuddered and stopped.

— Full house this morning, the driver said.

He leaped down to help, with much pinching, pushing, hand-slipping and laughter, the two hitchhiking girls to climb to the cab. Through chokes of laughter one of them said: Thank you, sir.

She was a stumpy, dull-eyed, pasty-faced, unhealthy-looking blonde.

— Thank you kindly sir, the other said.

She was redheaded and bucktoothed. She had bony knees.

He closed his eyes to the sight of them. They had nothing to offer to a man whose visions had been of bodies that had had the best treatment that money galore and southern sun could give them on broad beaches, skyscrapers of luxury hotels in the background. Using her own words he said to Cathy, pitying her as he pitied himself, not blaming her for not being other than herself: Someday the two of us will be dead. That's the only thing we could find now to agree on. Live with your ghost then, your dead soldier, live with the dead. Forget you ever dreamed about life. Shatter the dream before it grows to be a living child.

He shivered as he spoke to her. He was surprised, indeed, that nobody in the cab could hear him. His lips had moved. But nobody had heard a sound, or noticed his shivering or his moving lips. They were talking about the black man.

— Not us, said the redhead. We heard about what happened. But we don't know those girls.

— We wouldn't, said the blonde, have anything to do with blacks.

— We have more sense, said the redhead.

— Wise girls, said the driver.

— They're not sanitary, said the blonde.

— In America now, said the driver, they have great trouble with the blacks. And they'll have more. They gave them too much of their own way. Give a black man an inch, he'll want a mile. What I'd do now if I was president…

Respectfully the driver's mate annotated: He lived ten years in America.

— What I'd do now is to send the bloody lot of them back to Africa where they came from. Let them make their own way there. They had Africa to themselves once, and devil the much they made out of it. Walking about on their dirty black feet on hills of diamonds and they never knew the riches were there until the white man came along and discovered them.

The driver's mate said: He was out in the Middle West, too.

— I sure was, the driver said. Six years in Iowa. That's where you'd see the farms. The nation's bread-basket, I heard it called. Twelve feet of rich black topsoil that would grow anything.

— And no weeds, said the driver's mate.

Leading remark and following speech seemed part of their ritual of the road.

— Clean as a whistle, the driver said. They don't know what the word weed means. Do you know this...

Caught up by his subject he turned his eyes from the road and fixed Christy with a squinting stare.

— Do you know this? If it hadn't been for Christopher Columbus and his dirty Spaniards with their dungyard boots there wouldn't be a weed in the New World, not a weed.

He beamed his stare back again on the roadway, a second too late. His mate said: He's in the ditch, boss, but it was his own fault, a queer-looking fellow with a helmet on a bicycle.

Thirty yards ahead the driver parked the groaning quivering galleon. He said: Go back and see is he injured.

The girls were in giggles. With effort the redhead controlled herself: Excuse us, sirs, from laughing. But we know the fellow in the ditch. He's a crazy from Cosmona with only one eye. He's never out of the ditch.

— Once in a while he is, said the blonde. He was yesterday.

They were off again into spluttering convulsions. The footsteps of the driver's mate went away from them, the sound of a car approached, then stopped at a distance. They waited five minutes, ten minutes. To their right a field of ripe oats, hedge-high, golden, waited for the reaper. To their left lazy cattle stood and lay under a beechtree, ready in their shelter to face the heat of the day. The driver switched off the engine. The girls were calm again. The driver had spent his eloquence. Christy clutched his box, looked now at the oats moving gently in a light breeze, now enviously at the cattle: a short life but an easy one, no decisions to make, no hopes to be disappointed. He had nothing to say to the girls or to the driver. In the silence he could hear voices at a distance, then the returning footsteps of the driver's mate, then the engine of the car starting again.

— Not a scratch on him, said the driver's mate. Sound as a bell.

They drove on. The black people of America and the black soil of Iowa had been dealt with and forgotten.

— It was his own fault he got in the ditch, the driver's mate said. As blind as a bat in one eye and crazy. He said he was trying to break the speed record to Dublin. A doctor fellow, a fine young man, drove up and said he would look after him.

They drove through a village that was lazily awakening and unshuttering.

— As queer a looking specimen as you'd see, said the driver's mate. Helmet and goggles and all, dressed up, to ride the wall of death, weights on the spokes of the wheels, a real highflyer.

The girls were giggling again.

— Let us in on the joke, said the driver's mate.

They controlled themselves. The blonde said: You don't know the half of it.

She wiped tears of laughter from her cheeks. She said: It was something funny that happened yesterday.

— Cosmona, said the driver's mate, must be the great place for fun.

— We couldn't tell you, said the redhead, for blushing.

— Make the tea, said the driver.

— Tell us after the tea, said the driver's mate. There's nothing I like better than a funny story.

— But don't look at me when I'm telling it, the blonde said.

— Spare her blushes, said the redhead.

— Strong and sweet, said the blonde. I like my tea strong and sweet.

— But not black, said the redhead. She's mad about milk.

§

She had expected him to be gone in the morning.

She bathed and scrubbed, washing away the sweat of the night. The words of an old song tormented her: But, lo, when she woke with the merle in the morning no lord was beside her that e'er she could see.

She had, she admitted to herself, hoped that he would be gone in the morning for there was no hope, that she could see, in beginning anything over again, least of all with a man like Christy.

He'd fled in the nighttime and left her to founder and fill a lone grave by the bonny green tree.

But unlike the soft girl in the song she wouldn't founder, she would fill no lone grave. Something, she knew, had happened in the night that not even Christy could run away from. He had told in the end a truth that he could never deny, and she knew and she knew, and she knew that women did know.

Strong Man Hoban's people, the tinkers, had their own way of finding out when a woman of the clan was pregnant. They'd scatter ears of oats on a plate and the way the ears settled told them what they wanted to know and even whether the child to come would be male or female. Someday she might ask Dancing Annie to step down from the seat of the chair and scatter the oats and foretell the sex of the child she knew, she knew, she was going to bear. Women did know. She had felt the planting as she would have felt a blow in the face. A gipsy woman would break an egg in a deep bowl, without separating yolk from white, and spray over it water from her mouth and drown it, and if the egg next morning was floating on the surface she was pregnant: with a son if the white was separated from the yolk, with a daughter if the white and yolk were mixed. She needed no such test. She knew. She knew. She didn't need to walk, as country wives too long barren had been known to do, on cattle pasture in summer evenings in the hope that a bullet might lick them, or to sit by the hearth hoping that a cricket might alight on them, or to stand by marshland to study signs in the flights of wild duck or geese. She knew, she knew, she needed no signs, women knew.

One day years ago in the bar she had overheard two country-men talking about Guts Armstrong, a local small-farmer, and his cousin Susan. The Armstrongs were a rough lot, infamous for inbreeding. One man said: There'll be another shotgun wedding in the Armstrongs.

— They were always great people for keeping it in the family. Who told you?

— Who but Guts himself.

— From the horse's mouth.

— He said he had Susan's rump raised the other night on a lap of hay in Coll's meadow.

— Not for the first time.

— And when he rolled off her she sat up in the hay and said Guts you fixed me good and proper this time.

— How did she know?

— They say that women do know.

— A bell rings.

— No, a whistle blows.

As you might expect that ended in laughter every bit as coarse as the Armstrongs, where cousins always seemed to be marrying cousins and with more than customary haste. But Susan Armstrong had had, in truth, known, and Guts had made an honourable woman or a decent girl out of her, if that wouldn't be an extravagant way of talking in relation to the Armstrongs. Over the years the cousinly couple had had several children, begotten in bed and not in the hay-meadow, and in spite of the kind prognostications of the neighbours, dear hearts and simple rural people, not one of the children was born with two heads or a hare lip or the face of a cretin.

Women knew, women knew, she almost sang to herself and went, against her usual routine, to the bar to study the extent of the wreckage of the day before. For Cosmona it had been an unusually busy day. Any one of those four gentlemen of the press could drink enough for three normal men, and hold it too. Their company and talk had been a break in the routine although she'd have liked it better if they'd stopped short of making Peejay as drunk as themselves. But then it didn't take much to make Peejay as drunk as it took gallons to make them, and a splurge might do the manikin good and set him painting dancing girls instead of weeping women for the holy nuns and that prig, Mr. Lane, above at the hospital. The idea set her laughing as she descended the stairs and walked along the stone corridor. The darkened bar smelled of drink gone sour and smoke gone stale. She switched on the light and stood for a long time refusing to be hurt or shocked or angry, refusing even to be annoyed. For what could you expect from Christy except something so pitiably mean, so childishly malicious that you were driven to pity him as much almost as he pitied himself?

The toy policeman lay on his back on the counter. His face was gone. Beaten in. The hollow head had been filled with brandy, she sniffed to make certain, that had mostly seeped through to moisten and stain the counter. He bled brandy. A little way to the right Little Boy Blue was obscenely impaled on the handle of a beer pump. He might recover but he would never be the same again. She didn't need to run to the attic to know what fate had overtaken the placid blonde girls, the toy piano, the music box, the toy soldiers, the teddy bear, the menagerie of animals that had waited for so long lonely for a child to play with them. She poured herself a brandy and saw the space where last night two bottles of whiskey had been. She didn't need to look at the cash register. She knew. This time he had closed the door on himself forever. But the poor besotted proud miserable fool who thought always that he was too good for the only world that ever bothered to find a space for him: even in closing the door forever he had done the only job for which he was born and for which he came into the world.

She swept the brandy-sodden faceless corpse of the dead policeman into a large clean wooden box, a fresh coffin for the little people who for so long had kept her company. She didn't need them any more and when the time came they would have replacements, but at least she owed them a decent burial. She eased Little Boy Blue as gently as she could from his agonising impalement but, gently as she worked, the legs came off and she dropped legs and trunk and trumpet into the box on top of the policeman. She drank the brandy and walked to the attic and swept up the fragments of the little girls, nobody else was injured, and thought of King Kong trampling on running terrified people, and for a brief moment allowed herself to hate. Yet what was the sense in hating some faceless shadow who moved away from her in another room behind a door closed never to open again? These old musty rooms had their own lovable heroic ghost.

The month before her child was born she would buy new toys. For a boy, for a girl? Dancing Annie and the magic ears of oats could answer that question.

In the stone corridor she stuffed the box with wood shavings and carefully hammered on the lid. Light as a feather it would float for a long time. She carried it back to the bar and poured herself another brandy, sipped it, decided she didn't need it or never again would need to lean on the strong red arm of Beau Jolais. She had her own strength coming to her, it could be, from a hope for the future and the memory of a young man of her own blood and breed who had faced up to death on the fields of Flanders. Even Substance, her brother, might be stupid and at times tongue-tied before her raillery, but he was no coward, no thief in the night. She poured the brandy back into the bottle. Charles Roe, her chief consumer of brandy, could have it at the listed price.

Not even King Kong could trample on the treasure she carried in her belly, and Christy's pitiful malice, his pathetic self-pity, driving him to try to leave wreckage behind him everywhere he went, had only served to make her more certain that last night in one sweating moment he had for once justified his existence and built up more than he could ever destroy even if he was as big as King Kong.

The first sentence on top of what was left of the pile of leaflets told her that she was, or would be, the mother of fair love and of fear, and of knowledge and of holy hope. She accepted it all except the fear. She had no fear that her son would be a half-Hanafin. The cowardly thieving father had not meant what he had done. But she had. There would be no father. For the sake of safety she would, gently but firmly, breed any taint of Hanafin out of the young bones. He would never be as Christy was. There was more of real manhood in Gabriel Rock. Her son would never be as the miller's son had been, patiently rotting to death in bed. If he had to die ever in war, he would, in his death, bring back out of the shadows the ghost of the lost warrior who haunted her imaginings, he would be a hero, an airman, a man with the wings of an eagle.

Did daft Nora feel as she herself felt that something new had happened? Did Nora carry away with her to the care of the nuns, alas, the secret of the soul of a poor devil who had at least tried to fly even if it was only on a bicycle?

Never burn friendship, her grandmother had told her over and over again, but cast it on the running water: fire destroys but water bears friendship on into eternity. She had a sort of stubborn liking for that angry old woman who, in the same stubborn black-blooded way, had, Cathy knew, a care for her granddaughter's welfare.

From her grandmother, Cathy had adopted that superstition: letters from friends were never crushed and cast on the flames but torn into tiny pieces and flushed down the lavatory bowl to seek eternity in a septic tank. She saw the absurdity of it but still went on doing it. For a long time now there had been few friends to write letters. When the rare letter did come she treated it solemnly to its dismemberment and watery funeral, but wrote no answer. Until this moment she had had no good news to tell. In the time to come, as her child grew up, things would be different. Here at the moment she had in this box the last mortal remains of little people who had been the friends of her loneliness. Those remains were not for burning. They would go a royal flowing road to a heaven all their own.

There was no sign of life in the grassgrown innyard. The door of Peejay's hut was open and she began to tiptoe and to hurry with the precious box nursed carefully before her. But then she thought: What did it matter now if Peejay knew how vile Christy was, or if Cosmona knew, or the world? Cosmona didn't think much of him as it was. The world had given him the reward that showed what it thought of him. She had no compulsion, no duty to protect him any more. She had better things to do. He was no more to her than the chickweed among the grass under her feet. So she detoured to the hut and looked in at the open door but there was no sign of Peejay or of Gabriel Rock that she had sent there to hide. The weeping women of Jerusalem had the place to themselves.

Beyond the green wooden gate at the end of the yard a field path went for a quarter of a mile to the bank of the river. Deep hedgerows protected her from the eyes of Cosmona if any eyes were yet, in that sleepy place, awake and open. The sun was up but the hedges were still wet from the night, and wet grasses brushed against her knees and leaned over the narrow pathway on which, try as she would to banish the sight, she could not help but see the broken brandysoaked body of the little policeman, the shattered fragments of the pink placid little girls. There was a girl not so long ago in Crooked Bridge who was poled by a fellow who left her and married another. When the bridal pair stepped in all their finery out of the church what should they see on the path before them but a doll broken and twisted out of shape, and the young wife's first baby had been born dead. That was a grim story. In the damp shadow of the hedgerow it took possession of her until she hoped that everywhere Christy went in the world he would see before him on his path the image of a broken bleeding child, that he would never know anything of the good deed he had unwittingly done.

Horrid thoughts belonged to the shadows. One horrid thought gave birth to another. She hurried to escape from them: from her memory of her reading of a sad English queen who had, growing in her belly, the tumour that would kill her and who thought, against all reason, that the growth was a child. In every room of her palace, the history book had said, there was some record of her hope and agony. Even her prayer book, dropped from her hands at a moment when faintness overcame her, and wet with her desperate tears, was found to be open at the prayers for women in childbirth. No bloody wonder the poor tormented thing, and her Spanish husband hadn't been much help to her, had burned heretics by the hundred.

The hedgerows ended. She was almost running. But she was out into sunshine on the banks of the delightful river. The shadows were behind her. She would school herself to think no more of Christy Hanafin. Her husband would be, as indeed he had been for so long, the ghost of the Flanders soldier come back with the wings of an eagle to walk in old rooms where he had been happy as a boy. His son and hers would grow up happy in the same rooms, his youth brightening them, happy on the green slopes above by the Moat, on the heathery places over the closed caves, happy by the river or in the old mill listening to the wisdom of Martin Mortell who would live forever, or at least until the son to be born was grown to full manhood.

Stepping stones crossed the river that was here, for a brief space, wide and shallow. She sat on the first stone. With the long good summer and little rain it was high and dry on bare brown earth scuffled by the cattle that came here to drink. She watched the play of the water, the trailing and twisting of weeds that had grown around the stones.

For sure it was an omen that no longer than a week ago she had read an article written, for expectant mothers, by a lady doctor in a woman's magazine. Those nine months matter, the doctor began, and went on to say that the realisation that she was going to have a baby might come to a woman in one of several ways. Mrs. Guts Armstrong and herself and daft Nora, perhaps, could say amen to that. In common with many other happily married women (the lady doctor held) a woman might know the glad news instinctively before there were any symptoms to guide her. This certainly could come to her in a wave of such deep awareness and contentment that just for a moment it would seem that time stood still. That was what the lady doctor said. Just for a moment by the river in Cosmona time stood still.

But for other women, the doctor said, even though they were equally sensitive and alert, there might be no such inward knowledge. They might never know they were pregnant at all until certain obvious symptoms presented themselves such as tingling, irritation, tenderness and fullness of the breasts, a frequent desire to spend pennies (the doctor coyly said), and sometimes, but only sometimes, early morning nausea or actual sickness.

On the same page in the same magazine there had been an article about tennis elbow, its cause and cure. She hadn't read it. It had no special interest for her. It didn't seem to apply to her life in Cosmona. But she had read and re-read the article on the nine months that mattered and wondered, laughing to herself, if she shouldn't give Johnny Connell his way and trap him into something that he would be too childishly proud of to wish to escape from. It would be his boast in crowds of men, his solitary pride.

Time enough when the morning nausea had established itself to break the news to Granny, time enough when she had first given to Johnny Connell that there thing, as the song said, that he was seeking, just enough of it and often enough to lead him by the long wet nose and to pleasure herself, but not so as to run any risk to the load she carried, but just enough to give Johnny, and Granny who had the money, the notion that Johnny was a fine anonymous father, deprived of his rightful title only because Cathy had once been foolish enough to marry a wastrel who still lived. There were days or nights when she too had willed Christy dead. But a superstitious terror of thinking anyone expendable so as to make life easier for herself had chilled her. Her black wish might return to herself.

In the end, despicable as he was, and unworthy to live, he had passed the secret of life on to her. He was that much of a man.

Johnny Connell was a man too, wasn't he? He would have his uses. He wasn't the worst. If Christy took to himself the liberty to lie and steal and destroy dreams, there were surely some liberties that the woman he'd abandoned could claim for her own: so as to build, not to destroy. She was protecting someone not yet born. To do so it would be wise not to let the old woman with the money know that her grandson would have in his veins any of the weak blood of Christy Hanafin. She had a wedding ring if she cared to wear it along with her horseshoe ring. She had a married name. That much Christy had, before the world, provided her with. A poor shape of a man it would be that couldn't give a woman at least a plain gold ring and the use of his name.

On a high wide-topped stone halfways across the river she knelt down and placed the box gently on the restless water, held it for a while, then launched it with a push on its way to eternity. It spun at first with the twisting current, listed a little towards the stern, then found its course and sailed away from her, rocking slightly, rocking the children to sleep. Spots of froth danced around it. The sun was strong on the water. She knelt and watched until her eyes were flooded with sunshine and tears.

There was a woman in one of Charles Roe's oft-told tales whose husband went to complain about her to the holy virgin, Brigid, the saint of Kildare, the worker of wonders. His complaint was that his wife would not sleep with him and intended to leave him. Would the saint give him a spell to make his wife love him again? That was a rare thing to ask from a virgin. Should she have asked Sister Bruno or Sister Grignon de Montfort for a pill to put in Christy's drink?

The box was so far away now and her eyes were so moist that she couldn't be sure whether or not it still floated, whether the white blob she saw were froth or wooden box. But then a ray of sunlight caught it, high and dry and waterproof, going away from her around a curve of the stream.

So the holy virgin of the oakwoods of Kildare, where her round tower still stood where Christy would see it on his mean miserable journey back to Dublin, blessed water for the man and told him to take it home with him, and put it in the food and drink and on the bed. Before God, whatever was in that virgin's water – Charles Roe always relished so obviously the telling of that part of the story – the man couldn't, from that moment out, beat the wife off him with a blackthorn stick, and it was much to be hoped that none of the nuns of Kildare ever sampled the brew by mistake, or out of curiosity, or they'd be pulling the black breeches of the curates or of the parish priest, his reverend self.

One day the man set out on a journey. To get a rest, Charles Roe said, but Cosmona knew that Charles Roe was afraid of women. The wife rose up and followed him until she saw him and there was a strip of sea between them, and she called out to him that if he would not come back to her she would walk into the sea that was between them.

History was silent, Charles Roe said, as to what the man did.

The box was gone out of sight. She wiped her eyes and stood up on the flat stone, startled for a moment to see a man standing on the far bank. But it was only Peejay. He came towards her along the stepping-stones. He was barefooted. He wore corduroy pants and braces, a grey collarless workman's shirt, a straw hat. He carried a spade on his shoulder. The blade was stained with fresh clay. He showed no surprise at seeing her there, at that hour, standing up from her knees on a flat stone in the middle of the water. That was the beauty of Peejay: everything to him was ordinary.

— You're early at the digging, Peejay.

— I had a funeral to attend to, ma'am. The white cock died on me.

— Peejay, I'm sorry.

— So am I, ma'am. He was lucky. There was good luck, I always felt, in the touch of his claw.

They crossed to the bank and walked back towards the hotel. She led the way, keeping on the sunny side of the hedgerows: no more horrid thoughts. She asked Peejay how his head was this morning.

— The drink is a curse, he said. Those four quare fellows are a disturbing element in Cosmona. It could be that all those things wouldn't have happened if they hadn't come here looking for stories.

— You could root them out of bed now, Peejay. Get them on the road to Dublin to tell their tale of a day in Cosmona.

Had the touch of the claw of the white cock, the King of Cosmona, brought to her the blessing of ripeness? Like Christy, Peejay's cock had done her a good turn before he died. It was sad to think that the white crowing King was dead, and buried beyond the water.

— If they only knew the half of it, Peejay said, they'd have the real story to tell.

— Tell it to them, Peejay.

— Some of it I will, he said. All the news that's fit to print.

With struggle and effort one of the visitors was opening a rickety window, shoving his head out to gulp in the morning. He waved and yodelled at them. It was the small young man called Ned.

— I suppose it's hard to blame them, Peejay said. They live an unsettled life, drinking, roaming from place to place, racing deadlines.

— An early morn, Ned roared. The top of the early morn to you, Peejay.

His head and shoulders were withdrawn into the room as if somebody had pulled him by the heels. Then the stout man called Bob appeared and crowed like a cock and flapped his arms like wings and also vanished abruptly.

Art Finlan came walking down the yard towards them, camera on shoulder, his pipe going. Peejay said: Is Mr. Hanafin gone, ma'am?

— He's gone, Peejay. I didn't know you knew.

— There isn't much escapes Peejay. Eyes and ears of Cosmona.

— A picture of the two of you, Art called. Hold it.

He unslung the camera.

— Don't fret, Peejay said. One is often better alone.

— I won't be alone forever, Peejay.

— You're a young woman yet, ma'am. You could make a good home for a man.

— That's what I'll do, she said. I'll make a good home for a man.

§

— Here I am sitting peacefully at the preliminary to breakfast, Lord Laurence said, muddling without overmuch enthusiasm at my oaten-meal porridge, as prepossessing as a linseed poultice, and I raise my eyes and lift up my heart and look across the table and what do I see but you, Peejay?

— Come to cheer you up, Mr. Collins. It's a heavenly morning outside. It's a great day for the rocky road to Dublin.

— You are barefooted, Peejay.

— The dew on the grass, Mr. Collins, is the best thing in the world for the feet to cure corns and banish bunions. Christ himself went barefoot.

— John the Baptist, who may not, of course, have been a reliable witness made a passing reference to latchets and shoes. Would that imply that Christ was sometimes shod? At good times, perhaps, when the carpentry was prospering. Did it ever occur to you, Peejay, that Saint Joseph may also have been the village undertaker?

— They just wrapped them up, Mr. Collins. In grave clothes or cerements. Like parcels. No coffins.

— A point well made, Peejay. You're sharp this morning.

— There isn't much, Mr. Collins, escapes Peejay. He was barefoot when Mary Magdalen did anoint his feet and with her hairs did wipe them. They grew the hair very long in those days, do you see.

— A woman's hair, Peejay, was then her crowning glory.

— Oh, no razor cuts or Eton crops or hussies going about with heads like boys. He's barefoot in all the holy pictures I ever saw. I'm painting him barefoot myself.

— The last word, Peejay, has been said on the matter. You speak as one with authority.

Bearing two glasses of whiskey and a carafe of water Bob Gunning made a slow careful entry, placed one glass and the carafe before Lord Laurence, sat down stiffly at another table, took a newspaper out of his pocket, unfolded it, began to read, drank the whiskey neat in one steady draught, shuddered, coughed, crowed like a cock, went on reading.

— Did either of you, said Peejay, ever hear the one-man juke-box of Cosmona and Crooked Bridge?

He took from his hip-pocket a tin whistle and fixed it firmly in the left corner of his mouth. He took from a table two tea-spoons and rattled them rhythmically, rounded back to back, in his right hand. He blew the whistle, deftly controlling the stops with the fingers of his left hand. He hopped from foot to foot in an uncouth jig. All at one and the same time he sang out of the right side of his mouth and blew out of the left side and jigged and rattled the spoons. He sang: One, two, three, four, five. Hunt the hare and turn him. On the rocky road and all the way to Dublin. Whack folaldeedee.

From behind his newspaper Bob Gunning prayed: Sweet Nellie of Holy God, keep our heads in the state of grace.

Lord Laurence applauded. From the doorway, Ned, whiskey in hand, joined in the chorus. Behind him, Art, lowering his camera to the floor, joined in the applause.

— High up or low down, Art said, I can't find the white cock, Peejay. The hens are there, but no cock, no king to rule the roost. What did you do with him, Peejay?

Peejay put away the whistle. He returned the spoons to their places. He said with dignity: Mr. Finlan, am I my brother's keeper?

— Where did he go, Peejay?

— Be your age Art, Ned said. You're a married man. Where would a cock go in the early morn? He's over by the aqueduct playing games out of school.

— One last picture of him I wanted, Art said, as Chanticleer. Welcoming the morning. All Cosmona almost I have here in this box.

He patted his camera affectionately, carried it to his own separate table and sat down.

— But not all, only almost, said Peejay.

— True enough for you, Art said sadly.

He relighted his pipe and puffed and hoped that somebody would soon bring to him something resembling breakfast. He said: No picture of the ghost could I get. No picture of the pair on the Tower. I hadn't the long distance lens. But I have the girl who saw the ghost and from here to Paddington Green she's the prettiest little Polly Perkins of a nursling that ever was seen. The neatest little legs. Ned, that's where you should have been. Not wasting your time in the haystacks with the lower orders.

From behind his newspaper Bob sourly agreed: Exactly what I said. Lower orders. The gutter. But he led me on, or dragged me down. Any port in a storm, he said, and when all fruits fail, welcome haw. I said to him: Ned, no, not good enough. Keep the few shots we have left in the locker only for the best. We're not getting younger.

— Speak for yourself, Ned said. And as for pictures I have the world copyright on the picture of the year. Peejay's cock in piston action, one two, one two, in Cosmona at the aqueduct. The caption is a poem by the Venerable Laurence Collins, Order of Preachers. When lovely woman spreads her feathers. Recite, Laurence.

— You are too young, Laurence said, and too early in the morning.

— That pretty little nursling, Art said, from Paddington Green. As beautiful as a buttercup and as proud as a queen. Oh, her pretty little Polly Perkins.

Crestfallen, Ned said: My teeth water.

— Teeth, said Bob. Always thinking of your belly.

He folded the newspaper. He said: Food, Peejay, and no more bullshit. We're off to Dublin in the green and the blue and our helmets glitter in the sun. No bloody news in the paper this morning. No lead story. They had to fall back on a speech made by a minor politician.

— I'll give them a lead, Peejay said. Listen to this.

He walked to the dark doorway behind the snack-counter and shouted: Minnie girl, the gentlemen of the press need viaticum.

Food for the road, he explained to the unseen servant.

He took from the right-hand pocket of his pants a roll of ruled paper. He smoothed it out. This was clearly his great moment. He said: Hear ye. Hear ye. Mr. Broe in his merry way may tell me that I'll never make the grade as a newspaper man. But while ye were all asleep or whatever ye were at I got the story of the week. A real beat.

Art asked: Is it the black man?

— 'Tis not. Although the sergeant in the barracks says there's a ship's officer and a detective and another sailor can talk his lingo coming today from Dublin City to collect him. That should make a good picture. They can get him for jumping ship.

— By God, said Ned, he jumped more than the ship.

— Peejay, Laurence commanded, give us your big story.

— Obedient to the senior member, Peejay read: Travelling entertainer and roadshow strong man, Patrick Hoban, of no fixed abode, and his wife, both stated to be hawkers, were apprehended at the Cawley residence, adjacent to the picturesque and historic village of Cosmona, and charged with assault and battery, drunkenness, malicious damage, and conduct liable to lead to a breach of the peace.

Peejay explained that in the well-written news-story the gist of the story was always in the first sentence.

Laurence agreed and said that C. P. Scott could do no better.

Peejay read: They are charged with assaulting Mr. Ignatius Cawley, Senior, and his two sons, Owen and Ignatius. Mr. Cawley said that after midnight when he was asleep in bed Hoban came into the house from a shed where he (Cawley) had permitted him (Hoban) and Hoban's wife to sleep and demanded more drink by menaces. He (Cawley) refused and Hoban then used strong language and struck him (Cawley) over the eye. Owen Cawley and Ignatius, Junior, then pushed Hoban, with great celerity and at great personal risk, out the door. Hoban then procured an axe, broke two windows, came in again through one of them and again assaulted Cawley, Senior, also Ignatius Cawley, Junior, and Owen Cawley who was rendered unconscious. Asked by Sergeant Smith, who apprehended him and with whom he went in an orderly fashion to the station, to make a statement Hoban pleaded in extenuation that he suffered loss of memory and had been excited by the events of the previous day. He had considered that Cawley or somebody had insulted his wife and he would give nobody, not even the King of Spain, the right to insult his (Hoban's) wife.

— Fionn MacCool of ancient Ireland, Ned said, isn't a patch on his long drawers.

— A King and the son of Kings, Laurence said. Why indeed should the King of Spain be entitled to insult his (Hoban's) wife?

Peejay read: Interviewed by our reporter, who was first on the scene, a young Dublin lady, then resident in the Cawley abode, said: Jesus, Mary and Joseph, get me back to Dublin, to somewhere where I know somebody. They're animals here. The country is a horror.

— Her statement, said Peejay, is reported verbatim. End of story.

He folded the paper and gave it to Ned. He said: Mr. Broe, put that in your pipe and smoke it.

— You mean Finlan, Ned said. He has the pipe. But I must hand it to you, Peejay. You're the coat and vest, and the rest are nowhere.

With a sweep of his arm and a reverend genuflection he passed Peejay's manuscript on to Lord Laurence. He said: The greatest story ever told. The giant wrecks the bloody castle. And, as usual, we missed it.

— But we got enough Art said, to fill a book or the *News of the World*. All human life is here. Count our many blessings, count them one by one. A white cock that can shake hands. A darling girl that saw a ghost. A tinker woman can dance on the seat of a chair while her husband holds the back-rung of the chair between his teeth. A dying man who was kicked by Japs into the River Kwai. A Peeping Tom performing in full view of all. Ned and Bob happy with the town whores.

— Rusty Nails and Blotting Paper, Bob said. They had the rarest ideas about how to stay not pregnant. That little blonde wore a miraculous medal and swore that nothing could happen to her while that medal was on a string around her neck. Nothing.

— It didn't, said Ned, save her from you, you brute.

— And a rape, Art said, a grade-A rape performed by a sailor, and a black one at that.

— There was a drunken bumblebee, said Laurence, and a man who crawled on his hands and knees and stole a bottle of brandy, and a homing pigeon that stopped to rest in a bar. Before me on the table no breakfast so far, Peejay, but three copulating flies, ménage à trois, infinitesimal thrills on a white American cloth beside a lake of cold spilled coffee. Peejay, get that girl and a damp cloth and have this table cleaned. Jump to it or, before God, I'll clean it with your priceless manuscript.

Responding to the voice of the master, Peejay jumped. The dark doorway swallowed him. There was a sizzle and smell of frying, a muttering of angry voices.

— Raped on the Railway, said Laurence, was the name of an old book I saw once in London in an exhibition of rare books. Raped on the Railway, or, A True Story of a Lady who was first Ravished and then Flagellated on the Scotch Express.

— He killed that cock, Art said. I'll swear he killed that cock.

— Another book was there beside it. It may yet be of interest to Ned and Bob. It was called…

From his notebook Laurence read: The Charitable Surgeon, being a new way of curing without Mercury, the several degrees of the Venereal Distemper in both sexes, with a new discovery of the true seat of Claps in Men and Women. Likewise the most certain easy way to escape infection, though never so often accompanying with the most polluted companion.

— He killed that cock, Art said. I feel it in my bones.

— Then when I was on my travels in the great U.S.A., Laurence said, I noticed that rape was very fashionable. Any female from two to eighty-two could have the privilege. In Atlanta, Georgia, there was a public benefactor, a coloured youth, who went about forcing fifty-year-olds at bus stops. Since Atlanta's not a city but a suburb lost in a forest, he had plenty of privacy.

— He killed that cock, Art said. I know he did.

— We may have it for breakfast, Bob said.

— I had meant, said Laurence, to ask the woman about that pale young soldier in the photograph. All those musical melancholy names, Ypres, Loos, Arras, Bethune, Saint Quentin, Neuve Eglise, Bapaume, Bourbon Wood, Péronne, Monchy.

— And Cosmona, said Art. Forget not Cosmona. He killed that cock.

Perhaps I could still ask her, Laurence said, after breakfast. Over our last drink. Which I will buy, for you young men. Just one for the road, one, two, three, four, five, hunt the hare and turn him on the rocky road to Dublin.

§

The bridge over the canal at the fringe of Cosmona and on the rocky road to Dublin is humped and narrow and much like any other old, humped, narrow, eighteenth-century bridge that crosses that weedy, water-lilied canal all the way from the spreading Shannon (sung by Spenser) and its chain of lakes, to that masterpiece of small-bridge architecture, in its own class quite as wonderful as the soaring Golden Gate Bridge of Joseph B. Straus who so admired the Creator's handiwork in the giant redwood trees of Northern California that he wrote a poem about them: The greatest of earth's living forms, tall conquerors that laugh at storms, their challenge still unanswered rings through fifty centuries of kings...

...to that masterpiece, as I was saying, in Dublin, in Percy Place, not far from the salt water, and called Pessary Place by a jocular friend of mine who once had there an apartment much given over to the purposes of unlicensed love.

The four newspapermen, two to each car, bumped over the hump of the Cosmona bridge and proceeded eastwards, and God go with them and the message they bring to Dublin and the world, or the part of the world that reads the newspapers they work for. Knowing them, they will, I know, try to tell the story as colourfully and accurately as they can. Their telling will have certain advantages over mine: they weren't present at every event, they spent too much time talking and drinking in the bar, but to offset that, they had the cameras of Art and Edward to give testimony that no words, however eloquent, could give. What, for instance, was the exact background when Peejay's cock sinned by the aqueduct and brought upon himself the wages of sin: was the hayshed to the left of the farmhouse or to the right, where were the barns and the stables, were there trees in the distance or clouds in the sky? Could it happen that when Art Finlan descends to the darkroom he may see, standing with the night-matron and the nurses, another nurse, an elderly woman, long-skirted, her veil not flowing but tied in a knot?

These and other things I could only find out if I followed the four to the city which, for reasons too tiresome to mention, I am unable to do, being left by them for the moment leaning on the canal bridge, Father Jarlath to my right, Martin Mortell to my left, the hounds, Bishop, Deacon and Martha, below us: Martha dancing on the towing path, Bishop and Deacon, bursting with the force of hippopotami through trailing weeds and floating lily-pads, in pursuit of some other form of life. A waterhen? A rat? Or could that still, dead, artificial waterway rise to a regal otter?

On the towing-path Martha voices her encouragement.

Father Jarlath is saying that the manner in which, and the extent to which, dogs enjoy the morning is one of the few things that have kept him believing in the existence and goodness of God. Another of those things is that men can now fly, although God, to compel his creature to exercise his god-given ingenuity, had created him without wings.

— Fly like the birds, Martin. Fly like the angels.

He had himself flown in a tiny one-engined crate until the bishop had forbidden him, said that it was disedifying to the faithful, the faithful of Cosmona mark you, the Cawleys and the country farmers, that it was giving downright scandal to them to give them to say that a priest of God was spending money on an aeroplane. The old crate cost no more than a Baby Austin and he could service it himself.

— Not a word by the way, Martin, about what his lordship himself spends on a limousine and a uniformed lackey to drive it. Not that the lackey gets much for his pains. Did anyone ever hear of a bishop that paid anyone a living wage? Although they'd talk about Pope Leo and social justice and Rerum Novarum and Rerum Devilmaycarum until the cows and the crows came home. And if that limousine broke down neither his lordship nor his lackey could do anything to start it again, short of making a novena or giving it a kick or paying the garage out of the hard cash provided by the faithful.

And it was a prayer in itself, he argues, to rise into the air, to feel the force of the lift, to see the fields like a green tide drifting away below you. The Lord himself must have had that feeling when he took off from Mount Olivet and headed home, his work done, to report to the da.

— Man will never be truly happy, Martin, until he flies more than he walks. Here am I, plodding about in my big boots when I really desire and deserve to fly. There I was, in the mud of Flanders envying the Royal Flying Corps because they went like angels soaring above the clay.

That was why and how he had learned to sympathise with Gabriel Rock who had been buried in mud by the villainous Cawleys and had tried to escape from that mud by trying to fly, God look to his wit, on a bicycle, leaden weights on the spinning wheels, the nearest things to wings the poor boy could think of. The doctor would look after Gabriel, the doctor was a decent man, and Father Jarlath would stand behind the doctor in anything he said or did.

— But as for those Cawleys, Martin, a bad breed. In all Christian charity I will scourge them off the face of the earth as our divine Lord scourged the money-changers out of the temple. I'll finish what Hoban and the sailor began.

— Dogs and ducks and birds he always envied, he says.

— As happy as the angels. Dogs enjoy the morning.

He calls and whistles. He calls: Bishop and Deacon and Martha. To heel. On to the hospital.

With no particular relevance, but speaking rather at a tangent, Martin Mortell (still leaning with us on the bridge, for the happy dogs pay not the least attention to the priest nor does he reinforce his demands by a second shout) points up at the heathery slopes above the Moat of Cosmona and tells a story of a man of the local gentry, a man seven feet seven inches in height, who had served in the armies of that Frederick of Prussia, who had the regiment of men all eight feet tall. The man of Cosmona grew to dislike that army and everyone in it and Prussia and its tyrant King. In the end he deserted and, after great hardship, made his way through France to the sea, and so to Ireland. And ever afterwards on the birthday of the King of Prussia, the Cosmona man would leg it up to the summit above the caves and fart three times in the direction of Berlin.

— A royal salute and no mistake, says Father Jarlath.

— If every man, he vehemently says.

He hammers the parapet of the bridge as if he was in the pulpit. He hammers it so vigorously that I am forced to stand back a little to give him elbow room.

What he has to say is simply this: That if every man would do the same as that seven-foot-seven gentleman of Cosmona – he might have been an ancestor of Charles Roe on the maternal side – and fart at Kings, and fart at armies, and fart at all brief authority, there would be no wars except the sort of farting wars and competitions they used to have in the County Kerry in the olden times. The miller's son, Stephen, would thus be alive today.

— Did you never hear, Martin, you that knows so much of the old ways, of the Kerry farting competitions? Gold cups and red rosettes for the longest and loudest. It's in the nature of Kerrymen to fart. Big men, and windy with ignorance. Like Texans, they say, in the U.S.A. Strict rules were laid down, too. No corned beef and cabbage. Fart fair or not at all. 'Twould be the good idea to revive those contests, to settle all international disputes in open competition at the International Farting Festival of Farranfore in the heart of the Kingdom of Kerry.

The miller, who is dusting the dust of the stone off the elbows of his good black suit, is saying that he had indeed had his interest in the old ways, and had prayed, as much as he had ever prayed, for a son who would have the same interests. But now his son is dead and the world is going nowhere and the millwheel will stop when the miller stops. There had been a time when to throw down or demolish a mill was esteemed a capital crime. That was when men knew what was what. The grain grew red and dry. The river flowed smooth and strong. The wheel turned like a song. Good bread was baked by the open hearth. That was a time when the mill was the centre of the country, cargoes on queues of carts and drays, rich farmers coming to pay their respects. All men knew the miller and believed in him and, even in days of damp harvest, he could give them good oat meal and flour.

— But that's all gone now, Jarlath. I might as well be as dead as Stephen. That unfortunate wretch, Christy Hanafin, might have made a better son for me than the pathetic victim that's dead up there in the bed, and he not the weight of fifty pounds. Christy Hanafin can recite a good poem about a mill. But when I listened to him, Jarlath, it was like as if I was listening to the son of the devil saying a prayer, and I could see nothing but the dead and rotting bodies of women and children lying all along the jungle route that Stephen walked on his bare feet, as if he was a beggar and a slave and not the son of a man who dressed his own mill-stones in one of the richest valleys in Ireland. He chewed brown paper soaked in piss to try to get the saline moisture into his system. There was a man stole another man's cat and killed it and ate it raw, claws and guts and all. That's the world of today for you, Jarlath, your great world in which man can fly like the angels. Claws and guts and all. A raw cat.

After a considerable silence during which the three hounds not only end their capers and come to heel but even go quietly trotting, and sniffing at each other's arseholes, towards the hospital, Martin asks Jarlath what Jarlath thinks is the worst thing that could happen to a man. Jarlath says that he, being what he professes to be, should answer: Eternal Damnation. But he had once heard that a man in America, whose son was hanged for a brutal quadruple murder in the State of Kansas, among the wheat fields, the red dry grain, said that the worst thing that could happen to a man was to have his son hanged. That was a weird thing for any man to say. For wasn't that exactly what had happened to the Eternal Father: His only son was hanged.

The miller says that sons should stay at home, that men should keep their feet on God's good earth and leave flying for the birds, that he will walk on now to the hospital to ask the nuns for their prayers for the repose of Stephen's soul, and ask Peter Lane and the patients also for their prayers.

— You're just like the bishop, Martin, who thinks I should keep my feet on the ground. He didn't silence me. He grounded me. He said: You're no angel.

We all laugh at that and then, remembering that the death of the miller's son has been mentioned, are silent for a while.

— On with us then, says the priest. 'Tis my day to hear the nun's confessions. Scruples is the height of it. And I waste my breath preaching them thundering sermons about the sins of the flesh in the hope it might put something into their heads worth listening to: a real temptation, instead of a scruple about fervour in mental prayer. That Peter Lane is damn near as bad. A sort of mealy-mouthed Jesuit or a Methodist. Mental prayer, I ask you.

— Tell them all to stick to the earth, Jarlath. Feel the grain and you'll know what it will produce. Smell the straw and you'll know if the oats will be good. Flying will get them nowhere.

We laugh again; and on they plod, priest and miller, earthbound, and leave me looking at the water. I may not see them again for a long time. But inland waterways have always been among my chief delights, and I am happy here. Lakes and rivers, I prefer, because, mostly, they made themselves without the aid of man, and seldom or never depend on him for their continuing life. Yet these old canals are very beautiful in their decay. Is there anywhere such peace to be found? A slow barge or a white pleasure-cruiser stirring reeds and weeds once in a blue moon. In the arch of the bridge there, the deep groove cut, over the years, by the towing-rope as the horse hauled the barge through the eye of the needle, the horse to pull, the man to guide, a mark made on stone by a centaur. A shoal of rudd passes, glittering in the sunny water, perhaps that selfsame shoal of rudd that Laurence and Art saw by the aqueduct.

So let me sit here and forget for a while my own life and all its works and pomps (I don't yet know about your lives) and forget even the lives of those who, for some reason or other, I have been trying to tell you about. Should I have told Jarlath, though, that the next time round the confessional ring, Peter Lane, if at all he rides according to the rules, should have more to confess than scruples about the state of his mental prayer? Jarlath who must, because of his coat and his collar, ride by the rules, must ask Peter Lane the time-honoured question: Did he cause pollution? Art Finlan, kindly and always a gentleman, would think that that was a poor way to talk about the prettiest little Polly Perkins that ever was seen. But perhaps Peter Lane will keep his and her secrets to himself. He never, anyway, did think much of Jarlath as a confessor.

Peter Lane is not the man he was when, eighteen months ago, he came to this hospital to have the bones of his back healed by modern orthopaedic methods. White linen aprons swaddling young round limbs may have made him to think that there are more altars than that marble altar with its cold linen and candlesticks and flowers, and the little cave or box where God, it is said, hides. God can hide in the oddest places. Peter Lane, I suspect, will never make that altar. Feeling between the nimble legs of Nurse Walters he has discovered that there are delightful things particularly forbidden to sworn celibates and, by them, very hard to come by.

Howandever, on my way I must go, and my way is not back to Dublin, with the four, pleasant as that might be. We all have our particular destinations, and mine is back to Cosmona to meet the doctor, whom I like, and that bouncing little wife of his. Ahhahaha you say – but it is not as you think. After all Gabriel Rock was – wasn't he? – the most important person in our view of Cosmona, and I am merely anxious to know from the doctor what will become of Gabriel. Although it is true that there is more to be found out about the doctor himself, a good man, contented, spreading contentment, selfish but also generous because he has never been so stressed that his selfishness has had to reveal itself. There is more, too, if you must have the admission, to be found out about his wife, particularly in her present mood, and bless her little round pudding of a bottom. More too about why Edward did, indeed, take a photograph, with one of those tiny cameras you can tie around a waistcoat button, of Stephen Mortell on his deathbed; more about the sort of cousinship between Charles Roe and Lord Laurence, a something not uncommon in their country, a bond of booze and big words and gentlemanly ways and nothing much to show for it; more about the Island of the Living where Jarlath and Martin are now standing and talking about Mount Athos, that far peninsula in Northern Greece, crowned by a marble peak seven thousand feet in height, a land of bleak hermitages and ornate monasteries stored with the wealth of Byzantium. No woman, child or eunuch, no female creature of any kind, except for an occasional panicky hen, has been permitted here for more than ten centuries. Charles Roe, they are saying, is the man really to talk about Mount Athos.

But the morning sun is momentarily clouded. A cold shivery breeze is blowing from the east, ruffling and darkening the water, making the weeds appear solid and impenetrable, sinister as a jungle.

In his travels in the U.S.A., about which Lord Laurence is so fond of talking (he, instead of Christy Hanafin, should have met that truck-driver), he came, he said, to a place in Florida where, to clear the weeds out of the waterways, the Floridians were employing manatees or seacows or dugongs, those ungainly aquatic mammals that, being seen by drunken sailors, gave rise to the legend of the mermaid, the siren creature, half fish, half lovely woman (like a lot of women) sitting on a rock in the salt sea, combing her long hair, enticing the mariner to his doom. The legend isn't much of a compliment to women or to fish. For the dugong is, says Lord Laurence, an earless, often barnacle-encrusted behemoth with sunken eyes, bristly moustache, blubbery upper lip and spade-like tail. It grows fifteen feet long, weighs a ton, and measures more than seven feet around the waist. But the female manatee is a good mother. She carries her baby in armlike flippers and nurses it at her breast much as a woman does, when a woman does – that is.

When Lord Laurence was in Florida, if he ever was and if he didn't just read it all in the papers, he says that it had been found that a seacow could eat per day one hundred pounds of underwater plants, mostly water-hyacinths – a delicate and delightful diet, I'd say. The Sudanese at that time were thinking of turning the manatees loose in the Upper Nile which gets so matted in places with the water-hyacinth (lavender variety) that you can walk on the water like Jesus or dance on the water like the saint of the Island of the Living.

Just think of the Cosmona canal solid with hyacinth, of Charles Roe walking on the water or Miss Grace dancing, of mermaids by the million living on blossoms and singing their siren songs. It is a dream better suited to Peter Lane, in the loving mood he's in, than to a dry stick of a mortal like myself.

But now, thanks to me, you know about the manatees or seacows or dugongs and the weight of water-weed that one of them can eat per day.

They are, also, sociable and rarely quarrel. The male is a good husband and devoted father. Consider the case of Matthew Arnold and his forsaken merman.

A baby manatee weighs sixty pounds and is delivered under water.

But, on my way. There's a shower coming from the east.

Later in the day the sun will return stronger than ever. Over the grain-fields of the Cosmona Valley the sunlight will be as golden and crisp as the crust on good homebaked bread.

§

Peter Lane at the moment is reading the Revelation of Saint John the Divine, burning love on Patmos banished, and it isn't frankly revealing much to him: except that he which hath the sharp sword with two edges considereth that he (Peter Lane) holdeth the doctrine of Balaam who taught Balac to cast a stumbling-block before the children of Israel, to eat things sacrificed unto idols and to commit fornication. He is reading the Revelation not with any sense of remorse, but for the sake, he hopes, of the poetry. He is tailor-squatting on his bed in his pink corner, comfortable in pyjamas and dressing-gown, his crotch at ease from the cutting fulcrum of the pants of that black suit which he has outgrown in eighteen months, as he has also outgrown everything that it stands for. Because he is unrepentant (you see he hasn't died in the night like the princely little boy who was about to become a Jesuit but who fell from grace and fornicated at his farewell party), and because he has a vacuum under his belly-button from an exultant sense of liberation and expectation, he is reading the Revelation not in the Douai but in the Authorised Version. He is doing this, he hopes, for the prose.

He wonders is he cold or hot, or cold or hot in what, and what is cold and what is hot. Or is he lukewarm, and, if so, about what, and thus only fit to be spewed out of the mouth of he that hath the seven spirits of God and the seven stars? He reflects that Saint Charles of Sezze, that holy Franciscan lay-brother who, along with Long John Silver, is one of his favourite characters, was once rude enough to say to the devil that if he didn't close his mouth and stop tempting him he would fill his (the devil's) mouth with dung. The hagiographer did not specify the nature or quality of the dung.

Cold, or hot, or lukewarm? Quietly in his corner, he tailor-squats and feels himself and knows that he is hot, sizzling hot, and as stiff but not as knobbly as a blackthorn stick. Seven stars, he thinks, and seven golden fiddlesticks. Afar on the grass by the Tower some coltish, young, blue-and-white nurses are exercising, laughing, calling to each other, trotting in circles, white veils flapping. In fond imagining he trots with them. Basically they are all made like the Mouse, be they blond or brunette, red or golden or mouse-coloured, slim or plump, small, medium or large. He has made a discovery. It is a general issue.

Neither repenteth he of his sorceries or fornications, in spite of the threat from locusts big as horses, and wearing breastplates, and having stinging tails like unto scorpions. It hadn't, for God's sake, even been a full, final and complete fornication, and now he is still alive on a fine harvest morning, with fields to be opened and reaped and all life before him; and with all due respect to the beloved John, raving crazy on the Isle of Patmos, he would do better next time.

When the shower comes, that had threatened as I walked away from the canal bridge, Peter Lane abandons beloved John, hobbles from his pink corner and helps the nurses wheel to the shelter of the glass roof the pink-covered beds that had been dominoed all over the open balcony. He is a man again. He can walk. He can do things. He has a true love whose secrets are all his. He loves all the nurses, too. They all are her sisters. No voice from clouds above lone Patmos will ever say to him: Nevertheless, I have somewhat against thee because thou hast left thy first love.

For true love, he knows, endures. Beauty is truth, truth beauty, and so on, and, oh, the dazzling wonder of the green sparkling world when the shower has blown on towards Dublin. It overtakes Laurence and Edward, Arthur and Robert, in the town of Naas, sacred to running horses, but as they are happy in the Five Lamps Bar it doesn't affect them and they don't even notice the huge truck that they had passed out on the wide-open plain of the Curragh of Kildare, lumbering into the lead again.

Thereafter there enter unto Peter Lane, Brothers Kennedy and Keegan, led by the sharp-tongued nun, Sister Francesca, her green parrot on her shoulder. To rattle the holy brothers she points out to them that Brother Lane is drifting into heresy by reading the Authorised Version. Then merrily she goes her way while the parrot calls and calls to the delight of the boys: Tippity toes. Tippity toes. Lie down in your beds. Be good, be good, be good.

The two holy brothers and the prodigal son walk slowly in the nun's wake – her black robes billow, she is in full sail and laughing – from the noisy balcony to the peace of Treasure Island. Inspired by Andy the parrot, Brother Keegan talks of pieces of eight and Long John Silver's parrot, Cap'n Flint, than whom, according to Long John, only the devil had seen more wickedness, who had sailed with Cap'n England the pirate, and been at Madagascar, Surinam, Providence, Portabello, and who, although she looked like a babby, had smelt powder. From the large pocket of his knee-length clerical coat Brother Kennedy hauls up a copy of the tale of Long John Silver, and says that the effect of the paintings that Sister Francis Regis has done on the glass walls of the playroom has been to set everybody in the seminary remembering his boyhood and rereading the book.

They sit surrounded by coloured glass. They recall their boyhood. They talk of Treasure Island. The doctor passes on his morning rounds and waves a greeting. Brother Kennedy, looking after the doctor, points out that Billy Bones at the Admiral Benbow considered all doctors as swabs who knew nothing about seafaring men, or about places as hot as pitch, with mates dropping around you with Yellow Jack, and the blessed land aheaving like the sea with earthquakes. Peter Lane, although he doesn't say so, is in fair agreement with Billy Bones. He remembers with annoyance, still warm, the familiar way in which the doctor on the previous day had patted the buttocks of Nurse Walters. Trespass, trespass he should have shouted. Hadn't the doctor at home his own private rumpleteetum to pat if he felt so inclined?

Brother Keegan, in a desperate effort to edify, and since not one word has yet been said about Abbot Marmion of Maredsous and his contention that Christ is the Life of the Soul, says that all life is a search for treasure, spiritual treasure. Treasure Island was shaped like a fat dragon standing up. What, Brother Keegan wonders, was the shape of the Island of Patmos. Nobody is able to enlighten him and Peter Lane couldn't care less. Peter Lane knows very well where treasure is to be found. So opening the book at random he reads to himself while the others talk, how Long John is saying that if he had had the use of his two legs he could have chased the runaway man in Bristol and come up alongside him, hand over hand, and broached him to in a brace of shakes. Peter Lane in his mind alters the sex of the fugitive. The image of himself as the ruthless pirate vessel and Nurse Walters as the helpless treasure-craft to be overhauled, stripped and pillaged is a rewarding one. For not yet has he seen her stark naked. Saint Thomas Aquinas now had had more luck although he didn't appreciate it. Didn't his obliging family, in an effort to keep him out of the cloister and turn his mind unto other things, send in unto him a naked woman, but holy Thomas drove her out again with a burning brand? Peter Lane would never be so churlish. His day would come. The burning brand was good and ready.

In terms of Treasure Island, Kennedy, who is a wit, speaks farewell. This will be their last visit to him in the hospital. Soon he will go out into the world to convalesce and rehabilitate, then to rejoin them, they pray, in their godly work. Peter Lane has other plans or, at any rate, other aspirations.

Kennedy says: Everybody knows you was a kind of a chapling, Brother Lane, yet there were few could hand and steer as well as you. You liked a bit o' fun, you did. You wasn't so high and dry nohow but took your fling like a jolly companion.

Then off they go laughing, forgetting in their assumed merriment – for they are, indeed, sorrowful at parting – to take the book with them. When they have well gone he goes on idly reading, remembering his boyhood. He is twenty and a bit now and the world is before him. He approaches it in his fancy much as Jim Hawkins, seated by the fire in Squire Trelawney's in the days before the voyage of the *Hispaniola*, used to approach the treasure island from every possible direction, explore every area of its surface, climb a thousand times to the top of the hill called Spyglass Hill and, from the top, enjoy the most wonderful and changing prospects. Sometimes the island is thick with savages to fight, sometimes full of dangerous animals. But Peter Lane knows that there is treasure there, not Keegan's spiritual treasure in which he has no longer any particular interest, but a quick-stepping girl with small hands, a heartshaped face, a lilting Munster voice and her own way of saying: Some people. The cheek.

The island is all for her, and the landscape of the island as he watches it becomes the landscape of the summer of the black cat and the green girl. She gives a new, harmless, laughing meaning to the three teasing women and the redfaced goat with the buck-teeth and the bicycle clips but no bicycle.

That morning he has tried to write a poem to her, but nothing much would come of it except a sort of bawdy rhyme about going to sleep upon the stormy heath, the sky above me and yourself beneath. No, that won't do. Who in hell would, anyway, want to sleep upon a stormy heath? The Mouse would laugh at that until she burst her belt: Some people. The cheek.

The ground is dry again underfoot. He walks to the Tower. He thinks of her in terms of Sister Grignon de Montfort's and Sister Bruno's leaflet: He that loveth her loveth life. He that watches for her shall embrace her secrets. There is great delight in her friendship and inexhaustible riches in the works of her hands and in the exercise of conference with her. She is more beautiful than the sun, and above all the order of the stars. Being compared with the light she is found before it. Take hold on her and she shall exalt thee. Thou shalt be glorified by her when thou shalt embrace her. Come to her with all thy mind. Keep her ways with all thy power. Then shall her fetters be a strong defence for thee, and a firm foundation, and her chain a robe of glory. For in her is the beauty of life, and her hands are a healthful binding. She will strengthen him, and make a straight way to him, and give him joy, and will disclose her secrets to him.

He thinks that if he knew music to that he could sing it.

Walking back from the Tower he can see beyond the hospital the windows of the nurses' home. He knows which window is hers. The curtains are drawn. She sleeps, making ready for the night.

He thinks that if he should ever come back to this place without her, the grass, the stones of the Tower, the pink and blue coverlets, the mingled, jumbled voices that are all one voice, would cry out to him to tell him it was not the same place. He does not yet know that places can be as forgetful as people.

In an hour, or a little less, the rooks will leave their hunting in the fields, their talking around the Tower, the ruined abbey, the churchyard trees, to cross over for lunch to the coloured balconies. He will be able to time the sun by them and their comrades-in-arms, the cunning grey-headed jackdaws. They may not however be as plentiful or ravenous as usual. More and more harvest fields are every day being opened for the reaper. Harvest fields are happy hunting-grounds for foraging birds.

The Cards of the Gambler

Benedict Kiely

'An astonishing book.'
Thomas Flanagan, author of The Year of the French

to gamble — 'this is the desire that halts the heart, that sets the soul swinging between fear of loss and hope of gain . . . .'

Imaginative, mythical, fantastic, yet real — with *The Cards of the Gambler* Benedict Kiely holds the reader as only a great stroyteller can, weaving the ordinary and everyday with gleaming threads of Irish folklore into the deep pattern of a modern Faust.

It is the story of a Doctor who loses everything gambling and thinks he is damned; who meets God in one pub and Death in another, where a pact is made . . . .

Introduced by Thomas Flanagan, author of *The Year of the French*, *The Tenants of Time* and *The End of the Hunt*.

ISBN 0 86327 477 3